DEATH REIGN OF THE VAMPIRE KING

They came at night—the clouds of blood-thirsting, poisonous vampire bats—led by a strange man-thing who flew high in the black sky, directing their horrible slaughter. Blood was their desire, and they sucked it from the veins of helpless infants, from the white throats and breasts of frantic women, from the hands and faces of terrorized men. While the authorities doubted and dallied, one man—Richard Wentworth, that brilliant aristocrat who, as the dread *Spider,* strikes terror in the Underworld—realized that this was another of the devastating onslaughts of lawless genius. Never before was the *Spider* so badly handicapped. With his beloved Nita captive, his loyal servants out of the battle, himself unarmed and pursued by law and criminal, he must fight the greatest battle of his life when every chance seems lost and every hope is gone . . . !

THE PAIN EMPEROR

The beautiful young woman was preparing for bed. She smoothed a cleansing cream over her face, rubbing it in well. And a second later, she was writhing on the floor, whimpering with agony—for the unguent contained a powerful acid which destroyed the girl's beauty forever. And at the same time, while countless women were disfigured for life, thousands of other persons were dying wretchedly from poison in tinned foods, in medicines, and in candies! And Richard Wentworth, champion of humanity, was termporarily powerless to help his countrymen in this hour of their great need, for a bitter enemy called the Avenger had arisen to oppose him. Harassed at every turn, his servants helpless to aid him, his life and honor horribly imperilled, can the *Spider* deliver his native land from the greedy clutches of the underworld's master-brain?

Also available from Carroll & Graf:

THE MASTER OF MEN!™ #4
SPIDER

Grant Stockbridge

Carroll & Graf Publishers, Inc.
New York

First Carroll & Graf edition 1992

Carroll & Graf Publishers, Inc.
260 Fifth Avenue
New York, NY 10001

ISBN: 0-88184-898-0

Manufactured in the United States of America

This volume is dedicated to
Batman and Spider-Man
and all other superheroes
who were inspired by
Harry Steeger's
action-hero creation—
The Spider

Death Reign Of The Vampire King

Never before had greedy, criminal genius loosed so loathsome and deadly a weapon! The Bat Man—leading a band of savages, releasing clouds of bloodthirsty vampire bats—planned to make himself a greater conqueror than Napoleon or Jenghiz Khan! One man stood in his way—Richard Wentworth, who, when the law fails, sallies forth as the dread SPIDER to spread red death in the Underworld. And the SPIDER—his beloved Nita forfeited, his loyal servants captive, his own life ever in horrible danger—must battle both the Bat Man and a broken heart!

CHAPTER ONE

The Bat Man

Twenty men with shotguns patrolled the wide lawns of Robert Latham's mansion, crouching in the black shadows of night. Their hands were tightly clamped on their weapons and they cringed close against the walls of the house. They watched the moon-drenched sky fearfully.

From the dense shadow of a shrub a score of yards away, another man spied upon them. He was a hunched, grotesque figure and his long black cape made his body blend with the darkness. He held no weapon, but beside him was a large bird cage. On his lips was a thin, tight smile. . . .

Those guards feared different terror, but if they could have seen this lurking man, they would have fled screaming in panic behind the protecting walls of the house. Not even their ready shotguns would have reassured them. For they were men of the Underworld and he who watched preyed upon their kind. He slew and left a mocking vermilion seal upon their foreheads to show that full vengeance had been exacted by the champion of oppressed humanity—nemesis of all criminals—the *Spider!*

The smile lingered on the *Spider's* lips as he surveyed the mansion, blazing with a hundred lights, and watched the men move about furtively with their deadly guns. He was determined to enter that house, though he knew that discovery within those walls would mean certain death at the hands of these men whose fear of him was matched only by their hatred and their desire to kill him. Yes, his entrance must be secret . . . for a while.

The *Spider* rose slowly to his full, bowed height, lifted the cage at arm's length and removed its bottom. For perhaps thirty seconds, nothing happened at all; then a black form dropped from the cage, spread leathery wings and flitted off erratically into the night. Then another and another, until six bats had taken wing. The *Spider* laid the cage gently on the earth, crouched again into the shadows to wait. The lights of the mansion would attract insects and those bats fed on small, flying vermin of the night. When the bats flitted between those men and the sky, the panic of terror would reign. . . .

The *Spider* nodded. They had reason for fright, these men. Within two weeks, a dozen race-horses and four men who frequented the tracks had been killed by the bite of vampire bats!

Useless to say that vampire bats never had been known outside of the tropics; useless to state that they never killed. There could be no mistaking the type of wound, the tiny area of skin peeled away by the keen, painless teeth of the bat. But the bodies of the victims had not been drained of blood. They died instead . . . of *poison!*

The *Spider* smiled coldly in the darkness. His bats were not poisonous—not even vampires—but the men who watched the home of Robert Latham would not know that. . . .

Abruptly, one of the armed guards cried out shrilly. There was more than warning in the shout. There was panic, fear and dread. His shotgun belched flame and lead upward into the darkness; then another man also screamed and fired. A ground-floor door flung open in the mansion and the men streaked toward it, shotguns bellowing.

*   *   *

This was the moment for which the *Spider* had played. He wrapped his cape tightly about his body lest its flapping betray him and ran fleetly forward. When he burst into the moonlit ring about the house, he was shouting more loudly than any of the other panic-stricken men. He went in through the door with the rest, mistaken momentarily for one of their number.

Swiftly, he backed across the room in which the terrified guards were huddling. A man turned toward him:

"Geez!" he gulped, "the boss was right. Them bats—"

So much he said before he realized that this sinister, capped man with the hunched shoulders—with cold eyes gleaming beneath the wide brim of a black slouch hat—was no comrade of his. His mouth opened to cry out. His eyes stretched and terror glanced across his countenance. The *Spider* was recognized!

If this man shouted aloud the *Spider's* name, a dozen shotguns would blaze at once. These men feared him, but like cornered rats, they would shoot him down. . . .

The *Spider's* action was as swift as his thought. His left hand shot forward, the first two fingers rigidly pointed. They struck basic nerve centers in the throat. With the cry unuttered on his lips, the man collapsed. In two leaping strides, the *Spider* crossed the room, plunged through a door. The other men, staring fearfully out into the darkness, while the last of the guards still raced for cover from the threat of those harmless bats the *Spider* had loosed, saw nothing, knew nothing of the more frightful menace among them—until they turned and saw their companion on the floor. Even then they did not understand, but cried that bats—the vampire bats—had slain again!

Within the house, crouching now in the shadow of a stairway, the *Spider* heard that cry with tightened lips that knew no mirth. If the gods were good, he would find here tonight an answer to this mystery of vampire bats whose bite was fatal. Newspapers, even reputable scientists, talked of a new species of bat carrying the poisoned fangs of snakes. . . .

The *Spider,* waiting there in the darkness for the excitement to die, shook his head slowly. There had been other such foolish theories as this whenever the criminal great turned their hands to slaughter. In his many battles to protect mankind against them, the *Spider* had unearthed drugs that drove men mad, and others that made them docile as dogs; explosives which performed the impossible by absolutely disintegrating whatever they blasted; there had been a gas that destroyed steel as termites do wooden beams. . . . And now there were vampire bats which killed like snakes! No, he did not believe in such vermin. There was something far more menacing behind this nascent terror than a new species of bat.

The *Spider* was ever alert for new outbreaks of crime. It was only by constant vigilance that he had averted, a dozen times over, the desire of the Underworld to rule over the nation; the slaughter of untold thousands. . . . It had seemed to him now that perhaps some ring of race-track gamblers had conceived a new, horrible weapon and was using it, at present, to destroy personal enemies and to frame races. If that were true, it was no more than a routine job for the police; but suppose . . . suppose the criminals behind this strange new terror, turned their thoughts to nation-wide conquest!

The *Spider* had seen many overwhelming reigns of terror begin thus trivially. He had learned the wisdom of striking quickly and terribly. So he had come tonight to determine what Latham knew of this strange, new, killing instrument.

The turmoil below was quieting. Soon the patrol of the grounds would begin again. The *Spider* had no fear that the man he had struck would regain consciousness and betray him. The jiu-jitsu blow would be effective for at least an hour and by that time, the *Spider's* presence would be known to them all!

A slow smile crossed the *Spider's* straight lips as he crept stealthily up the service stairway of the mansion toward the second floor sitting room, where, he knew,

Latham kept his watch. There was a shotgun guard in the wide, upper hall. The *Spider* drew a length of silken line from a pocket of his cape, rope less than the diameter of a pencil which yet had a tensile strength of seven hundred pounds! The *Spider's* web, police had dubbed it. Well, he would use it now to catch a fly!

Carefully, he looped the cord, carefully tossed it. The unwary guard felt gossamer brush his throat; then he was yanked off his feet, his shotgun clattering to the floor. The *Spider* was beside him in an instant and once more he struck swiftly to render the man unconscious. He freed his line and, in two long bounds, was at the door behind which Latham lurked with his bodyguard.

That noise of clattering gun had been intentional. After its sound, all was utter, waiting silence. Then, abruptly, the door the *Spider* watched snapped open. A man with a gun held rigidly ready sprang out into the hall. He grated a curse as he saw the prostrate guard, moved toward him cautiously. The *Spider's* fist lashed out, caught him hard on the jaw. While the man still wavered on his feet, the *Spider* had yanked away his gun, was through the open door, had closed it, and the automatic was covering the room.

"Ah, Latham," said the *Spider*, his voice flat, mocking. "Let me compliment you on the efficacy of your guard!" He laughed softly, and that sound, too, was taunting, blood-chilling.

There were three men in the room and they sat—one of them half-stood—in attitudes of frozen fright. Only Latham's gun was in sight, upon a small, nearby taboret which also held whiskey and a soda siphon. He held a glass in his right hand and, the first to recover, he began presently to slosh the liquid about in it slowly. He was spare, but full-faced and distinguished with his smooth, brown hair which had whitened upon the temples.

"Damn' glad you've come, *Spider*," Latham said calmly. "Perhaps you know some way of stopping these damned bats."

"Just keep on drinking, Latham," the *Spider* said. "I wouldn't think of interrupting your pleasure."

The *Spider's* voice was gentle, but the grim, gaunt face with its lipless mouth and harsh beak of a nose was threat enough. Latham gazed at the sallow face, the hunch-backed figure in black cape that crouched behind the ready gun and his pale face became grayish. His glass moved jerkily away from the taboret and he touched tongue to his dry lips.

"Good God, *Spider*," he said hoarsely, "I . . . I was just going to set my glass down."

"Certainly, Latham," the *Spider* agreed. "Tonight, Latham, you have no reason to fear me. I simply want to ask you some questions. . . . *Whose stable shelters the vampire bats?*"

Latham contrived a smile. "The guard I've got here tonight should prove to you that mine doesn't, *Spider*," he said anxiously. "Hell, my men just drove away one attack . . . !"

The *Spider's* lipless mouth parted a little, but he did not explain the bats. Abruptly, tension whipped his body. He half-crouched and his gun jutted toward Latham's chest. Pounding footsteps were racing down the hall. In the darkness outside, a man screamed—a cry that choked off in mid-shout. With the suddenness of lightning, the lights clicked out and somewhere, wailing, quavering through the night, came a mourning note that was like the moan of a tortured soul in hell.

"Oh God!" screamed Latham. "It's the Bat Man!"

For fifteen seconds after the first beat of footsteps, the *Spider* had suspected a trick. Perhaps someone knew the method of quickly reviving the man he had knocked out. There was a way. . . . But the sound of Latham's voice, the inarticulate fright in the cries of the others, convinced him that their terror was genuine.

The Bat Man . . . no need to inquire what they meant. He had suspected human agency behind the attacks of the vampire bats. These men knew and they called the master of the winged killers . . . *the Bat Man!*

The *Spider* waited tensely for this oddly-named man to show himself. His guns were ready. . . . Instantly, instinctively, the *Spider* had sprung from the spot he stood when the lights went out, but no one moved to attack him. There was a wild stampede of feet toward the door. Latham cried out.

"Keep that door shut, damn you!" His gun streaked flame out of the darkness. Near the door, a man groaned and thumped to the floor.

"Keep away from that door!" Latham shouted again, his panic barely under control. "I'll shoot the first man who touches it."

The *Spider* realized abruptly that the running in the hall had ceased. Either the man had seen the bodies there and fled in terror, or . . . *or the bats already had struck!* The *Spider* crouched to the floor, so that he caught the gray light of the window across the room— so that he could watch movement about him. No one budged. A man whimpered off to his right near the door and the one who had fallen at Latham's shot breathed with rattling breath. Latham had aimed well. He was cursing monotonously.

"You see, *Spider*," he whispered. "You see, he's after me. The Bat Man . . . !"

His voice was drowned in the bellowing blasts of shotguns just outside the window. There was a tearing, ripping sound of wire screen and the *Spider* saw against the gray square of the window the fluttering form of a bat!

"Cover your throat, Latham!" he shouted. "A bat just came in the window."

Even as he cried the warning, a half-dozen more of the black, loathsome things dodged in through the torn screening. A shuddering moan came from Latham.

"You can't tell when they bite," he whimpered. "You can't tell. Oh, God . . . !"

With his teeth set, the *Spider* whipped out his fountain pen flashlight, squeezed out its widely diffused ray.

15

He saw a dodging, leathery-winged beast within inches of his face. The bat flicked away, but the *Spider's* bullet was swifter than its flight. The creature was torn to bits by forty-five caliber lead and the *Spider* pressed back against the wall, watching, watching. . . .

Abruptly, he became aware of two things. Within the house, all was silence. And there, but dimly heard, came a shrill, monstrous squeaking, as if a giant bat called to its kind!

It sounded again and black bat forms fluttered through the beam of the *Spider's* light, whirled toward the window and were gone.

One more of the creatures the *Spider* smashed with lead; then he was alone with the thumping of his heart, the reverberations of his shot. He lifted his gloved left hand and touched away the moisture that had oozed out through his facial make-up. He acknowledged to himself that in those few seconds, crouched against the wall, he had known the cold touch of fear. Bats with poisoned teeth . . . ! He fought down a shudder.

On swift, silent feet, the *Spider* crossed the room and peered out of the window. The entire mansion was dark and on the grounds nothing visible moved. The squeaking which clearly had recalled the bats had now ceased and far off, toward where the moon sank, a dog howled. Upward, there was nothing except the blackness of the sky. . . . Suddenly, the *Spider's* teeth shut upon a curse, his guns swirled upward. But he knew that shooting would be vain. His eyes were narrow as he stared. . . .

No bat ever had that wing spread, nor flew with that gliding, motionless ease. And yet, sliding effortlessly across the starry sky, the *Spider* beheld a creature *with bat wings fully ten feet across!*

Even as he watched, the thing steeped its angle of dive and sped out of sight over the close, clustering trees that reached upward toward the sky. For long moments after it was gone, the *Spider* crouched there at the window. He was aware of his quickened breath, of the aching in the forearm of the hand that held his gun.

"It was out of range," he whispered to himself. "Out of range!"

He jerked his head angrily, reached up a gloved hand to shut the window, then turned back to the room. Almost the *Spider* doubted his eyesight. No, no, he had *seen* the thing. His eyes had been too well trained in a thousand situations where life and liberty, a thousand lives, hinged on the accuracy of his vision. Breath hissed noisily out between his teeth. Latham had cried, "The Bat Man!" Was it possible that what he had seen was a . . . a man with wings!

The *Spider* spread the light of his torch over the floor. There was no doubt in his own mind of what he would find, but the horror written largely on Latham's twisted features tightened his own grim mouth. Latham had covered his throat, so the bat had fastened to his hand. He was dead.

Slowly, the *Spider* turned the beam upon the other two in the room. They were dead, too. He found the instrument which had smashed out the screening of the window—a spear with a special collar of light, steel blades which extended fully nine inches all around the haft. It must have been hurled with terrific force, for the screening was double, a heavier screen mesh outside the usual lighter wire.

The *Spider* made his way swiftly through the darkened house, avoiding the bodies of men that were everywhere scattered in distorted, tortured attitudes of death. There was no use in carrying the bats he had killed with him. He had recognized them as vampires of an ordinary variety, *Desmodus rufus,* a tiny creature whose body was no more than three inches long, with a wing spread of only seven inches. He could recognize it by its reddish-brown body and the black wings with edging of white. The heavy bullet had smashed the animal too badly for him to examine its teeth. However, that was scarcely necessary. The *Spider* was terribly sure now that human agency was behind the murders.

17

At the outer door, the *Spider* paused for a moment, his eyes dark and narrow. Twenty-seven men had died here tonight by the bite of non-poisonous vampire bats. He himself had seen the attack. A cold fury swept him as he realized what havoc these same tactics would wreak if they were used against the populace at large. So far, the Bat Man had confined his attacks to a few gamblers, also creatures of the half-world like the bats. The *Spider* could not mourn their loss to humanity— but suppose the man went power-mad? Suppose the agency behind these attacks turned loose his murderous creatures upon cities, upon entire countrysides . . . ?

The *Spider's* lean, taut-skinned face set in determined lines. It was his job to keep such things from coming to pass!

His gun was in his hand as he stepped outside the door. A blazing light slapped the *Spider* in the face. From the close-pressing shrubbery, a man called hoarsely:

"Hands up, it's the law!" The voice broke off in a gasp. "Good God, it's—the *Spider!* The *Spider* sent them bats!"

"That's the man," broke in a girl's voice, a deep, emotional voice.

Then another man, shrill, almost hysterical with his discovery. "It's the *Spider!* The *Spider!*"

CHAPTER TWO

"Death to The Spider!"

The *Spider's* gun was ready at his side when the police behind the light challenged, but he did not fire. The *Spider* did not fight the law. He might go outside it in a thousand ways, kill, burglarize, kidnap. . . . But when he did, it was to smash criminals, to assist the law in its great work, because the police and other enforcement officers were hedged in by too many restrictions to operate effectively. He would die before he would fire upon one of the law's men.

Yet capture meant death for the *Spider;* it meant a revelation of his real identity and disgrace for his comrades and the one woman in the world who knew his secrets, Nita van Sloan. It meant even more than that. It meant that the law, for all its myriad successes against petty, customary criminals, would be without a means of combating this new terror that had arisen from the Underworld: the Bat Man, whose existence as yet they did not even suspect!

The thoughts flashed through the *Spider's* brain in the second he closed the door and felt the assault of the light. Useless to attempt a retreat. Before he could open the door and duck from sight, a dozen bullets would smash through his body. There were at least twenty men in the shrubbery out there. He could hear their rustling, their murmur as his identity was shouted hoarsely into the night. He might shoot out the light. It would give him an instant. But the night was scarcely dark enough to hope that he could flee unseen.

The *Spider* shrugged his shoulders, dropped the gun and raised his hands shoulder-high.

"I'm the *Spider,* all right," he admitted calmly, "but you'll have to hunt someone else to take the blame for the bats. I thought Latham was the man, but I was wrong."

Two men were coming out from behind the light now, walking wide lest they come between the guns and the *Spider.*

"What do you mean, wrong?" asked the hoarse voice that first had spoken.

The *Spider* allowed his straight lipless mouth to twist into a smile. "You'll find out when you take a look inside."

The two men were close now. Each had fastened a handcuff to one of his own wrists and held the other cuff open, ready for the *Spider's* hand. His eyes turned cold as he saw that. He could escape from handcuffs that were fastened between his own wrists, but if he were chained to two men . . . !

"We'll look into that," the leader growled. "But it'll take more than your say-so to clear you. This young lady seen you comin' in here with a cage. . . . Stand still. There's ten guns on you!"

The *Spider* had started uncontrollably at the information that he had been seen entering the grounds. Why, this was utterly damning! How could he convince these men that the bats he had let escape had been harmless?

"Who accuses me?" he demanded sharply. "Let me see the one who accuses me?"

The leader's voice dropped a note. "Never mind that now. You keep out of sight, young lady. He's up to some trick."

The *Spider* frowned, his heart thudding in his breast. He had had no definite plan in mind, but it was apparent these men were alert for any trick. They would be eager to kill. . . . The two men approaching him, both of them broad, tall farmers, were within a foot or two with their ready handcuffs. They were his only chance, the *Spider* knew. He must somehow use these two to escape, for once those handcuffs closed about his wrists. . . . The men behind the light were watching keenly, for they understood the situation as well as he.

The *Spider* extended his left arm toward the man who approached from that direction, smiled at him with a thin parting of his lips.

"Come on, come on," he said impatiently. "What are you waiting for? You couldn't be afraid of the *Spider?*"

The man's young face flushed a little. He braced himself visibly and, holding the handcuff in both hands, stepped within reach of the outstretched hand, slapped the shackle about the wrist and fumbled to close the cuff. It was the very instant for which the *Spider* had waited. By offering his wrist so placidly for the bracelet, he had partially disarmed the man. But, even more important, he had obtained a hold on one of the men before the other had quite reached a place where he could act.

While the man still fumbled with the cuff, the *Spider's* fingers closed upon the chain between the shackles and, without a visible preliminary tensing of muscles—without a change in his face—he yanked savagely upon the bracelets. In his timidity, the man was leaning forward off-balance and the jerk pulled him directly in front of the *Spider,* between him and the guns that threatened.

The second man leaped forward and the *Spider* slammed his captive against him, slipped his wrist from the still-unfastened cuff and skipped backward through the door into the house. An excited man fired a shotgun and one of the struggling pair cried out in pain. The *Spider* heard all that as he slammed and bolted the door, then he raced to a window on the same side of the building.

The law men were already battering on the door. A

window had been smashed in and gunshots were pouring death into the building. Guards were racing to surround the mansion. The *Spider* opened his window and waited. A guard started past the casement, paused and stared at it uncertainly, then inched forward. The silken rope snaked out of the darkness, yanked him to the window. A single blow knocked him out and the *Spider* was through the window and away. . . .

Once he was amid the shrubbery and trees, he was safe. Not even his namesake, the spider, could move more soundlessly than he. At the high, iron fence that surrounded the estate, he whistled softly in a weird, minor key. Seconds later, a shadow glided to the opposite side of the fence and a rope ladder, made of the same soft, silken cord, came swinging over. A moment later, he was speeding with that other shadow beside him, toward the hidden lane where he had parked the car.

"Wah! *Sahib!*" whispered the one beside him, "are we mice that we flee from battle?" He spoke in the Hindustani that was native to him.

The *Spider* chuckled. "They are men of the law, Ram Singh, more to be pitied for their stupidity than slain."

The turbaned Hindu, the *Spider's* servant to the death, grunted, but made no other reply. To Ram Singh, all men who opposed his master were game for his swift, keen knives. *Wah!* Mice!

The *Spider* flung into a black, low-slung Daimler sedan and the Hindu leaped to the driver's seat, sent the powerful car almost silently through the woods lane. In the tonneau, the *Spider* dropped his hand to a button beneath the left half of the cushions. The seat slid smoothly forward, turned half about and revealed in its back a closely hung wardrobe. The *Spider* folded upward a mirror about which neon lights instantly glowed. He pulled out a tray filled with the equipment of disguise. . . .

Five minutes later, as the car slid to the concrete highway which skirted the front of Latham's estate, the

22

Spider—who was the *Spider* no longer—slid the cleverly contrived wardrobe into place, lounged back against the luxurious upholstery and drew a cigarette from a platinum case. When the police stopped him a hundred yards further on, he leaned forward politely to speak to the sergeant.

"Identify myself?" he said in the rich baritone that was his natural voice. "Oh, decidedly, sergeant!" He drew out a wallet, extracted a card and presented it between two perfectly manicured fingers.

The sergeant scowled at first, then his face cleared. He actually smiled. "A thousand pardons, Mr. Wentworth," he murmured obsequiously. "I've heard of you in New York, working with the cops to stop some of them crooks. Something here might interest you, sir. Them vampire bats killed about twenty men over there. . . ."

Richard Wentworth listened attentively. This was no masquerade, but his true identity. Scion of a wealthy family—its last surviving member—he had long ago pledged himself to the suppression of crime. He had created that other sinister character, the *Spider,* so that the Underworld might be additionally cleansed by a healthy fear.

Richard Wentworth, clubman, sportsman and amateur criminologist, was a friend of Governors and of Presidents, a man eagerly sought after by Commissioners of Police whenever the ugly head of super-crime was lifted. He sat there, his bronzed, strongly chiseled face keenly intelligent as he listened to the sergeant's account of the deaths at Latham's mansion. Finally he nodded gravely, a pleasant smile on his firm lips, his gray-blue eyes merry.

"Thank you, sergeant," he said, "if you will pass me through the gates I would be glad to look over the scene."

It was wasted time, Wentworth—the *Spider*—knew, but it would be suspicious to pass without inquiry. He hurried the inspection as much as possible, on fire with eagerness to pursue his quest. It was pretty well known in police circles that Latham had a tie-up with Red Cullihane, a Philadelphia brewer who in prohibition days had been one of the leading big-shots of the East. Wentworth no longer believed that Latham was connected with the Bat Man, but it was pretty obvious that Latham had been a target for especial animosity. It might well be that Cullihane would next be the target.

After leaving the grounds, he stopped once on the way northward through Maryland to send a night-letter. It began *Ma Cherie* and was addressed to Miss Nita van Sloan, Riverside Towers, New York City. Part of the message said *Dinner Thursday at the Early Quaker*. The rest of it seemed to be lovers' words but actually it bade the woman he loved—his ablest ally in the battle against crime—to hasten to Philadelphia with his speedy Northrup plane and bring with her his chauffeur, Jackson, who was much more than a chauffeur in the plans of the *Spider*.

Then the low, black car of the *Spider* sped northward again. To any one who gazed upon the man in its back seat, he would have seemed a bored member of the class of idle rich. To be sure there was a strength and intelligence about his face and a singular directness of gaze, a confidence of bearing that had nothing to do with a bank account, which might have surprised the onlooker. But, certainly, his face gave no evidence of the grim thoughts that were racing through his mind. . . .

Until now, Wentworth had had little opportunity to consider the events of the evening and now that he reviewed the attack of the bats, he felt a mounting sense of dread. There could be no doubt at all of human agency. Even without the wailing cry which had heralded the attack, the shrill squeaking as of a giant bat which had called the killers home, there was the spear which had smashed through the screening so that the bats would be able to enter and do their assassin's work. Yes, in that one venture, the *Spider* had confirmed his fear that a new menace had arisen for humanity.

Wentworth glanced at his watch, then leaned forward to turn on the radio. There was a news broadcast about now. . . . The announcer's voice came to him with unexpected harshness. There was excitement beneath the calm ordering of carefully enunciated syllables:

"Jack Harkins, ladies and gentlemen, bringing you the extraordinary news of the day. . . ."

Innocuous phrases, but the man's words were fraught with tension, with terror. Harkins had a stimulating voice. He talked in pounding short phrases that seemed to bring the action he described into the very room with his listeners.

"Does the world face another of those overwhelming madman's attacks which have struck terror to our hearts in recent years? May God in His mercy will that it is not so. But it looks as if it is. These winged horrors of the night, the vampire bats, have struck again! Twice tonight, in two widely separated parts of the country, they have struck. And, ladies and gentlemen, *one hundred and ninety-five people are dead!* Think of it, one hundred and ninety-five!"

Wentworth, listening to the hurried, staccato rhythm of the newsman, felt his hands clench in hard white knots. None could have detected the idler in his face now, for it was white and rigid with anger and his blue-gray eyes were almost black with fury. Then what he feared had already come to pass! The Bat Man had not been content with his attack upon Latham. . . .

"At first there seemed to be no danger except to those who were associated with horses in some way. It is a well-known fact that the vampire bat confines itself largely to horses, prefers their blood to most others. But tonight, that hopeful idea was dispelled once and for all, and terribly dispelled. In Centertown, Pennsylvania, the bats flittered down and kissed the throats of lovers in the parks, they tasted of the blood of brave policemen on their beats, brought their poison death to the gay crowd before the motion picture shows. A dozen people were killed in the panic, in the dash to escape, but many, many more were prey to the vicious poisoned teeth of these blood-thirsty little beasts. . . ."

There was more, much more of that sort of thing, all melodramatic, highly-colored and calculated to help the work of the Bat Man, whatever that was, by spreading the terror of the bats. Wentworth shook his head. There was no reason for the *Spider* to visit Centertown. Nothing to be gained by gazing on more bat-slain human beings. He must hasten to Philadelphia, hoping against hope that he had guessed right about the next target of the Bat Man. Abruptly his attention was pulled back to the radio. . . .

"And now, folks, to the most exciting part of the whole thing," the newsman went on. "And something you won't know whether to believe or not. The *Spider* was seen at Latham's place. Yes, sir, the *Spider!* And a girl whose brother was killed a week ago by the bats, says she saw the *Spider carrying a cage full of bats!* Now, what does that mean? Is it possible that the *Spider*. . . ."

With a grated curse, Wentworth shut off the radio and sat rigidly, staring straight ahead of him into the blackness of the night. No need to ask what lay ahead. Once more the nation would go mad and hunt the only man who could save it from the monster who had loosed his flying killers on the people. It would blame the *Spider* and throughout the country would ring the blood-thirsty cry of . . .

"Death to the *Spider!*"

A hard bitterness descended upon Wentworth. Damnable to have the very people for whom he had sacrificed so much—for whom he hourly risked death and disgrace—turn upon him in this way. He should have become accustomed to it by now, he who had served without stint in the face of persecution by law and criminal and civilian, but somehow the thought could still rankle. Not that the *Spider* ever wavered in his devotion to the pledge he had made so long ago. . . .

He caught up the speaking tube which communicated with Ram Singh. "I must be in Philadelphia within the hour," he ordered quietly

He saw the tensing of the Hindu's broad shoulders, saw the turbaned head bend a little more over the steering wheel and heard the bass thunder of the engine deepen a full tone. The wind whispered past the car, but there was no other indication of its great speed except the occasional whine of tires on a curb. Within the hour. Yes, it was necessary to hurry. Wentworth had not anticipated that the Bat Man would strike again so quickly. Now that he had shown his versatility, there was no reason why he should not attack Red Cullihane, Latham's associate, at once.

Wentworth realized that it was merely his assumption that Cullihane would be attacked, a slim thread of hope. But there was no other clue to follow. It was desperately necessary that he find some more definite lead to this Bat Man immediately. If he could only be on the scene when next the vampires struck, he had a plan. . . .

When Ram Singh drew the powerful Daimler to a halt on a street that paralleled Philadelphia's waterfront, it was not Wentworth who alighted from the car, but a hunched and sinister figure whose very appearance was a threat . . . the *Spider*. The *Spider* knew—it was a part of his self-imposed duty to know—much about Red Cullihane. He knew of his home in the Heights and his gambling salon near the Early Quaker hotel where Wentworth had appointed a meeting with Nita the next evening. Actually it had been Latham who ran the place with Cullihane to provide protection

Then there was a great, gaunt warehouse upon the hill overlooking the Quaker which was used as a depot for distribution of the Golden Stein beer which Cullihane now manufactured legally. It was this warehouse which Wentworth now approached for here was Cullihane's stronghold and, if he feared attack, it was the place where he would be most likely to barricade himself.

Swiftly, the *Spider* advanced on the building, invisi-

27

ble in the black shadows with which he merged himself, and, from an alley mouth across the street from Cullihane's warehouse, he stood watching. Three minutes passed and a black coupé cruised slowly past, turned a corner beside the warehouse and vanished. Four minutes later, it appeared again and followed the same course. The *Spider's* thinned lips parted a little, showing the white gleam of his teeth. He was right then. Cullihane was frightened. He had taken up his position here and the coupé was a patrol, a sentry on wheels, against attack.

When the coupé had crawled out of sight again, Wentworth darted across the street. . . .

"*Spider!*" It was a woman's voice, high, challenging.

Wentworth did not turn toward the call. It was too old a trick, that crying a name to attract attention, to cause a moment of motionless waiting while deadly lead was poured into a victim. He went flat down on the pavement of the street. The crack of a light automatic sounded strangely loud in the deserted street. The bullet splatted against the bricks of the warehouse. He had a moment to wonder at the attack, then he sprang to his feet. Jumping sideways, as the girl fired again, he charged straight toward her!

Dangerous work this, racing into the muzzle of an automatic, even though it was light in caliber and a woman handled it. But like everything the *Spider* did, it was a maneuver shrewdly planned in his lightning-swift mind. There was no cover for him there in the middle of the street. Within seconds, Cullihane's sentry would arrive at the scene. Only one chance and he took it, charging straight on the gun.

He had two hopes, one that his charge would confuse the girl. The other. . . . With his left arm, he billowed his cape wide to that side. In the darkness, his long cape, which almost swept the ground, would make him a confusing target as it spread out to one side—would make it hard for anyone to judge the position of his body.

28

The muffling folds of the cape served him in good stead. His charge did not frighten the girl, nor did the booming discharges of his automatic which he fired deliberately wide. But the cloak did the trick. The *Spider* felt two bullets tug at it. The failure of those bullets did what his charge could not. It terrified the girl. While the *Spider* was still twenty feet away, she turned and fled. . . .

Wentworth raced after her, his feet silent while hers beat a panicky tattoo upon the cement. The *Spider's* jaw was tight set. He sprinted at his best pace—and in his university days, Wentworth had broken an intercollegiate record! There was desperate need for haste. Any moment now, that prowling coupé with its two men, undoubtedly heavily armed, would be upon them. And that must not happen. It must not. . . .

The girl twisted her head about as she ran, saw his figure with the cape streaming from broad shoulders as he rapidly overtook her. She screamed, high, piercing sounds of terror. She fired blindly, uselessly behind her . . . and the *Spider* pounced upon her. He knocked the gun arm up, slapped an arm about her waist. He did not check his speed, but lifted her bodily from the ground and sprang toward a doorway a half dozen feet ahead.

Even while he hastened for the shadows that would mean life or death to them, the girl began to struggle. She could not strike with her fists, since her back was toward Wentworth, but she did use her feet. Her heels drummed against his shins. The *Spider* could hear the roar of the engine as the automobile he feared raced to the scene. He heard the squeal of skidding tires. . . . With a vaulting leap, he gained the doorway, thrust the girl into a corner and held her there.

"If you move, you die," he ordered sharply—and realized his mistake. The two men—the coupé which had rushed up the street—was not the patrol at the warehouse. It was a police radio-car with two uniformed men in it. But the *Spider's* action, his order, caught them unaware. They had both jumped from the car, both stood beside it. And though they held guns in hand, the *Spider's* weapons alone were ready to shoot. They could not know that he would not fire on them.

"This way," Wentworth ordered tightly. "Drop those guns and walk this way."

Their recognition was apparent in the whiteness of their faces. They hesitated, their guns tightly clenched. Wentworth saw the struggle in their faces. Should they submit, or lift guns and shoot it out with this arch-killer? If they were lucky enough to win in the gun battle, untold rewards would be theirs. Fifty thousand dollars had been posted on the *Spider's* head. There would be promotion. . . .

Wentworth's left hand automatic spat flame and the gun flew from one policeman's hand, rattled against the coupé. He gripped his numbed arm, cursing.

"Drop that gun!" Wentworth ordered again, quietly.

The second policeman obeyed and the two moved slowly toward the *Spider* at his order. Wentworth's eyes were probing the darkness beyond them. Where were Cullihane's two killers in the other coupé? Obvious that they had ducked out of the way when the police car had shown up, running silent under orders. But the men would not have gone far. They were even more vitally interested in the cause of the shooting than the police. . . .

Wentworth's hope lay in the throbbing police-car at the curb. If he could get the girl into that, escape would be certain. The girl, whose identity he did not yet know, might yield some secret. . . . The *Spider* became abruptly aware that the eyes of one of the police had flashed to the doorway behind him and that now the man was doing his best to pretend he had not looked there at all.

There was but one explanation. The girl was creeping out of the doorway, still bent on his destruction, as she had been when first her gun had spat at his back. Yet he could not turn to meet her with these two police before him. He could hear the girl's shoes making small

30

rasping noises on the gritty pavement. Damn it, why couldn't she use sense? If she jumped him from behind. . . .

He shook his head. If she jumped him from behind, she would succeed in what she wished. She would achieve the *Spider's* death. She herself would suffer nothing. The footsteps crept closer. . . .

CHAPTER THREE

The Winged Death Again

The two policemen now needed no prompting to move toward the *Spider*. Both had seen the girl creeping upon him from behind and they wanted to be near enough to attack when she distracted the *Spider's* attention. He let them come while he listened acutely to the girl's stealthy approach. There was a way out, but it would have to be perfectly timed. . . .

The footsteps of the girl were very close now. One more step and she would probably leap upon him. The final step was delayed and, with a quick tensing of muscles, the *Spider* lunged to the side while his guns swung with alert readiness on the two police. He was just in time. Even as he sprang, the girl catapulted herself upon the spot where he had stood. Thrown off balance, she reeled against one of the police and the two sprawled together to the pavement.

Wentworth turned the flurry to his own account. With a quick stride, he was beside them. His gun flicked out and the policeman collapsed, unconscious, upon the pavement. The second man sprang to the attack, but stopped a blow which felled him also.

The *Spider* took handcuffs and uniform caps from the policemen, jerked the girl to her feet and thrust her into the coupé. He secured her to the door post with the handcuffs, then sprang behind the wheel, hurled the car forward and traveled at maximum speed for a half dozen blocks before he cut the pace. He put one of the uniform caps upon the girl's fluffy, black hair, pulled the other down over his own head. The interior was dark and it was unlikely that anyone would see more than the silhouette of the occupants' heads. It would prevent detection for a short while. He glanced toward the girl. She sat rigidly, staring straight ahead. Her jaw was set and there was furious anger in her face. She was surprisingly pretty in that moment . . . abruptly the *Spider* recognized her. She was the girl who had accused him at Latham's place, whose brother, according to the radio, had been killed by bats. But how in the world had she come here so swiftly? How had she known so accurately where to lay her ambush? Wentworth's pulses quickened. Did not all this mean that she was an ally . . . of the Bat Man? He must find out. Even her brother's death did not preclude the possibility. He turned to the girl.

"Your name, as I recall it," Wentworth said quietly, "is June Calvert. What was your brother's name, Miss Calvert?"

The girl jerked her head about toward him. "Have you killed so many that you can't remember the names of your victims?" she demanded, her deep voice vibrant.

"I didn't kill your brother," Wentworth said. "If I had, I should not bother to deny it. There are enough kills on my conscience to make one more unimportant."

The girl's lips curled though her face was very white. "You have the courage to sit there and admit . . . admit . . . !"

"Those I kill always richly deserve death," said the *Spider*. "I did not kill your brother."

Something in his quiet tone seemed to pierce the girl's contempt and anger. The contempt left her face, leaving in its place a puzzled question.

"I saw you with a cage of bats," she said. "Bob Latham . . . I thought he might have a hand in Dick's death, I was going there to . . . to . . . I saw you with the bats.''

Wentworth nodded slowly. "Yes, but if you saw, you also saw that none of my bats killed. It was fully half an hour after I went into the house that the vampire bats came. Mine were ordinary insect-eating bats that I captured to create a diversion there and open a path for my entrance.''

His quiet manner seemed to be convincing the girl against her will. June Calvert's head sagged forward, her chin trembled.

"If you know anything about me at all, Miss Calvert," Wentworth continued quietly, "you must know that the *Spider* keeps his oath. I give you my word of honor that I did not kill your brother. I give you my word, also, to kill the man who *is* responsible!"

Slowly, the girl's head came up. She turned her dark, intent eyes upon him, her wrists, bound by the handcuffs to the doorpost, closed and opened nervously.

"But why," she whispered, "why are you trying so to convince me? If, as you say, you have already killed so many, how does one accusation more or less affect it?" The *Spider* had his eyes on the street in the flash of the headlights. He laughed shortly, bitterly.

"I do not mind just accusations," he said, "but when they are false . . ." He shrugged. "You will hear plenty against me from now on. You will hear that I am responsible for all the deaths that occur from these poisonous bats. Even when I kill the Bat Man himself, the idea of my guilt will not be entirely dispelled . . . Oh, forget it! Will you tell me how you happened to be waiting there for me?"

The girl lifted her shoulders in a slight shrug. "There is no magic in it," she said. "I knew that Cullihane and Latham were allies. Because Latham was attacked by the bats, I thought Cullihane would be also. I thought you'd be there to . . ."

The girl broke off as a shrill, rising whine came from

34

the radio beneath the dashboard of the car. It ended and the announcer's dry voice intoned a call.

"Call two-thirty-five, car two-three-five, go to Seventy-first and Sullivan streets. Bat scare. That is . . ."

The announcer's voice broke off in the middle of the signature, then came in again, stronger, more alert.

"Calling all cars. Five men killed by bats at Seventy-first and Sullivan streets. Cars two-three-five, one-seven-four, Cruiser one-eight, go to Seventy-First and Sullivan. . . ."

A ragged curse forced itself out between Wentworth's locked teeth. Even as he feared, the Bat Man had struck again at once. The plans that he had laid for tracing the killers was nullified by a simple lack of time. A new thought struck him. The new point of attack where five citizens had been killed by the poison bats was nowhere near the warehouse of Cullihane, nor any other of his strongholds. Why then had the bats been loosed?

Wentworth started to whirl the car to race toward the spot where the bats were killing. That movement undoubtedly saved his life. From behind him came a stuttering drumroll of gunfire. Bullets tore the side of the car, pocked the windshield, then smashed it into glittering, slashing fragments. A shard stung his cheek . . . The *Spider* glimpsed his assailants in the rear-vision mirror, but already he was in action. He cramped the wheels of the car still further and drove head-on for a building on his right. The car behind him was Cullihane's prowl coupé. The men in it were still shooting. They must either have spotted him, or revived the police and learned from them that it was the *Spider* who kept watch.

As the coupé drove head-on for the building, Wentworth shouted to the girl to crouch to the floor and himself slid down behind the wheel, stomped his foot on the brakes. The force of the collision with the building wall half-stunned him, but the attacking car was already roaring away, convinced its work was done.

35

Wentworth slapped open the door, leveled one automatic and fired three times carefully.

The gun car went out of control, skidded into a side street, and out of sight, hit something with a loud, splintering crash. Under the dash board of Wentworth's car, the radio was still squawking. . . .

"Calling all cars! Calling all cars!" the announcer's voice was harsh and excited. "Close all windows. Patrol cars put up curtains. Kill bats when possible. Warn all pedestrians to get behind closed doors at first opportunity. Twenty-two have been reported dead from the bats . . . !"

Wentworth's teeth locked. His eyes were hot flames. He freed June Calvert from the handcuffs. "Get under cover at once," he ordered.

He raced away from the wreck. He would have to cover a dozen blocks before he could reach his own car. Talking with June Calvert, he had traveled further than he had thought away from where he had left his own car. Small chance that he'd be able to get a taxicab. . . . He became abruptly aware that June Calvert was running after him. The sound of her limping steps, one foot encased in a shoe, the other only stockinged, was close behind. Wentworth whirled.

"Get to cover," he ordered. "You must protect yourself or those bats . . ."

The girl stooped and snatched off her other shoe, came on toward him in her stocking feet. Her eyes were wide, determined.

"Wherever the bats are," she said, panting a little, "will be the killer of my brother. I'm going with you."

There was no time to argue with her. With a shrug, Wentworth turned and hurried on, hearing the quickened breath of the girl beside him. He kept an alert lookout for a cab, but none appeared. He ran lightly, conserving wind and strength. The girl presented a problem in more ways than one. If he reached his car, with her still beside him . . .

He sprang out into a cross street and halted, pivoting

to the left. His Daimler was there, rolling softly swift, toward him with Ram Singh behind the wheel. But he could not permit the Hindu to greet him lest the girl who had proved herself shrewd enough to anticipate the *Spider's* next move, suspect his true identity.

Wentworth flipped an automatic into his palm, pointed it at Ram Singh and ordered him to halt. For a moment, surprise glared from the Hindu's eyes, then the girl burst out from behind the corner and he understood. His jaw trembled in simulated fear as he drew the car to a halt for Wentworth and the girl to enter. "Don't shoot, mister," he pleaded.

Wentworth hid a smile as he motioned June Calvert into the car, climbed in himself.

"I see there's a radio here," he said dryly. "Turn it on and let's see where the fight is the thickest."

Wentworth felt a keen disappointment while his heart was wrung with pity, with a bitter fury, at the knowledge of what must be happening here in this city at the moment with the winged death of the Bat Man fluttering from the sky. He had not anticipated any such wholesale attack as this, but he had expected Cullihane's place to be assailed by the Bat Man. He had hoped that when it happened he would be in a position to put a certain plan into effect, but this surprise assault had left him without recourse. Nita and his plane were far away. . . .

The radio came in with the clicking of the button. ". . . all cars. Calling all cars. *Spider* reported seen in neighborhood of Water Street and Sycamore. Suspected of connection with the vampire bats. . . ."

Wentworth's laughter was sharp and bitter. He was always fugitive from the law, but now once more the entire forces of a hundred cities, of the nation, would concentrate on his capture while the real persons behind the depredations of the bats went unhampered. Once more, it would depend on the *Spider* alone to find and destroy this new and overweening menace to the nation—handicapped by a thousand enemies bent upon his death. How the Bat Man must be laughing now!

*   *   *

The radio was squawking without ceasing. New reports of the bats sweeping death over the city. Now they were on Walnut Hill, now at Twelfth and Market streets. . . . As that last message came through, Wentworth leaned forward toward Ram Singh on whose back he kept the automatic centered.

"Get to Twelfth and Market Streets at once," he ordered flatly. "And make it fast or I'll give you a slug in the back to remember me by."

Ram Singh sent the Daimler hurtling through the streets. Wentworth leaned back against the cushions, apparently relaxed. He fingered a cigarette from a platinum case and lighted it with a snap of a lighter. Outwardly calm, he was aflame with anger. Twelfth and Market! It was in the heart of the downtown section. A few blocks away, the theaters would be loosing their gay crowds into the streets. There would be a mighty harvest for the bats this night, unless, unless . . .

He leaned forward. "That cigar store on the corner. Stop there!" he commanded sharply.

He handed an automatic to June Calvert. "Hold the car here," he said and sprang out without waiting for parley. He knew he risked death in the moments while he raced toward the store with his back toward the girl's gun. She was still not wholly convinced of his innocence. He had read that in her eyes, but she thought it wise to go with him in hope of learning more. This opportunity with a gun in her hand. . . . But the *Spider* had not acted without forethought. The very fact of his arming her and turning his back would militate against her suspicions. Wouldn't she hesitate to shoot a man who trusted her?

The drug clerk pulled up a startled head as a hunched figure in a black cape went past him toward the phone booths. He kept staring as Wentworth dropped a coin and dialed a number. The *Spider* watched him through the door which he opened just enough to extinguish the light within the booth. If he had been recognized, the police cars would soon have another errand than warning the people of the bats. . . .

Richard Wentworth, clubman and dilettante of the arts, was a personal friend of Commissioner Harrington of the Philadelphia police. The *Spider* called his home, got through to Harrington. He wasted no preliminaries.

"The *Spider* speaking," he announced, his voice flat, crisp. "You probably already know that the vampire bats are loose in the city. I think they are intended to attack the theater crowds. It would be wise to order all theaters to lock in their audiences until the bats are gone. You may save thousands of lives by that order. . . ."

So much Wentworth got out in a quick rush before Harrington interrupted. The *Spider* smashed through his words with sharp tones of command.

"Keep quiet, fool! Seconds are precious!" he snapped. "Send out loudspeaker cars to shout warning along the streets. Get a plane with a loudspeaker if you can. Don't forget that most of your people have not had a chance yet to learn about the bats."

Harrington was spluttering with his anger now. Wentworth's lips thinned to a smile. He could imagine the expression on Harrington's heavy face. It had been many a day, Wentworth thought, since anyone had dared to take that tone with the man. But it had served its purpose, had kept him silent while the message of the *Spider* was poured into his ears.

"For God's sake, act quickly," Wentworth urged, then he hung up softly and sped back out to the car. The cigar clerk stared at him, then staggered back a step against the wall. His eyes stretched wide and he pointed a trembling finger.

"The *Spider!*" he gabbled. "The *Spider!*"

He turned and ran toward a narrow door that opened in the back wall of the room, his voice going incoherent, turning into an hysterical scream. Before he had reached the doorway, the *Spider* was beside the car. He sprang into the rear, past June Calvert.

"Twelfth and Market!" he ordered again. "Split the road wide open."

He took the automatic from June's hand. Her dark eyes were frowning on him.

"What did you do?" she almost whispered.

Wentworth told her with clipped sentences while his eyes searched the way ahead.

He would do more when he reached the scene of activity, but what he wanted more than anything else was a chance to strike at the man behind these atrocities.

What was the reason behind this new threat against humanity? There could be no question that greed for money lay somewhere in the background. Money was responsible for all organized crime and, heaven knew, there was organization here—incredibly acute organization. . . .

The Daimler was gliding through the business section of the city now, all dark save where the sparkling of theater lights threw a multi-colored glare against the heavens. A police radio-roadster, curtains tightly drawn, raced by with siren screaming and, at a word, Ram Singh followed. The radio still howled its incredibly mounting toll of deaths. Nearly a hundred human beings had been slain and the police undoubtedly could not discover more than half the victims so soon after the tragedy had begun. It was seemingly impossible that so purposeless a slaughter . . .

The Daimler swung a corner and a woman's screams rang out. Wentworth could see her, a dark, dodging form, as she ran frantically toward him along the street. She held a child in her arms and was bent far over it, protecting it with arms and head and bowed body. Wentworth could not see the cause of her terror, but he had no need. About her head, one of those poisonous vampires of the Bat Man must be flitting, seeking an inch of bare flesh in which to sink its deadly teeth.

Incredible that vampires should behave in this way—bats that were rarely seen, but came silently in the darkness of the night to flutter down on sleeping men and

40

animals and take their toll of blood. But these bats were attacking as if they were hydrophobic—or as if they were starved! Yes, that must be it. Vampire bats starved until they would attack any living thing, against any odds, to obtain food!

The thought was a flash of light in Wentworth's brain. He had needed to shout no order to Ram Singh. The Daimler already was sprinting toward where the woman stumbled in a heavy, hopeless run, her screams despairing as she shielded her child against the attack of the flying beasts. Wentworth whipped open the door, felt the wind snatch it from his hand and slam it back against the body of the car.

"This way!" he shouted. "This way! I'll save you!"

The woman cried out in joy and ran with increased speed toward the braking Daimler. Once let her get inside . . . Wentworth's automatics were in his hands. If he could only spot the bat that menaced her. Ah, a glimpse of a fluttering black form. The *Spider's* automatic blasted, hammered a bat into extinction. The woman was running toward him eagerly. She lifted her face, held the child out from her body in an effort to get it first into the protection of the car.

It happened in a heartbeat of time. Before the woman's face, a black shadow flitted. Leathery wings covered the baby's head. Wentworth could not shoot. He sprang forward and another of the loathsome black things flicked out of the darkness. The woman's scream rose high, higher, shrilling terribly. She stopped and stood rigidly, arms lifting the baby high. Its cries had ceased now and abruptly her own scream strangled into nothingness. She crumpled to the pavement while the *Spider* was still ten feet away.

As if it echoed her dying scream, another cry broke out. It was shrill, wailing and it ached downward from the heavens. It rose, wavering, to crescendo that made the cold flesh creep along Wentworth's spine, then died into a minor note that was like a death sob. The *Spider* shouted a curse. He knew that sound. It had heralded the death of those score of men in Latham's mansion. Hearing it, Latham had cried, "Oh, God, the Bat Man."

The Bat Man! Wentworth's eyes quested upward toward the muggy skies that threw back glare of street lights. Instinctively, he flinched. A bat dodged at his face and Wentworth's gun blasted upward deafeningly. The beast was hurled upward by the impact of lead, thudded softly to the pavement. The air was suddenly full of them, dodging, diving, sweeping on the *Spider*. His guns spoke deliberately, with a fearful accuracy. Through the night once more rang the wailing, blood-chilling cry of the Bat Man.

"Master!" Ram Singh shouted. "Master, quickly come to cover. A cloud of bats!"

Wentworth darted toward the Daimler, while his eyes still searched the heavens. Nothing moved there for the space of a half-dozen seconds, then far up there where the lights just touched him, the *Spider* saw again the incredible image of the huge bat-like thing he had spotted against the moon when Latham had died—Good God, was it only a few hours ago?—Wentworth's twin guns spat a deadly hail upward toward that gliding figure. But he knew it was futile, knew even as he continued to smash lead upward until his guns were empty.

"Master!" Ram Singh screamed the warning this time.

Wentworth sprang toward the car. He felt a gentle touch on his shoulder and brushed frantically with a gloved hand, knocked off a vampire bat. Then he was inside and the door thudded shut behind him. He was not a moment too soon. A cloud of bats blotted out for an instant the street outside, fluttering past the closed window.

A shudder swept over the *Spider's* body. He was no coward. No man in the world would ever call him that. But the sight of those hundred deadly little beasts with their soft flight and their teeth whose kiss meant death shook him as no gunman's lead had ever done. The black cloud lifted and he saw that the body of the

42

woman and the child was a moving, black mass of leather-winged creatures. . . .

Beside him, June Calvert was sobbing, her face buried in her hands. Ram Singh was muttering harsh Hindustani curses under his breath. Up there where this dark side street intersected the brightness of Market, there was a sudden, dark rush of screaming people. Over their heads danced a myriad black, deadly forms. Wentworth's lips were motionless, thin against his teeth as he stuffed fresh clips of bullets into his automatics. He would do what he could, but in heaven's name, what could he accomplish with the slaughter of a few bats? Something like a groan of despair pushed its way out between his clenched teeth.

Up there in the heavens, that winged monster watched the work of his kindred fiends, the bats. And . . .

Once more came that wailing, mocking cry. Damn it, the Bat Man was laughing, *laughing*. . . . *!*

CHAPTER FOUR

Bat Man vs. The Spider

Ram Singh thrust the Daimler toward where the crowd milled and slapped the air to drive off the deadly bats. Wentworth beat his knees with clenched fists. His guns were so futile against the hundreds of flying things. There *must* be some other method of fighting against them. . . . !

As the car rolled out into Market Street, men and women grabbed at the handles and sought to force their way inside. Wentworth had locked the doors. It was necessary if he were to accomplish anything at all. He might save a half-dozen persons inside the car, but that would keep him from work which might save hundreds. . . . He saw a fire-alarm box on a corner and shouted sharply to Ram Singh to halt.

He sprang from the car, fought his way through the crowds. The bats hovered just overhead. Now and again, one would dart downward and a man or woman would scream and die. Wentworth wore gloves, as always when he was in the *Spider's* disguise, and now he dragged his long, black cape up over his head, tearing a hole through which he might look. Twice, he felt the feathery touch of a bat lighting upon the cape and the hint of their poisonous death tightened his lips grimly. He reached the alarm box, jerked open the door and

44

yanked the lever. If the firemen could smash through, there might be a chance. . . .

Across the street, a theater was gay with many-colored lights. Police stood behind the closed, glass doors, he saw. Despite his anger, Harrington had taken the *Spider's* advice. Perhaps a few hundred who might otherwise die terribly would be saved as a result of that.

Wentworth dared not uncover his head, lest the bats strike at him and without better vision, he could not shoot. Still, he did not dare return to the car lest he not be able to give the firemen the only suggestion that he thought might help. If they put on smoke helmets and covered their hands, they would be virtually immune to the attack. . . .

A crashing blast across the street pulled his startled gaze to the theater. He heard the crash again and saw one of the inner doors crash outward, saw an axe glitter coldly. Even as the police whirled with their nightsticks ready, other doors crashed outward and the entire audience of the theater came streaming out into the street.

"Bats!" a man screamed. "The theater is full of bats!"

Wentworth saw a woman attempting to cover her bare shoulders with a cape, saw a bat settle like a loathsome, black flower upon her bosom. The woman fell. He started across the street, but a new rush of terrified men and women drove him back. The hoarse sirens of the fire engines cut through the medley of terror and pain. The trucks were literally ploughing their way through the crowds. Wentworth saw that the men already had donned their smoke helmets. He nodded approval. If he could find the man who had ordered that, he wouldn't have any trouble putting over his idea. . . .

A battalion-chief's car jangled its way through solid ranks of screaming, dying people and the chief sprang out. He dodged as a bat flitted at him, ducked back inside the car and put on a smoke helmet. Wentworth rushed to his side, spat out his idea in swift words.

"Get hoses going," he shouted. "Knock people

45

down and keep the streams going above them. Bats can't get through.''

The battalion-chief was a gray-haired man. Wentworth saw his shrewd, smoke-narrowed eyes through the goggle eyes of the helmet. The driver of the car was rigid with fear, fear of the bats, fear of the man whose face he glimpsed when Wentworth lifted the hood of his cape. The chief nodded. He took off the smoke helmet long enough to shout orders. Wentworth dashed back to his car, ducked inside and began shooting.

"Get in front," he ordered June Calvert. "In front, but leave the glass slide open."

The girl hesitated, then clambered over the back of the seat. There were two panes of glass that slid in grooves between front and rear of the car. She left one open. Wentworth took off his hat, then flung open one door of the car. For long, dreadful seconds nothing happened, then a bat flicked into the interior, dropped toward Wentworth's face. He swept his hat swiftly up and knocked the bat to the seat. It would be helpless there. Bats have no way of taking off from a horizontal surface. They cannot take off from a porch which is less than several feet from the floor, for a bat takes off by dropping free, spreading its wings, then gliding. With its wings already spread, it might take off from a lower object, but the seat would not permit that. Wentworth waited, his hat poised, his split-second muscles set for the perilous task of capturing bats whose merest bite would be fatal.

One hose already was hissing out its stream of water into the crowd of Market Street. Men and women were bowled over and bats were washed out of the air to flutter helplessly on the pavement. Given time, they might work their way up the side of some building and fly again, but they would be given no opportunity for that.

Time after time, Wentworth's hat swept a bat from midflight to the seat and finally he slammed the door, crawled into the front section of the car and closed the glass slide. He sat looking over the water-flooded street. Many of the crowd had caught the idea of the hoses— a dozen were operating now—and were throwing themselves down beneath the protecting streams. The battalion-chief had evidently sent in a call for more trucks for the hoarse cry of their sirens filled the air.

Crowds were streaming now from every theater with cries that they were filled with bats. Wentworth's heart was heavy within him. It had been at his order that people had been kept prisoner in those theaters. Harrington would be glad to give the excuse that the *Spider* had advised the action. He could hear the man's grandiloquent voice now.

"Gentleman of the press, you all know what the *Spider* has done for us in the past. I thought him an honorable man, fighting for the law in his own peculiar way. Naturally when he advised a thing, I considered it seriously. Hold the people in the theaters—yes, it seemed a good idea. How could I know that the *Spider* had turned into a mad dog who should be exterminated on sight? I have given my men orders to that effect. To shoot the *Spider* on sight. . . ."

Yes, Harrington would talk like that. The *Spider* had tried to serve and he had led the people he sought to protect into a trap for the Bat Man. Regardless of whether he had convinced June Calvert, her earlier testimony that she had seen the *Spider* carrying a cage of bats would be revived. Wentworth laughed grimly. It only made his task more difficult. He closed his eyes, pressed them with heavy fingers. There was so much death, so much tragedy all about. What, in heaven's name, could be the purpose behind this wholesale slaughter of the innocents? If only he could have foreseen what was happening, have had Nita here earlier. . . .

Wentworth pulled up his head. There was work to do. Not yet had the Bat Man called home his charges with that thin, gigantic squeaking. . . . He turned to Ram Singh.

"I must thank you for standing by the *Spider* in time of trouble," he said crisply. "Many men would have fled from the scene of disaster the moment a gun was taken away from their back. You must tell me your master's name that I may commend you to him. Meantime, get us away from here at once. Miss Calvert, I am sure that soon it will be safe to go abroad. I am going to put you in the protection of some building. . . ."

Wentworth's words cut off as he met the black, blazing regard of her eyes. There was hatred there, more than suspicion, certainty. Good lord! Had she penetrated his subterfuge with Ram Singh? Had she detected the fact that they worked together, that the Hindu was in reality the servant of the *Spider?* If she had . . .

"You, you fiend!" she choked. "You almost tricked me. But it was *you* who kept those people in the theaters so that the bats could kill them. You are the Bat Man, and. . . ."

Wentworth shrugged, motioned to Ram Singh and the great car purred away from the spot where the dead lay in the streets beside the panicked living who crouched beneath the protection of the fire hoses. June Calvert ceased to talk and only glared at him angrily. Luckily, she had no gun. . . . She was put out presently at the entrance of a subway that would shelter her from bats. Wentworth spun to Ram Singh.

"Find me a taxi immediately," he said sharply. When the Daimler surged forward, Wentworth rapidly instructed the Hindu in the course he must follow. Moments later, the Spider, stripped of cape and hat, part of the disguise removed from his face, sprang into a cab.

"Fifty dollars if you make the airport in twenty minutes," he ordered. "Ten more for every minute you shave off of that."

The taxi's forward lurch hurled him back against the cushions and he eased to a more comfortable position, drew out cigarettes and lighter. If only the Bat Man would delay for a while his signal to the bat horde. . . . He shook his head. There was small hope of that. Already the attack must have lasted for over half an hour, the hungry bats were becoming sated. Probably he would have no such luck.

The motor of the cab snarled with speed. They shot over the bridge toward Camden and the hiss of the wind increased. Wentworth had not doubted that Ram Singh would do his part. He had known just where to send the Hindu for the materials needed. . . . The Spider's mind was weary with futile contemplation of the tragedy he had seen, the hundreds laid in writhing death in the streets. He had certain lines of investigation he could start. That spear which had been hurled through the window of Latham's home. He had noticed certain of its characteristics and was pretty certain that it was of a type used by the headhunters of the extreme reaches of the Amazon, the Jivaro Indians. A ridiculous idea, that those fiercely independent Indians could have been brought to America, or could have come of their own accord. But then it was ridiculous, too, that vampire bats had invaded the temperate zones. Neither seemed possible . . . yet hundreds had died of their poisoned bite this night. Yes, literally hundreds. He glanced at his watch, then out at the dark buildings streaking past. The taxi was making good time.

Finally the lights of the airport came in view. The driver slammed up to the administration building, twisted about to blink behind horn-rimmed spectacles.

"I think you will find the exact time about seventeen minutes, sir," he said in polite, precise English.

Wentworth tossed him a hundred-dollar bill and raced toward the main building. He glimpsed a low-winged monoplane on the tarmac of a nearby hangar, its motor ticking over and swerved in his race. Minutes were precious, terribly precious. It was barely possible that the Bat Man had not yet sounded the recall for the bats. Even if he had, swift action might yet win the day for the *Spider*. . . .

*   *   *

Wentworth reached the plane in a pounding sprint. A mechanic stood with a pilot at the door of the hangar and they turned in amazement at sight of the running figure. Something of his purpose they must have guessed, but not in time to accomplish anything. Even as they started forward, shouting, Wentworth toed the wing, sprang to the cockpit and instantly yanked the throttle wide. The plane's engine spluttered, then bellowed. The ship began to trundle down the tarmac. It was a Lockhead, a type with which Wentworth was entirely familiar. He jockeyed to gain speed rapidly. For seconds, there was danger that the pursuing pair could reach the tail and nail it to the ground. Then the ship gathered way. An air-liner was circling the field for a landing and the operations officer atop the administration building's conning tower flicked a red light at Wentworth frantically. The *Spider* glanced aloft, gauged his distances and sent his powerful monoplane off the ground downwind.

For seconds, the ship climbed sluggishly, then its speed picked up and he sent it racing at low altitude toward Philadelphia. He could not have wished for a better plane, but he longed for the machine guns of his scarlet Northrup. No way of knowing into what peril he flew tonight.

The lights of Philadelphia sprang at him. Within minutes, he was circling over its streets, peering down into the canyons and seeking the square to which he had directed Ram Singh. It was difficult at night, but after five minutes of circling, he located the place. His altitude was no more than four hundred feet. He drew an automatic and fired two shots. Staring down at the square, he saw the flashes of Ram Singh's answering gun.

Suspenseful moments passed then while Wentworth hung the Lockhead in the sky, watching, watching. . . . His panted breath of relief was almost a triumphant shout when, against the blackness of the square, he caught a dozen flitting bats which glowed as with phosphorescence. Ram Singh had succeeded then, had obtained the radiolite paint and sprayed the vampire bats with it, afterward providing them perches so that they could wing from the Daimler at the proper time. Now, if the *Spider* could keep them in sight and follow them to whatever place they had been kept, it was likely the Bat Man would not be far away!

At first, the glowing spots that were the bats flew about in seeming bewilderment, then they turned westward and, grouped loosely together, flew steadily in a straight course. Three times, the bats turned from their steady flight and each time a man in the streets died beneath their teeth. Wentworth, circling grim-lipped in the heavens, saw and could do nothing. But he swore a hard oath that the Bat Man and his followers should pay for each of these lives. They were martyrs to the cause of justice. . . .

Finally, the last of the houses of Philadelphia were gone from under Wentworth and still the bats winged on into the darkness. It was easier to follow them since the city lights no longer blinded him. It was necessary for him to swing in tight circles. The bats flew much more slowly than the plane, yet if he swung wide he might very well lose sight of their glowing bodies.

The flight moved on and on westward. Wentworth almost despaired of any definite goal for the bats. It seemed impossible that they should have been released so far from the city and yet sweep so directly there. Yet they flew fairly close together and bats generally traveled in pairs at most, generally alone. There must be some reason for this group migration. . . .

Suddenly, through the vibration of the plane's motor, Wentworth heard a shrill, wailing note that he recognized instantly. It was followed immediately by the squeaking rasp, as of a giant bat. The glowing flight below him faltered in its steady progression. He realized that they were no longer pushing forward, but were climbing straight toward him!

It was impossible. No one could so direct and guide bats, and yet—and yet here they came directly toward his swift plane! The answer came to him almost with the realization of their approach. The shrill squeak of the giant bat had come *from his direction!* The bats only flew toward the sound, then—then . . .

With a cold chill of apprehension racing up his spine, Wentworth tilted back his head to stare upward into the heavens. Then he kicked the rudder violently. The Lockhead rocked, spun to the left and Wentworth snapped a gun into his hand, staring with incredulous eyes at the black shadow that had seemed to float above him in the heavens.

Above him, almost within pistol range, was the huge creature that he had seen twice now upon the scene of vampire murder. Even as Wentworth spotted the thing, he saw flame streak from somewhere near its head and a rifle bullet cracked past his head!

An oath squeezed out between the *Spider's* locked teeth. No longer was there any doubt the thing was human. It might have wings, might skim the skies like a bat, but it was human. No bat could fire a rifle. With the thought, Wentworth yanked back the stick and drove straight at the thing, automatic ready in his hand. . . .

Once more the rifle cracked and the bullet dug into the fuselage beside Wentworth's shoulder. The *Spider* kicked the rudder, skidding the plane about. He was within range now and the *Spider's* lead never missed. . . . His automatic was ready, but its muzzle swept empty air! In the instant it had taken Wentworth's plane to wheel about, the Bat Man—it could be no other—had disappeared! Even as he made that discovery, lead whistled upward past his gun hand.

The *Spider's* lips twisted against his teeth. He shoved the stick against the instrument panel and the Lockhead dropped her nose like a plummet. In a heartbeat, he had lost two hundred feet. But he had not caught the Bat Man. He had a glimpse of him in the instant the ship's nose had gone down. The Bat Man had stood on his tail for that shot upward at the ship and as Wentworth swept by, he was in the midst of a whipstall. . . .

As the phrase *whipstall* snapped through Wentworth's brain, he gasped. Gasped even as he threw two swift shots at the Bat Man. Thère was time for no more. He was dangerously close to the ground and the Lockhead was heavy, its wing spread proportionally small. Down, down she went while he maneuvered rudder and aerolons. The Lockhead came out of it with twenty-five feet to spare. Wentworth zoomed, *viraged* to spot the Bat Man. . . . He was gone! As quickly as that, in the few seconds while the Lockhead dived for earth and zoomed out of it, the flying man had vanished.

Wentworth eagerly scanned the earth below, but there was nothing there, no movement, no sound—and no place where a plane might land even if the Bat Man were down there. Sudden wild hope sang through Wentworth's brain. Had those two swift shots, thrown in the midst of a power dive of terrific speed, knocked down the Bat Man? Slowly, the *Spider* shook his head. It was barely possible, but even his extraordinary aim would scarcely be equal to that task. Besides, he was certain that his zoom, his *virage* would have been quick enough to spot a Bat Man tumbling to earth. However, if he had dived. . . .

Wentworth's mind turned back to the idea that had flashed through his brain as he had darted past the Bat Man. *Whipstall!* That described the performance of the winged man. It was a phrase applied to planes that, rising too steeply, slapped straight down to the ground as if the tail were the handle of a whip and the nose the lash. A bird couldn't perform an operation such as that if it wished, nor could a bat.

To Wentworth that meant only one thing. That Bat Man was an ordinary human being. . . . *with wings attached to his body like a plane!* As the idea struck, a memory came to the *Spider*. Recently, at Miami, a "daredevil" had dropped from a plane with triangular canvas wings stretching from arms to his body and another fin between his legs. With their aid, he had looped and stunted in the air, finally using a parachute to land.

53

Why wouldn't it be possible, by extending those wings to each side with struts and braces, to operate precisely as a motorless glider?

By the gods, the thing sounded possible! There was no time now, of course, to figure weight per square foot, gliding angles. . . . While he thought, Wentworth had been scouring the country below him, hoping against hope that he might catch some glimpse of the blowing bats. But it was in vain. The Bat Man had accomplished his purpose. He had almost killed Wentworth with his rifle, operated in what way God only knew, and he had distracted him until the murdering bats could escape.

Spider and Bat Man had met—and it was the Bat Man who had won!

CHAPTER FIVE

Dinner With Death

Wearily, Wentworth turned the Lockhead back toward Camden airport. Undoubtedly all fields had been warned to watch out for a stolen ship. He smiled slightly, took the stick between his knees and stripped off the remnants of his disguise. Many things could be forgiven Richard Wentworth, especially if he paid well. . . .

He had no more trouble on landing than he had anticipated and found Ram Singh waiting for him with the Daimler. He settled gratefully into the cushions. A half hour later he was asleep at his rooms in the Early Quaker, an ancient and quiet hotel on the waterfront. He was astir early, found a note on his bedside table that Nita van Sloan already had arrived in response to his summons. A smile touched his lips. He lifted the note, in Nita's own handwriting, to his lips, and crossed to the telephone, got her rooms at once.

"Darling," he cried jubilantly, "could you find it in your heart to have breakfast with me, oh practically at once?"

"I thought the invitation was for dinner," she told him, "but it's just possible that I'm not engaged. . . ."

It was pleasant in the informal dining room of the Early Quaker. Its flooring was the ancient boards of a wharf and extended out over the river. Mooring rungs were still fastened there, and there was always the pleasant suck and murmur of the tide among the piles. The wharf had been glassed in and, open now, allowed the warm, morning sunlight to stream through.

Nita's smile, as Wentworth greeted her in the lobby, was warm and welcoming. Her violet eyes were deep and the bronze-lit curls that clustered about the perfect oval of her face were incredibly lovely. Wentworth told her so in a soft murmur as he took her arm and led her toward the sunlit dining room. Nita's lips were curved in a remembering smile. Their pleasurable moments together were all too brief. Greatly they loved, but the *Spider* could never marry. How could a man take on the responsibilities of wife and children when any moment might find the disgracing hand of the law upon his shoulder—when any night might bring his death at the hands of one of a hundred enemies?

No, Wentworth had sacrificed his hope of personal happiness for the sake of the thousands of others who would be denied peace, perhaps even life, if the arch-criminals that now and again arose, were not put down by the *Spider*. He had never regretted his choice, but their were times when bitterness touched his soul. . . .

At a table where they could gaze out on the blue of the Delaware River, Nita touched Wentworth's hand, her violet eyes gravely on his.

"I see that they blame the *Spider* again," she said.

Wentworth shrugged. "It is inevitable, I suppose. How do the newspapers explain the *Spider's* calling fire engines and directing the firemen to save the people with their hoses?"

Nita glanced toward the approaching waiter. "They don't explain it, Dick. They don't mention it at all."

Wentworth grimaced. The battalion-chief, then, had taken credit for the idea. Well, it did not matter. He began to tell Nita the events of the night before. He had no secrets from her. Often she helped him in his battles and more than once she had herself worn the *Spider's* mantle, and made the *Spider's* kills. . . .

The day passed without further event and Wentworth

spent the time conferring with police officials, seeking some clue to the reason behind the wholesale slaughters of the Bat Man. He found no motive, but he learned one thing that made his lips thin with determination. The Crosswinds Jockey club was holding an annual banquet at the Early Quaker this evening.

It was a quasi-social affair and he decided at once to attend. Even though the Bat Man had been striking at random at humanity, it seemed likely he would still follow the aim of his first attacks—the race track. Even if there were no new assault, it was possible that Wentworth might pick up some lead to the killer. Certainly, the man must be some one familiar with racing and the coterie connected with it. He might very well still be associated with the turf himself. . . .

An invitation was easy to arrange and the dinner he had planned with Nita was shared with some hundred other persons, social celebrities and turf men. Commissioner of Police Harrington was there at the head table with Wentworth and Nita. His red-jowled face was far from pleasant. It was plain that the overwhelming tragedies of the last twenty-four hours weighed heavily upon him.

Wentworth had scarcely seated Nita when a blond, handsome man who towered even above Wentworth's six feet came eagerly to them.

"I say!" he cried. "Aren't you Nitita—I'm sorry—Nita van Sloan?"

Nita looked up questioningly then sprang to her feet and held out both hands.

"Piggy!" she cried. "Piggy Stoking. In heaven's name . . . !"

Wentworth stood politely by, smiling slightly, estimating the taper-shouldered strength of the man, taking in the youthful but determined face. Nita turned toward Wentworth, flushed a little.

"This is Frederick Stoking, who was my first beau," she told him, laughing. "He used to pull my pigtails when . . . when I wore pigtails. Richard Wentworth, Fred.''

The two men bowed, shaking hands, taking each other's measure. Wentworth decided Stoking was intelligent, and steady, just as his wide-set, blue eyes were. There was a deep cleft in a firm chin. Without consciously willing it, he compared himself and this man who had been Nita's first beau. They were very much of an age, he and Stoking, but the trials he had undergone, the woes and the pains, had taken their toll of Wentworth's face. There were lines at his mouth corners, a sharpness to his nose. Stoking was gay.

"You must join us after the banquet," Wentworth said cordially. "I'd like very much to hear about Nita's pigtails."

Stoking's eyes were grave despite the laughter about his mouth. "They were just as lovely as her curls are now," he said. "I pulled them, but I assure you it was reverently."

Nita laughed at him. "None the less painfully!"

Stoking left and Wentworth and Nita both watched his superb figure as he moved back to his own party. Wentworth looked down at his plate, reflecting a score of yellow lights. His mouth was unconsciously grim. He was not thinking anything definitely, but there was a darkness, a depression, of his spirits.

Nita's hand touched his arm. "Why, Dick!" she whispered, "I do believe you're jealous!"

Wentworth straightened his shoulders, put a smile on his lips, but he spoke very quietly. "Darling, I am jealous for the normal happiness that might have been yours if you had never met me. Why should you be burdened down, as I am, with the cares of the world?"

Nita's hand tightened on his arm. "If you don't stop that, I shall kiss you right here in public," she said fiercely. "Perhaps I prefer to be burdened."

Wentworth laughed, patted her hand, and shrugged aside his depression. He leaned toward Nita, named all the celebrities present. "I am suspicious of all small men," he told her. "There's that jockey over there at

58

the third table. An ex-jockey, rather, turned stables owner. He's very successful and bats haven't killed any of his horses. Sanderson is the name. He still doesn't weigh above ninety pounds.''

''Why small men?'' Nita asked.

''I've estimated the wing spread of the Bat Man, gliding angles, weight per square foot. He couldn't perform in the air as he does with that wing spread and weigh much over a hundred pounds. For instance, the man next to him, another ex-jockey named Earl Westfall, couldn't possibly manage himself on the wings. He's put on a lot of weight for his height, must weigh about a hundred and eighty to judge from his girth.''

Nita's hand still clung to his arm. She tightened her fingers. ''That red-headed man bending over Commissioner Harrington's shoulder . . . ?''

''Red Cullihane,'' Wentworth said briefly. ''Partner of Latham, who was killed last night.'' He felt a tingling race over his body as he studied the stubby, powerful build of the man, a tingling of apprehension. Cullihane's presence here spelled danger for all of them. Suppose the Bat Man should strike at him tonight, at this banquet? If the man's intention was merely promiscuous slaughter, the gathering here offered an excellent opportunity, especially if people connected with the turf were still mainly his targets. Wentworth's eyes tightened, his hands beneath the table clenched into hard knots. He was suddenly sure that his premonition was correct, that there would be slaughter here tonight. . . .

He glanced swiftly about the banquet hall, built out over the Delaware river on piles, an ancient wharf actually. The glassed sides were open wide and through them now and then came the moan of a tug whistle, but there were tight-fitted screens. They could be smashed out by the same means that had been used at Latham's home, but Wentworth doubted that method. It would allow too slow ingress for the number of bats necessary to dispose of the entire gathering. . . . Nevertheless, he was certain that the attack would take place.

Wentworth's smile tightened, thinned his lips. Queer, these premonitions of his. They were rarely wrong and he had come to believe them to be based on the intuitive workings of his subconscious mind. He no longer strove to trace out the reasons, merely accepted the conclusion thus presented to him. There would be an attack here tonight.

Somehow, his mind refused to apply itself to the problem of defense. There was no reason for the lethargy. He was thoroughly rested after the strenuous activities of the previous twenty-four hours. Yet, instead of planning strategy, he found himself gazing time and again at the man who had been Nita's first beau. Fred Stoking's eyes kept straying toward Nita, too.

Nita's hand touched Wentworth's arm. "What's the matter, Dick boy?" she whispered.

There wasn't anything the matter, except that he felt a vast reluctance for the encounter that was approaching. Good God, would there never be an end of this ceaseless fighting?—Never an end of the warped madmen who sought nation-wide dominion through crime? He knew a strange rebellion that he, and he alone, should meet these terrors. . . .

"Nita," he spoke abruptly, "I want you to join Stoking's party and get them to leave here at once on some pretext."

Nita's fingers tightened on his arm. "What is it?"

"There's going to be a bat attack here," he told her, barely breathing the words. "I know it, but I couldn't persuade anyone to believe me. I don't even wish to prevent it. If I don't permit the attack, I won't be able to trail the Bat Man."

Nita started to protest, but a glimpse of Wentworth's bitter eyes stopped the words on her lips. She looked at him a bit curiously. His desire to remove her from the path of danger was understandable enough, but why Piggy Stoking?

Wentworth smiled at her slightly, reading the question in her eyes. "I rather like the lad," he said. "Besides I want to check up on your past and if he were killed, I couldn't do it."

He rose to his feet and Nita, perforce, stood also. She looked up into the lean, tanned face she loved, the smile fading from her lips. So often, so often they had parted like this on the eve of peril and death. . . .

"Be careful, Dick!"

"For you, sweetheart!"

Many eyes followed Nita and Wentworth as they crossed the floor to Stoking's table. They made a brave couple, those two, alike in proud carriage, with that touch of arrogance in the poise of the head, confidence like an accolade upon their shoulders.

"I'm called away unexpectedly," Wentworth told Stoking. "I'm sure I can trust you since there are no pigtails to pull."

"I make no promises," Stoking warned him. "Those curls tempt me, too."

Wentworth bowed his way from the table, his smile lingering mechanically on his lips. From the antechamber, he sent for Commissioner Harrington. The man came heavily toward him, shorter than Wentworth, a frown between his eyes.

"What's up?" he asked crisply.

Wentworth's face was as grave as his. "Bats," he said. "At least seventy-five per cent of the guests tonight are associated with the race track. They got Latham. Cullihane, with whom Latham was associated, is present."

Harrington tried to laugh it off. "You're of the belief then, that these attacks are sponsored by some crooks or another? You believe in this Bat Man?"

Quick anger throbbed over Wentworth. It was the unbelief of men like this, the slowness of authorities entrusted with the protection of humanity, that necessitated the activities of the *Spider*. Oh, for the keen strength of Governor Kirkpatrick in a time like this!

Kirk, who had been police commissioner of New York City for years, had never hesitated. . . .

"Very well," Wentworth told Harrington coldly. "Doubt me and watch your friends die." He turned on his heel and strode away.

Commissioner Harrington came after him hurriedly. "No offense intended, Wentworth," he said. "Surely, you must realize it's hard to believe in a man with wings . . . ?"

Wentworth turned toward him. "It's no man with wings," he said shortly. "But a man who has rigged a bat-like glider. You've heard of motorless gliders, haven't you? I fought with him last night and he outmaneuvered me. Naturally, the shorter the wingspread, and axis, the more quickly the craft can pivot or dodge." He recounted briefly his battle with the Bat Man the night before. He stopped once to bow as Nita and the Stoking party passed them. His eyes saluted Nita for her achievement, then he turned back to Harrington and continued his story. When he had finished, the Commissioner frowned heavily, staring at the floor, standing with braced legs hands locked behind his back.

"I cannot doubt you," he said. "I know what you've done in New York, of course, against criminals. You must pardon my hesitation. The conception is a bit bizarre."

Wentworth acknowledged that with a short nod. "Quite, but I do not make statements unless I have ample reason for them. I tell you that the bats will attack here tonight. I do not know when, but. . . ."

His words broke off as a piercing wail, a sobbing moan swelled into the antechamber where the two men stood.

"The Bat Man!" Wentworth rasped.

As if his words had been a signal, the lights blinked out and a deathly stillness fell upon the gabble of the banquet hall, upon the entire hotel. Then a woman screamed.

"The bats!" she cried, and a panic roar followed her scream.

Wentworth's hand closed on Harrington's arm. He felt the man's start at his touch. "Perhaps next time," Wentworth shouted at him, "you *will* believe!"

CHAPTER SIX

Waters of Doom

Wentworth's face was grimly set as he raced to the battle against the poisonous bats. If only he had begun earlier his attempt to persuade Harrington! But it was useless to reproach himself. He had acted immediately after the discovery of what impended. Only one thing to do now: attempt to save the lives of these trapped banqueters.

He fled headlong for the outer door and as he reached the curb, the long, low form of his Daimler rolled forward, jerked to a halt. He snapped open the back door, reached inside and snatched out a large drum-like object of glittering chromium. As he started back for the door of the hotel again, the driver sprang to the street and reached his side in long strides.

"Stay here, Ram Singh," Wentworth ordered. "Throw the switch as soon as I get inside."

The turbaned Hindu scowled at being barred from the battle, but there was no hesitation in his movements. He leaped back into the car. Wentworth shouldered open the doors of the hotel and instantly a wide beam of light blazed out from the drum-like object he carried. He hurried with it to the door of the banquet hall and its powerful ray illuminated the entire room.

The air was filled with the fluttering small messengers of death and streams of them poured upward through traps opened in the floor. Wentworth cursed. He should have seen that method of attack. The wharf floor had been preserved in its original form. "Atmosphere" for the hotel. The Bat Man had merely opened the trap doors that once had been used by workmen and released his hordes of killers. Wentworth thanked the gods for his foresight in putting the powerful searchlight into the car. He had not expected this attack tonight, but had prepared for future frays. Now the blazing white beam was blinding the bats. Many of them were fluttering back into the pits from which they rose, while others swung blindly about the room in their heavy, laborious flight. Two score of men and women lay upon the floor, dead from the bites of the starved vampires—but the light had saved a hundred others!

Wentworth did not delay on the scene after placing the light. A single glance had pictured the hall indelibly upon his mind, then he turned and raced for the outer doors again. It would be impossible, he knew, to attack from here the men who had brought the bats. It would be certain death to attempt to descend through those bat-crowded trap-doors. But there was another way. . . .

As he sprang to the street he saw Ram Singh's knife glittering in the air. Four men were trying to slice the cable that fed current to the searchlight. Wentworth's twin automatics flew to his hands. He shot twice. Ram Singh's blade had disposed of the other two. His teeth flashed white in a smile as he faced his master.

"My knife is thirsty, master," he cried in Hindustani. "It has but sipped a drop or two . . . !"

Wentworth had not paused while he shot. Now he thrust his guns back into their holsters and, with a gesture to the Hindu, raced for a wharf from which he could reach the river. Ram Singh loped along beside him. He was chanting under his breath, a war song in which the exploits of his wonderful knife figured large.

A high board fence bordered the wharf. Wentworth sprang upward and seized its top. Instantly, Ram Singh caught his feet and helped him. Stradling the top, Wentworth reached down a hand to the Hindu. Below him the water was black with wavering white shadows of lights upon its surface. Under the piles which supported the dining room of the Early Quaker were only shadows. . . .

Wentworth stripped off coat and shoes. He thrust his automatics into Ram Singh's hands.

"Thy knife, warrior!" he ordered.

Ram Singh wiped the blade across his thigh and Wentworth gripped it between his teeth, dived into the black water. There was scarcely a splash to mark his smooth entrance. Ripples spread quietly and lapped against the piles, making zig-zags of the light's reflections. But Wentworth's head did not break the surface again. Under water, he stroked for the darkness beneath the Quaker wharf. Under there somewhere were the men of the Bat Master, loosing new killers upon the people above.

When he rose to the surface, it was with his fingers against the barnacle-studded base of a pile. His head lifted without a sound and he peered, narrow-eyed, through the darkness. Rays of light escaped from the banquet hall overhead. By that faint illumination, Wentworth made out the shadows of four boats. In each a man crouched beside a high cage from which the bats had been released. Even as he spotted them, the boats began to ease away from the trapdoors.

Noiselessly, Wentworth stroked toward the nearest. As he approached, the man in it slid over the side and vanished into the black water. Wentworth whipped the knife from between his teeth and dived. It was not the kind of weapon he liked, but this was no time for niceties. This man in the water was a knife at his back, a threat of death. What Wentworth sought was a live prisoner, but this swimming assassin. . . .

There could be no vision under this black surface, but Wentworth had marked the other's course and his knife fist groped before him. He touched living flesh, felt it flinch away and stroked mightily forward at the

65

same time lunging with the knife as with a sword. Its keen point bit deep. He wrenched free and struck twice more, then swept backwards. There was a great, kicking commotion that made the water boil. The dying man's head breached and Wentworth heard a gasped cry in a language he did not recognize. Instantly the other three men took to water. . . . diving toward the *Spider!*

Wentworth stroked softly away from the spot where his victim had sunk. He must fight this out in the water for the air was filled with a soft fluttering of bats, and their hungry squeaking. He glimpsed one against the faint light from above and dodged beneath the surface as it fluttered toward him. His lips shut in a thin line, his eyes narrowed against the darkness. Death above from the fangs of a myriad bats; and in the water, death at the hands of three men whose companion he had killed. If only he had his automatics, dry and ready for action! But he had only Ram Singh's knife. A round head broke water within a yard of his face. . . .

On the instant, Wentworth flung himself toward it, his knife flashing in a cutting swing. The head flinched back out of range and instantly disappeared. But not before Wentworth had caught a glimpse of a knife between its teeth, a knife that now would be reaching for his groin!

Useless to try to flounder backward out of range. The knife-man would have the speed of a dive behind him. Wentworth did the only possible thing. He plunged forward and to one side at the same time. He had a glimpse of two other men moving toward him, then he pivoted to strike at his immediate assailant. The man's knife broke water first, thrusting toward the spot where a moment before Wentworth had been.

Wentworth did not wait for the whole man to show, but dived with the knife pointed for the body behind that arm. This time he felt his knife bite home. He did not attempt a second stroke, but swept on past the man, dragging his knife with him. Deadly blind work, this fighting in black water beneath a black, wooden roof. No telling where the knife had struck but no death flurry threshed the water above his head. . . .

Wentworth stroked cautiously beneath the water, knife hand feeling ahead for obstructions. He touched the shell-roughened surface of a pile, circled it and allowed himself to drift upward. His lungs were bursting, there was a heavy heart-pound in his ears. But when his head eased above the surface, he dared not let the air escape rapidly. Behind his post, he waited, listening as the humming in his ears subsided.

Not a sound broke the silence save the squeaking of the bats. Up there in the banquet hall was silence, too. But Wentworth did not push out into the open. Probably the two, or possibly three, men left were doing as he was, clinging to piles and waiting for the enemy to betray himself. Well, the *Spider* still had a stratagem in reserve. Without a sound, he submerged and swam toward the spot where he had entered under the wharf.

It was laborious work. He dared not dive, lest the splashing betray him. He must waste precious time submerging, pushing off from the base of a pile and groping ahead lest he ram head-on into another. Twice he submerged before, in the dimness, he could detect open space ahead of him. Then he exhaled loudly, began to swim with small, secret splashings, deliberately making noise. Behind him all was silence.

He swam on, not too swiftly. He gasped out words in Hindustani that sounded like curses of despair to his pursuers. He ordered Ram Singh to shoot when the men appeared, yet spare one. When he had gone fifty yards from the edge of the wharf, he peered behind him. With the speed of fish, two men were swimming after him. He began to flounder, as if helpless with fatigue. The knives in the mouths of his pursuers were visible now, glints of steel. But only two. . . . Well, then, his knife thrust had gone home.

From the top of the fence, Ram Singh's automatic spat red flame. There was a thin, inarticulate cry and one of the heads vanished. They had been very close to Wentworth and with the shot and cry, he spun about and sped in a racing trudgeon toward the remaining man. The knife-man paused uncertainly, turned and began to swim back toward the wharf but at a pace that was markedly slow and burdened. Triumph shot through Wentworth. He changed to a powerful overhand so that he could watch his victim . . . and his sense of triumph lessened. Seconds before the man had been swimming swiftly, easily. Even fear could not so quickly destroy his speed. . . .

The thought had only half-formed in Wentworth's mind when he dived to one side, stroking with all his strength. He felt the faint concussion of Ram Singh's second shot and burst above the surface to find a second knife man beating up the water in a death-flurry. The original swimmer was making better time now for the wharf. It was obvious that, even as Wentworth's glancing thought had told him, the fellow's floundering was part of a trap. He had led Wentworth on until his companion could dive under water and knife Wentworth from behind. Only the *Spider's* keen powers of observation and split-second action had saved him. His face was set, hard. He raced on after the man whose antics had so nearly trapped him. . . .

The man's efforts were feeble again, a great deal of splashing and small progress. Wentworth overtook him speedily, but delayed just out of his reach. The man turned and hit out impotently with his knife. With a quick grab, Wentworth had his wrist. A wrench and the weapon was sinking to the bottom. But the battle was not so soon over. He did not wish to kill the man, nor to die himself. The other seemed too determined to drag him down, even at the cost of his own life.

As he lunged, Wentworth had a first clear glimpse of his features. He frowned in bewilderment even as the man reached out to seize him. The man was obviously an Indian, short of stature with a flattish face and black, heavy hair. But he had no time for speculation, for the Indian fastened upon him with arms and legs and they instantly sank below the surface.

Black water closed over them and they drifted lower and lower toward the bottom. Wentworth struggled desperately to free himself, to free even one arm, but the Indian clung with the strength of a madman, arms and legs wrapped about him, head buried under Wentworth's chin. Already, the *Spider's* lungs seemed squeezed with iron torture bands—already his blood was humming in his ears. Hope of capturing the man alive fled from him. It seemed possible now that he himself would not escape from this fight alive!

Colored lights danced in the blackness of the water and he knew that they signified approaching unconsciousness. But unconsciousness here meant death for the *Spider*—destruction for many thousands of others from the onslaughts of the Indians and their murdering bats! The Indian's arms seemed to lock more tightly about him. . . .

CHAPTER SEVEN

Poisoned Ambush

Wentworth, suffocating beneath the waters in the grip of the Indian, had only one recourse. The knife between his teeth. He could not free his arm to wield it, but the Indian's head was beneath his chin. Slowly, with a sense of timelessness and enormous effort, Wentworth began to twist his head to one side, to turn the point of the knife between his teeth toward the Indian's neck.

The noise of his own laboring heart was thunderous in his ears. His lungs strained, strained. He blew out a little breath through his nostrils to relieve them, but instantly they were paining again. And he twisted his head, squirmed it sideways so that the long blade of the knife turned downward. All thought was done with now. Consciousness was almost gone, but still Wentworth's will drove his head to that slow twisting motion.

He was conscious of no movement, either in his own body, nor that of the Indian. They were resting on the slimy bottom of the river, but he did not know when they had touched there. With a final exhaustion of will, he achieved the position of head that he desired and jabbed downward with the knife. There was a pain in his neck, a stabbing brilliance of agony that made him think he had knifed himself instead of the Indian, then there was a vast, absorbing darkness. . . .

Even through that blackness, he had a sensation of lifting upward, though it seemed the Indian's arms were still about him. Impossible to know how long that oppressive darkness lasted, but finally he was looking up into the face of Ram Singh. The Hindu grinned widely.

"By Siva, sahib," he cried, "nothing can kill thee!"

Wentworth thrust himself up and found that he was inside of his car, the windows closed while black things hovered against it, the vampire killers of the Bat Man.

"Thy servant dived to help thee, master," Ram Singh went on, "but did not find thee until thou arosest thyself."

Wentworth took account of himself slowly. His brain came flashing back to full life ahead of his laggard body. He had succeeded then in puncturing the Indian's spine and relaxing his death grip. But even then, he would have drowned had it not been for the ever-vigilant Ram Singh.

"I'm afraid," he whispered, "that I lost thy knife, O warrior!"

Ram Singh held up the glistening blade. Wentworth was rapidly regaining his strength. His maneuver against the Bat Man had failed through the bravery of the monster's men. Indians. He recalled suddenly the Jivaro spear which had been driven through the window of Latham's mansion. He fumbled a flask of brandy out of a pocket of the car, took a long swig.

Ram Singh, squatting on the floor, was busy rewinding his turban.

"Wah! Those demons of Kali!" he exclaimed. "Thy servant was forced to hide his face in his turban to keep the bats from feasting on his blood while he sat upon the fence."

The potent liquor revived Wentworth's body, made his heart beat strongly. He leaned forward to his radio, tuned it carefully. From it issued a series of musical monotones . . . Ram Singh ceased the wrapping of his turban and listened. Wentworth began to smile.

"Quickly, Ram Singh," he cried. "That is Jackson in the plane. I set him to keep watch above on a chance that the Bat Man would strike. Jackson has followed. . . ." Wentworth stopped to catch the rhythmic beat of wireless signals: ". . . followed a plane from which the Bat Man dived. It was over New Jersey. Quickly, Ram Singh, by way of Trenton. . . ."

Ram Singh climbed over the front seat and dropped behind the wheel. Wentworth had seen at a glance that the lights blazed now in the Early Quaker hotel and he severed the cable that connected with the searchlight he had carried into the building. The Daimler was instantly in motion. . . .

For a while Wentworth rested. When Ram Singh had reached Roosevelt highway and was racing through the outskirts of Philadelphia toward Trenton, he opened the wardrobe behind the seat and substituted dry clothing for his ruined evening clothes. He donned dark tweeds. When the time came, he would add cape and broad-brimmed black hat, alter his face . . . and the *Spider* would step forth from the car in all his sinister fearful majesty. . . .

The wireless signals from Jackson continued to drum on his ears, repeating the message first sent and giving the new positions of the plane. Even if Jackson did not trail the ship to a hiding place of the Bat Man, they might capture the pilot and learn something from him. If they found a headquarters for the Indians . . . Well, there would be a new battle.

It was like the *Spider* that he should press on this way while his body still had not recuperated from a struggle that had nearly cost his life.

Because he was tired, he urged Ram Singh to greater speed in the pursuit. He warned the Hindu that, since they hunted Jivaros, they must be on the watch for poisoned blowgun darts.

"The Jivaros are headhunters," he explained. "They strip the skin from the skull, stuff it and smoke it down to about the size of a doll's head. If you don't want that turbaned skull of yours to be hung up at an Jivaro feast, be careful!''

Wentworth knew that Ram Singh was laughing. . . .

The Daimler rolled past a deserted, darkened air field and at Wentworth's quick order, Ram Singh whirled the mighty car about and sent it toward the hangar. It was necessary to use guns, even when Wentworth offered to buy a plane, before the single man on guard there could be persuaded to part with a fast ship. Wentworth left a check and sent the plane rocketing through the night. The ship was equipped with radio and Wentworth flashed a message to Jackson, received his joyous response. The Bat Man's ship was still boring steadily northward. . . .

Twenty minutes later, Jackson's wireless spluttered rapid signals: "Attacked by two ships with machine guns. Over Shrewesbury River near Red Bank. They're good and. . . .''

Then silence, blankness in the dark night above New Jersey. Wentworth caught at the throttle, but the plane already was doing its best, blazing through the black sky with its motor revving at dangerous speed. The *Spider's* mouth was a hard, uncompromising slit. Had Jackson, brave Jackson, paid the penalty of all who fought side by side with the *Spider?* A price of pain and blood and death? The empty sky gave him no answer. He pictured Jackson flaming down into the shallows of the Shrewesbury—Jackson who had fought with him in France, who had saved his life, and had his own saved in turn, a dozen times upon the battlefields of earth and sky! Jackson was battling for his life, had perhaps crashed in flames . . . !

Seconds dragged into minutes, each of which saw three miles of dark countryside slip past beneath hissing wings. Finally the dark shimmer of the river showed on the horizon and beside it spurted a bright gout of flame. Wentworth leaned forward in the pilot's seat, but he could make out no details of the scene below, no trace of hostile ships in the sky. At long last, he was circling over the spot of fire. It was the wreckage of a plane, but it was impossible to tell whether it was the Northrup. . . . Wentworth put the ship into a steep dive, circled and landed on the meadow by the light of the burning ship.

The *Spider* sat motionless in his plane, the motor just ticking over, and stared at the wreckage. It was a biplane as his Northrup was, but beyond that he could tell nothing. He climbed out of the cockpit and Ram Singh vaulted to the ground beside him. Slowly they made their way forward. . . .

"Master," said Ram Singh, "you warned me beware of blowgun darts."

At the words, Wentworth stopped short, a new thought striking him. Was this a trap? He had been so wrapped up in the idea of Jackson's battle, of his crash and death, that he had not paused to think of trickery. But now he threw swift, piercing glances into the shadows that ringed the plane's fire like waiting jackals at a kill.

"Thanks, Ram Singh," he said quietly.

He led the way even closer to the ship. Its structure greatly resembled a Northrup, but Wentworth could not be sure because of the smashing of structure by the crash. He became aware of automobile headlights speeding along a nearby road and turned heavily back to his own plane. They left the ring of dying red fire, stepped into the darkness, twice black now since their eyes were narrowed by the flame, and . . .

"Duck, major!"

Jackson's hearty deep voice rang out of the night somewhere. Even while a leap of joy convulsed his heart, Wentworth snatched Ram Singh's arm and pulled him to the ground with him.

"Roll," he shouted. "Roll toward the plane!"

Over his head, he saw tiny three-inch darts sail past. Off in the darkness, came the popping of blowguns, as if corks had been pulled from many bottles. As he and Ram Singh rolled desperately toward the ship, more of those butterfly harbingers of death buried their poison points in the earth beside them. Wentworth sprang to his feet and ran zig-zag toward the ship, snatched the throttle wide. Instantly a hurricane of wind whistled past him and Ram Singh stood beside him, hands locked on the wing. Wentworth had set the brakes, but with the propeller bellowing, the plane might get loose.

Leaning against the slip-stream, Wentworth pulled his automatics. He could no longer hear the popping of blowguns, but he could trace the course of the featherlight tiny arrows. He and Ram Singh were safe now, protected by the wind as by a sheet of steel, for the darts did not carry enough force, or weight, to penetrate that hurricane. Wentworth's guns began to speak rhythmically and screeches of pain came from the night. His heart beat joyous rhythm to his shots. He had thought Jackson dead and now he was restored. His lips moved grimly at each bullet he pumped into the darkness.

"Jackson," he called. "Come to the ship!"

"Coming!" Jackson's deep voice echoed, then he burst zig-zagging into the circle of light, crossed it and raced toward the ship. Wentworth's guns sought out the sources of the darts that flew for him and presently Jackson was beside him, his thick chest heaving from his run. He stood stiffly as the soldier he was, wide shoulders braced, broad face expressionless.

"Lost the Northrup, sir," he shouted above the roar of the propellers.

"Saved our lives!" Wentworth shouted back at him. "Into the plane, sergeant. Ram Singh, at the controls."

Ram Singh loosened his hold on the wing. The ship was quivering with the battle between propeller and brakes. Released, it bounded scarcely seventy-five feet before it lifted its nose toward the skies. Wentworth, crowded into the forward cockpit with Jackson, fitted on headphones and handed a pair to the sergeant.

"Report," Wentworth ordered briefly.

"Yes, sir," said Jackson, his voice at attention even though he himself was seated. "You know how I picked up a plane and followed. Got here, two other ships laid for me. Plane I followed kept right on. Tried to follow and two ganged up on me. Shot out my radio. Incendiary bullets got gasoline. Bailed out and parachuted into river. Got to wreck in time to see them sneaking devils trying to ambush you.''

"Planes go away?" Wentworth inquired.

"Think they landed, sir," Jackson responded. "Not in sight when parachute opened."

Wentworth peered overside and found that Ram Singh was circling slowly, recalled he had not ordered any particular destination. Even as he looked, lights flared out over a field and three ships scuttled through it and bolted into the air. Wentworth laughed. Useless to attempt to fight three planes, when those ships had machine guns and he had only his automatics. But there was another way. He leaned forward and tapped Ram Singh's shoulder, shook his fist toward the lighted field.

Ram Singh twisted about and showed his gleaming teeth. While he still looked, the ship dipped nose down for the earth, diving straight toward the three rising planes!

CHAPTER EIGHT

Triumph of the Bat!

The fantastic courage of that unarmed dive upon three machine-gun planes stupefied the pilots of the attacking ships for a space of seconds. They scattered from under the headlong plunge of the *Spider's* plane, breaking their formation, darting in all directions to escape what seemed a suicidal attack.

Wentworth's plane, under the steady hand of Ram Singh, flashed past them toward the field before they realized their mistake. When they whirled to the assault, it was almost too late. Ram Singh was floating in to a landing near the hangar at the upwind end of the field. The three planes, machine guns stuttering, swept in together on the slow-moving ship.

Watching them bullet-dive toward him, Wentworth saw certain death for his valiant men and himself. Their ship made a perfect target. He snatched out his automatics and sprayed lead at the lights that flooded the field with pale lavender illumination. His bullets smashed them into blackness and he sent his shout against the beat of the propeller, the lowered hum of the motor.

"Ground loop!"

He felt the ship tilt to the left as Ram Singh threw over the stick. There was a rending crash, the snarl of a bent propeller and Wentworth was hanging in his straps from an overturned plane. He was the first out and Jackson and Ram Singh were scarcely a second behind. They were jarred, but unhurt, and they followed Wentworth in a dash for the darkened hangar a hundred feet away.

Over their heads, motors roared and machine guns chattered. There was a beating of hard, leaden rain upon the earth near them, but none came too close and they reached the hangar in a hard run.

Inside the hangar, the liquid pop of a blowgun was incredibly loud. Wentworth cursed at this new attack. His gun answered almost of its own volition. There was a gasped cry and, after that, silence.

"Ram Singh!" Wentworth ordered sharply. "There must be a car outside. Get in it and speed away from here."

"Where to, *sahib*?"

"Philadelphia. Shake off pursuers there, not before. Report to *missie sahib*."

There was a movement of shadows, a muttered: *"Han, sahib!"* and Ram Singh had salaamed and vanished. Within a minute and a half, an automobile engine roared and dwindled rapidly into the distance. Wentworth and Jackson stood with their backs against the left wall of the hangar and waited.

"Any orders, major?" Jackson asked quietly.

"Just wait," Wentworth told him. "It's their first move. Must be more men here than the one Jivaro with the blowgun. Some will follow Ram Singh, thinking we've all escaped. When the others leave, we follow. The headquarters must be somewhere near here." Wentworth was hard put to hide the elation in his voice. He had played in luck tonight in spite of the destruction of his Northrup and his failure to capture a man alive in the battle under the wharf.

The machine guns had ceased to fire now and from the drum of the motors, it was apparent the planes were circling the field. Minutes dragged past, then a single flood light sprayed its ray over the ground. A second and a third followed and without waiting for complete illumination, the three ships swooped to a landing, rolled toward the hangar. From behind the lights, a dozen Indians in short scarlet kirtles ran toward the planes.

Goggled men sprang from the cockpits and the Indians prostrated themselves upon the ground. Wentworth watched, frowning, from the shadows of the hangar where, with Jackson, he crouched behind a gasoline drum. He was frowning, but what was going on out there was obvious enough. The Indians believed these flying men were gods. . . . One of the Jivaros leaped to his feet and raced off across the field. Moments later, all was dark again, but the planes were not trundled toward the hangar. There was absolute silence. . . .

"Something's up, sir," Jackson whispered.

Wentworth's eyes were tight and hard as he strove to accustom them to the darkness. No doubt that what Jackson said was correct. In some way, the Indians had detected his trick of sending only Ram Singh away as a decoy.

"Looks like we'll have to fight our way out," he said quietly. "Try to capture a white man. The Indians wouldn't know anything and wouldn't talk if they did. There must be a side door. . . ."

Leading the way, with Jackson just behind him, Wentworth crossed the dark hangar toward its opposite side. He found the door all right, turned the knob cautiously. That silence outside was prolonging itself suspiciously. . . .

A voice called hollowly from the main door and Wentworth wheeled that way, guns ready. No one was in sight.

"Surrender!" the voice called again, "or you will be killed instantly."

Wentworth pushed open the side door and slipped outside. Jackson was close behind him and they stood, waiting, peering into the darkness that crowded close upon them. A dozen yards away was a thick woods. Nothing moved. . . . With the abruptness of a gunshot, light bathed the entire side of the hangar, outlined the two men against it like black silhouette targets. Wentworth's gun blasted even as he flung himself to the earth. The light went out but behind him Jackson cursed raspingly.

"Got me, major. Blowgun dart. . . ." His voice faded and was punctured by a series of popping sounds there in the edge of the woods. Wentworth's guns blasted, his lips thinning back from his teeth. Jackson, good God, Jackson hit by a poisoned dart! . . . Two darts pricked his own skin, one on the throat, the other on his cheek. A dozen more thudded gently against the galvanized side of the hangar. With a shouted roar of anger, Wentworth leaped to his feet.

God! So the *Spider* had got it at last, dying not by the guns of the Underworld, but by poison on the end of a primitive arrow! His automatics blasted deafeningly. Screams beat upon his ears through the thunder of his weapons, but it was the end. No mistaking that this time. Here was no death trap, no plant he could wriggle out of, here was only death. . . .

Already a cold numbness was stealing over him. He wavered on his feet, squeezing the triggers of his automatics again. They kicked from his hands. For long seconds more he stood there, feeling again and again the prick of the darts, piercing his clothing, kissing his hands. By sheer will force, he fought down the numbness that washed up his limbs, that groped with cold fingers for his heart, his brain. . . .

A fierce, ringing cry welled up from his lips. The *Spider* fell. . . . A single glimmer of consciousness remained. He felt a great peace, a welling happiness of spirit. The battle was ended at last. Nita, *Nita*. . . .

He was dead, and yet he continued to realize dimly what was going on about him. In this fumbling way, he felt that he was lifted and carried. He remembered vaguely that *curare,* the poison with which the South American blowpipe users tipped their darts, paralyzed instantly, but did not kill for almost twenty minutes.

He was passing through that intermediate stage of death now. . . .

Something pricked his throat. What the devil, were they injecting more poison into his veins? But there was no need for that. He was already. . . . But was he? The numbness was receding, the blackness withdrawing from his eyes. He could not understand all that was happening, but he could not doubt it. Had these Indians then found an antidote for the poison that had no antidote?

He heard a voice as harsh and grating as the squeak of a bat ranting impatiently. Then someone systematically began to slap his face. He opened his eyes and peered up into the impassive face of an Indian. The eyes glittered like points of obsidian knives. . . . Hands gripped his shoulders and hauled him to his feet. He was in an immense black room where the light was dim and red. The grating voice came from a great bat upon a throne of skulls. . . . what, a bat? But it wasn't possible . . . !

Wentworth shook his head violently to clear it, peered again at the throne. He saw now that it was a man seated there, a man with great leathery wings stretching from his shoulders. Now and then he waved them back and forth languidly. Wentworth saw these things without actually taking them in, but presently the last of the fogginess lifted from his brain, leaving it brilliantly clear. He peered into the face of the creature on the throne and, uncontrollably, a strong shudder plucked at his muscles. Was this the Bat Man then?

The face was incredibly hideous, the nose sliced off, the whole countenance drawn up toward that wound into a striking and hideous semblance of a bat's convulted face. He had even attached huge, pointed ears to his head, and those wings. . . . Wentworth pulled himself together with a bracing of his shoulders, a lift of his chin. There was that about the man and his face that made his blood run cold, but it was trickery. It must be. . . .

He looked about him with steady eyes, saw that Jackson stood nearby with four men clinging to his unbound arms even as Wentworth realized he also stood. About them stood ranks of impassive Indians, each kirtled in brilliant red with a belt about their waists of some curious whitish leather. . . . The monstrous squeaking of the Bat Man pulled his head toward the throne sharply.

"You are wondering why you are alive," he rasped. "It is not our habit to kill such prisoners as come our way—that is, not at once. You were shot with narcotic instead of poisoned darts. You see, our bats must have food."

He said the words simply, so matter-of-factly that for a moment the meaning did not penetrate. Food for the bats. . . . But these bats were vampires. They fed on blood! Wentworth's eyes tightened against a tendency to widen. He could feel the quivering of the muscles in his temples, but Wentworth forced his stiff lips to smile.

"I have considered many ends," he admitted casually, "but supplying oral transfusions to bats was not among them!"

He was conscious of Jackson's white face, his knotted, wide-muscled jaws, but he dared not look that way lest his sternly held composure desert him. The Bat Man made no direct reply to Wentworth's jibe, but the already contorted face was made revoltingly hideous by a frown. Jackson's breath was audible to Wentworth, a hissing, strangled sound. Somewhere behind the throne, a gong lifted its singing note and the Bat Man's frown faded. He smiled and lifted his right hand. . . .

Behind the throne, a door opened, revealing hangings of golden silk and through those portières stepped a woman with glistening black hair that fluffed out from beneath scarlet fillets. She wore a scarlet robe, but one milk-white shoulder was bare, her breasts were outlined in bands that criss-crossed over her bosom in Roman style. Wentworth's teeth locked tightly.

"June Calvert!" he whispered.

82

The girl smiled down on him haughtily, her dark intelligent eyes half-veiled by their lids.

"Who is this?" she asked imperiously.

The Bat Man's rasping voice seemed to soften a little. "Richard Wentworth, my dear, who is either a confederate of the *Spider*, or the *Spider* himself!"

Wentworth controlled the start that his muscles involuntarily made at those words. What, had he been discovered so early in the fight? His fists knotted and the Indians to each side, feeling his muscles harden, gripped more tightly, put their weight into their holds upon his arms.

"One of my men," the Bat Man was explaining, "saw the *Spider* knock bats into a car driven by a Hindu and later the Hindu released those bats coated with radioactive paint. This man attempted to trail them from the skies. The Hindu is this man's servant. . . ."

A remarkable change had come over June Calvert's face. It was still imperious, but it was twisted with hatred and rage. Her eyes, half-veiled, burned with living fires of anger and her hands became claws.

"The *Spider!*" she whispered. "The *Spider* who killed my brother!" Her hand slipped to her girdle and whipped out a curved dagger. She moved toward Wentworth on slow, crouching legs like a cat.

Wentworth smiled at her. "I am not the *Spider*," he said quietly, "but if I were, I could not have killed your brother. He died by the bite of the bats."

June Calvert laughed and the sound was more like a snarl. "Yes, bats killed him. His own bats. He was a partner of the Bat Man, but you turned the bats upon him. It was you, you, *you* . . . !"

"Calm yourself, my dear," Wentworth shrugged. "I'll admit that anger becomes you . . ."

June Calvert sprang toward him with her knife uplifted. The Bat Man squeaked. It was precisely that—not words, nor articulate sound—simply a squeak of peculiar timber. An Indian sprang between Wentworth and June, offered his breast to the knife. For a moment, it seemed she would strike him down to reach the man behind him, but the Bat Man was speaking now.

"My dear," he whispered raspingly, "I have another, juster, more delightful death in store for our friend here, be he *Spider* or not. As you know, the appetite for human blood of our cutely starved bats must be whetted. Sometimes when we have no prisoners, we are forced to call for volunteers from among our company, but now there is no need for that. Would you not consent, my dear, to feed him to the bats instead?"

June Calvert stood panting, just beyond the human barrier which shielded Wentworth. Gradually the hatred and rage in her face became more subtle, gave place to a cruel joy.

"Splendid!" she whispered. "Oh, splendid!" She turned toward the throne and bowed low. "Grant that I may watch the . . . bats feed."

The Bat Man's laughter was squeaky, too. It ascended the scale like the grating of a saw-file until it became inaudible in the ultra-human range.

"Yes, my dear," he whispered. "You may!"

He lifted his left hand in a peculiar gesture and Wentworth's captors wrenched him backward and pinned him to the floor. Other Indians tore his clothing from his body. To his right, he could hear Jackson cursing and fighting futilely against similar treatment. Then, birth-naked, they were thrust across the darkened room. Behind them, came a long file of Indians, marching, chanting a harsh paean. Their joy was obvious. On the throne at the other end of the long room, the Bat Man laughed and laughed his squeaky, unearthly mirth and June Calvert stood, proud in scarlet, with a cruel smile on her lips.

Wentworth and Jackson marched side by side now. Jackson twisted about his head. "Good God, what a woman!" he whispered. "She's mine, major. Mine! I never saw a woman who could stir me so. . . ."

Wentworth looked curiously as this staid soldier who

had fought beside him through so many life and death struggles. A steady man, reliable and unimaginative. But now his chest heaved with something more than his exertions, and there was a set, determined jaw. He did not even seem to consider what lay in store for them.

"When we get out of this," Jackson said heavily. "I'm coming after her. I am."

Wentworth smiled thinly. Jackson said *when,* not *if,* we get out of this. But then, Jackson was depending on the *Spider* who had wrested him from many a fierce and loathesome doom. Wentworth felt the grimness of his own locked jaw, but he was fighting against an overwhelming despair. To be locked in a cage, naked, with starved vampire bats, could mean only inevitable death.

A steel grating was opened in a chamber whose walls were steel-mesh wire. Wentworth was hurled forward, Jackson behind him. They sprang to their feet as the door clanged shut, got their backs against a wall and strained their eyes into the twilight of their death-chamber. There on the floor were stretched two things that had been men. Their flesh was shrunken and folded in upon their bodies. Cheeks were sunken and shriveled lips bared locked teeth. But more than anything else, it was the *pallor* of the bodies that mocked Wentworth and Jackson in the cage of bats. Those bodies were . . . bloodless. . . .

Jackson still seemed in the daze which the beauty of the woman had afflicted upon him. Wentworth slapped him violently on the cheek.

"Later, Jackson, later," he said sharply. "Now, we must fight for our lives, unless you want to be as they are." His rigid pointing arm, indicating the bodies on the floor, snapped Jackson to attention. He paled. A shudder convulsed his shoulders.

"Good God, major!" he whispered. "What can we do?"

Wentworth shook his head slowly. There were Indian guards outside the cage with ready blowguns. There was no escape there. June Calvert had had a chair brought to the door and she sat there, languidly waiting for the torture to begin.

"What in God's name can we do?" Jackson whispered again.

Already above them in the dark upper reaches of the mesh prison, there were premonitory squeakings and fluttering. A bat winged through the air near them, circled, and swept toward Jackson. He struck savagely with his fist, then cursed and gripped his hand.

"The devil nipped me," he growled.

Wentworth laughed and there was a touch of wildness in the sound. The bats' teeth were not poisoned, it was apparent, since Jackson had been bitten and still lived. But how long could they survive the blood-draining battle with the bats? There were thousands of them up above, to judge from the sound. But he knew the answer. It would be a matter of time only.

"We could make a barricade of those two bodies," Jackson said, without hope.

They did that, crouched behind the blood-drained corpses that warned them of what the future held. They settled themselves to fight for their lives. Abruptly the air was filled with a myriad black flutterings. Jackson and Wentworth flailed the air with their arms. Utter loathing gripped the *Spider*. The stench of the bats was nauseous and the thought of dying to feed such beasts. . . .

Jackson screamed with a hint of hysteria. "Take him off! Take him off!"

Wentworth smashed a bat that had fixed on the side of Jackson's face, then he felt leathery wings touch his throat and tore a vampire from his own flesh. Black wings were beating in his eyes. His breath came short and hot in his throat and it strangled him. He fought with locked teeth, without hope, but with desperation. Good God above, what an end for a man . . . !

CHAPTER NINE

The Wooing of Nita

Nita was reluctant to leave the Early Quaker with Fred Stoking and his party, knowing, as she did, the battle that impended. But there was nothing she could do to help Wentworth when the bats came, so she went at his bidding. The evening dragged at the night club to which they went and at midnight the group broke up. Newspaper boys were shouting extras when Fred Stoking helped Nita into a taxicab. The headlines screamed of the massacre at the Quaker.

Stoking looked at Nita, sitting erect though pale in the dim rear of the cab, then leaned toward the driver and ordered him to make all possible speed to the Quaker Hotel. Nita thanked him with a glance. There could be no news of Dick there, unless . . . unless, she forced the thought, he had fallen prey to his enemies. But she must know that much with all speed. She was scarcely conscious of the blond handsome man beside her, whose eyes were so attentively on her face. Her thoughts were all of Dick. . . .

The Quaker was a shambles and police sought to bar Nita and her escort, but Stoking was equal to that emergency. He and his family were influential; Commissioner Harrington was a personal friend. . . . They went in, but found no news of Wentworth. Nita brightened a little. He had found a trail then, and followed it.

Stoking led Nita into a small lounge off the main lobby and seated her there.

"I'm sure you won't go to sleep for hours," he said.

Nita acknowledged that with a faint smile. Did she ever sleep when the *Spider* was abroad? Well Wentworth knew that and he would phone her when there was opportunity. . . . She sent word to the desk where she might be found. . . . Stoking found his way to the deserted bar and brought back drinks he had mixed himself.

"Now, Nitita," he said, "let's talk."

There was something in his tone that pulled Nita's head toward him, that penetrated her consciousness. She often worried about her Dick, but it seemed tonight that her fears were greater than usual. It was almost as if she sensed that at this very moment, far away in New Jersey, Wentworth was being thrust into the cage of famished vampires. But she could not know that of course. She forced herself to attend to Stoking's words. . . .

"Nitita," Stoking said again, using the name that he had given her long ago in pig-tail-pulling days. "Nitita, you are unhappy." He rushed on as she tried to protest. "It is not a secret, you know. When I came back from the Orient, you were the first person I asked for, and I heard such tales! Nitita, you have no right to be unhappy."

Nita laughed a little unsteadily. She looked up into the handsome face bending protectively toward her. Fred Stoking had always had nice eyes. They had acquired authority and depth with the added years, and they were tender on hers now.

Nita said, hesitantly, "Why, Fred, I believe you're making love to me!" She knew instantly that it was the wrong thing to have said. Stoking leaned closer.

"Nitita, you'll say I'm a romantic fool, but I always have loved you. Ever since . . ."

Nita lifted her hands in mock horror. "Not that line, Fred, please. The fiction writers have abused it so!"

Stoking refused to banter. He reached up and touched Nita's gleaming hair with a caressing finger. "I'm very serious about this, Nitita."

Nita was silenced. There was an intent directness about this man that could not be turned away with jests. She looked into the depths of his eyes and believed him. Her hand went impulsively to his.

"Don't, Fred," she said quietly. "I appreciate what you say, more than you can know. But I'm engaged to another man."

Stoking threw back his head and laughed. There was an edgy bitterness to the sound that was not pretty. "Engaged!" he said mockingly. "For how many years, Nita, have you been engaged to Dick Wentworth?"

Nita took her hand away and twisted her slim white fingers together in her lap. She looked at them, writhing there, and she smiled. "It's quite a while," she said quietly.

"He has no right!" Stoking declared fiercely. "I stayed away because I know of this so-called engagement, but as it went on and on, I began to hope. Nita, I came home for you. I am going to take you back with me. No man has a right to inflict such unhappiness on any woman. . . ."

Nita lifted her head proudly. Her hands were quiet now. There might have been a time when domineering thrilled her, but she was a woman who had . . . good God, who had killed men! These slim white hands of hers could throw a bullet with accuracy that almost rivaled the *Spider's*. Her muscles were hardened by the physical instruction Wentworth had insisted she undertake when, defying his own opposition and the dictates of her own longings for normal, human life, she had pledged herself to the hard road of the *Spider*. Why, if she wished, she could tie even this powerful man beside her into knots with jiu jitsu! No, she could not be cave-manned.

Stoking saw his error at once. "Forgive me, dear, if I sound too excessively masculine," he said, with a touch of whimsicality, "but you can't guess how long I've eaten out my heart with longing."

"Stop, Fred," she said softly, "you make me very unhappy!"

Stoking laughed again, harshly. "Then I will stop. You have enough unhappiness. . . . Oh, my dear, I could give you so much. I know you do not love me, but you would, Nitita, you would! Don't tell me that you don't like the things I do, the far ends of the earth when you wish, and a fireside and children when you don't. Unhappiness!"

Nita's full lips straightened themselves with compression. "You are talking rather foolishly," she said, for all the stab of pain he had given her. Fred Stoking could read her all right. "Very foolishly. After all, I am, as the saying goes, free, reasonably white, and considerably over twenty-one. . . ."

"Twenty-six," Stoking said harshly. "Can you tell me anything about you I don't already know?"

"A great deal," Nita smiled into his eyes, so directly, so steadily that his own faltered a little. "A very great deal, Fred. But what I am saying is this: I am not unhappy in my present life. If there are . . . other things I would like, you must not think that I took my present course without great thought. It may be that Dick and I shall never marry. Dick warned me of that when we found we loved each other. He was unwilling for me to face that, but I insisted. We . . . love each other. I don't know what more to say." She reached for his hand, confidently now, steadily and he gripped it hard with both of his. "Fred, I've told you a great deal more than any one else has ever heard. I tell you so you won't foolishly nurture a vain hope. . . . If after all you're not merely . . . but that was unkind. I believe you and what you say."

Stoking held to her hand fiercely, his face drawn and lined with his struggle for control. His voice came out hoarsely. "All right. I accept what you say. But that doesn't mean I give up. Not if Wentworth said the things you indicate. And he would. I know it now. He would be the first to give me encouragement!"

Nita gasped, her hand flinching from his grasp. Before her rose the face of the man she loved, not the gay smiling Dick who first had won her love, but the white-faced battler whom peril created. She saw the hard bitterness that wrenched his lips, the cold, gray-blue strength of his eyes, and she could hear him saying just what Stoking declared.

"Darling, you know it is hopeless," he would say. "I love you. God knows I do. Love you enough to give you up. Seek happiness in normal living. The hell in which the *Spider* lives is not for a glorious woman like you. . . ."

Nita buried her face in her clenching hands. "No!" she cried, her voice muffled. "No, no, no!"

Stoking sat silent beside her, a little frightened at the emotion he had stirred, but his lips were grim-set. He was a fighter, too. Presently he touched Nita's arm.

"We'll forget it for the present," he said, "but don't think I've finished. I don't give up so easily."

There was a bleak coldness in his own blue eyes. He looked up abruptly as a movement caught his gaze. A bellboy stuck his head in at the door. "Phone call for Miss Nita van Sloan!"

Nita sprang to her feet. "Where?"

The boy turned and swaggered cockily across the lobby. Death nor tragedy, nor weeping women in the hotel lounge, could dim the brass that shone upon him—and not alone from his uniform buttons. Nita hurried to the telephone he indicated, aware that Stoking followed at a discreet distance. Now, Nita thought, now I'll hear Dick's voice. Dear Dick . . . !

"Hello," she faltered, then she straightened, her hands tight on the telephone. The happiness went out of her, but something else entered, the white, tight-lipped determination that was the other woman beneath

91

her soft and lovely beauty. She spoke in Hindustani, her voice crisp, decisive.

"Is he in his own identity, Ram Singh, or . . . ? That helps some. Where are you? Wait there then. I'll come as quickly as possible. No, Ram Singh, there is nothing you can do now but wait."

She turned from the phone and Stoking strode toward her. He checked a half-dozen feet away, recognizing the change in her. It was present even in the way she walked. Still graceful she was, but there was business and determination in her pace.

"It's trouble," Stoking said flatly. "I've heard how you've gone to rescue Wentworth on occasion. You'll have to count me in on this."

Nita hesitated and her appraisal of him was as swift and competent as a marine captain's. "Very well," she said. "Get the fastest car and the fastest plane in the city. Have the car at the door in five minutes; the ship ready when we reach Camden field. Dick has been captured by the Bat Man!"

She moved swiftly to the elevators and, for a space of seconds, Stoking stood and watched her go, his eyes admiring, filled with longing, then he sprang to a telephone. . . .

It was just four minutes later that Nita stepped from the elevator, but Stoking was ready. He caught her elbow and was conscious of the bulge of a gun beneath the smart, tailored fit of her dark-blue suit. Stoking felt distinctly out of place in his tail coat and faultless evening dress, but he made a joke of it.

"I carry armament, too," he told her gayly, "part of which you would probably disapprove. It is a knife strapped to my left forearm."

Nita said briefly, "Knives have their uses. Ram Singh has saved my life a dozen times over with his. Is the rest of your armament a revolver? If you have no firearms, I have an extra one in my purse for you."

They were in the car by now—Stoking's own, with a respectful chauffeur at the wheel—and the machine, which was a rakish Minerva, was muttering at close to top speed through the deserted streets. Stoking lounged on the cushions beside Nita and she noted with approval that he had the same manner of facing crises that so distinguished Wentworth, a calm, bitter readiness. Nita herself was tense.

"Don't you want to tell me about it?" he suggested quietly.

"You'll have to know if you're to help," Nita conceded, as if reluctantly. She told him of Wentworth's flight, the crash, and of Ram Singh's being sent away in a stolen car. "Ram Singh knew that he was supposed to be a decoy," she went on, "and when the Bat Man's crew didn't pursue, he stopped. He heard some fast, deliberate shooting and recognized Dick's guns. Then he heard Dick cry out. . . ." Nita paused, pressing her hands tightly down on the bulging black handbag in her lap. "Ram Singh does not scare easily, but he said that it . . . it sounded like a devil's death cry."

"Dick isn't dead," Stoking said quietly. "You would have known it, if he were."

Nita's voice was very low. "Yes, you do know me, Fred. You're right, I would have known. What Ram Singh said confirms it. He saw Dick and Jackson carried into two planes and flown away. Ram Singh tried to steal the third plane, but found the propeller had been bent in landing. He just escaped the Indians and came to phone me. He's in Flemington. We're flying there. Have to make a landing in a field with magnesium flares."

"I've got a two-seater Lockhead Vega," Stoking said casually. "I'm an indifferent pilot, but I understand you can handle ships."

"I have a thousand hours—transport license," Nita replied, tight-lipped. That was Dick's doing, too, teaching her to fly. Dick had been thorough. . . .

"I want to apologize again," Stoking kept his tone light, "for trying to caveman you. It was not the right tactic—not at all!"

Nita felt her tension easing a little beneath his banter.

He was doing his part well, but even he knew that the ultimate effort must be hers. Well, she had never failed Dick yet.

The Vega was fast as Nita could have wished, but it seemed scarcely to move toward Flemington. She made a safe, though rough, landing on a meadow near the town and Ram Singh raced up in a car while they still clambered from the plane. The Hindu hesitated at sight of Stoking but, at a sign from Nita, accepted him and began to spill what supplementary news he had in a virtual downpour of words.

"What were the Bat Man's planes used for?" Nita asked abruptly.

Ram Singh lifted his shoulders in token of ignorance. "Perhaps, *missie sahib*, to distribute bats. There was a cage of them in the plane left behind."

Nita laughed exultingly. "To the field quickly, Ram Singh!" she cried as she sprang into the car Ram Singh had brought. "We must have that cage of bats!"

The car was fast enough, but scarcely comfortable. Stoking and Nita jounced miserably as the intrepid Hindu streaked over dark Jersey roads. He battled curves with squealing tires and motor roaring wide open, flew through unlighted anonymous towns that were no more than sounding boards for the car's engine.

"Why this wild enthusiasm for bats?" Stoking inquired mildly. "I must confess the poisonous little beasts don't interest me in the least."

"Later," Nita snapped. "Look for barbed-wire fences. If you see one, sing out. Ram Singh, stop at the first cry. *Stop, Ram Singh!*" Nita sprang from the car, groped in a pocket of the front door and got pliers, then strode to a barbed-wire fence on her side of the road. Within brief minutes, she was back with a coil of separate strands of wire. But still Stoking had no time for questions. Nita demanded his handkerchief, then the lining from his coat. Finally, she tore the up-

94

holstery of the car with the pliers and pulled out gobs of curled hair and padded cotton.

Ram Singh was traveling more slowly and silently. Everything in his manner suggested that they were near the field and that no chances must be taken of discovery.

"Bring me the cage of bats," Nita ordered.

Ram Singh sprang from the car and salaamed profoundly, lifting cupped hands to his forehead as he bowed in respect. *Wah!* This woman was a fit mate for his master—a tigress whose claws were as deadly as those of the old one himself. Bring back the bats? He would bring back heaven and hell, let her but command it!

As he strode off into the darkness, Nita sprang from the car and took the cap off the gasoline tank. She had fastened the torn bits of cloth to strands of the barbed-wire and now she dipped each one into the gasoline. When Ram Singh returned, she was ready. At her command, the Hindu maneuvered out one of the bats and held it so it could not bite. Nita fastened a string made of torn cloth through a small slit she made in the bat's inter-femoral membrane. The string was attached to wire, which in turn wrapped a bundle of gasoline-soaked cloth.

All climbed back into the car, then Nita touched a match to the gasoline rag and ordered the bat released. With the torch blazing behind him, the bat rose bewilderedly straight upward for a short distance. Then, with side excursions in which it tried to shake off the blazing tail that had been given, it made a laborious way southward. Nita watched until the ball of fire gave her the right direction, then she sent Ram Singh forward.

The Hindu was smiling broadly. *Wah!* Had he not said she was a veritable goddess? Wentworth *sahib* had sprayed bats with luminous paint and followed them. The *missie sahib* lacked the paint, but did that hinder her? By Siva, no! They would follow these bats to the hiding place of this unclean creature who flew through the air, then, by Kali, the destroyer, there would be an accounting! A hand stole to the hilt of the keen knife at his sash. . . .

They traveled five miles southward before Nita released the second bat. That left her three more. When they were gone. . . . But before that, they must have a clue to the Bat Man's whereabouts. They *must!* One by one those bats with their trail of fire fought upward into the sky and winged their way off into darkness, charting a course for the Bat Man's headquarters. The way was still southward. The next to the last bat had almost escaped them when the rays of an approaching car's headlights blinded them, but finally they detected the flying creature deviating from a straight, southern course, heading slightly eastward. They were near now, very near. That much was obvious, but how would they find the place with only one more bat? They might arrive within a hundred yards of the place and then. . . .

Resolutely, Nita prepared a larger bundle for the torch, burdened the final bat until it could scarcely lift itself toward the sky. It would be forced to fly slowly; the longer burning of the torch would help. Nita signaled a stop, alighted and stepped behind the car to dip the cloth in gasoline. As she struck a match to the torch, she breathed a little wordless prayer. If this hope failed them. . . . The bat struggled upward. Nita watched it go with aching eyes, then whirled as footsteps grated in the roadway. Flashlight glare assaulted her eyes and a gruff voice that carried the obvious burden of authority, rasped at them to: "Put them up!"

"We've got you, you damned murderers!" another man rejoined. "You was seen turning loose them bats along the road. Guy passed you and saw you. And now we catch you at it."

One man was on the running board with a gun against Ram Singh's side. Nita did not answer. She barely heeded them or realized their presence now, for she was watching the ball of fire that marked the bat's heavy flight as it moved directly eastward. . . .

"You're completely wrong about this," Stoking said sharply. "We have nothing to do with the poisoned bats. We. . . ."

A policeman's stocky figure came out from behind the light and his billie slapped Stoking unconscious to the ground. "Any guy that would turn loose them bats. . . ." he muttered, then turned to Nita.

Nita realized abruptly that, though she had at last approximately discovered the hiding place, at least of adherents of the Bat Man—the spot where possibly Dick was held prisoner—she was now helpless to render him any assistance. She caught the policeman by the arm, tried to explain what they had been doing. He only scowled and growled at her.

"Listen, baby," he said. "Only one thing int'rests me. You was turning loose them bats and you are going to jail. Come along!"

Nita gazed despairingly into his face. He couldn't mean what he said—but it was obvious that he did. She *must* get away. She had to save Dick—who must be very close now.

With a wrench, she freed herself from the policeman's hand and darted for the shrubbery at the side of the road. She reached it, but the bushes were thick and blocked her retreat. She snatched for the automatic beneath her arm, her breath sobbing in her throat. Dick never fired on police, not even to save his own life, but, but . . . this was for Dick!

She lifted the automatic. The policeman's stick slashed down on her wrist. Agony raced up her arm, then the policeman had her. Her arm was twisted behind her back until she moaned with the pain of it. She was tripped and thrown flat on her face, then handcuffs pinched home on her wrists. She lifted her head and saw Ram Singh unconscious on the ground beside Stoking. That hope was gone, too.

"Baby," growled the policeman, "when I say jail, I mean *jail!*"

Utter despair shook Nita. Sobs rose in her throat, but she choked them down. Surely, this time, destiny conspired against Dick! Was this, then, the end which the *Spider* and his mate had known must come some day . . . ?

CHAPTER TEN

In the Vampire's Cage

It seemed to Wentworth, in the cage of the vampires, that he and Jackson had fought for hours against the bats. His arms became leaden with the ceaseless flailing against never-tiring wings. The upper half of his body was bleeding from half a hundred tiny wounds, but as yet, none of them was serious. Both men were panting through brassy throats.

"Can't . . . keep it up . . . much longer, major!" Jackson gasped beside him. The ceaseless whipping of his arms lagged for an instant and five of the brown furry beasts broke through his guard and darted at his face and throat. Jackson shouted, seized one in his fist and beat at the others with it. The captured bat squeaked and squealed and other vampires drew off, fluttering just out of reach of the defending arms of the men.

"Make it keep on squealing," Wentworth ordered sharply.

Jackson did, and while the bat shrilled its fright, the others held back.

"It won't last long," Wentworth panted.

"No, and there's no way out . . . unless Ram Singh comes."

Wentworth shook his head. "Sent him to Philadelphia. We'll have to get out of this ourselves." It was as if he knew that at this minute, within five miles of the house, Nita and Ram Singh and Stoking were helpless in the hands of the police. He knew a sickening despair. If he could only think. . . . Already the truce of fright was ending and the bats were fluttering to the attack again. Through their black cloud, Wentworth gazed toward where June Calvert still sat watching. She was leaning forward, her face cruelly smiling.

"Behold your love, Jackson!" he cried, "how she enjoys your torture!"

Jackson, flailing again with weary arms, peered toward her and, even in the midst of pain, Wentworth saw that she still drew him; that the strange attraction held. A glimmering of an idea began to shine in his brain.

"Jackson," he said quietly. "We're going to the door, back to back. You face the door. . . ."

Jackson turned a bewildered face toward him. "We'll be more exposed, sir."

"Quite," Wentworth conceded. "I'll stand first. Set your shoulders to mine and we'll walk across to the door."

Jackson was used to obedience. He knew that if Wentworth spoke, it was in furtherance of some definite plan. He did not question the strategy. After all, he had been a soldier. As Wentworth stood, Jackson sprang to his feet, and set his back against Wentworth's, walked slowly toward the door while they both struck out with their arms and kicked off the bats that flew low to attack their legs. They reached the grilled opening and Jackson pressed against it.

"Now, what, major?" he asked. His voice was strained and difficult.

Wentworth struck down a bat that bit at his face, caught another in his hand and held it, loudly squealing, before him. For a while the others held off. Wentworth laughed.

"Behold, Jackson," he cried, "the woman you love!"

Jackson did not answer, but Wentworth could hear

his heavy, strained breathing. The bats continued to circle and with regular sweeps of his arms, he drove them back. He waited. It was a faint hope that he entertained. Jackson's instantaneous, passionate interest in the woman was a strange thing, but its reason was clear. The woman herself was intense, strongly emotional. The sight of her fancied enemy undergoing the torture of the bats made her breasts heave quickly. If she saw Jackson's overwhelming fascination, was it not barely possible that she might respond?

Jackson was a vigorous, handsome man, with a rugged, wide-jawed, wide-browed face. His chest was banded with muscle and the glistening perspiration caught every high-light, emphasized every ligament contour. There was something primitive about both of them: this savage fighter who had been an incorrigible in the army until he fell under Wentworth's firm hand, and this woman who could delight in torture and death. Elemental, both of them.

The *Spider* could not turn to watch the woman's face or actions. The bats would not permit, and even a glimpse of his own watching eyes might disrupt the spell he sought to weave. He could feel the quicker pumping of Jackson's sides, and finally, because he strained his ears through the ceaseless squeaking of the bats, he caught June Calvert's whispered words.

"Why . . . do you look at me . . . like that?"

Jackson made no answer. If he had guessed at Wentworth's plan, he gave no sign of it. Wentworth supposed that he was too much preoccupied with emotion to think at all.

The woman spoke again, more strongly. "Why do you look at me like that?"

Jackson boomed out his deep laughter. "Because I hate you!" he cried.

Wentworth's eyes tightened and he nodded slowly. A bat broke through his guard and fastened on his throat. He tore it loose and felt his flesh rip, too. He

100

laughed softly, battled on. The woman's voice was closer now.

"You don't hate me," she said. "You don't! I can see it in your eyes!"

Jackson said nothing and when the woman spoke again, Wentworth started, she was so near!

"Why do you look at me like that?" she whispered.

No sound from Jackson, no more from the woman. Wentworth could hear the breathing of both. He seized a bat and made it squeal in pain. The sound was piercing, hurt the eardrums, but it no longer drove back the vampires. They lanced in over Wentworth's arms. One got past him and fastened on the side of Jackson's throat; but Jackson did not move to knock it off.

"The bat!" the woman whispered. "There's a bat on your throat. Take it off; please take it off!"

Jackson laughed again. "There will only be another. Let him stay and take his three ounces of blood."

"Please take it off," June Calvert cried. "Oh, there is blood on you, all over you."

Deliberately, Wentworth allowed another bat to slip past him and fasten on Jackson's upper arm.

Jackson spoke to the woman. "Come in here."

"No, *no!*" The woman was panting.

Jackson laughed, triumph in its sound. "You must."

After that, long silence, then Jackson's laughter again, the muscles tightening across his back. Presently, the woman sighed.

"You're hurting me," she whispered. "The bars. Wait, I will open the door."

Her footsteps hurried away. Jackson's weight sagged against Wentworth's back. "She's a devil," he whispered. "She takes my strength away. God, she's wonderful, wonderful . . ."

Wentworth said nothing, his mouth tightening as he continued the battle against the bats. Not much longer, thank God. A little more and they would be out of this cage of death. Even then, there would be fighting—but against humans, and a limited number of them—not against the winged vampires. . . . He made a mental note that Jackson, after this, would be useless to him against the Bat Man.

The woman's footsteps were running when she returned. "I had to kill the man," she sobbed. "I had to. He wouldn't give me the keys."

Metal rasped and Jackson sprang through the door. Wentworth whirled and went after him, slammed the cage shut. Jackson thought nothing of his escape. There was still one bat fastened to his arm, but it was the woman, leaning back in Jackson's embrace, who removed that. She pinched the vampire's throat and held it for a while, then dropped it to the floor. There was a smile on her red lips as she looked up into Jackson's face. She would have to go with them, Wentworth thought, or the Bat Man would put her in their place in the vampire's cage. He cast swiftly about the black-walled room for a means of escape.

His clothing still lay upon the floor and he donned such pieces of it as were not impossibly torn. The bites of the bats were beginning to pain now. He was wrapped in their torture. He went back to Jackson and June Calvert.

"June, if you want him to live," he said sharply, "we'll have to get you both out of here quickly."

June Calvert looked at Wentworth without comprehension for fully thirty seconds, then she pulled herself out of Jackson's arms.

"Good God," she stammered, "what have I done? I have freed my brother's murderer!"

"I am not his murderer," Wentworth told her quietly. "I had nothing to do with his death, but you have freed us. If the Bat Man catches you, it will mean your death as well as ours."

June seemed still in a half-daze. She looked from Wentworth to Jackson and her gaze lingered longest there. Her face softened.

"You are right," she whispered. "We must escape. Come, I'll lead the way."

Wentworth motioned Jackson toward the remnants of

his clothing upon the floor and, with a bound, he reached them and pulled them on. Wentworth had no weapon, nor did Jackson and June had only her curiously curved dagger.

"Are there any weapons we can get?" Wentworth asked.

June shook her head slowly. "The Bat Man allows none," she said. "None save his own and the blowguns of the Indians."

Wentworth thought grimly that the Bat Man did not trust his allies overmuch and nodded at the idea. That would be a help, perhaps.

"We would better leave at once," he said. "Soon the Bat Man will come back to see if we are dead, and then. . . ."

June Calvert nodded. She led the way with the stealth of a cat toward a curtained wall, pulled it aside and revealed a narrow passageway. "At the end of this are three doors," she whispered. "The one to the right leads outdoors. After that, there is no way to escape save by fighting through."

She walked ahead, carelessly, with assurance and behind her Jackson and Wentworth made no sound. Wentworth had no intention of leaving, but he must have a weapon before he could carry out his plan to kill the Bat Man. Jackson and the girl must go. . . .

There was no warning at all, but suddenly the hall ahead of them was crowded with the short, kirtled figures of Indians and a dozen blowguns were aimed at Wentworth and his companions. He whirled to retreat, but that way was blocked in the same way. There was no escape, not even by sacrificing his companions could the *Spider* win through to kill the Bat Man and rid humanity of this newest and most terrible scourge. For, to hold either girl or Jackson as a shield, would merely expose his back to the other force. . . . Wentworth shrugged.

"We surrender," he said shortly.

From somewhere nearby, but out of sight, the Bat Man squeaked an order. "To the bat cage with them.

Strip the woman and throw her in with them. She is a traitor. That was for your benefit, my friends, now I shall repeat the order in their own language. . . ." The Bat Man broke into a gabbled tongue of the Indians. Instantly, they moved forward, half of them almost crawling to keep clear of the blowguns which the other half held ready.

Wentworth knotted his fists, his jaw set rigidly, but he knew it was useless. He would only bring on his own death, whereas if he submitted . . . But what hope lay that way? There would not again be an escape from the fangs of the vampires. He locked his teeth to hold back the curses of despair. Now, surely, there was an end of hope . . . !

If Wentworth surrendered philosophically, June Calvert did not. She swept, raging, toward the line of Indians and they parted before her, and seized her from behind, swept her helpless to the floor with a garrote about her throat.

A hoarse shout tore from Jackson. He hurled himself toward the struggling girl. Her dagger was out and she slashed about with it, hamstrung an Indian so that he dropped, screaming, to one knee. She took a second man in the groin with the blade. Jackson seized an Indian about the throat with his powerful hands, lifted him high and tossed him upon his fellows. Then a tiny dart blossomed on his shoulder, the hollow pop of a blowgun echoed down the hall. From his place of concealment, the Bat Man laughed squeakily.

Wentworth had shouted a warning when Jackson first charged in, but he had known in advance that it was hopeless. Yet he could not stand back while these other two fought. . . . The *Spider's* manner of fighting differed from theirs. Instead of rushing in against the blowguns, he threw back his head and laughed, an echo of the squeaky, bat-like mirth of the leader. While he laughed, he walked toward the place where Jackson and June still battled.

The girl was almost unconscious now, with the bite

of the garrote on her throat. Jackson was staggering and Wentworth thought from his behavior that the dart which had pierced his shoulder carried the narcotic, not the deadly poison. . . . Wentworth continued his laughing advance. He could see that the Indians were puzzled, that they did not know whether or not to shoot. The Bat Man continued his mirth. Apparently, he could not see what went on in the narrow hallway. Wentworth stood now over Jackson, who had fallen, and the girl. Both were unconscious. Lord, it was so hopeless. What could he hope to accomplish, unarmed, against ten savages? Two lay dead on the floor, one still moaned over the gashed and useless leg. . . .

Wentworth helped the injured Indian to his feet and, still making squeaking noises, led the man down the hall. The blowgun men were puzzled, and as he continued, parted their ranks. Hope began to thrill through Wentworth, but it died in an instant. Apparently, he had shown himself to the Bat Man, for suddenly a high, shrill squeak rang out. Instantly, a flood of Indians hurled themselves upon him. Blowguns were forgotten. It was hand to hand, twist and wrench and punch. An Indian seized Wentworth's right wrist and attempted to twist it behind him. The man was powerful and his very grip was painful. Wentworth hurled himself bodily backward, tossing the Indian against the ceiling with the impetus of his fall.

The trick was a mistake. Though the man he had thrown fell unconscious, and probably dead, to the floor, four other Indians dived bodily upon Wentworth before he could rise to his feet again. He held one off with a kicking foot, got his elbow against the throat of a second, but the other two hit solidly on his chest. One got his fingers on Wentworth's throat and pressed crushingly on the larynx. Darkness began to whirl before Wentworth's eyes. He pulled up his hands, got hold of a finger with each and shredded the throttling hold off of his throat. He heard the fingers break and the Indian whimpered.

Another of the small, fierce men crawled into the

battle. He had June's bloody knife and he moved its blade gloatingly toward Wentworth's throat. At the same time, five more Indians hurled themselves upon him, seizing arms and legs, kicking at his sides. Pain rippled over him. The knife caressed his neck . . . and a gun barked!

The sound of the pistol was deafening in the narrow confines of the hall. The Indian with the knife jerked to his feet and crashed down again in a crumpled heap, his forehead smashed by a heavy bullet. Three pistol shots smashed out together and three more of the small, savage men were slain. Wentworth hurled a body from his chest, bowled over another Indian and sprang to his feet.

"Catch, Dick!" It was a woman's voice, and an automatic arched through the air to his hand. A woman's voice . . . Who could it be but Nita? Wentworth threw back his head and laughed joyously. Nita . . . and a gun in his hand again.

"Brave work, Nita," he cried. He charged down the hall where the Indians were scrambling for their blowguns. He fired once as a man got his long tube to his lips, then he ducked from the hallway into an opening to his right. He no longer heard the squeaking laughter, or sharp orders of the Bat Man, but the creature could not be far away. Back in the hall, Nita's gun and those other two he had not identified were slamming death into the Indians. . . .

Wentworth was racing down a corridor between narrow walls, toward a twilight dimness that seemed to recede before him. He stopped abruptly, listening. The shooting and the shrieks of wounded and dying still came to his ears, but that was all. Nevertheless, he ran on, hoping against hope that he might find the Bat Man. Something clicked beneath his feet and he ducked backward, sensing an opening above his head. He went back three slow paces, eyeing that hole in the ceiling.

Suddenly he understood. A black form had dropped from the opening and leathery wings fluttered toward him. He cursed and fired a quick shot. No need to wonder whether the teeth of those bats were poisoned. Why else would a trap be set with them? He fired twice more in quick succession, then pulled his coat over his head, covered hands in pockets and raced past the spot where the bats whirled. He dared not use more of his bullets, lest there be none left when finally he came face to face with the Bat Man himself.

He burst suddenly into the open through a swinging door and stopped, peering about him. In the east, the sky was graying with dawn. In the woods that grew close to the house, sleepy birds were twittering with the promise of day. Wentworth looked down to the grass. It was wet with dew and here and there upon the blades, spiders had woven webs which were beaded with moisture. Straight ahead of him, a spider web had been torn.

With a cry that he scarcely suppressed, Wentworth sprang forward. The trail in the dewy grass was plain now. This way, the Bat Man must have fled. Abruptly, as he ran, Wentworth halted, made a circuit beneath a tree. There, for some reason, the tracks had left a gap as if the Bat Man had sprung into the air for a distance of ten feet. Even so, Wentworth barely escaped the trap he more than half suspected. His feet jarred the hidden trigger and from the tree overhead a sprung branch hurled a spear deep into the earth where, moments before, Wentworth had narrowly missed treading. If he had stepped there, the spear would have drilled him from neck to groin. Thereafter, he went more cautiously along the woodland path. He had gone perhaps seventy-five yards when, ahead of him, a plane roared into life. Wentworth sprinted for the clearing which he could see now vaguely through the trees, but as he burst into the open, the ship he had heard was just lifting from the earth, despite a cold motor, and climbing rapidly over the tree tops. . . .

The automatic jumped and slammed in Wentworth's hand. He was certain that he hit the plane twice before it slid out of range, but he could not have scored on the pilot for, though there was a slight faltering on the flight after the second shot, the plane kept steadily on. Wentworth cursed with disappointment. There could be no question that the Bat Man had escaped in that ship. He proceeded more cautiously along the trail back and found another trap which he had missed by sheer luck with his long, running stride. He discharged a small bow which hurled a poisoned dart.

Well, once more the *Spider* had met the Bat Man and this time, though he had failed to capture or kill the leader, he at least had not utterly failed. He was light-hearted as he loped back to the gaunt, low building where Nita had come to the rescue. The long, dim halls were as silent as before, more so, since cries and shots no longer echoed. For no apparent reason, an unrest seized him. His pace quickened until he fairly sprinted toward the place where they had battled.

Before he reached the spot, he saw bodies of red-clad Indians sprawled in the doorway. None of them even groaned. Surely, by now, he should hear the murmur of Nita's voice, the sound of her walking. But there was nothing. . . . He hurdled the stacked bodies, halted motionless in the middle of the hallway. Save for the dead—and the unmoving body of June Calvert— the place was empty.

"Nita!" Wentworth sent the cry echoing. "Nita! Nita!"

He waited and the echoes died and silence flowed back to his waiting ears. He sprang toward the spot where she had stood, shooting down the foes that crowded against his back. On the floor there, he found a scrap of lacy white that was her handkerchief, found two abandoned automatics. . . . He straightened with his face gone hard and white, his eyes glittering like deep glacial ice. There was no mistaking those signs, but, good God, Nita could not have been captured thus with those other two with her to help her fight! It wasn't possible . . . !

And then Wentworth saw another thing that filled his

heart with leaden despair. The wall was pricked in half a dozen places by blowgun darts. A groan came from the depths of his soul. He whirled and ran through other dim corridors, burst outside and circled the building, but nowhere was there any trace of Nita. Finally he came to a standstill again where her guns lay upon the floor. He lifted his clenched fists toward the ceiling and shook them twice. He had thought at least a partial victory was in his grasp, and in the moment of elation, he had lost everything . . . !

CHAPTER ELEVEN

Against All Hope

Wentworth turned once more to look about the hall and his eyes fell upon the supine body of June Calvert. Was she dead, then, with that garrote about her throat? With sudden hope, Wentworth approached her in long strides, looked down on her sullenly beautiful face. If it had turned blue with strangulation, then the stagnant blood already had been dissipated. . . . He flung down on a knee and felt for the pulse, held his polished platinum cigarette case before her lips. There was no indication of life either way, and yet. . . .

Swiftly, he turned June over on her face and began resuscitation, hands pressing down on her short ribs to expel air from her lungs, releasing sharply to suck in oxygen. Artificial respiration. He was desperately anxious that she survive. If she was seriously interested in Jackson, she might well reveal the Bat Man's secrets!

It was heart-breaking work, this resuscitation of an apparently lifeless woman. If she should survive, he might speed the rescue of Nita, the smashing of all the Bat Man's demon plans. But if his work was useless, precious minutes were being wasted. For over half an hour, he continued the slow rhythm of breathing. There was a frown upon his forehead and curious, straight hardness to his lips. Almost he had despaired when there was a faint sigh from June's lips and, sluggishly, reluctantly, her lungs took up their work again.

She was alive! Wentworth almost cried the words aloud. He had no stimulant to administer, but he used what means of restoration he had, bathing her temples with cold water from a tap he found. Fear widened her eyes when first she beheld him, but presently she appeared to remember the situation. She tried to look about her, hand gripping her throat. . . .

"The Bat Man kidnaped them all," Wentworth told her harshly. "The woman I love, the man you love."

June Calvert thrust herself up on stiff arms and stared about the passageway, saw the heaped bodies of dead Indians and nothing more. Wentworth helped her to her feet and she began to stumble through the deserted halls and rooms. Finally, she sagged weakly against a wall and sobbed there, shoulders jerking spasmodically.

Wentworth watched her narrowly. He must judge her mood exactly if she was to be of help to him. Weeping was the wrong note. He jeered at her.

"I didn't expect you to spend time crying," he said. "Don't you realize that every second wasted brings the man you love that much nearer to the cage of vampires?"

June lifted her dark, disheveled head and stared into Wentworth's eyes. Her shoulders still jerked, but no sound came from her lips.

"Help me," Wentworth urged, "and we will save him."

Resolution hardened on the girl's face, a faint smile twisted her full lips. "You are not interested so much in saving him, as in capturing the Bat Man."

"Not capturing him," Wentworth corrected softly, *"killing him!"*

June Calvert's dark eyes widened a little, but she made no comment.

"But you are wrong about my not wanting to save Jackson," Wentworth continued. "He has been my comrade in arms for years. My Hindu servant is also a captive—and the woman I love. Come, June, the Bat

Man ordered your death. You can no longer have any loyalty toward him. And there is Jackson. . . ."

"Jackson," she whispered. "A soldier? What's his first name?"

Wentworth fought for calmness. Seconds were so precious, but if he took a wrong move with this girl. . . . He smiled a little. "Jackson won't want you to call him by it," he said. "It's Ronald."

June was immediately indignant. "Why, I think it's a lovely name. Ronald," she tried it on her lips, softly. "Ronald Jackson."

Wentworth lost patience. "You'll never have a chance to call him by it if we don't hurry," he snapped. "Don't you realize that Jackson is going to be killed . . . by the Bat Man? Even while we stand here talking, he may be. . . ."

June shuddered. The tremor shook her shoulders, jerked over her entire body. "Yes, yes!" she whispered. "But I know so little. I don't know who the Bat Man is or where his other headquarters are, except that he boasted that only he could reach his hideout in the Rocky Mountains unless he went first and prepared the way . . ."

Wentworth was silent, letting her talk now that she was started, but bitter disappointment gripped him. Despair was a cold weight in his breast.

". . . I think," June was frowning, "that he was . . . quite fond . . . of me. He had a strange diffidence and made me rather timid offers to sit beside him when he ruled the world. Oh, it's not as unlikely as you think. He intends to practically destroy the United States. . . ."

A jagged curse forced itself from between Wentworth's lips. "But why? In God's name, why?"

"He intends to demand tribute of all the nations of the world," June said slowly, "in return for a promise not to loose the bats on their peoples."

"Preposterous!" Wentworth snapped. "They wouldn't pay." Then he frowned, remembering. There

112

had been a time when nearly all the maritime nations of the world had paid tribute to the Barbary pirates of the Mediterranean, bribed them not to attack ships flying their flag. Only the United States had refused, and had sent great battleships to uphold that refusal. And that had been less than a hundred years ago. Only the United States had refused . . .

"He thought," June went on, "that the United States would refuse to pay, so he would make an example of her to the rest of the world. I think he plans to save New York for the last. His next attack. . . ."

"You know that? Good!" Wentworth began to know hope again. "Where will that be?"

"Michigan City," June replied briefly.

Wentworth uttered a sharp exclamation. Michigan City was an amusement resort at Chicago to which the city's population flocked in tens of thousands for swimming and other amusements. And in the entire place, there were not a half-dozen buildings into which the bats could not enter. In Chicago proper, it would be different. But in Michigan City, literally thousands would die. . . .

"Come," he said sharply, and hurried down the hall. He heard June's footsteps just behind him.

"Where are you going?" she demanded.

"Michigan City!"

"But you promised to save Ronald!" the girl cried.

Wentworth nodded, never slackening his pace as he pushed out into the morning that was reddening with sunrise. June Calvert caught his arm, tried to pull him about.

"You promised!" she cried.

Wentworth stopped and faced her. "Do you know where Jackson is?" he demanded.

"No."

"Do you know where the Bat Man is?"

"N-No."

"Then, June, we have to go to the only place you know of that the Bat Man will appear, don't we?"

* * *

113

June sobbed, pressed a clenched hand to her forehead. "Yes, yes," she whispered, "but before that, Ronald may be . . . may be . . ."

Wentworth's tanned face was drained of all color. June Calvert lifted her head slowly and looked at him. "Ah," she whispered, "I forgot. The woman you love is there, too!"

Wentworth said dully, "Yes." He turned and hurried off toward the airfield where, almost an hour ago, the Bat Man had winged into the dawn. June caught his arm.

"There are no more planes," she said. "There is nothing at all here to travel in, but there's a highway about three miles to the west."

They tramped in silence through the damp woodland, crashing over underbrush, jumping brooks, fighting thickets. Finally, they burst out in the highway and stopped, staring. There were two automobiles parked on the opposite side of the road. In one of them, two policeman sat.

Wentworth walked toward them and the man behind the wheel twisted about an angry face.

"Hey, buddy," he called. "Come here and get us loose, will you? We're all tied up."

Wentworth stopped beside the car. "How'd you get tied up?" he asked curiously.

"We was chasing them guys what's turning loose bats," the man, red-faced and angry, declared. "We has them all tied up, girl with them, too. Then one of them gets loose and pulls a knife on me and we can't do nothing."

Wentworth tackled the ropes, shooting eager questions at the policemen, but as the story unfolded, his eagerness died. It was apparent now that it was Nita the men had almost stopped. Nita and Ram Singh and Stoking. All of them were in the Bat Man's power now, food for bats. Wentworth's jaw tightened. . . . The police took him and June back to town, casting many curious glances at the girl's strange scarlet dress. When they had found the dead Indians there in the woods, they would remember this meeting, because of that similarity of dress. . . . Wentworth shook his head grimly. There was no time now to explain, even though trouble would follow later.

At Flemington, he found the plane Stoking had rented. He appropriated it and sent the ship racing into the West. At dusk, the attack would be made on Michigan City. There was ample time to reach Chicago by plane. Ample time, if there were no mishaps. . . . Persistently, Wentworth's thoughts reverted to Nita. She was in this situation, prisoner of the Bat Man, because she had striven to help him. God, this was no life for a woman! Better a thousand times, if they had never met. Better if she had married this Fred Stoking, who had been her childhood sweetheart. . . .

His bitterness came back overwhelmingly. What right did he have to wreck Nita's life this way, perhaps to bring about her death? If she had never met Dick Wentworth. . . .

Wentworth was snapped from his reverie by a spluttering motor. He glanced sharply at his instruments, but nothing was wrong there and the engine was drumming steadily again. He peered over the side. Beneath him lay the wild reaches of the Alleghanies. Good God, if he were forced down here, it would take him days to reach even a mountaineer's cabin! Days more before he could reach Chicago! The Bat Man would have struck and vanished. . . . The motor coughed and missed again!

The *Spider's* face became hard and rigid. No use to conjecture now. The engine was failing. It was only a question of selecting a spot to crash. A bitter curse squeezed out. He leaned over the side, staring down at the jagged, forested sides of mountains below him. He realized grimly that it was not merely a question of landing in a spot from which it might be possible to reach civilization, it was even doubtful if they would survive the landing!

There was not a fifty-foot clearing anywhere in the tangle of mountains—not a roadway, nor a fire lane. The motor was missing badly now. Even though he pulled the throttle wide, the plane was losing altitude. Not rapidly, but losing none the less. He would have to make his decision quickly.

A mountain-top glided by beneath him, its trees no more than seventy-five feet under the fuselage, and the valley beyond opened. Wentworth knew a thrill of hope, for there was clearly a break in the forest down there. He swept a rapid glance over the country. No sign of smoke, or of human habitation. He laughed sharply. Would it not be better to smash against that rocky precipice that thrust out of the opposite mountain? When finally he escaped from these mountains, Nita would be dead—and Ram Singh and Jackson. . . . Every one dear to him would have died through his failure. Resolutely, he sought to close his mind to those facts. He was, he told himself, no longer a human being, but a cause. He was the *Spider!* He must live to defend humanity. . . .

Time after time, he had been compelled to abandon Nita to her fate while he battled new monsters of crime. For a single instant, however, his mind broke from his rigid control, and he pictured her thrown helpless into a cage of vampires, saw her white body fall under the fluttering black hordes. . . .

He screamed curses into the air, shook his fist at the skies that arched pitilessly above. By God, it should not be! It should not! The final splutter of the motor, the whir of the dying propeller snapped him out of his bitter tirade. He had been handling the plane sub-consciously, directing it toward that clearing in the valley which alone offered hope of safe landing.

Behind him, June Calvert's high voice beat on his sound-deafened ears.

"What's the matter?"

"Motor conked out," he called back to her, then leaned over the side to stare down at the clearing. It

116

was a lake, full of black, jagged snags. The trees grew right to its shores. Once more Wentworth laughed, hardly, bitterly. It would be better if he did die—but he must strive to live. He sent the ship down in a sharp dive. . . .

CHAPTER TWELVE

Race With Time

As the plane sloped toward the lake, Wentworth's eyes swept the wooded shores hopefully. There was no beach anywhere. The retractable landing gear already had been lowered. Now Wentworth set to work to crank it back into the fuselage by hand. The hull of the plane would not resist water long, but he could use it as a pontoon in landing whereas the wheels would catch and tip the ship forward on her nose. His danger, without the wheels, would be in snagging a wing in the water since they would be so close to the surface. Fortunately, the craft was a Lockhead Vega, a high-winged monoplane, so even that danger was reduced. . . .

Swiftly the plane neared the mirror-like lake. The steep, wooded mountains were reflected and white clouds made their images below. It was strangely peaceful, but Wentworth knew no peace, only bitterness and mounting rage. . . . Another hundred feet and the Vega would breast the lake. Wentworth kept the stick waggling gently from side to side, leveling off the wings. He swept in over the tree-tops with scarcely a dozen feet clear, put the nose down and swooped toward the surface.

Down the center of the lake, there was a space fairly clear of snags and Wentworth had picked that as the only possible landing place. Now, as the ship settled in a stall, only inches above the surface, he spotted a submerged log fairly in his path. There was no help for it. He must drive straight for the log. The stick had already gone soft in his hand. . . . The ship squatted down on the water with a heavy impact, ran twenty feet and snagged the log . . .

"Let go and dive!" Wentworth shouted.

The nose went down, the tail whipped up and over, hurling Wentworth and June Calvert like catapult missiles through the air. Wentworth struck head first in a shallow dive, whipped to the surface and peered about for the girl. She broke water a few seconds afterward, smiled at him, white-faced.

"Don't worry about me," she gasped. "I can swim."

Side by side, they struck out for the shore. The plane, on its back, already was settling deep into the water, buoyed for a while by partially emptied gasoline tanks. But the pull of the motor was rapidly overcoming that. Even as Wentworth reached the shore and stood erect in the edge of the woods, the water lapped over the last inch of canvas and the plane disappeared.

Wentworth, his face set, leaned forward to assist June Calvert to her feet and she looked despairingly into his face.

"We're beaten," she said dully. "Beaten before we fairly start!"

Wentworth's lips moved in a slight still smile. "It's ten o'clock. We have almost ten hours to reach Chicago."

June Calvert gazed into his strong face, with its locked jaw and determined eyes and her own despair lessened. "But what can we do?" she whispered.

Wentworth turned and looked up the steep slope of the mountain, toward the bare outcropping of rock near its crest. He nodded toward it.

"From its top, we may be able to spot some help," he said. He turned toward the thick alder bushes that crowded close to the water's edge, the white-stemmed

119

birches beyond. With a curt word, he started forward, wading first through swamp that rose to his knees. Among the birches, he stopped for a few minutes, whittling on two smaller trees with his pocket knife. Presently, they went on again, each with a staff.

The thickets continued and briars snagged at his clothing, tore his hands. He stopped and gave his coat to June Calvert. She thanked him with softening eyes, but his smile was thin.

"It's not chivalry, but wisdom," he said dryly. "You can travel faster with your shoulders protected."

She laughed at him and they went on again, Wentworth crashing through ahead to break a way. There was a hard desperation in his soul. He had to fight to keep from plunging forward at a mad run that would have exhausted him within minutes. A trotting horse travels farther, he reminded himself. God alone knew how much of this tramping there might be, but if he could get hold of a fast plane within the next six or eight hours. . . .

After they left the low shores of the lake, the underbrush was thinner, but the grade was steepening. It took a half hour to reach the crest of the hill, Wentworth discovered with a despairing glance at his watch. Then twelve such hills. . . . But there were the descents and the valleys to cross. Five, six such hills and his margin would be reduced to nothing.

"We'll have to run down this hill," he said shortly. "Jog, don't race."

He set the pace, the half-trot, half-lope that the woods-runners of the Indians had used over these same trails years ago. Half way down the hill, they struck a small path and June cried out in happiness.

"See, a path!" she panted. "Someone must be near!"

"Game trail," Wentworth threw over his shoulder.

But he swung along its course. As long as it went in the direction he wished, it would be swifter traveling. Unconsciously, his pace quickened. At the bottom of the hill, he realized that there were no footsteps behind him and halted. A hundred and fifty yards back, running doggedly at the pace he first had set, was June Calvert. Her red dress had been torn off at the knee and the coat looked strange with the silk robe, but she was plugging steadily along. She looked up, saw Wentworth.

"Go on, go on!" she cried. "I'm all right."

Wentworth waited until she was near, then ran on. The game trail stopped at a small brook in the valley, but another slanted up the hill, Wentworth pushed on, no longer running, but slowly regaining his breath as he pulled the hill. He had hoped from the ridge just passed, that he might detect some signs of human habitation. The hill ahead inspired him anew, but he said nothing. . . . The next valley was empty of hope, too. Wentworth stole a glance at his watch, an hour and a quarter gone. . . .

Doggedly, he held himself back as he loped down toward the valley. The game trail was gone now, wandering off down the valley and the way was constantly impeded by shrubbery. He kept his lips locked against the urge to pant. He could hear June Calvert gasp for breath. But, damn it, there could be no stop, no resting. Within a few hours, the Bat Man would strike. If the *Spider* did not then take his trail, it would be too late to save Nita and those two gallant men who had thrown in their lot with him. It might even be too late to strike at the Bat Man, for if this chance failed, future contacts would depend on luck alone.

These thoughts worked maddeningly in Wentworth's brain as he loped downhill, and labored up the next grade, the third. If this one also proved an empty hope . . . But it would only mean pushing on to the next and a further reduction of the possibility of success. He scarcely dared look at his watch.

It was hot in the woods where the trees choked off all breeze. Black flies and midges danced about his perspiring face and his shirt clung damply to his body. Nor were his shoes fitted to this type of walking. The soles speedily grew slippery on leaves and the fallen needles of pines so that walking became an exhausting labor. At the top of the third hill, June was three hundred yards behind him and he himself was panting through stubbornly resisting lips. Almost he dreaded to peer into the valley beyond and search the opposite slope, but hope urged him on. He looked—it was empty . . . !

June Calvert toiled up to him, glanced and passed on, pushing herself into a labored run. She was panting, too, but there was a stubborn set to her chin. Wentworth loped after her, drew abreast.

"What time?" she gasped.

Wentworth looked reluctantly at his watch. "Half past twelve."

June said nothing and they ran on. At the bottom of the hill, a spring bubbled water into a small brook. Wentworth halted and they drank sparingly and pushed on. The three hours that followed were nightmares of exhausting action. There was no more running down hills and at the crest of each they stopped for long minutes. The heat had increased, and they dared not drink heavily lest cold water bloat them. When they struck a game trail, they followed it, but mostly there was dense underbrush that must be circled or crashed through and in the bottoms, alder bushes made almost impenetrable thickets.

Each hill had burgeoned hope of what might lie beyond, but each crest brought disappointment, so that Wentworth scarcely dared to gaze on the scenes below. The seventh hill seemed interminable, its crest was a bare ridge where rocks jostled the clouds. Twice, on the climb, Wentworth halted and June Calvert toiled to where he stood and went past him. The third time, he was just on the edge of the barren ridge that crowned the rise.

He stood there, gathering strength for the last pull, for the disappointment that must meet him from its top and once more June moved up beside him. Not even glancing in his direction, she traveled on heavily. Her stockings long ago had ripped from her legs and the flesh was torn and lacerated by thorns. Her head sagged so that her black hair half-hid her face and she moved with the steadiness, the stiffness of an automaton.

Wentworth watched her mount toward the crest; then he tramped on himself, head hanging, the white birch staff helping him up the grade. He did not look again at June, but abruptly he stopped, his down-gazing eyes seeing June upon her knees, head sagging, hands clasped together before her. He lifted his eyes and saw slow, blue smoke rising from the opposite slope of the hill. Was it already too late? He said nothing, but looked wearily at his watch. It was half-past four. If he could get a plane by six . . . It would take a half hour or more to reach that smoke.

He bent down and raised June to her feet and together, his arm supporting her, they went down the hill. The bottom was incredibly overgrown, but nothing could have stopped Wentworth now. He crashed through like a bull. On the far side, he stopped, peering upward. Laurel grew thickly ahead of him, screening the ground from view, but he could still see the smoke above the trees. What it portended, he did not know since there had been no house visible from the opposite ridge. But surely there were men here. They would be able to speed him on his way.

He turned, waited for June; then he pushed on again toward the laurel. He was looking at the ground when a rasping voice called out.

"You can stop right there, furriner!"

Wentworth glanced up sharply. A rifle muzzle yawned at him through a thick clump of laurel. . . .

Wentworth looked very calmly into the muzzle of the rifle. He had looked into similar eyes of death many times, but it was not that which calmed him now. It was his determination that nothing should stop him.

"Our plane crashed in a lake seven hills back," he said shortly. "I want a horse or some other means of getting to the nearest town. I'll pay for it . . . by check." He mentioned the method of payment as an afterthought. It would be very easy for the hidden man to shoot if he thought there was any chance for loot.

"We ain't got no hawses," he said flatly. "I reckon you better mosey back over them thar seven hills."

June Calvert was at Wentworth's shoulder. "Stop being a damned fool, Lemuel," she said. "We're not going back and you're going to help us to get out."

"Yuh know Lem?" another hidden man asked cautiously.

June Calvert said, "Oh, go to hell!" She walked to the right of the bushes where the rifle was poised. Wentworth was as puzzled as the rifleman obviously was, but he followed June. Two mountaineers came cautiously out of the laurel, tall, lanky, with squinting blue eyes.

"Where'd yuh ever meet up with Lem?" he demanded.

"I reckon I'll let Lem tell you that," June said steadily. "You tell him June Calvert said you were a damn'-sight faster with your rifle than you are with your brains. We want a flivver and we want it quick."

The older mountaineer blinked at June Calvert's words, moved his feet uncomfortably and spat tobacco juice at the bole of a tree.

"Wa'al," he mumbled, "if yuh know Lem, I reckon you be all right. We got a flivver over the hill a piece. You wantin' me to drive it?"

June shook her head, started up the hill. Wentworth followed her lead and the lanky mountaineer stood, with his arms folded over the muzzle of his rifle watching them go.

"Just leave the flivver at Pop Hawkins' store!" he yelled after them. "Tell him I'll be after it directly."

Wentworth felt the weariness drop from his legs. He went up the hill as freshly as he had started hours before. He ranged up beside June, glanced at her curiously. Her lips were curved in a wide smile and she seemed hard put to choke back a laugh.

"You tricked him," Wentworth whispered wonderingly. "How in the world did you do it?"

They topped the hill before June spoke, then she laughed. "I used to teach school in the mountains," she said. "There isn't a family of them that hasn't got a Lemuel in it. If there wasn't one in this family, the chances were that they knew somebody pretty well who had the name. It wasn't half as wide a shot as you might think. They've got a whiskey still on the hill. That's the reason for the rifle."

At the crest, Wentworth swept the valley beyond with a quick glance. It was fully five miles across and far down toward the north was the smoke of a small town. But, best of all, there was a narrow, rutted road only a few hundred feet down. They went toward it rapidly.

"It was a very clever trick, June," Wentworth said. "I owe you one for that."

"You owe me nothing," June said sharply. "I was as much in danger as you were. What time is it?"

It was five minutes after five and Wentworth's lips drew tight and hard against his teeth as he hurried toward the ancient Ford that was parked in the middle of the road below. Wentworth had to crank it, but once started, the motor ran smoothly. He backed up a sharp embankment, wrenched the wheels about and sent it bounding down the steep hill.

The road twisted and wound between trees and rocks and bulging roots of trees. There were two ruts and between them grass grew. A more modern car would have scraped off its crank case in the first mile, but the high-wheeled Ford bounded as lightly as a goat from bump to bump and they made incredibly good time. Once a creek, which they forded, splashed water as high as the carburetor and almost stalled the engine, but it caught again and hurled them joyously down the valley.

Five miles of that and the road swung into a wider, dirt highway in which two cars could pass by running one wheel into the ditch. Three miles more and they came to a town of a dozen shacks with a general store labeled: "P. J. Hawkins, Merchandise, Groceries, Dry Goods, Seeds, Plows, etc." Wentworth jerked to a halt before it and went inside.

The town was Hawkinsville, Penn., and the railroad was twenty miles straight down the valley. Pop Hawkins wasn't sure whether there was an airport there, but there might be one at Pittsburgh. He said *Pittsburgh* as some people whisper *Heaven!* Yep, one of the boys did hire his car out sometimes. He went to the porch.

"Lem!" he shouted. "Lem Conley!"

June, from the auto, winked at Wentworth. It was ten minutes before this Lemuel backed a wheezy Dodge from the stable and sent them rolling down the valley at a mad thirty-five miles an hour. Ordinarily, Wentworth would have enjoyed this out of the way corner of the world, but there was no time for dalliance. It was close to six o'clock. . . .

It was seven, and the sun was slanting toward the hills, when the Dodge wheezed up to the railway station of Dry Town. There would be no more trains that night. Airplanes? Well, now, over the hill there in Goochland County, they was having a fair and a fellow did some dad-fool stunts up in the air. . . . No, 'twasn't fur, no more'n ten miles.

Wentworth almost despaired. He was dubious of the plane, too. Ships used for stunting, would not be the racing type he would need if he were to reach Chicago before the Bat Man loosed his hordes upon Michigan City. But there was still a chance.

The Dodge labored up roads that seemed perpendicular, finally crested the mountain and swooped down into Goochland with bolts rattling like castanets. The aviator at the fair wheeled out an old Waco that would make ninety miles an hour in a pinch. . . .

The red ball of the sun was balanced on the horizon and they took off into its eye. A half hour later, they set down at Pittsburgh and Wentworth chartered a fast Boeing, the only speedy job available on the field. Two

126

hours from Chicago. . . . and it was already deep twilight. How long before the Bat Man would release his murdering hordes?

Wentworth blindly watched the dark landscape sliding beneath the plane, the yellow lights of homes prick out. Those windows would be dark with death soon if the Bat Man were not overpowered. Michigan City was the only hope of contact with him, and yet—did Wentworth have the right to risk the lives, nay to sacrifice lives, at the amusement park tonight so that he could meet once more with the Bat Man if he was not already too late. It was true that many hundreds would die if he did not find and kill the man, but was he justified? Was he not thinking more of the urgency of rescuing Nita and Jackson and Ram Singh, than of those thousands at the park tonight?

Wentworth's lips twitched, became ironically twisted. He got heavily to his feet and walked through the cabin to the cockpit. There was only one pilot on this chartered trip and Wentworth dropped into the co-pilot's seat.

"Radio or wireless?" he questioned.

"Only wireless is working," the pilot yelled above the engine roar, "but I can send for you if you wish, sir."

Wentworth shook his head and leaned forward to the key, began tapping out the call signals for Chicago police. He had been wrong, he acknowledged to himself, in delaying so long with the warning, but he had hoped against hope that he could reach the city before the fatal hour.

HXW, he called, HXW, until, closing the circuit, he heard the answering call, WT, HXW, WT, HXW. Then he began to pound out his warning, identifying himself first of all, for he was known to Chicago police also.

"Bat Man raiding Michigan City tonight with poison bats," he rapped out while the pilot glanced at him, admiring his sending fist. It was rapid, but clear and rhythmic. "Have information from escaped prisoner of

127

Bat Man. Suggest that park be cleared instantly and information put on radio to keep windows shut, throughout city.''

"Commissioner MacHugh sends thanks,'' the wireless buzzed back at him. "Will follow suggestions.''

Wentworth signed off and switched off the set, leaned back in the seat with his eyes gazing off into the black sky. Well, it was done. He had thrown away the only chance he had of saving Nita from the death of the vampires. He argued with himself that he could not have behaved otherwise, but his heart felt cold when he lurched to his feet and stumbled back into the cabin.

June Calvert frowned at his white, drawn face. "What's the matter?'' she demanded sharply.

Wentworth shook his head. No use in destroying her hopes of Jackson's rescue. Actually, he was despairing before there was need of it. It still was possible that the plane would reach Michigan City before the bats flew their lethal way through the night. He walked restlessly back and forth along the aisle of the ship, hands locked behind him. June caught his arm as he passed and stopped him.

"Something has gone wrong!'' she said. "I know it.''

Wentworth shrugged. "We'll be too late, you know that. The Bat Man will have attacked and gone before we get there.''

"No,'' June protested, her dark face flushed despite the drain of fatigue. "He couldn't do that.''

"Why not?''

"He just couldn't, not after the struggle we've put up. Why, things don't work out that way!'' June was desperate.

Wentworth smiled at her wanly. "I hope you're right, June.'' He resumed his pacing. Abruptly, the door of the pilot compartment flung open. "Chicago police calling you,'' he shouted.

Wentworth ducked into the cockpit and fitted the headset to his ears again, waited until police had ceased signaling, then sent his answer winging through space, followed by a question.

Chicago's reply came with staccato speed. "Please repeat warning. Commissioner MacHugh, seven others in headquarters killed by bats."

Wentworth leaned forward tensely as he hammered out his message again. Chicago answered that Michigan City was in hand, advised him to fly to Elgin, Illinois, and land at a field that would show a light. The Bat Man had been seen there, the police continued. Wentworth thanked them and signed off, but sat for a considerable while without ordering a change of course. An hour had rolled by and Columbus lay behind the plane. He turned to the pilot.

"Did that last sending seem the same tone, the same strength as the other?" he asked.

The pilot turned toward him, dropping the companion headset that he wore about his neck. "Funny you should mention it," he said. "I had the same feeling about it—that it wasn't the same."

Wentworth's lips parted in a grim smile. "A decoy message, if I'm not mistaken," he said flatly. "Hold for Michigan City."

The pilot nodded cheerfully. "Yes, sir. Will there be a fight?"

"Pretty apt to be," Wentworth nodded. He got to his feet and started toward the cabin. He heard something hit with a rapid hammering thud just behind him, heard the pilot gasp and whipped about. The pilot was sagging forward over the controls, his head and body a mess of blood and across the twin windshields of the cockpit ran a stitching of bullet holes where machine gun lead had struck . . . !

CHAPTER THIRTEEN

When the Bats Fly!

An instant after the discovery, Wentworth was hurled toward the front of the ship as it answered the pilot's push on the controls. Wentworth's lips moved with his furious curses as he fought to reach the co-pilot's seat. A glance at the altimeter showed him that he must move swiftly, for already the ship had plunged a thousand feet. The gauge showed nine hundred feet!

No need to wonder about the shooting. That decoy message actually had been used to trace his plane so that a killer from the Bat Man could locate him with a radio direction-finder and shoot him down. And it would have succeeded had he moved a moment later or a few minutes sooner. Had he left the cockpit, he could not have reached the controls in time and had he been later, the bullets would have sewn him to the seat as they had the pilot.

The altimeter read five hundred feet when Wentworth got his hand on the stick and began to ease it back. The ship continued to drop at terrific speed and the wings shook with the strain of his attempt to lever out of the dive. For long seconds, it seemed the mighty ship would plunge its engines into the earth, but finally the nose began to lift. Something scraped along the fuselage, tossed the ship wildly. Wentworth tripped off the lights, peered downward through the bullet-pocked windshield and saw the treetops just beneath. The plane's momentum pulled it through.

In a trice, it was zooming and Wentworth caught a glimpse of fiery exhaust blossoms high up in the heavens where the murder ship was circling to watch the finish of its work. Wentworth was grimly thankful that his own exhausts were muffled, so that his flight would not be detected. He made the big Boeing hop hedges for a dozen miles before he dared to let it surge upward toward the skies again. He had no means of defense but he thought it probable that he could outrace his attacker in a straight-away pursuit. He did not sight the plane again as he drove on his course toward Michigan City.

He could turn now to the pilot in the seat beside him, but there was nothing he could do there. The man had made no sound or movement since the bullets had drilled him. His breath had not even rattled in his throat. There could be no doubt he was dead. Wentworth's face was impassive, but there were cold fires of rage in his blue-gray eyes. Another man who served the *Spider,* even though briefly, had died. Was he forever to bring only death to those who helped him?

Grimly, he tugged the throttle of the ship wide until the motors were raving out there in the darkness and the propeller whine rose viciously. He must reach Michigan City before the Bat Man could strike and flee.

It occurred to Wentworth suddenly that June Calvert had made no sound since the shooting and he peered back into the cabin, saw her stretched on the floor with a bloody wound across her temple. It did not seem to be deep, but Wentworth could not leave the controls to investigate. He bent more tensely over the wheel.

Ahead of him was the glow of Michigan City, its thousand lights reaching up challengingly toward the sky. Still the radio did not speak of an attack there. Perhaps he was in time after all! He realized the ship was vibrating dangerously, as he continued to push it at peak speed, but he could not slacken off now. Within fifteen minutes, he would be circling over the myriad lights. . . .

The radio squealed into action. "Calling all Michigan City cars. Calling Michigan City cars. Two men reported killed by bats in front of caroussel. Car twenty-four investigate. Proceed with caution. All others stand by."

It had started then, this new mad murder-jag of the Bat Man. His warning had come too late. . . .

He berated himself bitterly for his neglect, his selfishness in keeping the secret so long. Now Death would stride with seven-league boots across the park, taking great swaths of lives with each sweep of his keen scythe. . . . Wentworth was directly over Michigan City now, swinging in great circles about its borders, searching for some trace of the Bat Man. He could see the bats, even from his height, clouds of fluttering killers. A touch on his shoulder startled him. He looked up into June Calvert's face. It was very pale and he knew that she had seen the pilot's body. The air made a keen hissing through the bullet holes that effectively prevented speech.

Twice more, Wentworth swung about the resort, then, suddenly, he spotted his enemy, the Bat Man. With great wings spread, he was gliding over the fleeing thousands who left many dead behind. With a great shout, Wentworth gunned the ship, put the nose down and dived directly on the Bat Man. If he struck him, the propellers would be ruined, motors would fly apart, death would hurl the ship downward. Wentworth knew those things, but it did not matter.

This black, gliding thing was the creature who had destroyed so many hundreds of lives, who had killed this brave man beside him, who had snatched Nita from his side. There was a snarling smile on the *Spider's* lips as, resolutely, he hammered downward at the Bat Man. Only two hundred feet from him, now only a hundred and fifty and the motors bellowed like hungry lions.

When Wentworth was only a hundred feet away, the Bat Man glided smoothly to the right. Wentworth wrenched the plane about in an effort to follow, but his momentum was too great. He shot on past the slowly moving man and plunged toward the milling crowds below. With a frantic effort, he pulled the great ship's nose upward, whirled it in a *virage* and darted to the attack again. He was handling the powerful Boeing as if it were a light pursuit ship and the wings quivered and vibrated, the engines labored.

The Boeing dodged under the Bat's flight, whirled upward toward him with clawing propellers, the touch of which would slice the man in two. Wentworth had a glimpse of the drawn, frightened face of the Bat Man, saw a rifle spurt flame from near his head. He caught no bullet wind, but the man's effort pushed him just out of reach of the propellers. Savagely, Wentworth whirled the ship about and spotted the Bat Man fluttering downward like a wounded bird, sliding from side to side, whirling. Had he sliced the devil, then?

Wentworth took no chances. He sent the ship plunging toward the Bat Man, though they were now only two hundred feet above the earth. Even as he dived, he saw the Bat Man straighten out of his fall and speed earthward in a straight, controlled glide.

Grimly, Wentworth recognized that pursuit was now hopeless, for he saw the Bat Man glide downward between the high-reaching ferris wheel and a switchback structure. No chance for the Boeing there, but he was quite sure the Bat Man could not wing his way upward again. Those wings would not provide him with enough lift for soaring. He whipped about toward June Calvert.

"I'm going to land on the beach," he rapped out. "Got to follow him. Go to the tail and strap yourself down."

June Calvert smiled slightly. "A parachute would be faster," she said. "I can handle the ship!"

Wentworth's smile was a cheer. He slipped out from behind the wheel and June Calvert took it with practiced hands. Within a minute, he was strapped into the parachute.

"Land it on the beach," he shouted at her, then went to the cabin door. He fought it open against the slip stream, crouched and dived below the tail group, snatched out the ring at once. June had shoved the ship upward, but the altitude was barely adequate. Wentworth landed heavily behind the switchback, sliced through the parachute shrouds with a keen pocket knife and raced for the open. He wore a flying helmet with goggles from the ship and his coat collar was turned high. Only the lower half of his face was exposed to the attacks of the bats, for his hands were gauntleted. Even so, he kept alert for the flying death.

It had been impossible to watch the landing of the Bat Man, but Wentworth had traced out his course and now he ran swiftly toward the spot his calculations indicated. He had gone a hundred feet when a revolver spat from the darkness ahead. Wentworth fired at the flash and zig-zagged on. The revolver lanced flame at him again. Wentworth wasted no more shots. It was evident that the man who fired was behind some bullet-proof shield. For the Spider's lead always flew true to the target. . . .

Twice more the revolver was fired and only once did the lead hum near. The man was a wretched shot, Wentworth thought. He raced on, heard his opponent flee crashingly through formal shrubbery that was planted nearby.

As he ran swiftly in pursuit, Wentworth saw that the man's shield had been a concrete bench. There was a strange odor of bat musk on the air and Wentworth's eyes were narrow. Certainly, the Bat Man did a thorough job of impersonation! He went lithely through the shrubbery, hurdled a hedge, raced along a gravel path. . . .

Out of the darkness came the screams of men and women fleeing in panic before the bats. Wentworth owed his escape thus far from the poison vampires to

134

the fact that all of the killers were hovering where the crowd was thickest. He realized this and saw, too, that the chase was leading directly toward the concourse of the amusement streets. Did the Bat Man then have some means of protection against his small assassins?

Changing his course, Wentworth ran parallel to the flight of his enemy. If he could outline him against the light from the thousand electric bulbs which still beckoned their invitation to the crowd, there would be an immediate end to this slaughter. As if the fugitive guessed his purpose, he doubled back on his trail and fled again toward the formal garden and the switchback.

As they turned, Wentworth saw the huge Boeing slant to a landing on the sands. It bounced violently, but did not loop. Wentworth guessed that June Calvert had never before handled so large a ship, certainly not at night. She had courage! He had a new proof of that fact almost at once. The ship, once landed, did not remain stationary, but turned toward the park and trundled forward, its propellers lashing the air. June intended to shelter as many fugitives as possible in the cabin. . . .

Now, at last, Wentworth caught a glimpse of the man he pursued. Good lord, the Bat Man still wore his wings! Wentworth flung lead after him, saw him trip and fall. A great shout welled out of the *Spider's* throat. He dashed forward, then abruptly, flung himself flat to the earth also. From the shadows ahead came the liquid pop of blowguns. The Bat Man had led him into an ambush!

Wentworth lifted his head and grimly leveled his automatic. He realized that the Indians were moving rapidly to surround him. They would close in slowly until sure that the *Spider* was dead. He had eleven cartridges and there were easily thirty Indians . . . !

CHAPTER FOURTEEN

In the Bat's Trap

The feeling of despair that had never been far from Wentworth's heart since the first battle against the Bat Man surged over him again, but it received a sudden check. Unbidden, without preliminary, the thought rose in Wentworth's mind: *Nita is not dead!* And there was a reason for the thought. The Bat Man had not had time to go to more than one bat depot— and the bats of that group must be kept hungry for the night's attack! No, Nita had not yet been fed to the vampires.

With the thought, Wentworth felt a flood of new vigor come into him. If Nita lived, he would save her, despite this ambush of poison darts. There was one way . . . They would not begin to close in until they had completed the circle about him and there was yet an opening of twenty feet in the rear. Wentworth made no move toward it. Instead, he rapidly began to wriggle out of the parachute harness from which he had sliced the shrouds, rather than discard it in his need for speed.

He gouged out a deep hollow in the ground, set the butt of his gun in it and packed the earth down tightly about it. He fastened an end of the parachute harness, whose straps he had cut to stretch it to the greatest possible length, to the trigger of the automatic and the other end he held in his hand as he crawled straight toward where the Bat Man had fallen!

When he had gone a few feet, he pulled gently on the harness until the automatic fired. He smiled grimly. He was giving the poison darts a target, but it was a false one.

The rain of darts increased behind him as he crawled to the attack. There were four shots in the automatic. They lasted him twelve feet, half the distance to the Bat Man. He tried then to drag the empty pistol to him but the strap slipped loose and he was compelled to abandon it. To return there through the fire of the Indians would be fatal. Besides, the circle was complete and the blowgun men were beginning to close in. Unarmed, he pushed rapidly on.

The innocuous seeming pop of the deadly guns sounded strange against the background of panic screams out there where the bats were thick. Through the middle of sound, he caught, too, a distant rumble as of a train. Were police coming by rail? But that was foolish . . . He realized abruptly that the sound came from the switchback where cars were running wild, empty, about the tracks, abandoned by the operators who had fled, or been killed by the bats. The scent of bat musk was heavy all about him.

Already, Wentworth could make out the black hump that marked where the Bat Man lay. The sight tightened his mouth, narrowed his eyes to a steely hardness. He was only six feet away—now only three! He hunched himself up on tense thighs, hurled himself bodily upon the middle of the wings! He fell on fabric. A metal brace prodded him in the side, but that was all. *The Bat Man was gone!*

The sound of Wentworth's leap had not passed unnoticed. While he lay, half-dazed by his fall, an Indian called in a nasal shout that was a challenge. Wentworth could not answer. He did not know the language. A bat-like squeak in the wrong tone might be equally betraying. But there was a way out. He thrust himself to one side of the brace which evidently supported the wings, got to the edge of the queer contraption and crawled underneath it. His lips were smiling. Even the light fabric of the wings would be enough to protect him from the darts—if the Indians dared to fire at the spot where their master had been!

Wentworth began to wriggle along flat on his stomach, carrying the wings with him. His acute ears heard the advance of the blowguns as their popping grew louder. When they were almost upon him, he halted. When they passed, he began again the slow crawling. Fifteen feet outside of their circle, he slid out from under the wings and, bent double, raced away on silent feet.

Where had the Bat Man gone? Wentworth found himself sprinting toward the high, spidery structure of the switchback. There, he could escape the Indians.

Under its shadows he crept, and crouching there, he became aware again of that strange, over-powering scent of bat musk which he had detected earlier in the night. He twisted his head about, sniffing like a dog. Unless he was fooled by the wind, the scent was stronger toward his left. Without hesitation, Wentworth crept in that direction. The Bat Man was armed and the *Spider* was empty-handed, but it would have taken more than that to turn him back tonight!

The scent was stronger now. Wentworth crouched low, seeking to outline his enemy against the sky but there were only the slits of the switchback. He pushed on. The scent grew fainter. He pivoted back again, frowning in perplexity, angry in frustration. Then there was an infinitesimal squeak, as of leather on wood, almost directly above him. He tilted back his head and saw, outlined like a spider in a squared web of wood against the sky, a man climbing among the braces of the switchback.

Strangling down the cry of triumph that rose in his throat, Wentworth sprang to a horizontal brace just above his head, and swung up, clambered to his feet.

The structure was built with high verticals and horizontals like the floors of a house. Then in each oblong made by the crossing of uprights and crosspieces, there were X-braces, stretched diagonally from corner to corner. It was a simple matter to walk up one of these diagonals, using the crosspieces as a handrail. Wentworth clambered swiftly in the wake of the little man who was making panicky speed for the top.

Wentworth recognized the Bat Man's plan. At the top of the first incline toward which the man climbed, the cars moved at a snail's pace. It would be an easy matter for him to climb in and sail over the runways to safety before Wentworth could overtake him. There was one defect in his plan. He could get out only at the spot where he had entered, on the long initial incline up which the cars were drawn by a chain—unless one of his henchmen could operate the brakes which ordinarily stopped the cars, but which were independent of the cars themselves.

The Bat Man was half-way to the top now, climbing like a monkey among the cross-braces. Wentworth was fully thirty feet below him. He abandoned walking the X-braces and started scrambling up them like a ladder, X-brace to crosspiece, to X-brace again. It was dizzying work and every second increased the distance above the ground and the peril. Out there in the darkness, the flying cars squealed on curves or rumbled down inclines that were almost perpendicular. At the bottom of the incline, a car was beginning its clanking rise to the peak which the fugitive sought.

Wentworth realized with a despairing cry that the Bat Man would reach the top in time to board the car, and that he himself could not. He threw a sharp, estimating glance about as he fought upward at top speed. The rails of the first dip were only about half the distance of the top from him, and to walk the crosspieces to it would take only seconds. The string of cars, four hitched together, would be gaining the momentum for its entire run there, but the point opposite Wentworth was less than half way down the swoop. It would be accelerating—not yet at its peak speed. . . .

Grimly, swiftly as always, the *Spider* made his choice. Already, he was footing it along the cross-piece. He reached the track before the car arrived at the top of the incline where the Bat Man was even now scrambling. While there was yet time, Wentworth scrambled ten feet higher along the track. Then he crouched and waited for the car. There was a railing here and he poised on its top, which would be barely on a level with the side of the car seats. It would be a perilous undertaking!

Wentworth's jaw locked rigidly, the muscles in his thighs tautened. . . . The cars had reached the crest. The Bat Man scrambled in and, with a rising roar, the train plunged down the rise toward where Wentworth waited.

The Bat Man saw him, raised up in the front seat with his revolver in his hand and a despairing cry in his throat. There would be a split-second when he was directly opposite Wentworth—when he could shoot at him at point-blank range. He would, at that time, be moving at about thirty miles an hour. Wentworth estimated his chances, crouching there on the rail, and his lips drew back from his teeth. The cars roared toward him . . . !

Wentworth was not standing broadside to the cars, but was facing the same direction in which they were traveling. He had no way of estimating the velocity of his leap, but it could not reasonably be more than fifteen miles an hour. That difference was enough to make it damnably dangerous. Added to that was the fact that his footing, both in jumping and landing, was extremely uncertain. He did not need that threatening revolver to make it a life-and-death attempt. He must spring into the air at exactly the right heart-beat of time. There must be no hesitation, no slip-up.

And yet, as the car hurtled toward him, Wentworth flung his laughter into the air—reckless, taunting laughter. The Bat Man leaned forward, stretching the revolver out before him. He was almost upon Wentworth.

"Look out, fool!" Wentworth shouted.

His cry was at just the right moment. It caught the Bat Man squeezing the trigger—the front of the car almost level with Wentworth. At the same instant, Wentworth jumped. If he could, he meant to hammer the Bat Man to the floor with the bludgeon of his body. But he miscalculated—either his own speed or that of the train—for his feet caught on the back of the cushion of the third car. The blow smacked his feet out from under him and hurled him, headfirst, into the seat of the fourth car.

The car whirled sickeningly around a curve, jamming Wentworth over against one side of the seat; then it straightened out for another dive. The rush of wind helped to clear Wentworth's brain and he thrust stiff arms into the cushions, shoved himself erect. He was almost thrown out as the car plunged again. He peered ahead, saw the glint of a revolver and pulled his head down as the bullet whined.

The *Spider* still did not have complete control over his body, but there was no time to be lost. The moments when he could crawl forward to the attack were terribly limited, for the track led under the cross-braces of other tracks and to stand up would mean a broken neck. Likewise, the sideway of the U-turns would hurl him off by centrifugal force.

Nevertheless, Wentworth set himself grimly to climb forward. He jerked the cushion from the seat and, when next there was an instant of clear overhead, he hurled it forward against the blast of the wind and threw himself head first into the third car of the train.

The cushion did not reach the first car, but it had made the Bat Man duck and before he could shoot, Wentworth was under cover—one car nearer the front! He thought that the next cushion he hurled would reach its goal.

Already, the train was starting the last and lowest circuit of the structure. Wentworth realized that he would have no further chance to advance on his enemy until a new circuit was started. Meantime, the Bat Man would have the long, slow climb up the incline in which to escape. His hands clenched with determination as he crouched behind the protection of the car's front. If the Bat Man attempted to get off this car, he would have the *Spider* on his back!

"If you jump out," Wentworth called to him, "I'm going to push you off. I won't have to touch you. A cushion. . . ."

Wentworth did not again lift his head above the seats, but he leaned far over to the side and peered toward the front car. He saw a foot thrust out cautiously. He started to shout a warning to the man to get back, but shut his mouth grimly and held his cushion ready. The Bat Man's foot reached out farther. They were almost to the top and he must hurry if he was to get away before that. Wentworth saw the foot lift a little and hurled the cushion.

The heavy combination of wood and leather struck the walkway beside the track just as the Bat Man stepped down, hit the same place. The Bat Man screamed, lost his footing and fell flat. He rolled against the side of the car, bounced toward the low guard railing. Wentworth sprang to his feet to hurl himself upon the man, but at that moment the car gave a lurch and surged over the top of the incline!

Wentworth cursed, peered back and saw the Bat Man roll onto the tracks which the car had just quitted, then the train carrying Wentworth whipped down into that first, terrific dip. The *Spider* sat and cursed under his breath the entire way around the switchback. The circuit that last time had been so swift—stretched out interminably—but at last the train swept toward the chained incline. Wentworth sprang out, peered eagerly upward and—*The Bat Man was gone!*

Both the Bat Man and the Indians had vanished. Heavily, he turned toward the plane, and while he went, by back-ways where the bats were not, he heard the piercing, gigantic squeaking which he knew was the

142

recall signal for the vampires. There was no tracing the sound. It seemed to come from everywhere. . . .

Wentworth broke into a run. The battle was not yet lost. If all roads were blocked and all small men detained for examination. . . . At the plane, he found a group of uniformed police and, inside their circle, Commissioner MacHugh, of Chicago, was shooting questions at June Calvert.

June was taking it languidly, leaning against the side of the Boeing with a glint of humor in her dark eyes. She had taken advantage of the interim to fluff her black hair about the piquant oval of her face. But her beauty was only a mask for grim determination. That much, Wentworth knew.

He thrust through the circle after MacHugh had identified him. MacHugh was small, but he had a big, hearty manner. His energy was tiring to watch. He sprang forward to grasp Wentworth's hand. "By all that's holy, Wentworth!" he shouted. "I was about to string the girl up by her thumbs because she wouldn't talk. How do you pick 'em, my boy? How do you pick 'em?"

Wentworth grinned into the Commissioner's face. The man was infectious. "Commissioner, the Bat Man was here just a few minutes ago. I fought with him, but he got away. I suggest that we stop all roads and search for small men, not above a hundred pounds. . . ."

MacHugh made a move. His complexion was dark and his frown made his face ugly. "I escape by one pound! Is the Bat Man small?"

"He is," Wentworth said grimly. "After all the small men are together, I want to look them over. There's a bare chance I might identify him."

"I say, there, Commissioner MacHugh!" a man's voice piped. Wentworth spun about to stare beyond the circle of police. He caught his breath. Sanderson, the weazened ex-jockey turned stable owner, was just outside the cordon, waving at MacHugh.

"Let him in," the Commissioner called. He turned to Wentworth. "Sanderson came out with me. We were at a show and just got here a few seconds ago. Sanderson wanted to look about."

Wentworth stared suspiciously at Sanderson as the little man sauntered up, swaggering a bit. His mind was racing. Both of these men were small—both had just arrived on the scene. Was it possible that . . . one of these men was the Bat?

Wentworth moved to June's side, turning his back on the others.

"When the big squeak was made," he whispered, "was MacHugh here?"

June shook her head, glanced over his shoulder at the Commissioner. "Do you think . . . ?"

Wentworth shrugged. "I don't know," he said, suddenly weary. Once more, the Bat Man had won. . . . There was no longer any need to starve the bats. Nita, dear Nita. . . .

CHAPTER FIFTEEN

A Clue at Last

A dragging weariness rode with Wentworth back to Chicago in Commissioner MacHugh's sedan. He sat on a kick seat beside Sanderson, who kept up a half-apologetic conversation on the horrors he had seen at Michigan City. The dead were estimated at three thousand five hundred.

"Some of them must have suffered horribly," Sanderson went on in his subdued voice. "One boy had strangled a bat in each hand, but he had at least a dozen bites on his face and neck. I picked up a bat, and ever since then, I fancy I smell like the damned things."

Wentworth said nothing, but his thoughts were swift. Now that Sanderson had called attention to it, he did catch a faint whiff of the bat-musk which had been so powerful in the vicinity of the Bat Man. Suspicion leaped full-grown into his brain. It wasn't possible that bat scent should cling so to a person who had only handled a dead one. He decided that Sanderson's movements should be watched, his whereabouts at other appearances of the Bat Man checked.

Where did the scent that the Bat Man used come from? Surely, not from merely handling bats, nor from the glands of the bat itself. To generate such a powerful taint of it, hundreds of bats would have to be slaughtered and certainly, the Bat Man could not have a great enough supply of bats to warrant such butchery. Only one explanation was possible then. The scent was artificial, and. . . .

Wentworth sat abruptly straight, spun toward Mac-Hugh. "Commissioner, will you have your men gather every dead bat possible at the park and rush them to me at the Blackstone hotel? This is important! It may mean the solution of the case!"

Sanderson shuddered. "I should hope so. Vampires! Brrrr!"

Fatigue and mental fag lifted from Wentworth's body. At last he had a trail which might lead to the Bat Man. And it was one that could be followed swiftly. . . . He engaged a suite of rooms at the Blackstone and, one hour after the dead bats had been delivered to him there, he left with June Calvert for the airport. The Boeing had been refueled and new windows substituted for those the machine gun had wrecked. At Wentworth's orders, these were bullet proof. The pilot was a United States Marine officer whose mouth was straight and pugnacious below a pointed nose. His eyes were direct.

"What the hell's up? And who are you?" he demanded when Wentworth entered.

Wentworth smiled slightly. He mentioned his title and regiment of the reserves, his name. The Marine came sharply to his feet, saluted with a crisp efficiency.

"Begging the major's pardon," he said flatly, "but they got me up out of the first night's sleep I've had in a week. Lieutenant Carlisle, sir."

"At ease," Wentworth told him briefly. "I asked for a pilot without nerves, who was reasonably good with an automatic and better than good as to courage. I'm satisfied. Take off at once. All possible speed for the Rocky Mountains, about fifty miles south of Hooligan Pass."

The lieutenant saluted, fairly jumped to the controls. The plane swept down the field, lofted gently and swung about in a bank that almost scraped off the wingtip.

146

*   *   *

Wentworth's face was drawn with harsh lines of fatigue. There were dark smudges beneath his eyes, a deeper crease at his mouth corners.

"We're going to the Bat Man's main headquarters," he said shortly. "The purpose is to kill him and save certain persons who are his prisoners."

"But how do you know where to go?" June demanded.

Wentworth smiled faintly. "I've got a good nose. I'm going to sleep."

It was not the least of Wentworth's miracles that he could sleep when all his soul and body stirred with anxiety. But there was nothing he could do now, and how many hours had it been since he had last slept . . . ? Two hours after the takeoff, Wentworth sprang up from the cushions. Many of the lines had been erased from his face and, after a swift toilet, he was fresh, and vigorous. He went into the cockpit, dropped into the co-pilot's seat.

"Mr. Carlisle," he said. "We're going to kill the Bat Man."

The lieutenant turned his head briefly. "Yes, sir."

"Do you know the Rockies, Mr. Carlisle?"

"Yes, sir."

Wentworth smiled faintly.

"Interrupt me if I'm wrong, Mr. Carlisle," he said. "About fifty miles south of Hooligan Pass, there is a section in which hot springs abound. Also, due to the action of this hot water upon limestone, there are large, far-reaching caverns. In the recesses of those caves, it is likely that the heat—due to the water—would approximate that of the tropical river regions of South America where vampire bats live. In those caves, vampire bats could breed just as they do in the tropics and thus produce the overwhelming numbers which have been loosed on America. Do you agree with me that far, Mr. Carlisle?"

"Yes, sir!" There was a rising enthusiasm in the lieutenant's voice.

147

"How long, Mr. Carlisle, before we'll reach that section?"

"Twenty-two minutes, sir!"

Wentworth nodded and got to his feet. "I am looking for a canyon in that district into which it would be impossible to descend, Mr. Carlisle. Signal me when you reach Hoot-Owl Center."

Wentworth returned to the cabin and found June Calvert sitting up sleepily. He crossed to a long paper-wrapped package that he had picked up in Chicago, which had been brought from New York by plane. He unwrapped it quickly and revealed a pair of wings, folded flat together. June sprang to her feet.

"The Bat Man's wings!" she cried.

Wentworth shook his head. "No, mine," he said, "but modeled after the Bat Man's. Because of my greater weight, I had to increase their size. Will you help me, please?"

He lifted the wings and adjusted the straps over his shoulders. The wings folded flat together and pointed out rigidly some nine feet along the cabin. There were straps also about waist and ankles to support his body. When he jumped from the plane, a jerk would snap the wings out to each side and lock them there. A kick would move the rudder into position just behind his feet. There were tip aerolons which he could operate by twisting his wrists and his feet rested on the rudder rod. There was no elevator. The aerolons and the shifting of his body would take care of dives. There would be little climbing.

June Calvert looked at him with wide eyes. "But why, why?" she whispered.

Wentworth laughed. "Didn't the Bat Man say no one but himself could reach his hide-out unless he willed it? Well, I am now the Bat Man so far as aerial navigation is concerned!"

From up forward came a queer hooting sound and for a moment, Wentworth did not identify it. Then he realized its meaning. Lieutenant Carlisle had signaled

148

that the ship was over Hoot-Owl Center. Wentworth smiled slightly as he released himself from the straps, leaned the wings against the wall and walked forward. The little mountain town lay beneath them and ahead lifted the barrier of the Rockies. A small, crooked road wove its way upward into the fastness and on it Wentworth made out three auto trains of seven or eight cars apiece. His eyes narrowed at the sight and he caught up a pair of field glasses and focused them on the road.

The cars were trucks and each carried big boxes that would be far too heavy a load for the vehicles if they contained weighty cargo. Furthermore, the men who manned the trucks were Indians, not the lithe, red men of the North American wilderness, but the stubby, fierce savages from the Amazon, each with his blowgun.

Wentworth's hand dropped on the pilot's shoulder. "These are the men of the Bat." he said. "Climb as high as possible while still keeping an eye on them. See where they go, and then—I have some twelve-pound bombs."

Lieutenant Carlisle said, "Yes, sir!"

Wentworth strode sharply back into the cabin with elation singing in his veins.

June Calvert stood up and moved toward him. "What is it?" she demanded, whispering. She had to repeat the words before Wentworth looked at her.

"We're close now," he said. "Very close." He moved toward the wings that were shaped like a bat's.

Carlisle's voice rang out from the cockpit, "Major!"

Wentworth hurried to him.

"They've stopped, sir," Carlisle said. "They're getting out."

Wentworth took the glasses and peered down. The plane had climbed three thousand feet, but was still easily visible to the men below. Their flattish faces were turned upward. Wentworth's lips thinned. He lowered the glasses.

"They've guessed we're following! Bomb them.

149

Drop down to fifteen hundred. I'll throw the bombs out of the door.''

Carlisle spun the ship about and Wentworth dragged out two wooden cases from opposite walls of the cabin, opened them and took out two bombs shaped like tear drops, but with fins on the tails to keep them nose down. He forced open the door and waited while the Boeing circled downward. Wentworth could see the up-turned faces without glasses now. He held the bombs ready.

June Calvert came and stood beside the box. "I'll hand them to you," she said.

The three motorcades had merged and were strung out along the road for over a half-mile. Wentworth waited until the ship was in position, then darted the first bomb toward the head of the line. It struck ten feet to the side of the road and splintered a huge pine. The second bomb made a direct hit on the second truck. The body went to pieces. The big cages of bats were tossed a hundred feet and the steel frame soared and crushed the front of the fifth truck in line.

The Boeing zoomed, viraged and swept back over the road again. Indians were scattering in all directions from the trucks, blocked permanently by the first bomb Wentworth had thrown. The last truck was trying franti-cally to turn about and retreat. Wentworth's third bomb hit close by, dug a pit under its wheels and flopped the car over on its side. Systematically then, Wentworth pelted the rest of the trucks until not one remained undamaged.

"One of the trucks got away," June told him tensely. "The first one in line. You missed it and it went up into the mountains."

Lieutenant Carlisle evidently had noticed it, too. The ship was sent hurtling after the truck, but Wentworth put his last two bombs back into the case, went forward to the cockpit.

"Keep the truck in sight," he ordered.

There was a drumming thud upon the roof of the

150

cabin. The hammering moved forward and in its wake appeared a seam of bullet holes. A machine gun! Wentworth cursed. He pulled June Calvert far back into the tail of the ship, saw the windows of the cockpit sliver under the hail of lead, but resist the attack. The tail of the ship whipped over, wind roared in through the open door as Carlisle put the giant Boeing into a side-slip to dodge the attacking plane.

The bomb case lurched toward the opening and, even as Wentworth darted forward to seize it, plunged outward into space. The roar of wind through the door abruptly checked and Wentworth knew the Boeing was sliding in the opposite direction. He saw a jot of earth leap upward where the bomb case struck. The road was blocked! That accidental discharge of high explosive had struck squarely in the middle of the mountain trail and dug a twenty foot pit across it. And the truck they were following was on the far side of that pit!

Now there would be no trail to lead them to the headquarters of the Bat Man. They would have to guess at its location. . . . Wentworth shouted forward. "Turn your port side to the plane!"

The Boeing zoomed, whirled in a vertical bank and, peering upward now through the open door, Wentworth had a glimpse of a speedy little monoplane diving toward him. There was a flicker of flame behind the propeller that showed his machine guns. . . .

"Up!" Wentworth shouted.

He felt the plane lift even as the machine gun fire dipped. The bullets missed. . . . The ship was close enough now. No need to aim. Wentworth held both automatics on the nose of the ship, held on the face of the man just visible behind the windshield of the attacking plane. He pumped the full charge of both automatics.

The monoplane zoomed, fell off on the left wing and screamed downward in a whipping, screaming tail-spin. Wentworth, stepping back from the doorway to reload his automatics, could see the pilot lolling helplessly back against the crash pad. The *Spider's* eyes narrowed as his lips parted in a smile. The man was dead. That much was obvious, but was it the Bat Man? Grimly, he hoped that it was, but he doubted such luck. The Bat Man usually made his attacks on his own wings. . . .

Wentworth slipped the loaded weapons back into his holsters and pushed forward. There was nothing to do now but follow the road and hope that they would be able to spot a canyon that might fit the description Wentworth had given. He dropped in the co-pilot's seat and waited while the Boeing made slow wide circles over wild, mountain country.

A squealing sound, not unlike the squeak of a giant bat, came from the wireless headphones and Wentworth, frowning, lifted them to his ears. The squealing continued, but now it was broken into short and long sounds. Wentworth cursed, pressed the phones closer. . . . It was Morse code! Swiftly, Wentworth deciphered the message:

"Unless you at once return the way you came," ran the dots and dashes, "you will forfeit the lives of three friends and the woman you love. Furthermore, I shall shoot you down, as I am in a position to do at this moment. Consider, *Spider,* the lives of four people against a strategic retreat. Which do you choose?"

The squealing stopped for a moment, then began again, the same message. Coolly, Wentworth moved the coil of the radio direction-finder. "Two points east of north," he said to Carlisle, "and very near. He is threatening to shoot us down. Keep a sharp eye out for attacking planes."

Wentworth moved hurriedly back into the cabin then and donned the wings, tightening all the straps. Just short of the tip aerolons, there were two holsters and into these, Wentworth thrust his automatics. He stood by the door, peering down at the mountains sliding past below him.

Carlisle shouted, "Plane is attacking ahead, major. Something funny . . . Good God, *it's the Bat Man!"*

Wentworth turned about and smiled at June Calvert.

"Tell Carlisle to dodge the plane and circle aloft. He'll have the ceiling of that monoplane. Tell him to look for a signal from that canyon we're passing over."

June Calvert nodded, staring at him with wide eyes. Wentworth shouted forward, "When I shout, kick the tail to starboard!"

"Yes, sir!"

Wentworth paused in the doorway, gazing downward, his hands moved over the buckles of the wings that jutted oddly from his shoulders. There was a grim, drawn tension about his mouth. He poised in the doorway like a diver, shouted at Carlisle, then sprang head foremost into space, with only those queer wings and his skill to save him from inevitable death on the rocks five thousand feet below . . . !

CHAPTER SIXTEEN

The Jaws of Death

Wentworth plunged downward at terrific speed, falling free, the wings of no more value than a tangled parachute. He spread his legs so that the fin between them straightened, the rudder whipped back into position. He was falling headfirst now and it was easy to pull the wings about into flying station.

He twisted the aerolons, kicked the rudder and immediately felt the lift of the wings. He shot forward on a level with the momentum of his plunge, peered about and a shout of anger and hate rang out. The Bat Man was diving headfirst toward the Boeing and, even as Wentworth shouted, the giant plane faltered, slid off on one wing and nosed down. It took only a glance to realize that the Bat Man's rifle had penetrated the bullet-proof glass and that the Marine pilot and June Calvert were plunging to their deaths!

Instinctively, as Wentworth saw what had happened, he tilted back his aerolons and zoomed up toward the Bat Man. It was not until then that the man saw Wentworth, flying on wings so like his own. When he did, he staggered uncertainly for a moment, his flying speed falling off. Instantly, he overcame his surprise and dived to gather momentum.

It was only then that Wentworth realized the difficulty of the thing he had undertaken. He had intended the wings to enable him to penetrate the Bat's hiding place, now suddenly, he found himself forced to fight in a field in which his opponent was easily the master. He was plunged instantly into a life and death struggle!

Wentworth realized these things when he prolonged his zoom too long in an effort to gain altitude on the Bat Man. He lost flying speed, whip-stalled and found himself plunging for the earth at a furious pace. Aerolons and rudder kicked him out of it, but he found the Bat Man sweeping toward him nose-on. The rifle which Wentworth now saw was strapped to the top of the wing and was aligned with the man's body. It spat flame and a bullet whipped past within inches of his head.

Wentworth's face was grimly set. If the Bat Man expected any armament at all, he would naturally conceive it to be of the same type as his own. Actually, Wentworth's automatics were pointed straight out to each side, slung in holsters through whose tip they could fire as readily as if held freely in the hands. As Wentworth wheeled out of the line of fire, he pointed a wingtip toward the Bat Man and squeezed the trigger. The recoil kicked the wing upward slightly and Wentworth had to twist aerolons to straighten out his curious craft. The bullet went wide.

Wentworth completed a circle but found the Bat Man had the speed on him, from his dive. His enemy shot about in an almost vertical bank which Wentworth would have believed impossible and the rifle was leveled once more. A bullet from the Bat Man's rifle struck the wing and tugged at Wentworth's sleeve. A second shot, close on its heels, struck the duralumin brace and whined off into space.

Wentworth dived. It was the only thing he could do. The Bat Man followed and the *Spider* saw that he had one advantage—speed of descent. In a vertical plunge, of course, both would drop at the same pace, but at a glide, Wentworth's greater weight, his higher ratio of weight to wing spread gave him the advantage. But he could not outfly bullets. . . .

Lead cracked over his head viciously. Wentworth kicked the rudder and dodged. He repeated that while bullets sang and whined about him. The wing was struck again. Wentworth twisted his head about and saw the Bat Man was gaining on him slightly because of his dodging. As he looked, the squealing, rasping signal that was a call to the bats rang out. Good lord, was the man summoning the vampires to his assistance?

Wentworth whipped about and tried once more to down the man with automatic shots, but his lack of lateral control handicapped him badly. He dared not empty his guns with such poor assurance of success and he was forced once more to turn and run. The *Spider* run from an enemy! It was incredible, but it was so. The man had greater skill.

They were dangerously close to earth now. No more than a thousand feet. Wentworth continued to dodge while he searched the earth with eager eyes. Over to his right was the deep slit of a canyon. Beneath him, all was dense woods. There was no spot to mark where the Boeing had crashed. Desperately, Wentworth searched the earth for some spot in which to land. There was none.

Abruptly, Wentworth remembered the reason for his wings. They had been for the purpose of entering the secret hiding place of the Bat Man, of invading the canyon cave in which, Wentworth deduced, he had made his headquarters. There was a canyon, and the attack upon him had been begun near it. He would have to chance a dive into its tricky and turbulent wind currents.

With his mind made up, Wentworth slanted directly for the darkened mouth of the canyon. Behind him, the Bat Man screamed again and it seemed to Wentworth that it was more than a signal. The sound held a touch of fright, perhaps of anger. The Bat pressed him more closely, dived steeply to intercept his approach to the cliffs. Wentworth smiled thinly. He had guessed right then. The hiding place was there! He would enter that canyon or die in the attempt.

The Bat pressed closer, closer, his rifle barking again and again. Wentworth watched him come with worried, angry eyes. There was death for one of them here on the lip of the cliffs, or in that narrow bit of air that led downward into the throat of the canyon itself. In that confined space, there could be little dodging, little hope of escape. Bullets would fly. . . .

On the point of darting downward into the canyon, Wentworth whipped upward into a zoom almost head on toward the Bat Man. He twisted the aerolons and side-slipped toward the valley below. As he slipped, holding his wings steadily vertical so that he plunged at terrific force toward the stony death below, he began to shoot. For the first time, now, in that perilous position, he had the stability he needed for accuracy. His first shot caught the right wing of the Bat Man. His second plucked at the man's clothing. But in his steady dive, Wentworth exposed himself to the fire of his enemy's rifle and the bullets whipped closer, closer. . . .

A knife of fire slit down Wentworth's right arm and his hand went utterly numb and useless. He knew that one of the bullets had touched him at last. It was a superficial wound, but it might well mean death! The crippling of that arm loosened one of the aerolons to flap as it would. It halved his armament . . . !

A wild challenging shout rang from the *Spider's* lips. Its echo battered at him from both walls of the canyon, but it seemed to him that there was another shriller voice shouting, too. He fought grimly to hold on with his numb hand to the handle of the aerolon. He did not seek to use it, merely to hold it stationary while with his other hand and the rudder he maneuvered his other wing uppermost. As the rudder turned him, first, head-down, then over again, he caught a glimpse of a black cave's mouth far below and, on the edge before it, several figures stood with arms uplifted. By the gods, if that Bat Man did not kill the *Spider* in the air, then the man's Indians would slaughter him when he landed!

Bitterly, Wentworth completed his whirl, thrust his gun-hand upward. If he died, he at least would not die alone!

His hands moved, his feet kicked the rudder. Before his eyes whirled the black opening of the cave he had seen and the gesturing figures. They were going to kill him, were they? He tried to kick a wing about so that he could shoot, but he forgot to bank or his hands failed on the aerolons when he did it. He skated sideways, twisting his head about to see the death that presently would strike into him.

In God's name, who was this who held out waiting arms to him? That face! Nita! *Good God, Nita!* He felt that he was still skidding sideways toward that lovely face that floated before his eyes. He saw men leap toward him, then . . . nothing!

Impossible to tell whether he was unconscious for an hour or a second, but the crooning of Nita's voice drifted away and returned to him in waves of sound. He pushed his eyes open, looked up into Nita's face. He struggled up. . . .

"The Bat Man! The Bat Man!" he cried. "Where is he?"

"Dead, darling," Nita told him. "You shot him down out in the canyon there, before you sideslipped into a landing here on the ledge."

Wentworth moved his arms stiffly and found a biting pain in the right one, found the left unencumbered by the wing. He looked about him. June Calvert was standing near, with Jackson's arm about her. Fred Stoking and Ram Singh smiled at him. The Marine lieutenant. . . .

"Mr. Carlisle," Wentworth said weakly, "how in the hell do you happen to be still alive?"

The Marine grinned. "I faked out-of-control and landed in the canyon valley. There's a rope ladder up here. Had quite a tussle with some of those vampire bats up there. They came out when that guy screamed up here in the air, but they couldn't see in the daylight very well and we got the best of them."

Wentworth sank back on the hard rock of the ledge gratefully. "Well, Earl Westfall will never be electrocuted then."

Nita smiled at him. "How did you know the Bat Man was Westfall? We found out when we came here that he wasn't the fat man he seemed at all. He had a rubber suit that he blew up. It made him look huge. And that Bat Man face of his—it was a mask."

Wentworth looked about, found June Calvert's eyes. "You ought to know how I found out, how I learned where the headquarters was."

June Calvert shook her head. "I haven't the faintest idea," she said happily, "but I don't see that it matters much as long as you did." She looked up into Jackson's wide, grinning face.

"Really," Wentworth complained, "won't somebody inquire how the great Wentworth learned the secret."

Nita laughed and brushed his forehead with her lips. "Tell me, darling," she whispered. "I'll always want to know."

"The bat musk secret," Wentworth said. "None of the Indians was ever attacked by the bats and there had to be a reason. It was because they smelled like bats."

They were interested now, all of them. Fred Stoking looked at Nita with wistful, but hopeless, eyes.

"It wasn't possible for the Bat Man—or Westfall—" Wentworth went on, "to get enough bat glands to make the odor, so he had to make it artificially. The bat musk was strangely like some perfume I had run across. Basically, of course. I identified the perfume—Chatou's Oriental—and found out where large shipments of it had been made. It came to Hoot-Owl Center, and would you believe it? Westfall actually had it addressed to his stable manager! But I had been suspicious of Westfall for some time. I found out from some of my newspaper clippings that he had recently been to a sanitarium for drug addicts and I looked up his weight there. It's exactly ninety pounds.''

Wentworth pushed himself to his feet. His side ached from a flesh wound and his right arm hung useless at his side, but there was a smile on his face. He put his good arm about Nita's shoulders.

"Darling," he said, "I think that—when I get out of the hospital—I shall go on a real bat."

Nita shuddered, laughed up at him. "I'm willing, but for heaven's sakes, let's call it something . . . something else than . . . a bat!"

The Pain Emperor

In a hundred thousand homes, families sat down together at the supper table. A few hours later, those persons were dead—killed by poison in canned foods! Thousands of women used cosmetics, and acid made their faces forever hideously scarred. A master criminal, daring and clever, was ruthlessly slaughtering Americans to win immense illicit profits for himself. Only one man was powerful enough and wise enough to stop this wholesale murder—Richard Wentworth, champion of oppressed humanity, better known as the *Spider*. And the *Spider* was engaged in the bitterest battle of his career, fighting the Avenger, a false, wily crusader who was determined to destroy him!

CHAPTER ONE

Marked for Death

The croupier called the winning number in an emotionless voice and Richard Wentworth's chips were raked in. He shrugged, rose with a smooth grace that spoke of perfect muscular coördination. "I'll be back, dear," he murmured.

Nita van Sloan's head tilted back so that he could look down into the violet depths of her eyes. "Don't be long, Dick," she said. Her soft lips were smiling, but not her eyes. They cried a warning. She knew that tonight, among these wealth-crowded halls, the *Spider* would stalk. And she knew, also that each time her Dick became even fleetingly that dread nemesis of the underworld, he took his life in his hands.

These were the thoughts that swarmed behind the veil of her violet eyes, behind the curving beauty of her smile. She said only: "Don't be long."

Wentworth's blue-gray gaze gave her assurance, and his glance about this room where danger lurked behind suave laughter was deceptively careless. Nita knew that the *Spider* would act tonight, but she did not know that he was walking open-eyed into a trap!

Tonight, Wentworth was trailing a man who called himself the Avenger. He was a mysterious underworld figure of amazing intelligence, and Wentworth recognized in him possibilities of great good—or diabolical evil. And he suspected that the evil dominated.

Somewhere among the excited groups of flushed, dry-lipped women and men with smiling lips and trembling hands, he knew the Avenger was waiting to strike, ready to spring his trap.

Wentworth did not know its exact nature, but he suspected that Stanislaus Mannley, the man who operated the gambling hall, was involved. It was like the first blind move in a unique game of chess. A gambit was offered, and Wentworth willingly accepted it to learn the Avenger's motives.

Ordinarily he would have waited for events to reveal the Avenger, but time was pressing. The day's news had brought a hideous revelation. It was either a tragic accident or wanton murder. Forty-three men and women had been killed by poison in their food. It was a matter which the *Spider* hastened to investigate, alert as he always was to suppress the super-criminals whose attacks left police dumbfounded and helpless. For Wentworth, in his rôle as the *Spider,* had dedicated his life to the destruction of these fierce menaces to humanity.

Yet no man seeing Wentworth's nonchalant saunter would have suspected the thoughts that swirled through his brain, knowing that he was walking into a trap from which he might not emerge alive. There was a ready strength in the swing of his broad, perfectly tailored shoulders, a touch of arrogance in the poise of his well-shaped head.

He bowed his way past a group of acquaintances and stepped into the hall, furnished with the exotic luxury that Stanislaus Mannley everywhere affected. His steps were slightly quickened now, his eyes flashed alertly about. At frequent intervals along the walls, tall mirrors flanked by dull red lamps increased his range of vision, told him that he was not spied upon. He paused a moment beside a black Egyptian bowl, from whose depths rose the thin thread of incense smoke, a spiced and sultry scent. When he passed on again, a signet ring had vanished from his finger and a rosette of the *Légion d'Honneur* was gone from his lapel.

His fingers were deftly busy now. From a small kit strapped beneath his left arm, he slid out a black mask that would cover his entire face and a blond wig to conceal the crisp black of his hair. He need not hide the faultless black and white of his evening dress. Fifty other men here wore it tonight.

Before a door that was without label or plate he halted to listen, then he thrust it wide and stepped inside. An automatic glinted dully in his right hand.

"I'll trouble you not to move, Mannley," he said.

A man sat alone behind a baize-covered table. He quit dealing cards for solitaire and said smoothly:

"Anything to oblige."

His jaw-heavy face was emotionless, without surprise, but there was a flare of light in his eyes. They flamed strangely with hate and that fact flashed a warning to Wentworth. Why should the man's eyes show hate? Surprise, fear, dismay; any of those might be expected, but not hate. Not hate, unless Mannley had been expecting him, the *Spider*. All criminals had ample reason to hate the *Spider*, who scourged their ranks ceaselessly, who slew without mercy to protect the nation and the people he loved from the forays of the underworld.

Yes, that flame of hate meant Mannley had been expecting the *Spider*, and that confirmed Wentworth's suspicions. This was a trap. His eyes hardened.

"You have," said Wentworth rapidly, "a check for three thousand dollars which was endorsed over to you by a boy named Shane Malone. I want it."

"You won't get it!" The gambler's heavy jaw thrust forward. He leaned slightly on the green-covered table and his slender, white fingers splayed out over the scattered cards. He was a corpulent man and there was a bulge in the breast of his stiff shirt.

"I see that you already know who I am," said the *Spider* softly, and he registered Mannley's start as one

165

more proof of the trap. "You know then that I am not averse to killing you. Will you surrender the check, or shall I take it from you . . . afterwards?"

Wentworth's eyes had whisked over the room, seeking the trigger of the trap. The place was empty except for chairs and this green-baize table, a liquor cellarette against the wall, a steel safe set into the wall. It was windowless, too, and the sole exit was the heavy door to Wentworth's left and slightly behind him. The room was sound-proof.

The gambler's hands pressed down on the cards until the finger tips spread in little balls.

"I'm not afraid of you," Mannley said hoarsely. "You're just a cheap crook, *Spider*. You pretend to be a sort of Gallahad fighting crime. You go around killing people and printing that little red seal on their foreheads. . . ."

Wentworth's left hand slid to his vest pocket and produced a platinum cigarette lighter. He thrust it out and touched its base upon a card that lay face up on the table. The card was the ace of spades and when he removed the lighter, a blood-red figure was sprawled across its black central pip, a figure that had crooked hairy legs and poisoned venomous fangs, the image of a spider.

"That was what you made reference to, I believe, Mannley," said Wentworth smoothly. Beneath the mask, his lips thinned into a smile to see the blood drain from Mannley's face.

The gambler licked his lips, began to talk more feverishly than before, spilling words that did not always make sense, heaping invective upon the *Spider's* head. Wentworth's lean, long jaw hardened. Small muscles bunched beneath his ears. The gambler was stalling for time. That meant the trap was to be sprung through some one's interruption, that it was not yet time for the intercession. He took a slow stride to the edge of the table, the automatic jutting from his fist.

"Quit stalling, Mannley," he said sharply. "I swear to you that if you do not give me young Malone's check within one minute, I shall imprint my seal again, the next time upon your forehead beside a bullet wound. I know this room is sound-proof. No one will hear the shot."

With the muzzle of his automatic, he gestured toward a thin expensive watch that lay on the green cloth.

"One minute!" he repeated.

Mannley's eyes dropped to the platinum dial of the watch, to the small golden hand ticking away imperturbably the seconds of his life. He looked at the sinister red seal blotting out the pip of the ace of spades. He glanced furtively toward the door and the tip of his tongue touched his lips.

The *Spider* caught that side-glance and his eyes tightened. It was from there the interruption would come—the blow of the Avenger? But he must not show that he had seen the glance, lest he betray his knowledge of the trap. His ear attuned to catch the first whisper of sound, his eyes boring into Mannley, he skimmed rapidly over the circumstances that had brought him to the gambler's private room.

His ostensible purpose was to recover Shane Malone's check. The boy had got over his head in gambling debts and forged that check. It was being held over his head to force him to do certain criminal tasks—or such was the story that had brought him here. Wentworth's chauffeur, Jackson, who had been his top-sergeant in France, had given him the information. In a restaurant, Jackson had taken the part of a girl named Patsy Malone when she was imposed upon by her escort. She had babbled out the story of her brother, Shane, and the check, and Jackson had attempted to wrest the check from Mannley by force.

While Jackson was confronting the gambler, even as Wentworth was doing now, the Avenger had barged into the room and shot Jackson through the shoulder.

"Lay off Mannley, he's my meat," the Avenger had said, and then had fled.

It was a clever build-up. Those who were familiar

with the *Spider's* crusades—and the newspapers gave him ample unwelcome publicity—would know it was precisely the sort of bait that would draw him. A young boy in difficulty with crooks, the *Spider's* own associate wounded. Yes, the *Spider* would hasten to make redress. But it was too perfect. And that was what had aroused Wentworth's suspicions, suspicions fully confirmed now.

The Avenger had publicized himself as a nemesis of the underworld, even as the *Spider* was. He had snared a number of criminals in a spectacular way, recovering thousands of dollars in loot. Other stolen property he had retained and spread broadcast over the city in the homes of the poor. Mostly they were gifts of money to the destitute that bore tags:

With the best wishes of the Avenger!

Newspapers had christened him the modern Robin Hood and Wentworth had been at first inclined to cheer him on—until the total of unrecovered loot had begun to reach enormous figures and he realized that large amounts of it must be sticking to the Avenger's fingers. Wentworth realized, too, what a threat to morality such a figure as the Avenger might become; how he might lead astray the youth of the land by his false example. And he had decided to investigate, to walk into this obvious trap and take the Avenger captive.

If the Avenger's answers indicated his efforts were honest, the *Spider* might even enter into a loose alliance for the suppression of crime. He bore no ill will against the man who was attempting to add the scalp of the *Spider* to his belt. But if, as he suspected, the Avenger's intents were to line his own pockets under the mantle of a bogus Robin Hood . . . Wentworth's nostrils thinned, his lips flattened against his teeth. Then, indeed, there would be a settlement.

But he would need to be careful. When the Avenger struck, Wentworth must move swiftly and surely. The Avenger was a clever fighter, his scheme bore the imprint of genius, and Wentworth had no desire that his scalp should decorate the Avenger's belt . . . His eyes flicked to the watch.

"Thirty seconds," he said flatly. "Thirty seconds to surrender the Malone check or die, Mannley."

"For God's sake," the gambler begged hoarsely. He lifted a perfectly manicured hand from the table and the fingers trembled. "Don't make me. . . ."

"Fifteen seconds!"

"All right! All right!" The words stammered from Mannley's lips. He moved the trembling hand toward his inside breast pocket. Suddenly his knees jerked upward. The top of the table bulged explosively and cards jumped. His left hand jerked into sight with a stubby, heavy-calibre revolver. It was a flashy, lightning-fast draw, but it was suicidal.

The *Spider's* automatic barked and Mannley jerked spasmodically. His chair went over backwards and his feet flew high. The table leaped into the air and sprawled upside down on the floor. Cards sailed in all directions. There was no compassion in Wentworth's eyes. A crook had met his just end, that was all. In a stride, the *Spider* reached the gambler's side. His quick fingers withdrew the papers from Mannley's pockets, and there was a smile that was twisted into mockery upon his lips.

The ace of spades, with its *Spider* seal, had fallen upon the dead gambler's breast.

But the smile quickly faded, gave way to a frown. The papers he sought, the check of young Shane Malone was not in Mannley's pocket. Perhaps, then, in the safe . . . Abruptly, the *Spider* whirled, alert eyes on the door of this private room. His gun's muzzle moved with his eyes. His ears had given him warning.

Even as he spun, the door flung wide and a half dozen white and frightened faces crowded into the opening, a half-dozen witnesses that the *Spider* had slain a man!

CHAPTER TWO

The Avenger Strikes

Crouched tensely, with the only exit blocked, the *Spider* nevertheless found time to wonder what had brought these people here. He knew that this room had been sound-proofed by the cautious gambler. It was here that he settled his crooked affairs, and he did not want the squeals of his victims—or perhaps a shot—to be heard by the innocents in his halls outside. Yet the *Spider's* shot had brought a rush of people. His lips thinned. Undoubtedly this had been planned by the Avenger. He hoped to trap the *Spider* without being himself exposed to danger.

The *Spider's* movements were a blur of speed. He reached the doorway in a long bounding stride, automatic blasting in his hand. His bullets, deliberately high, shattered the lintel above the opening. Hoarse cries of fright burst from men's throats. A woman screeched, throwing both white arms straight above her head. The *Spider's* shoulder thumped against the stiff white bosom of a man's formal shirt, slammed him against two other men and sprawled all three on the floor. Then he pivoted to the right, dived through a doorway to a window through whose pane the black iron tracery of a fire escape showed. He flung up the casement, then dived into a closet.

The door, shutting quietly, muted the excited shouts

in the halls and the pounding of running feet. That would mean that all the gambling salon had been panic-stricken. All persons would be dashing for the doors. He hoped Nita would flee with them as he had instructed her to do if an alarm were given. He must remain, of course, for he had not yet achieved the purposes of his visit. He had barely escaped the Avenger's trap; he had not yet obtained Malone's check, nor had he met the Avenger.

Wentworth believed he ran small risk of identification by any one in that crowd that had stared in the door at the *Spider*, a man with blond hair and a black mask on his face. Yet it had been a comparatively feeble trap. The Avenger would not be satisfied with such a flimsy device. No, there was more to come. The Avenger must have been more subtle than that.

Wentworth thumbed out the nearly emptied bullet-clip of his automatic and replaced the cartridges. He carried another lighter gun beneath his right arm, but it was best to be fully prepared. The Avenger was no enemy to ignore.

He swept the blond wig and black mask from his head, dropped them to the floor. Over them, he spilled the contents of a small vial he pulled from the same useful kit beneath his arm. Then, listening a moment at the door, he opened it and eased out. His signet was upon his finger, the rosette of an *officer* of the *Légion* on his lapel. He joined a group of men hurrying past the door.

There was nothing to connect this man with that nemesis of the underworld who killed in the night, the *Spider*. By now, the articles of his disguise had been eaten into a shapeless pulp by the acid he had poured upon them. A little while and nothing would remain but an evil smell. Nothing to connect him? Well, almost nothing. But the gun beneath Richard Wentworth's left arm would match the bullet that the *Spider* had sped into the gambler's body, if anyone should think to demand a test.

If Wentworth was worried over that possibility as he

followed in the wake of the hurrying crowd, it did not show on his vital, keenly alert face. His mind was still busy with the fact that his pistol shot had been heard outside the sound-proof room. There was only one explanation; the Avenger had planted witnesses!

A slight frown creased Wentworth's brow. This self-styled Avenger had sprung into being full-grown. One day, the man did not exist so far as the public knew; the next, his name was on everybody's lips. He had leaped into fame on the springboard of a famous kidnaping case. A prominent banker had been abducted, then freed when his ransom was paid. He had been unable to help police find his captors and the case had dragged along without new developments.

Then this man who dubbed himself the Avenger had called a morning newspaper and told the editor to go to a certain uptown apartment, and he would find the kidnapers, bound hand and foot, with the ransom money beside them. And even as the Avenger had promised, the kidnapers and loot were found. An hour afterward, the Avenger had called again.

A slight smile touched Wentworth's lips as he recalled the braggart phrasing of the Avenger's statement, as reported by the newspapers:

"I am a famous detective," the Avenger had said, "and I have ways of finding out what is happening in the underworld. From time to time, I will trap famous criminals and leave them for the police. I do not intend to act unless the case baffles all the authorities."

The Avenger operated differently than the *Spider*. He never killed. His prey were found always with the evidence of their crime beside them. In the month that had followed his initial effort, he had struck many times, snaring jewel thieves, payroll bandits, kidnapers, and once a murderer. He had promised next to turn up the slayer of a famous gang leader from Chicago, named O'Burke, whom police had sought vainly for several days. O'Burke had been shot down in New York.

Wentworth had watched the Avenger's progress through the newspapers—the Avenger reported every accomplishment directly to the press—and suspicion had begun to gnaw at his mind.

Then, on the day of the Avenger's biggest coup, these forty poisoning deaths had been reported, and, a day later, Wentworth's chauffeur, Jackson, had been shot. Wentworth had rushed to the hospital to find Jackson painfully wounded, but conscious and already out of danger.

"I'm sorry, major," the loyal servant had said, calling Wentworth by his wartime title. "I'm damned sorry, but I ran afoul this Avenger fellow and he blew me down."

Jackson's story of championing Patsy Malone and attempting to recover her brother's check from Mannley still struck Wentworth as fantastic. Jackson, a squire of dames? It was incredible! Jackson was as hard-boiled as they came. A good man, but hard. And now, he became excited over a girl's misfortunes!

"What's she like, Jackson?" Wentworth had asked softly.

"Her name's Patsy Malone, major," Jackson said. "Blue eyes, black hair curling around her face, about five feet two and peppery as tabasco. Why, she could have taken that bum to pieces if she hadn't been afraid of him, and. . . ."

Wentworth smiled. "Okay, Jack, now go ahead with your story."

It was softly said but Jackson flushed. His jaw became stubborn. "Damn it, major," he said roughly. "She's a square kid."

Wentworth made no answer and Jackson went on with his story. And so Wentworth had come to pay Mannley a visit, partly to avenge Jackson and help Patsy Malone, but more to meet this man who called himself the Avenger. There was small doubt in Wentworth's mind that the man was playing some deep game, and he was determined to fathom it.

* * *

Wentworth had separated from the panicky crowd fleeing from Mannley's. The gambling halls were nearly empty now and police had taken charge. A few men had remained, perhaps out of curiosity, or from sheer bravado. One of them might well be the Avenger. Surely the man would not give up without at least one more effort to snare the *Spider*.

Wentworth glanced about him, estimating those who had remained behind. Before this, he had found geniuses of crimes among his acquaintances. It was more than probable that the Avenger, also, came from that social stratum. He was too intelligent, his plans and their execution too clever for him to be classed as a common criminal. Wentworth had no description of the Avenger except that he was fully six feet tall and that his shoulders were as wide as a door.

He nodded greeting to a man who answered that inadequate description, Commander Samuels, a retired navy man recently returned from a business investigation in Russia. The man's round, jovial face, the light eyebrows like abbreviated hyphens, struck him abruptly as curiously mocking.

"Did you know Mannley had been shot?" Samuels asked, and in his voice, too, was that quality of mockery.

Wentworth raised his brows. "Really?" he murmured. He strolled on toward the door of Mannley's private room, spotting on the way two more men who might fit such a description, one a croupier named Larue with a green eyeshade across his brows; another was a minor police official, evidently called from some formal entertainment. The official, striding from Mannley's room, stared hostilely at Wentworth.

Wentworth swept an exaggerated bow. "Deputy Marshant," he said.

The man grunted and strode on. Wentworth nodded to the patrolman at the door, showing the police courtesy-badge he carried and stepped inside. An officer he knew, Inspector Trowbridge, stood staring grimly down at Mannley's corpse, but they were the room's only occupants.

Trowbridge glanced up, his over-sized head bobbing in greeting on his stringy neck. "A nice mess," he said, thin-voiced. "A helluva nice . . ." He broke off, staring past Wentworth.

A sudden blow between the shoulders sent Wentworth reeling forward. He heard the patrolman's startled cry choke off, heard his body slam down and a voice ring out from the doorway: "Hands up, everyone! The Avenger is speaking!"

Wentworth whirled, but his hands stayed clear of his guns. The man who called himself the Avenger had shut the sound-proof door and his shoulders matched its width. He was dressed in black from head to foot, black dress suit, a black priest's vest over his shirt, a black mask that was a hood tucked inside a black collar.

"Here's another crook for you, Inspector," boomed the Avenger's deep voice. "This Wentworth is the *Spider*. You'll find that bullet from gun under his arm will match bullet from gambler's body."

CHAPTER THREE

A New Horror

The Avenger's words sent a thrill of alarm through Wentworth's body. He had been conscious of the danger of that tell-tale gun beneath his arm, but he had thought it a minor risk. After all, how could anyone know that he still carried the murder gun? A tight wariness stiffened his muscles. Truly, the Avenger had planned well. It flashed through his mind that the Hooded One had prepared for all of this, even to the death of Mannley!

None of his swift fears, his mounting tension showed in Wentworth's face. There was mild mockery upon his whimsical lips and in his tip-tilted eyebrows. He bowed, clicking his heels. "Ah, the Avenger!" he murmured. "But you flatter me, sir, comparing my work with that of the *Spider*."

Through the drumming of his blood that was the tocsin of danger, Wentworth studied the man. He was attuned to peril and even when death gibbered at him his active brain reached ahead to the next move in the lethal chess that he played. He was seeking, even while he struggled for a way out of his dilemma, to find some characteristic to identify the Avenger. There was nothing except the man's size.

The Avenger was fully six feet in height, though the breadth of his shoulders made him seem somewhat shorter. His voice was thick with a suspicion of accent and he had the Russian trick of dropping articles before nouns. Commander Samuels might have acquired such a mannerism on his frequent expeditions to Russia. At the same time, either the deputy, Marshant, or the croupier, Larue, might assume such an accent.

But this was no time for speculation. He must worm his way out of this ingenious trap. The Avenger did not kill, but he might just as well loose the full contents of that ready automatic into his heart, as turn him over to police with the gun that could be identified both as his own and as the murder weapon. But there was no way out. The Devil! Was the *Spider*, for all his vaunted cleverness, to fall prey to this hooded Avenger in their first encounter? He heard impatience in the Avenger's voice.

"Come, come, Inspector Trowbridge," the hooded man snapped. "Handcuff Wentworth. You can get gun later."

Wentworth slipped out his cigarette case with fingers that did not tremble despite his tension. He tucked a smoke between his lips, snapped flame to it. His motions were sure and unhurried. Thoughts and abortive plans of escape darted about in his brain like imprisoned birds, but they all seemed useless. It would not do merely to attack the Avenger and flee, even if he could escape the menace of that leveled Colt's forty-five that was twin to the murder gun beneath his arm. To flee would be to confirm the accusation the Avenger had made. And Richard Wentworth, Park Avenue clubman, would become a fugitive from the law, his effectiveness against crime and criminals perhaps fatally impaired. Should he struggle with the Avenger, and in the confusion, toss the damning gun down the hall? He would still have a weapon, the lighter automatic beneath his right arm. No, that wouldn't do. Even if the murder gun were not found after he hurled it away, the empty holster under his left arm would accuse him.

A sense of panic strange to Wentworth shook him inwardly. Was there no way out then? Surely, this brain, these perfectly trained muscles on which he had so often and securely depended, would not fail him now! A pulse throbbed in the thin knife-scar upon his right temple. His whole body was tense with the need for action. He fought down his despair, made his voice cool and politely mocking.

"What are you waiting for, Inspector?" he asked. "Don't you hear the Avenger's orders?" Could he goad Trowbridge into open battle with the Avenger? It might help, though nothing short of Trowbridge's death could prevent a check-up of the gun. And Wentworth desired no officer's death, even if his own life hung in the balance.

Inspector Trowbridge had been standing, rigid with anger. Now his voice cracked in a curse. "Put down that gun!" he yelled at the Avenger. He thrust out his oversize head, leaned his angular body forward as he started across the floor. The Avenger's automatic swiveled toward him.

"Please to stand still," the Avenger barked. "I do not want to shoot you!" There was a flat menace in his voice that brought Trowbridge to a halt, his whole lanky body vibrant with anger.

"That's better," the Avenger said. *"Now put the cuffs on Wentworth!"*

Wentworth realized that only seconds had passed since the Avenger had forced his way into the room, seconds that had dragged out hours long. Either Trowbridge or the Avenger would be forced to act soon, but he still could not see how either could assist him. That damnable murder gun seemed to burn beneath his arm like white hot iron. Its twin stared at him with a black, death-greedy muzzle. The twin. . . .

The *Spider* tilted back his head to cover a sudden gleam in his eyes. He wafted a smoke ring toward the ceiling.

"By all means, Inspector," he drawled. "Put the cuffs on me. The Avenger has the upper hand and it will do no harm to humor him."

178

The inspector twisted his stringy neck and looked at Wentworth's smiling face, glowered back to the Avenger as if estimating the risks. The Hooded Man was no more than six feet away, but a charge in the face of that leveled automatic would be sheer suicide. Wentworth held his breath. He didn't want Trowbridge to attack the Avenger, not now. The Avenger must think he was winning. . . .

Wentworth held his breath. He dared not urge Trowbridge too much.

Inspector Trowbridge grumbled, cursed and fished out handcuffs from beneath his coat. As the official turned toward him, Wentworth blew out his breath softly and tossed the cigarette aside. He put his wrists together close to his belly.

Inspector Trowbridge angled toward him, followed by the Avenger's watchful gun. The policeman on the floor moaned softly and the Avenger drew back his foot and kicked the man behind the ear without once taking his eyes off Wentworth and the inspector. Trowbridge was quite close now, reaching out the cuffs for Wentworth's wrists. As his bony, thick-veined hands came out, Wentworth pivoted lightly on his left toe and slammed home his right fist in an upper cut. It cracked against the inspector's chin and sent him reeling backward with arms windmilling, reeling straight toward the Avenger!

Wentworth went in fast behind Trowbridge, thrusting him violently backward with both hands planted on his flat chest. The Avenger barked out a sharp warning, but as Wentworth had expected, he did not fire. He could not afford to have the wounding of a police inspector set against his name to dim the Robin Hood legend he was building. No such scruples would apply to firing on Wentworth, of course, especially when there was a murder gun in his holster that would identify him as the *Spider!*

The Avenger tried to spring aside, but the inspector was already upon him. The two men slammed against the wall and Wentworth leaped clear and struck with both fists, knocking aside the leveled automatic in the Avenger's hand, cracking a right into the hooded face. The blow was awkward, half blocked by the inspector's body, but the Avenger's shot went wild.

He fought frantically to free himself of the half-conscious inspector. He slashed with his automatic, but Wentworth danced out of range. His fist snaked through again, thudded against the hooded face. The Avenger's arms jerked upward for protection and the *Spider* struck twice with all his strength at the nerve center of the pistol arm.

The Avenger struggled clear of his entanglement with the inspector, but his automatic dropped from paralyzed fingers. Wentworth sprang backward, snatching for his own weapon. He did a strange thing then. Instead of snapping his Colt's forty-five—the murder gun—instantly from its holster as he knew so well how to do, he fumbled and barely got it clear in time to strike awkwardly as the Avenger closed in. The clubbing gun was seized in an iron grip and twisted out of his hand.

Wentworth dropped to one knee. His left hand flashed to the lighter gun beneath his right arm and pumped three swift shots upward past his assailant's face. The Avenger spun about with a hoarse, startled cry and plunged out into the hall. Wentworth was after him in a trice, but brought up short as he heard the heavy boom of revolvers smash out. The hall was empty. Commander Samuels, Deputy Marshant, everyone had disappeared.

Inspector Trowbridge struggled to his feet, stood staring vacantly about. He realized the Avenger was gone and sprang to the door, but the crash of shooting had already dwindled, the chase had left the floor and rushed noisily on. Trowbridge turned slowly about, his big head, dark gray hair awry, thrust forward. He stared at Wentworth and his eyes got hard and round.

Wentworth laughed and threw up both hands, palms outward.

"Now, Inspector," he said. "I apologize. I only hit

you because there was no other way of getting at the Avenger.'' He dropped his hands and offered a smiling jaw for the police officer's fist. "Go on, hit me," he urged. "I deserve it."

The hardness went out of the police inspector's eyes and they became speculative, suspicious.

"All right," he said slowly, "but pull your punches another time."

Wentworth nodded and, with that suspicious gaze still upon him, stooped to pick up the Avenger's gun— the twin of the murder weapon—which he had wrestled from the man's hand. He tendered it to the police officer.

"Here's my gun," he said. "You'd better check it just to make sure the Avenger was lying. This is the only forty-five I carry, and Mannley apparently was killed with a forty-five. My left hand gun—" he displayed it on his palm, "is a thirty-eight. You know I have permits for a half dozen various guns."

The inspector nodded sourly, accepted the heavier automatic, but still watched Wentworth. However, he gave grumpy permission for him to leave. He knew Wentworth by name because of his frequent visits to headquarters to visit his friend, Police Commissioner Stanley Kirkpatrick. Once out of the inspector's sight, Wentworth moved swiftly. In the gambler's quarters, he had spotted the safe which probably contained young Malone's note, but he knew that for hours it would be impossible to search it successfully. Meantime, there was other work for the *Spider*.

He had succeeded in routing the Avenger, but the Avenger had made it impossible for the *Spider* to pursue. But now that he could remain no longer, Wentworth would have to work like fury to find the Avenger and retrieve the weapon.

In order to escape from the trap, he had been forced to surrender into the Avenger's hands the weapon with which the *Spider* had killed. If the Avenger realized that, he need only send the automatic to police and his doom would be an accomplished fact. Also, if police

181

checked the number on the automatic Wentworth had surrendered to the inspector and found it did not belong to Wentworth, there would be trouble. He made a mental note to recover the automatic at the first possible moment from the police. It was barely possible he might obtain a clue to the Avenger's identity through it, though he doubted that a man as clever as the masked one would leave such an easy and clear trail.

A policeman warming his back against a steam radiator in the apartment building's foyer saluted Wentworth with his club as he pushed out into the night. Instantly a car started down the line and Nita tooled it to the curb.

Wentworth did not speak. He slumped back in a corner of the seat, hands thrust into his pockets.

He was sure now that the Avenger had deliberately set into action a train of circumstances, all implicating the *Spider* at the scene of the kill. Nor did Wentworth believe that it had been done purely as a publicity stunt for the Avenger, though he seemed hungry enough for that type of fame. Criminals, even psuedo-Robin Hoods, did not recklessly attack the *Spider* for such reasons, even though there was a fifty-thousand dollar reward on his head. A sudden thought struck him: the Avenger's most spectacular activity had taken place on the same day those forty-three poison deaths had occurred. Was it possible . . . ? Had the Avenger done that to reduce the publicity given to the poisonings?

Wentworth's head snapped up, his eyes narrowed. If that were so, the attack on himself must herald some incredible new visitation of death! Something that would pale those forty deaths into insignificance! The capture of the *Spider* would crowd all other news off the front pages of newspapers.

Wentworth cursed raggedly, leaned forward and switched on the radio, fumbled for a station which he knew at this hour was broadcasting news reports. He listened with thoughtful cold eyes as the announcer's voice droned through a grist of featureless news: a ship had thrown a propeller off Hatteras and been taken in tow by the Coastguard Cutter Mann; two boys had broken through the ice of a skating pond and been drowned when they tried to rescue a pet dog . . . the car was drumming up West End Avenue, now yawing at the corners as the gust swept up from the Hudson a block away. Nita braked to a halt as she caught a red light and the radio became suddenly louder.

"Here's a news flash," said the announcer. "Seventeen women have been rushed to the hospitals within the last hour, all with their faces terribly burned. Doctors said an acid apparently had been placed in some cosmetics. Many of the women will be permanently disfigured. For further details, read your local newspaper."

Wentworth smashed a clenched fist into his palm.

"That's it!" he said suddenly. "By God, that's it!"

"Heavens, Dick, what's the matter?" Nita asked fearfully. "It's a terrible thing, but. . . ."

"That's more work of the poisoners," Wentworth said flatly. "And, by Heaven, the Avenger is helping them!"

There was a cold horror writhing within him. Seventeen women with their faces fearfully burned. Acid in cosmetics! But why? Why should any criminal do such a thing? What profit could he hope to gain from disfiguring women? From poisoning scores of people? Wentworth jerked his head angrily.

Certainly, this crime seemed to confirm his half-guess as to the Avenger's motives. What man would lend himself to such infamy? And what was the motive?

The car spun a corner to the left, bored through a howling wind to Riverside Drive and coasted up to the entrance of a towering apartment building. Wentworth and Nita flung across the walk and into the foyer with a cold wind snapping at their heels. The rosy-cheeked hall boy recognized them by name and ushered them ceremoniously into the elevator with a swagger of incongruously wide shoulders. Despite the cold horror of this new crime, despite the turmoil in his mind, estimating motives, figuring his strategy against the estimating motives, figuring his strategy against the Avenger, Wentworth felt a lift of his heart as the cage soared toward Nita's home.

A slight boyish smile curved Wentworth's lips, his eyes softened, turned a little wistful. All his love was Nita's; all her heart was his. Yet few were the hours they might share. His pledge of service to humanity had been made before they had met and he had fought against their love as if it were a shameful thing. For the *Spider* could never marry. How could he, with the threat of arrest and disgrace, of execution in the electric chair hanging ever over him? No man of honor could ask a woman to share such a life with him, nor think of having a home and children when any hour might bring him shameful doom.

But that love had proved stronger than the combined great strength of both of them. They had made concessions to their happiness. She should fight with him for the things he held dear. So that others might have happiness and be protected from the poisonous beast that was the underworld, these two denied themselves the solace of their love. Wentworth had never regretted his decision for an instant, but sometimes desire for a peaceful domestic life nearly overwhelmed him; sometimes the cup of life seemed unendurably bitter. . . .

The elevator boy flung wide the door and Wentworth stepped into the hall. He darted aside abruptly, his hand flying to the automatic holstered beneath his arm. But even as his fingers closed upon the butt, he checked himself, frowning.

A man had straightened away from the wall beside the door of Nita's apartment, a husky figure of a man in a shapeless overcoat and a crushed hat. The man shambled across toward him, lifting a hand to cover a yawn. "Good of you to come so soon, old pal," he said. "Have you a statement to make to a gentleman of the press?"

184

"What the hell are you doing here, Blanton?" Wentworth demanded coldly.

The elevator boy stepped alertly into the hall. "Want me to throw him out, sir?" he asked brightly.

"How crude of you," the newspaper man murmured, but there was a hard glint in his eyes. It occurred to Wentworth that despite his slouch, Blanton was very husky and as large as the elevator boy. He refused with a curt shake of his head, a gesture of his hand that was dismissal. The elevator boy clicked a bow, stepped back into the cage and clanged the door.

"Now, Blanton," Wentworth said, "what do you want?"

Blanton had a blurred smile on his face, his eyes seemed sleepy, but there were shrewd wrinkles at their corners. His whole person was like that, careless and alert. His horsey face had a thin nose and his head was so narrow and long it seemed deformed. He smoked a cigarette in a holder at least twelve inches long.

"Wouldst have a word with thee," he said gently. "The city editor cracked his whip over the 'phone at me, routed me out of the hay and bade me scamper over to intercept thee. I, not you, am the one who should wax exceedingly wroth. You weren't routed out of a downy bed. . . ."

"What do you want?" Wentworth demanded again.

Blanton struck an attitude, left hand to his breast, right gesturing widely, but behind his mocking pantomime, his eyes never left Wentworth's keen face.

"Art angry with your little palsy?" His voice shuddered with mock horror.

Wentworth cursed impatiently and pushed past him toward the door of Nita's apartment. The reporter's hand rested lightly on Wentworth's arm and he peered with suddenly wide open eyes into his face.

"The Avenger says you are the *Spider*," Blanton said swiftly, clearly. "What statement have you in reply to that?"

Wentworth stopped and stared into the man's eyes. This play acting, this assinine behavior had not fooled

185

him at all. He knew that Blanton had one of the shrewdest minds among the alert set of news men who gathered information for the New York dailies. He knew that Blanton was a clever psychologist, used to worming information from reluctant and defiant sources. He knew, too, that Blanton had looked upon him with suspicious eyes more than once when the *Spider's* activities had come to light. The Avenger was striking again, and even more viciously. Newspaper publicity of this sort would hamper Wentworth's movements enormously.

"He says he has positive proof—concrete evidence—that you are the *Spider*," Blanton hammered on. "What have you to say, Wentworth?"

Wentworth smiled despite the sick thumping of his heart. The Avenger already had found out about the exchange of automatics! There could be no doubt as to his meaning. By Heaven, the man was shrewd! But why was he working this way, instead of turning the weapon over to police? Wentworth could not figure that, but he was sure that delay boded no good for the *Spider*. The Avenger undoubtedly was furthering some deep plan of his own.

Blanton's keen, sleepy eyes were studying Wentworth's face, but without profit. The secret services of the world had, on occasion, tried to pierce that mobile mask without success. Wentworth continued to smile. He reached out and pushed Blanton's chin with his palm so that the reporter's dinky, ridiculous hat slipped sideways on his head. There was just one defense, Wentworth knew, against the Avenger's round-about attack.

"Why say, Blanton," he told the reporter, gently mocking, "that the Avenger is absolutely correct. Of course, I'm the *Spider!*"

Wentworth threw back his head and laughed, heard Nita's smothered gasp. She stepped past and used her key. The reporter's eyes and mouth were wide open, ludicrous with surprise that was not all assumed. "May I print that?" he demanded eagerly.

Wentworth nodded graciously. "Certainly."

Blanton closed his mouth and glared at him. "You know damned well I can't print that!" he said savagely. "They'd laugh me out of the office if I 'phoned in anything like that. And I can't prove you said it."

Wentworth became apologetic. "I'm so sorry," he said. "I should have allowed the elevator boy to remain as a witness."

Wentworth bowed Nita through the opened door, waved a careless hand to Blanton.

"Come up'n see me sometime," Wentworth drawled. "And bring a witness!"

CHAPTER FOUR

The Spider Falls

The door closed behind Wentworth and his smile was instantly eclipsed. He faced Nita with a worried frown. A tawny, spotted Great Dane dog was prancing a boisterous welcome, but Wentworth greeted him only absently as they walked along the hall to the sprawling duplex living-room of Nita's apartment. A great studio window, with side drapes of warmly crimson velvet, filled the entire side of the room, showed the black, wind-swept Hudson, the yellow lights of the Jersey shore. But Wentworth had no eyes for that, though there were times when his gaze turned wistful at the warm homey comfort of the apartment.

"What made you tell Eddie Blanton that?" Nita asked breathlessly. "Even if he can't print it. . . . !"

Wentworth waved a hand wearily. "Blanton has been suspicious of me for a long time," he said. "I've seen it in his eyes when he hangs around Kirkpatrick's office. If I had denied it I would have given countenance to the Avenger's charges. This way, Blanton is left without ammunition. He doesn't know whether I'm joking or not."

Wentworth took both Nita's hands in his, looking deeply into her violet eyes while he told her rapidly what had happened at Mannley's club. Nita's gaze was quiet and unafraid now. She was a poised woman of the world; her head of clustered chestnut curls was carried high and proudly; there was dignity as well as beauty in her face. Her brow bespoke wisdom, and clear courage was in the modeled firmness of her lips, a fitting mate for this Master of Men.

Wentworth finished his recital and she moved from him with a slow grace, bending over to light a laid fire on the hearth. The flames towered swiftly. Flickering red lights danced over her hair and found new life in its gleam, shadowed her gracious figure against the flowing lines of velvet gown, colored like wine.

"I'll have coffee for you in a moment, Dick," she said. "Some excellent brandy. . . ."

Wentworth threw back his head and laughed sharply once. There was exhilaration, new life in the sound. Nita was always like this. In her he found a stimulus beyond belief. Her quiet courage spurred him to greater accomplishments. She smiled at him slowly now, the curve of her lips ineffably tender. Wentworth whirled, crossed the room with long, bouncing strides to a dressing room and a wardrobe behind a secret panel which held, behind a row of his own correct clothing, the garbs of his disguises. They were only a fraction of what filled the closets of his own Fifth Avenue apartment, but many times he had found it impossible to go there, had needed to draw upon this secondary depôt.

"Nita, dear," he called. "Would you 'phone Ram Singh please to rent a coupé and get here as swiftly as he can?"

While he asked her to summon his faithful Hindu body servant, he was busy before a mirror that was framed in white neon lights, constructing over his own firm, vital face, the sallow countenance of the *Spider*. The nose, built up with putty, became sharp and beaklike, the skin tautened until it emphasized the high cheek bones. Bushy thick eyebrows covered the suave line of his own. He draped a cloak over his arm, selected a wide-brimmed black slouch hat and thrust into a pocket a wig of lank long hair. Then he strode back into the living-room.

Nita came toward him with a china saucer in her hands. Her face was ashen as he held it out. A bit of gold chain lay in a pat of white greasy cream. Green bubbles stood up all over the chain and stained the grease.

"I bought a fresh jar of cold cream today," Nita said in a slightly muffled voice. "After I heard that radio broadcast, I thought I'd better test it."

Wentworth stared down at the green mess which the acid, acting on the copper in the chain, had made of the cold cream. His eyes lifted to Nita's dear face and a shudder shook him as he envisioned it welted and destroyed by the work of that acid.

"Thank God you tried it first!" he cried hoarsely.

Their eyes met and Nita set the saucer down and crept into his arms. Wentworth stared straight before him over her dear head. Seventeen women had been scarred for life by the work of these fiends tonight. Nita had barely escaped. What in God's name could be the motive behind such horror?

With an effort, Wentworth threw off the bitter anger that rose within him. When he spoke, his voice was flat and edged:

"I'm going to pay Patsy Malone a visit," he said briefly. "You remember the girl who got Jackson in a jam with the Avenger? I'm positive that through her I can get a lead to the Avenger. I've got to find him. If he isn't responsible for these . . . these horrors, I must know it so that I can hunt the true trail . . . And I must recover my automatic and destroy it. Never before has such damaging evidence got into hostile hands. I'm afraid . . ."

The hall boy rang from below and reported that Ram Singh had arrived with the car. Wentworth clasped Nita in his arms. Her hand stole across his shoulders, her fingers twined in his hair. A moment of happiness then Wentworth was gone, the disguised face that alone was changed now, half-hidden in a silken muffler.

Eddie Blanton pulled his shoulders loose from the

190

wall and ambled toward him, hands buried in the sagging pockets of his top coat.

"Give us a break, Wentworth," he urged. "Give me a serious answer for my paper."

Wentworth turned his back to him, stood facing the elevator door. "I'm tired of answering such fool charges," he said coldly. "Your paper would do better to ask the Avenger what he has done with the loot he hijacked from various crooks. Why is it that every time he pulls something especially spectacular and grabs off the entire front page of the newspaper, some other heinous crime is committed? Such as the disfiguring of those seventeen women today!"

"What do you mean, Wentworth?" Blanton was strangely excited, crowding up close beside him now, trying to peer into his face. The elevator door opened and Wentworth strode in, sent Blanton backwards with a swift thrust at his chest.

"Down," he ordered the boy shortly.

"Right you are, sir!" The boy slammed the door alertly, the roses of his cheeks redder than ever with excitement. The elevator swooped downward, while the signal buzzed continuously for the floor of Nita's apartment. It rang all the way down to the first floor.

"I'll take care of him, sir," the boy promised, with a slight straightening of his wide shoulders.

Wentworth said, "Never mind." He tipped the boy and strode out to the small coupé that Ram Singh held at the curb. The wind smacked him in the face and he grabbed his lifting hat, ducked into the car. The Hindu set it instantly in motion.

"Men from the newspapers have been at the house, *sahib*," he reported, his dark, hawkish face impassive. "They wish to know the *sahib's* answer to this pig of a pretender, this Avenger, who accuses the *sahib*."

Wentworth nodded thoughtfully. Whether the Avenger was trying to trap him, or merely to handicap him in his fight against the poison killers, he had taken a clever way. If the Avenger made out a strong enough case, newspapermen would dog his movements for days, might even set detectives on his trail. A heavy frown roughened his forehead. He must not be hampered. So many lives depended on his freedom to fight the poisoners.

Absently, he removed his hat, drew into place the lank, long wig he carried in his pocket, and cloaked his shoulders in a long, black cape. The coupé left Riverside Drive behind and let the wind blow it up Ninety-sixth Street across the dimmer lights of upper Broadway. Minutes later, it drew to a halt near a red brick tenement. Wentworth spoke briefly to Ram Singh in Hindustani, caught the acquiescent nod of the Hindu's turbanned head, his murmured, *"Han, sahib."*

It was the *Spider* who alighted from the coupé, a hunch-backed figure in a wind-flapped cape that shuffled his awkward way with deceptive swiftness along the sidewalk. A moment only was he visible; then the street held only a parked coupé and the sound of cold whining wind.

In the shadows of a dimly lighted hall, a twisted, sinister shadow moved. The *Spider* went with soundless speed and paused presently before a doorway. Behind it, a tinny radio blasted music but only made the quiet of the hall more oppressive. Despite the noisy instrument, the apartment within seemed still also—still with a waiting tension. . . .

A tight smile made faint lines about the *Spider's* lipless mouth. Was this the next trap of the Avenger? Had he figured that Wentworth would follow him here? Slowly, the *Spider* nodded. Oh, the man was clever! Wentworth faded away from that doorway and the black shadow drifted up another floor, and another until he could reach the scuttle and gain the roof.

From a compact tool-kit that he carried strapped always beneath his left arm, Wentworth drew a length of silken cord. It was scarcely as thick as a pencil, yet such was its cunning weave, and of such high quality were its fibres that it could lift seven hundred pounds.

With practiced speed, Wentworth looped the cord

about a chimney pot, threw its two ends over into space and, twisting the doubled line about his arms and legs, lowered himself with swift ease into the darkness of an air-shaft.

The winds of the heavens swept overhead and swirled down into the black pit. The *Spider's* cape swirled and flapped about him like the wings of a giant bat. But he steadied his body with feet touching the brick walls and went steadily downward until he was at the level of the apartment at whose door he had listened. Still that tinny radio shrieked and vibrated and still he could feel that tense waiting. A green shade full of tiny pinpricks of light covered the window.

Only one other window was lighted. It was a story below where he swung, across the areaway. Through it, he could see a girl before a dressing table mirror. She patted grease from a jar into her face. Wentworth bit his lips to keep from shouting a warning. Silly, of course. There wasn't one chance in a hundred that the girl had got hold of one of the acid-tainted jars. But she was so young, her face so fresh. Wentworth jerked his head in negation. No, he could not warn her lest he betray his presence. He was being foolish. Her cold cream was safe.

Still his eyes clung with fascination to the scene. The girl had pulled off her dress and wore a pale, sleazy slip of green that left her young plump shoulders bare. She stretched her neck, pointing her chin at the mirror as she worked the grease in thoroughly. Abruptly she stopped, her finger tips just touching her cheek. She frowned at her reflection in the mirror, felt her flesh in bewilderment.

Her face twisted in pain. She snatched a cloth and began to rub frantically, swabbing off the grease. She sprang to her feet. Through the glass window, Wentworth heard her cry out.

"Oh, God!" she screamed. She was dancing with pain now and Wentworth cursed with stiffly rigid lips. He knew, even if that girl down there did not, what had happened. Once more, the acid-laden cosmetics had

193

struck. He saw a man dash up to the girl, heard her screaming words, then the man snatched her from his vision. Wentworth cursed with slow, thick-throated violence. If only he had warned her! But he knew that he could not. White rage burned within him, rage at these fiends who struck at innocent women. This was not murder. It was lifetime torture that was being inflicted. Pain, then the horror of a welted, hideous face.

Lights began to spring up on the other side of the airshaft. A window directly opposite blossomed yellow. The *Spider* must move if he would escape detection. It was significant that the window shade already drawn down had not been raised. He was positive now that the Avenger lurked behind it. If that hooded one was responsible for these horrors that had been inflicted this night, heaven help him. . . .

Stiff with cold, the *Spider* got a foothold on the window sill, ducked his face into his arms and pushed himself violently out into the airshaft. He swung out three feet. He jerked up his knees to protect body and tight gripped hands and went through the window with a smash and a tinkle of broken glass. The spring roller of the green shade tripped and it slapped upward with a noisy, dying flutter. Wentworth landed on his feet, flung himself to the right until his shoulders struck a wall, and came out of his crouch with a gun in each fist.

"Stay just like you are," he ordered sharply.

Beside the closed door, the bulky hooded figure of the Avenger crouched, hand frozen half-way to his gun. On a rickety iron bed on the far side of the room a girl and a boy crouched miserably and in a chair a round-faced man hugged a baby against his chest.

Wentworth needed only a glance to know that the girl was the Patsy Malone whom Jackson had described, five-feet-two of tobasco. Danger signals were flying in her cheeks and in the bright anger of her blue eyes. The husky blond kid beside her must be the younger brother, the man with the baby must be a neighbor.

194

*   *   *

Wentworth's eyes narrowed on a slip of paper clenched between the boy's fingers, a slip of pink paper that was a check. The Devil! Had the Avenger played philanthropist and given the forged check back to the boy?

His quick question brought a wondering nod from the boy. One thing to mark up to the Avenger's credit then, but it could not change Wentworth's plans.

"Avenger!" he snapped. "You're coming with me. To the window, quickly."

The hooded, blank face with eyes glittering through the slits confronted him without words. The man was still crouched with his hand half-way to his gun.

"Quickly," Wentworth repeated, "or the police will take us both."

A sound like dry laughter came from behind the mask. "You have more to fear from police than I, *Spider*," said the Avenger grimly. "Let us wait for them."

Wentworth cursed, stalked swiftly toward the Avenger, a blackjack dangling from his left wrist while the automatic in his right held his prisoner motionless. He caught a quick movement to his left, saw that the blond youth was charging toward him in a head-down, desperate run!

"Get back!" Wentworth warned desperately. He didn't want to hurt the boy, but . . .

His dodge was too late. Young Malone slammed into him. The boy was powerful and sent him reeling, even as he struck with the blackjack. Patsy Malone cried out. The bed creaked as she leaped into the fight. The Avenger got his gun in his hand. Once more he laughed and came forward lightly, his heavy shoulders rolled forward in readiness to strike.

He was almost within striking distance when Wentworth finally fought clear of Shane Malone and allowed the boy to slump to the floor. The Avenger's gun was lifted to crash against the *Spider's* skull, but Wentworth was ready for him. He flung up his weapon to put a bullet through his assailant's arm, then hesitated. He could hit the Avenger's arm without difficulty. His perfection of aim assured that, but the bullet would plough on through, and behind the Avenger crouched the man with the baby in his arms.

Wentworth's hesitation undid him. The Avenger's gun raked out and struck him numbingly on the head. As he reeled backward, still hesitating to shoot on account of the baby, Patsy Malone flung herself upon him.

Dazedly, he heard a curse rip out from the doorway, heard the door slam inward and jerked his head about. A uniformed policeman stood on the threshold, revolver ready.

"Stop it!" he roared. "Hands up, the lot of youse!"

But Patsy Malone was past heeding him and Wentworth could not help himself. The girl flung herself upon him, sent him stumbling backward. Her clawing hands raked his face. Her light-slippered feet kicked at his shins.

"You've killed Shane," she cried. "You've killed Shane!"

Wentworth's head was beginning to clear. His eyes made a swift survey of the room as he went backward. The Avenger had whirled to face the door, his hands rising, his gun falling to the floor.

"That man is *Spider!*" The Avenger's deep voice rang out. "I am Avenger and I was taking him prisoner to turn over to police!"

The policeman's stride carried him almost within reach of the Avenger. Wentworth flung an arm about Patsy Malone and flopped down on his back, pulling her with him. As he fell, he hurled his blackjack upward and the lights crashed out. The policeman was silhouetted against a dim rectangle of flickering gas illumination in the hall, but the rest of them were in shadow.

With a heave of his body, Wentworth tossed Patsy aside. He sprawled forward to snatch the Avenger's gun

196

from the floor and saw the Hooded Man go forward, heard his fist thud and the policeman reel back. The *Spider* was off like a sprinter from his mark. As the policeman hit the door jamb, bounced and measured his length on the floor, Wentworth reached the Avenger and ground the automatic into the small of his back.

"Down the stairs fast!" the *Spider* ordered. His voice was low and there was steel in it.

The Avenger hesitated, then with a guttural curse moved toward the steps. Sharp heels beat the floor explosively behind Wentworth. He reached out to strike down the Avenger, to whirl toward this new menace, but he was too late. A woman's arms, Patsy Malone's, flung around his throat from behind.

"Run, Avenger! Run!" she panted.

The Avenger pivoted and slammed his fist full in Wentworth's helpless face. He went down and carried the girl with him and the Avenger's feet beat a hurried retreat down the steps. Patsy Malone scrambled erect, her breath coming fast. The *Spider* lay where he had fallen, unconscious. Patsy scooped up the pistol and held it in a trembling hand.

The timid, round-faced man, with the baby still clutched in his arms, stuck his head out of her apartment door.

"It's all right, Mr. Coxwell," Patsy said, somewhat scornfully. "The *Spider* is unconscious."

"F-f-fine!" stammered the man. "Keep him that way while I run for another policeman!"

CHAPTER FIVE

The Avenger Plots

While Wentworth lay unconscious, the Avenger made good his swift flight. He raced down the stairs, out through the back and into the next street through another tenement. As he passed through the second building, he removed his hat and yanked the masking hood from his head, shoved it into a pocket. Then he pulled the brim of his black hat low over his eyes, ducked his head and plowed along into the cold wind.

Two blocks farther along the street, he entered a parked sedan, climbed in under the wheel and waited. He drew out a tobacco pouch and, with a large piece of paper, made what the Russians call a "goat's ankle," a cigarette that held as much tobacco as a pipe. He lighted that, chuckled once as he blew out a great cloud of smoke. He wore only a light suit coat, yet he did not seem to find the frigid, still air of the sedan cold. He chuckled again as if there were something rarely amusing in his thoughts.

It was five minutes later that a second man, clad exactly like himself except that he wore a long cape cloak, opened the door, slid into the car.

"All goes well, Ivan?" the man asked, pronouncing the name *Ee-ván* in the Russian manner.

"All goes very well, Master," the man with the

"goat's ankle" between his lips agreed, and reported rapidly what had occurred in the Malone apartment.

"Good!" exclaimed the Master. "I have one more little errand for you tonight, Ivan. Take care of the O'Burke affair tonight. I'll 'phone the papers and the police can mark another crime as 'solved by the Avenger.' "

Both men laughed together. The interior of the sedan was thick with the smoke of Ivan's malodorous cigarette, the windows were misting over. Ivan puffed again, seemed to hesitate.

"Master," he said finally, "that is one thing I do not understand. Why did you have me kill O'Burke? He is a gang leader from Chicago, and you . . ."

"I am giving orders," the Avenger said. "It is your part to obey."

His voice was cold as the moan of the wind in the street. "This arrangement was your suggestion when I saved you from the police after you committed murder. You said your life was mine and that you would serve me faithfully in all things, even if you didn't know who I was, or why I did things."

"That is true, Master," Ivan said quickly, and his words were abject. "I do not question. My life is yours. I serve you as I would my chieftain upon steppes." His head was bowed before the burning regard of the eyes behind the mask.

"See that you remember it," the Avenger said harshly. "Tomorrow night," he went on, "you go to Chicago. I have heard that a rare shipment of diamonds has been received there, and I should like to add some of them to my collection. I don't believe any of the crooks out there would tackle it, so you'll take three men west from New York and I'll join you later. When you have the diamonds turn loose a narcotic bomb. Tie up your three companions and leave them to take the rap. Be careful you don't betray your identity."

Ivan nodded slowly. "You may trust me, Master."

If Wentworth could have heard their unemotional plotting to steal a fortune in gems and leave other criminals as prisoners to take the blame, his eyes would have blazed at confirmation of one theory. But the Avenger was going even farther than Wentworth suspected. He was no hijacking crook. He was committing the crime himself, then leaving the innocent to take the blame! Small wonder that he had no difficulty in solving crimes! But there was as yet no mention of that horror of which Wentworth suspected the Avenger—the poisonings and the injury of women.

The Master studied Ivan in the semidarkness of the car. Their faces were not visible, save that the glow of the "goat's ankle" gleamed momentarily on the Russian's high cheek bones, revealed a thin-bridged nose; revealed, too, that even while talking to this man, the one addressed as Master wore the hood of the Avenger.

He sat silently for a while, staring at the misted windshield which showed the street beyond only dimly. Things were progressing very satisfactorily. The *Spider* by this time must have been taken prisoner either by that policeman who lay unconscious beside him, or by other police whom the Malones had summoned. The news of his capture, coupled with the O'Burke affair would be smashed all over the front pages of the newspapers in the morning.

His fame would be greater than ever. That little Robin Hood trick of gifts to the poor had caught the imagination of the people and he was in small danger of capture by the police. At any time they closed in on him he need only to flee into someone's home and tell them he was the Avenger. They would hide him. Was not the Avenger the friend of the people?

Tonight had been a fair sample of that. Because Ivan had returned the check to Shane Malone, the boy and Patsy had knocked over the *Spider* for him. Ah, yes, these little philanthropies paid good dividends. A low dry laugh filtered through his black mask. His hand dropped to the handle of the door.

"Carry on, Ivan," he said lightly. "You have done good work tonight. That motion picture you took of the *Spider* killing that gambler, Mannley, turned out perfectly. It is too bad he was in disguise, but I think I have a way of solving that difficulty. The film should be in the hands of police in less than an hour." He paused, working the door handle up and down. It made a slight squeaking. "I'll look for you at the usual place in about four hours. We prepare that little excursion to Chicago."

"Master . . ." The Russian hesitated, held the last short fragment of his cigarette pinched between his fingers. "Master, who are these people who are killing many others with poison in tinned meat? Who are burning the faces off women with acid? Do you know, Master? It seems to me that they are very powerful, that we would better be careful lest we cross them."

The Avenger nodded slowly. "They are powerful," he agreed, soberly, then laughed suddenly. "Perhaps there may be some profit in that for us also."

The door clicked open and he stepped to the pavement. "I must make sure that the *Spider* does not escape."

Ivan coaxed the cold motor into life and drove rapidly southward, cut through an underpass beneath Central Park and pushed on toward the East River. Before a slatternly tenement, he parked the car. Five minutes later, he returned with a bundle over his shoulder—a bundle wrapped in burlap that was about five feet, six inches long and which squirmed with an independent life.

Ivan opened the rear door of the sedan, dumped the bundle roughly to the floor where it squirmed and made muffled groanings. Then he drove on. He came at length to a dim gray building about which the winds soughed mournfully, whose only light issued dimly from a cavernous door and served only to make the rest of the building, the tall barred windows, more dreary. Into the doorway, Ivan trudged with his now motionless bundle. And over Ivan's face had been drawn the black hood of the Avenger which showed nothing but the steely glitter of his eyes.

He leaned heavily on the bell and stood against the door so that the bundle on his shoulder concealed his masked face, but so that he could peer into the interior. From the doorway, a high, dim hall ran straight back to twin wooden doors that were black. On each side of the corridor was another doorway. It was from the opening to the right that a bent old man wearing a uniform cap issued presently. He carried a large ring of keys in his left hand and in his right was a flashlight.

Ivan jabbed the bell twice more impatiently, raising an echoing clangor within. The old man called something in a cracked voice and his shuffle became a little more rapid. He peered out, flashing his light so that it made a round white disc on the thick glass of the door. It was possible now to make out the metal legend that was attached to the front of his uniform cap. It read:

CITY MORGUE

The old man made querulous noises behind the glass and Ivan shook the door with an impatient hand. Finally the keeper shrugged and opened the door a crack. Instantly Ivan's shoulder swung it violently wide and he jammed a gun against the man's ribs.

"You will not be hurt," he said harshly, "if you obey. I am Avenger."

The old man reeled back with fright in his eyes. The door jarred shut behind the Avenger and his bundle began to make muffled sounds again.

"Quickly," said the Avenger. "Take me to the place where they've put O'Burke's body."

"What . . . what do you want?" the old man quavered. "There ain't nothing here except corpses. What's that you got in your bundle?"

"Hurry!" rasped the hooded man. "O'Burke's body!" He thrust the pistol menacingly forward. The old man stumbled down the hall, casting fearful glances back over his shoulder and the Avenger crowded close on his heels. His arm was clamped tightly about his bundle and its squirmings did not inconvenience him in the least.

Slowly the queer procession moved down the dim corridor, feet making flat echoes through the empty building. At the big double doors, the old keeper hesitated a moment, fumbling with his keys, then he inserted one in the lock and leaned against the door. He giggled nervously as it swung inward and he switched on lights.

"Reckon it don't make no difference to *them*," he mumbled. "And they do say you don't hurt folks, Mr. Avenger."

He shuffled across the tile floor. There was a damp chill in the air and the wailing of the wind crept into the room. Their footsteps seemed a violation of something that was both sacred and terrible. The thin, bent, old keeper giggled again, sucking his toothless gums.

"O'Burke won't mind neither," he cackled. "He may have been a hell of a big shot, but he's just a number now. Two-eighty-three."

Along the wall, chest high, ran a wide cabinet of white porcelain. In it were two tiers of deep drawers and over each was a small brass plate with a number on it. The keeper flashed his light on one or two of these, pointed a knotted old finger at one.

"In there," he said.

He turned toward the masked man behind him, then he let out a thin squeal and flattened against the chests. The Avenger's gun thudded on his old head and the keeper slumped to the floor. Ivan grunted and dumped his bundle down, caught hold of the handle of drawer 283 and pulled.

The drawer slid straight out and a gust of cold came with it from the refrigeration plant that kept those drawers, and their contents, at icy temperatures. The drawer was without sides, a white porcelain slab. On it a man's nude body and in his chest were four bullet holes. The morgue keeper was right. O'Burke wouldn't care about anything any more.

For a long moment, the Avenger stood look down at the body on the slab, then he bent over his bundle and

203

unwrapped it, spilled out a man who was wrapped in rope like a cocoon, whose mouth was stopped by a tight white gag. Swiftly the Avenger removed the gag. With it, he bound the man by his neck to the thigh of O'Burke's corpse.

"What . . . what are you doing to me?" the bound captive demanded. He had a childish face, warped by childish cruelty. His mental age could not have been above seven, but the dissipation that marred his countenance could not have been acquired in less than thirty years.

"What are you doing to me?" he demanded again, twisting his neck to see behind him.

"I'm tying you to O'Burke's corpse," said the Avenger, with a chuckle.

He drew an automatic from his pocket, holding it in a handkerchief, and deposited it in the bound man's lap.

"That's the gun you killed him with," he went on. "Your fingerprints are on it."

A squeal of terror gasped from the man's lips. "I . . . I didn't kill O'Burke," he shrieked. "You can't do this to me. You can't!"

Once more the Avenger chuckled. "I know you didn't kill him," he said, "because it happens I did, and with that gun. But the weapon is yours. You bought it two months ago. Your fingerprints are on the butt. Also you are member of rival mob. I think police will convict you of crime all right. This note—" he tied it deftly to the trigger guard of the gun—"will give them details."

"For God's sake, Avenger!" the man gabbed. "Don't do it! Don't . . . !"

The Avenger stepped back and surveyed his handiwork, the man with the young-old face, tied by his throat to the thigh of O'Burke's corpse; the automatic in his lap and the aged morgue keeper sprawled unconscious beside him. He chuckled again, turned on his heel and stalked from the room while the bound man shrieked and shrieked.

Within an hour, the papers would chant forth once more the praises of the Avenger. With his uncanny knowledge of the underworld, he had solved another crime that baffled police, found the murderer of that mighty gang leader, O'Burke from Chicago.

CHAPTER SIX

"This Is the End!"

While the Avenger went about his mysterious business, Wentworth lay unconscious upon the floor of the hall beside the policeman the Avenger had slugged. Patsy Malone, standing over him with the automatic in her hand, glanced anxiously at their supine bodies, turned her worried blue eyes toward the door of her apartment.

"Shane!" she called urgently. "Shane!"

No reply came from the darkness. The girl became anxious. She glanced down at the bodies in the hall again and neither moved. The girl turned and ran into the apartment. "Shane! Shane!" she called again.

In the hall was no movement save the shifting of shadows from the windblown gas jet. The two men, *Spider* and policeman, lay side by side and did not stir. Shrill voices made an excited gabble below. Tenants had heard the sounds of struggle. They were uncertain what had occurred or where it had happened.

Patsy Malone hurried back into the hall, called down the stair well: "Get a doctor!" she cried. "Go get Doctor Simmons. Shane is hurt!"

A man's voice shouted an answer and Patsy Malone turned back to stare down at the two bodies, the gun ready. Leaning her hips against the railing, she was a small, worried girl. There was a vertical pucker between her arched brows. Her black curling hair was disheveled and she brushed it up off her forehead with an impatient wrist. A tremor tugged at her chin, but she set her lips stubbornly. She began to walk up and down the hall, four short steps toward the head of the stairs, four short steps back. Her movements were light and graceful.

A low groan from one of the men stopped her, poised and alert, the automatic jerking up. The sound was not repeated and presently she resumed her anxious pacing. Feet pounded on the steps and Coxwell's ruddy, round face showed in the stairwell. He stopped, staring down at the two men.

"You took long enough," Patsy said tartly.

"I couldn't find a cop," Coxwell's breath was short. "I stopped by home to leave Junior, then I couldn't find a cop. I called them up finally and they wanted my life history before they'd send a radio car around. . . ."

"But they're coming?" Patsy demanded.

"They're coming," Coxwell nodded.

The words echoed like his own knell in the ears of the *Spider*. He had regained consciousness a few seconds before and had tested Patsy's alertness with a groan. He did not like the competent way in which she handled that automatic. She would know how to use it and even an excited woman could hardly miss him at this distance. But he must find a way out. If he were captured in this disguise, police would need no damning automatic pistol to convict him of murder.

He studied the scene beneath lowered lids. Perhaps, the policeman beside him would regain consciousness first and distract them—give Wentworth his chance. But it would have to be soon. Radio patrolmen traveled fast. It could not be many moments before the men showed up. The sound of tumbling feet gave Wentworth a brief chance to hope. But it was very brief. Shane Malone staggered drunkenly into the hall. When he saw Wentworth, supine upon the floor, he dropped the hands that gripped his aching head and slammed his foot heavily against Wentworth's side.

"You louse!" he growled, and drew back his foot again.

Wentworth stiffened his muscles. He must not wince. He must take this blow without flinching or he would betray the fact that he had recovered consciousness and all chance of tricking Patsy Malone and escaping would be lost. In his mind, he could imagine already the eager clamor of the newspapers over his capture, the boastful words of the Avenger.

"Stop it, Shane," Patsy ordered sharply. "There's no sense in kicking a man when he's down."

Shane grumbled, but he desisted and Wentworth had hard work to suppress a sigh of relief. The boy reeled toward the steps, muttering something about a drink and Coxwell stood over the *Spider*.

"You haven't tied him up," he said, his voice quaking.

"You do it," Patsy ordered. "I don't want to get close to him with this gun. He might be shamming unconsciousness."

Wentworth's eyes glinted beneath the lowered lids. That young woman knew tactics. But her efficiency meant his own doom. If he were bound, he would have no chance at all of getting away before police arrived on the scene. He must not be bound. He simply must not! But what chance did he have, flat on his back this way, with that gun keeping watch? He must act and act quickly.

Deep in his throat, Wentworth groaned. He rolled his head. If he could persuade Coxwell to make a hasty attempt to tie him up . . . Damn it! Coxwell was shrinking back, rather than advancing.

"Hurry!" Patsy snapped. "Tie him up. I won't be able to hold him after he comes to. He's slippery. Hurry, I tell you!"

Coxwell hung back a moment, then dropped on his knees and began to fumble with Wentworth's belt to use on his wrists. As he bent over, the *Spider's* arms jerked upward and clamped about his neck. Coxwell

208

uttered a strangled cry, tried to heave erect. He was a big man, wide-shouldered and strong and his jerk flung him to his feet, dragging Wentworth with him. His fists slammed against the *Spider's* sides, hammered his breath out in gusts between set teeth.

Wentworth had counted too much on the man's fear. Apparently, Coxwell was brave enough when he was cornered and his big fists were scoring painfully. And Wentworth was handicapped. He must keep Coxwell between his body and Patsy's automatic.

He wrestled Coxwell about so that together they blocked the hall. Patsy, hovering behind the big man with her automatic raised and ready, found it impossible to shoot. Abruptly, the *Spider* slammed the crown of his head under Coxwell's chin. The big man straightened with a grunt, went limp.

Instantly, Wentworth seized the rail with both hands, vaulted over to the steps. He landed in a sprawl halfway down to the floor below, twisted an ankle painfully. Men and women broke and ran screaming as he thudded. Patsy called out a sharp order to halt.

Wentworth seized the rail and vaulted again, landing in the hall and putting the ceiling between himself and that threatening gun. He almost cried out with pain in his ankle but he could not pause. Only one flight of stairs now was between himself and the safety of the street. He hurried painfully along, limping to favor his twisted ankle, darted down the last stairs.

Brakes squealed at the front door and two bounding figures in blue uniform plunged up the steps from the street. Wentworth cursed and spun toward the rear. A tall man in his undershirt stood there, gripping a heavy iron poker in both hands. As the *Spider* plunged toward him, he whipped it up over his head. But he had miscalculated the height of the ceiling. The poker struck, jarring his hands, breaking his swing. Before he could set himself again, Wentworth sprang upon him.

His right fist smashed home and the man reeled against the wall, not out, but momentarily dazed. Wentworth caught him by his shoulders and whirled him into the middle of the hall. While the man still swayed there, he pounded on toward the rear exit of the tenement. The police shouted excited warnings, but that hulking figure in the middle of the hall kept them from firing.

Wentworth dived out the door, reached a fence in a bound and gripping its top, flung himself over. As he landed, he whistled shrilly three times. It was a piercing sound that would carry a long way. It would signal Ram Singh to get the car under way, to look for him when he burst to the street and be ready for a quick getaway.

Wentworth whirled toward the next tenement, racing through it toward the front while the police pounded through the other building toward the back. He knew that other police cars must be racing to the scene. A half-dozen at least would be sent, if Coxwell had told them the *Spider* was stretched unconscious on the floor of the building. But for moments, the way would be clear, and with Ram Singh to pick him up from a flying start. . . .

He burst out of the front door, poised in the darkness while his glance swept the street for the coupé. It was nowhere in sight!

A harsh curse tore Wentworth's throat. He whirled toward the back of the building and heard heavy feet hit the floor. A policeman had climbed the fence in his wake. He swung out of the front door, leaping to the pavement.

"Hands up!" The order was howled from the other tenement.

Wentworth spun that way, looked down the barrel of a revolver held tensely in a policeman's hand. It was a moment for quick thought and quicker action. Within seconds, the other policeman would reinforce the first. Within minutes, other police cars would rocket into the street. And to be captured in the garb of the *Spider* meant death as surely as if those robes were lined with poisoned needles. Yet Wentworth could not use lethal weapons against the police. For all his lawlessness, for all his death-dealing to criminals, he had never fired on protectors of the law.

Nevertheless, his hand flashed toward his underarm holster and he cursed defiance of the policeman. The officer's face hardened, his hand contracted and the revolver belched flame and lead straight at Wentworth, who cried out in a choked voice, diving to the pavement, his legs jerking convulsively.

"I got him!" the cop yelled. "I killed the *Spider!*"

He sprang to Wentworth's side, caught him by the shoulder. Wentworth's arm flew out and the man's legs shot from under him. He came down hard and the *Spider's* fist, the rolling weight of his body, met his jaw. Then Wentworth was up and sprinting down the street. The police car was at the curb, but he ignored that, except to shoot off a tire as he raced past.

He had played a hair's-breadth game and had won. When he had gone for his gun, it had been for the sole purpose of forcing the policeman to shoot. The hardening of the man's face, the inevitable tightening of the mouth and eyes that betrayed the decision to shoot, had been sufficient warning. Wentworth had gone down with the flash instead of after it. His head had gone down under the bullet in the instant the policeman fired. A hole ripped in the back brim of his hat, a furrow across his shoulder burned by the same bullet bore witness to the closeness of his escape.

Behind him, a gunshot whip-cracked through the cold night and lead sang shrilly past his ear. Two more strides, once more the whimpering song of lead and he went around the corner with a bullet hole in the flapping tail of his cape. Seconds later, a radio car skated around the corner on hot rubber, roared toward the tenement. Wentworth spurted into a second cross street, loped on for another block and, changing his direction a third time, dropped to a walk, his chest pumping. He felt prickles of heat over his entire body at the narrowness of his escape and once more he was aware of the pain in his ankle. He limped heavily onward.

*   *   *

Twice now he had tangled with the Avenger, and the man had slipped from his grasp. He was no nearer knowledge of him now than he had been before, no nearer testing his theory of a connection between the man and the horrors that had been loosed on the city. That girl whose tormented screams rang now in his memory would be disfigured for life, her fresh youthful beauty ruined. Nita had barely escaped.

Mounting within him, Wentworth felt the familiar tide of white wrath against these unscrupulous criminals who preyed upon the innocent. He had foiled a hundred plots, sent a thousand criminals to their deaths, but still the wanton killing went on. Always some new monster lifted his head, devised some new means of squeezing money from the people by means of death and torture and mawkish terror.

Wentworth still felt convinced that the Avenger was in some way tied up with this new attack, but he had been stopped at every point in his efforts to make sure. He must turn from the pursuit of this phantom, pick up the direct trail of these poisoners—these destroyers of women's beauty. Such clues to the Avenger as remained must be followed by Jackson and Ram Singh while he turned to the trail of the poisoners.

But where was Ram Singh? Wentworth had left his faithful Hindu with implicit directions to remain ready for a quick getaway, yet the car and his man had been gone when he most needed them. Either Ram Singh had been seized, or . . . By heaven, that must be it! Ram Singh must have seen the Avenger fleeing the scene of their conflict, figured that his departure meant the end of danger for the *Spider* and followed the man!

Eagerly, Wentworth sought a dark doorway and divested himself of the main part of his disguise, shrugged the hunch from his shoulders and sought a 'phone. If Ram Singh had picked up a trail, he would communicate at once with Jenkyns, the aged butler at Wentworth's Fifth Avenue apartment. That was standard procedure. Eagerly, Wentworth put through his call.

"Yes, sir," Jenkyns' dignified old voice reported. "Ram Singh 'phoned. He said he had struck a hot trail and would call again."

Wentworth's step was buoyant as he left the 'phone-booth and took a taxi to his apartment. Perhaps after all, he was to have one more chance to try conclusions with this Hooded Man whom all the city idolized, whom the *Spider* alone suspected of duplicity. The new Negro operator of his private elevator smiled slowly, showing his white teeth, as he bowed Wentworth into the car and sent it smoothly upward fifteen stories to his penthouse.

"Lots of folks ask for you tonight, sir," the boy reported in his slow drawl. "Mr. Kirkpatrick upstairs. I shooed a lot of newspapermen away."

Wentworth nodded with a frown, his mind flicking back to the automatic that the Avenger still held, the automatic that would identify Richard Wentworth as the *Spider* and a murderer. Wentworth felt his muscles tightening, knew that subconsciously he had thrown himself upon the balls of his feet as if prepared for flight or battle. Had he escaped police and the Avenger, only to have Kirkpatrick come for him with the evidence to condemn him?

Slowly, Wentworth fought the tension from his breast, made his muscles relax. He did not want to question the operator, but he had said that Kirkpatrick was in his apartment and had not mentioned other police. Kirkpatrick would not have come alone if an arrest was intended. Furthermore, there had been no furtive shadows on the street to close in on his flanks. No, he was allowing his fears to betray him.

The operator slid open the door and Wentworth tightened again, feeling muscles quiver throughout his body as he spotted four men waiting in the hall before his door. Then he recognized them as newspapermen and he made his step nonchalant as he left the cage.

"Get out of here, bums," he said, and felt that his smile was obviously forced. He could not immediately shake off the fears that had gripped him.

The four men sighed in unison. "So you decided to come home at last?" one, a tall, hatless skeleton of a man jeered. "Come on, now, Wentworth, what you got to say about the Avenger? You know, he claims you're the *Spider*."

"No statement, boys," Wentworth said crisply. He stepped to his door, thumbed the bell button. He was frowning while the news men clamored about him. He could not operate effectively with all these men hounding him. Everywhere he turned, a newspaperman bobbed up at his elbow. They were keeping too close tabs on his movements, playing into the Avenger's hands.

Surveillance was the last thing in the world he wanted now. He must be free to operate against the poisoners, against the acid-destroyers. God alone knew how many more would be stricken if he did not strike at the criminals. His eyes narrowed angrily as a small, earnest youth with an excited gleam in his eyes thrust between him and the door.

"You can't defy the press like this, Mr. Wentworth," he said earnestly. "The people have a right to know the truth."

Wentworth shoved him aside gently, hiding his anger. "Take this infant away, Gallahan," he told the hatless skeleton, "and tell him the facts of life."

Gallahan guffawed. "He's a journalist, Wentworth," he said. "Just out of Columbia. But you better give us something to shut up the desk. Otherwise they'll keep us camping on your doorstep all night."

Wentworth hesitated. What Gallahan said was true. The news men were all friendly to him. He had met them a dozen times in his work as an amateur criminologist under his real name and when he visited his friend, Kirkpatrick, at headquarters. But they would have to stick until they got something that would pass as a statement.

"All right," he said, with resignation and grinned as the young journalist drew out a notebook and a pencil. None of the other newspapermen had even a piece of paper in their hands. They depended upon their trained memories and only jotted down a few important facts, usually after the interview was over. "All right, I've got just this to say: the Avenger is no Robin Hood. He has pocketed at least ten times as much loot as he has given to the poor. As to his charges, they aren't new. I've been accused before this of being the *Spider* because our trails crossed in working on the same cases. Your files will verify the exonerations."

He turned to find Jenkyns holding the door open. His ruddy old face worried beneath the crown of his silvery hair.

"But, Mr. Wentworth," the youngster crowded forward again, "that's no answer. Are you the *Spider?*"

Gallahan caught the youngster by the collar and pulled him away struggling.

"Want to answer that one, Wentworth?" he asked quietly.

"The answer is yes, of course," Wentworth said with a smile. "I'm also the Avenger in disguise and that long missing gentleman, Judge Crater. If you dig into my past, you will find suspicious indications also that I am the Lindbergh baby. . . ."

CHAPTER SEVEN

Death's Profit

He closed the door on the guffaws of Gallahan and peered sharply into Jenkyns' face. The old butler was very portly and dignified in his satin knee breeches, but his eyes were tortured. Wentworth surrendered his cape and broad-brimmed hat with a significant glance that told Jenkyns to dispose of them quickly.

"Mr. Kirkpatrick is awaiting you, sir," Jenkyns said impassively. "He has brought Ram Singh home. Wounded, sir."

With a startled exclamation, Wentworth strode into his living room, batting aside the portières with a sweep of his arm. Ram Singh struggled to his feet from a davenport and stood, swaying weakly, a white bandage about his throat.

"Be thou seated, O my wounded warrior," Wentworth told him in Hindustani, and strode across to clasp the hand of his friend, Stanley Kirkpatrick, commissioner of police.

"This was kind of you, Kirk," he said. "Bringing my boy home."

Kirkpatrick looked quizzically into his eyes. "That was not my sole purpose in coming, Dick," he said.

Wentworth lifted his eyebrows in surprise, but his masked gaze studied the saturnine countenance of his friend. Inwardly all was turmoil again. All his fears and tension returned. First, he had been struck with disappointment that Ram Singh had lost the trail when he had hoped to close with the Avenger. Apprehension for his Hindu boy was assuaged now, but the new menace in Kirkpatrick's voice and words shook him anew.

Yet he did not believe his friend had come to arrest him. Wentworth could not picture Kirkpatrick coming to perform that task yet delaying, before he left his office, to attach a gardenia in his lapel as he had. The man was groomed with his usual meticulous perfection, black mustaches waxed to needle points. The perfecto was held so steadily between his lean fingers that the pale blue thread of smoke from it rose straight and unagitated. But Kirkpatrick's blue eyes were shrewd beneath his level brows and there was a light in them that Wentworth could not quite interpret. Wentworth nodded, perfect amiability masking his inward questioning of Kirkpatrick's visit.

"If you will have a seat, Kirk, until I can make sure that Ram Singh is comfortable, I'll be with you. Jenkyns has already found your favorite Scotch for you, I see."

He crossed to Ram Singh and bent solicitously over his shoulder, asking a quiet question in English. His mind scarcely attended Ram Singh's reply in the same language. He still worried over Kirkpatrick's visit. But each thing in its time. He must listen to Ram Singh.

"I followed a Hooded One I believed to be this man who calls himself the Avenger," said the Hindu in his harsh, slightly nasal voice. "He went into the City Morgue and when he came out, he walked directly to my car. Evidently, he had seen I followed him. Before I had any warning of his intention, he smashed the window of the car with the hilt of a knife and struck at my throat. I had the engine running and jerked into gear at that instant so that his blade grazed, instead of piercing my throat. When I got from the car to attack, he had fled."

"It is considerably more than a graze, Dick," Kirkpatrick interjected in his dry way. "A half-inch to the left and you would be minus a valuable assistant. Luckily the jugular was not ruptured."

"Rest, O Ram Singh," said Wentworth formally. "Tomorrow there is much for us to do."

Ram Singh got weakly to his feet. He had lost much blood. But Wentworth offered no assistance, knowing that the doughty Sikh would consider a helping hand little short of an insult. The Hindu held his turbanned head proudly as he stalked from the room. Wentworth shook his head slowly, turned to Kirkpatrick with a smile that masked his concern over the commissioner's visit.

"I don't know what I ever did to deserve such faithful men," he said, "but my score with the Avenger is over-heavy now. He shot Jackson. Now he knifes Ram Singh. Furthermore, I believe him to be connected with the forty-seven poisoning deaths of the last two weeks and with the disfigurement of seventeen women tonight."

Kirkpatrick's alert eyes narrowed, his brows lifted. "Any evidence?"

"Not a scintilla," Wentworth admitted.

Kirkpatrick said grimly, "I should like to get evidence against someone in those deaths. They number ninety-seven now and two hundred and four women are in the hospitals with acid burns on their faces."

A startled oath ripped from Wentworth. Truly the criminals, whoever they were, struck with fearful and remorseless efficiency. Two hundred women ruined for life, nearly a hundred human beings slaughtered, and all for no apparent reason.

"By God," he swore, "these crimes must be stopped!"

There was fierce agreement on Kirkpatrick's face, but the quizzical gleam remained in his eyes. "It may be that the Avenger is behind it," he said slowly. "Certainly he does not hesitate to attack anyone. He has gone after the *Spider*, now."

Wentworth, feeling again the surge of anger that he had known on first learning of the horror the criminals had wrought, glimpsed sardonic amusement in Kirkpatrick's eye. Kirkpatrick knew beyond question that Wentworth was the *Spider* and had told him so to his face, but there never had been any final proof of that fact. Furthermore, Kirkpatrick admired and respected this killer of the night who struck swiftly and surely where the law's machinery, for all Kirkpatrick's brilliance, could move with only cautious tread. And he had declared an armed truce with Wentworth.

When he could, he would help the *Spider* in his battles against the underworld, but if ever there came a time when proof was put into his hands—such as that automatic which now the Avenger held—he would act with the full power and brilliance of which he was capable, even if that meant sending his closest friend to the electric chair.

That was why amusement brushed his eyes now, for necessarily these two always referred to the *Spider* in the third person, as if he were another entity; as if no peril lurked over Wentworth's head; as if that fact could never terribly split their friendship into bloody warfare.

Wentworth met his amusement with a swift question, a polite interest. His heart was drumming. He had been right then, in supposing that Kirkpatrick's visit had to do with the *Spider!*

"The Avenger delivered into police hands tonight," Kirkpatrick began slowly, answering Wentworth's question, "a damning piece of evidence against the *Spider.*"

Wentworth felt rigidity creep into his poise. Good God! Had he been wrong in his deductions? Had the Avenger after all given Kirkpatrick the automatic? He fought the rigidity, compelled his facial muscles to maintain that air of polite interest. He could not look away. He must keep his eyes on Kirkpatrick's.

"However," the commissioner drawled, "the evidence is not so helpful as it might be. It is a motion

219

picture of the *Spider* killing that gambler, Mannley. Unfortunately, the *Spider* wore his usual mask."

Wentworth drew a deep, slow breath as Kirkpatrick pulled his eyes away and turned toward the davenport where he picked up a brief case. It was bad, this latest blow of the Avenger, but it was not as damaging as he had feared. He had been careful to cover all identifying details. His eyes jerked abruptly to Kirkpatrick's compact, assured body as he caught a glint of metal and saw him extract an automatic pistol from the brief case. Some new evidence? But Wentworth was beyond further shocks now. The evening had been nerve-racking. Any new blow would be anti-climactic. Surely, the Great Playwright must see that! No more tonight.

There was a dullness in Wentworth's eyes, a slackness that extended throughout his body as he saw Kirkpatrick turn with the automatic.

"The bullets from this gun did not match with that from Mannley's body," said the commissioner and held out the gun.

Wentworth reached out his hand carelessly for it, but Kirkpatrick did not release it. His fingers tightened on the barrel which he held. Wentworth felt a numbing coldness in his brain. Good Lord! Some new issue to face? He forced a mild surprise into the lifting of his eyebrows, drove himself to meet his friend's shrewd, blue eyes.

"But," said Kirkpatrick softly. "I do not see why you found it necessary to rout the numbers off your gun."

Wentworth's heart gave a violent thump, then beat hard and slowly in his chest. For a moment he had believed the police had discovered that the weapon bore other numbers than his own. But this was just as bad. It was a criminal offense to remove the registered numbers from a fire-arm. He twisted his forehead into a puzzled frown as the automatic came free in his hand. He twisted it up to stare where the number should have been as if he could not quite believe the statement.

"Not just filed off, Dick," Kirkpatrick went on softly, "but routed out. That is a criminal's trick. As long as they are only filed off, certain acid treatments can restore the destroyed numbers by revealing the impression the die made in the basic steel fibres. Criminals have got hold of that fact and use a router which not only removes the number, but twists the steel fibres beneath so that not even the acids can restore the number. That is what has been done on this automatic."

Wentworth slipped a jeweler's loup' from a table drawer, and studied the surface of the gun closely with the glass screwed into his eye. He felt a mild sense of surprise that his hand did not tremble. Lord, what was the way out of this tangle? He doubted that Kirkpatrick would press charges on account of the routing, but it was a bad spot, especially if his own weapon should turn up later. Suppose the Avenger was keeping it to plant beside some murdered man to doubly damn him! He must disown this weapon. There was no other way.

"This is not my gun," he said slowly.

"It is the gun you gave Trowbridge as your own," Kirkpatrick replied sharply.

Wentworth nodded. "If you recall," he said, "the Avenger and I struggled in Mannley's room. My weapon was knocked from my hand and naturally I supposed when I picked this one up from the floor that it was mine. It is the same make and caliber and I did not examine it closely at the time."

"Than this is the Avenger's weapon?"

Wentworth shrugged. "I have no way of telling. As you say, it is obviously a criminal's weapon."

The two men stood facing each other, both frowning, their eyes masking true thoughts. The mouths of both were set and grim.

"I cannot doubt you speak the truth, Dick," said Kirkpatrick slowly. "I have never known you to lie to me even when the truth might incriminate you. But I must point out that if this is not your gun, then the

221

test of the bullet can not clear you of the Avenger's charges.''

Wentworth had expected that, but it was a type of charge he was prepared to meet. He seemed to become a half-inch taller as he drew himself up. His shoulders were braced stiffly, and his gray blue eyes were cold.

''I was not aware,'' he said stiffly, ''that the Avenger's charges were to be taken seriously. Do you wish to put me under arrest?''

Kirkpatrick stared his friend directly in the eyes and slowly the straightened corners of his mouth relaxed.

''No, Dick,'' he said, a little wearily, ''I do not wish to put you under arrest. I am just pointing out a fact to you, a fact that can be very dangerous. I don't know whether the Avenger took your gun or whether your gun fired the bullet that killed Mannley. But you are fighting the Avenger, that I know, and your gun in his hands is a peril to you. Dick, for God's sake, why don't you give up this dangerous life?''

Wentworth allowed himself to relax slightly. He crossed to the table where decanter and soda stood, poured Scotch into a glass and squirted soda into it. He needed a moment to steady himself before he turned slowly to face Kirkpatrick again. This was dangerous ground he was treading.

''Sooner or later, Dick,'' Kirkpatrick said seriously, ''you are bound to make a mistake. Evidence that you are the *Spider* will fall into my hands and you know that, even if afterward I killed myself for it, I would use that evidence as it should be employed. You seem to bear a charmed life where the bullets of your enemies are concerned. But it can't go on. Not forever!''

Earnestly, Kirkpatrick stepped toward Wentworth, placed a hand on either shoulder. For once Wentworth did not meet his eyes, kept his gaze on the pale amber liquor that he sloshed thoughtfully about in his glass. He knew in what deep affection the commissioner held him and he reciprocated it fully. Sometimes, it was good sport to match wits with him, but there had been times—as now—when it was not so pleasant. Times when it seemed inevitable that they must meet in life or death struggle.

If he did not meet Kirkpatrick's gaze, it was not because he could not. It was because he feared that the pain he felt at this meeting might be too plainly there, the pain that he could not answer his friend straightforwardly.

"I don't ask you to consider me, Dick," Kirkpatrick went on and his fingers ate deep into Wentworth's shoulders. "Men are men and can take the blows as they come. But, Dick . . . think of Nita. Think what your downfall would cost her. She would bear it proudly, because it is her blood and her heritage. But it would kill her, Dick, as surely as if the bullet that brought you down, the electric current in the chair, passed through her own body."

Wentworth was rigid under his grip now. The glass was clenched tightly in his hand, so tightly that it quivered slightly. Kirkpatrick was silent for a moment. When he spoke again, his voice was rasping and harsh.

"For God's sake, Dick, quit before it is too late. I feel . . . I feel that the end is near. I feel it here." He dropped his hands from Wentworth's shoulders and pounded a doubled fist against his chest.

A quiver ran through Wentworth. He was not superstitious, but he was a fatalist. He believed that in every man's life, the days were numbered. He believed that he, too, someday would come face to face with that day. When his muscles would falter in a crisis, when his bullet would not speed true; when his overwearied brain would make a mistake he could not rectify. For a moment the picture that Kirkpatrick had conjured up flicked through his mind. Nita, with him dead in the electric chair or bowled over by a gangster's bullet . . .

There was a sharp, tinkling crash and Wentworth looked down at his hand and saw that the glass had crushed in his grip. There was a tiny red gash of red across his fingers, an irregular damp splotch upon the golden pile of the carpet.

"Careless of me," he muttered.

The mask dropped over his face. He could not permit himself these thoughts. He drove the quiver of apprehension from his body, the sick thoughts from his mind, looked up with a quick smile.

"You know," he said, "I would have sworn it was impossible for a man to crush a glass in his hand. It must have been cracked."

Kirkpatrick stared at him with eyes that had grown haggard. His face seemed suddenly drawn and old. His head shook slowly; he sucked in a deep breath, then moved his shoulders wearily as though he adjusted them to an ancient and heavy burden.

"I knew it wouldn't do any good, Dick," he said dully. "But I had to try. I'm telling you the truth." Once more he struck his clenched fist against his chest. "I feel it here. This is the end!"

Wentworth's heart went out to his friend, but there was nothing he could do, nothing he could say. Even his expression of understanding would put an additional burden upon his friend, a bit of evidence against the *Spider* that he must ignore. And he could not turn from the path to which he had set his feet. Until the bitter end, he would drive on for the salvation of humanity, fight for the people against the encroachment of the underworld. When the end came—

He smiled slowly, a grimace that was stiff upon his otherwise expressionless face.

"Jenkyns," he raised his voice. "Bring another glass. And bring Mr. Kirkpatrick a gardenia."

Kirkpatrick looked slowly down to his lapel. The flower was crushed.

CHAPTER EIGHT

The Murders Go On

The two men stood silently while Jenkyns came and went. When Kirkpatrick spoke again, it was as if he had never brought up the subject of the *Spider*.

"Have you any idea of who the Avenger might be?" he asked quietly.

Wentworth made a grimace, told Kirkpatrick of the three men he had seen at Mannley's who might fit the description, Commander Samuels, the croupier Larue with his green eye-shade, and Deputy Marshant. Kirkpatrick jerked a hand impatiently.

"They're all out of the question," he said irritably. "How about young Shane Malone?"

Wentworth shook his head decidedly. "Just a kid, and besides I saw him and the Avenger side by side."

"But Ram Singh saw two men in the Avenger's disguise," Kirkpatrick pointed out. "That might easily have been framed as an alibi for Malone if the need arose."

Wentworth laughed, but the sound was a little shaky—emotion had left its mark. He crossed to the taborette to mix himself another drink. "Your guess is as good as mine," he said. "There is no clue except the Russian accent, and that might easily be assumed. The Avenger told the newspapers he was a famous detective, which probably means that he isn't. I suggest that we check on the movements of these men I have mentioned and see first whether they have alibis. But I'll admit that if any one of them had alibis for all the occasions, it would be more suspicious than otherwise."

Kirkpatrick brushed the whole matter aside, his saturnine face gone grave.

"Frankly, I am less interested in the Avenger's forays than in these poison murders," he said, his words clipped and brittle. "You have a hunch the two are connected, but that scarcely justifies our hunting for only one man."

Wentworth agreed with that. It was the decision he had reached himself. Despite the threat of the automatic that the Avenger held, he determined to throw all his energies into a quest for the criminals behind the poison and acid attacks. . . .

The next day found the death-toll mounting steadily and only when Kirkpatrick enforced a rigid embargo on the sale of both canned meat and cosmetics did the hospital reports dwindle.

Death broke out also in neighboring cities, in New Jersey, and even as far upstate as Albany. By night of the second day, two thousand were dead and the women whose faces were destroyed were nearly triple that number!

The canned meat company, to which the poison had been traced, was indicted for criminal negligence as was the cosmetic firm. Both were deluged with damage suits and bankruptcy was inevitable.

Wentworth was not permitted to forget the Avenger. Eddie Blanton and the other four newspapermen had been only an advance guard, for day and night, his doors were besieged by reporters. The Avenger had reinforced his charges against Wentworth by publicizing the motion picture film he had sent to police. Huge full-length pictures from it were printed by newspapers and showed the *Spider* killing the gambler, Mannley; showed him printing his seal upon the ace of spades.

One newspaper was running a series of full-page articles called: "Who is the *Spider*?" These detailed every battle which the *Spider* had fought with the underworld. They gave police records of the number of times Richard Wentworth had been put under arrest on charges that identified him with the *Spider*—and they printed in just as great detail, his exonerations. The *Press*, for which Eddie Blanton worked, was offering a ten-thousand-dollar reward for evidence that would convict anyone of being the *Spider*.

Added to the fifty thousand dollars which already had been placed upon the *Spider's* head, it made a small fortune. An army of amateur and private detectives camped upon Wentworth's trail, since the newspapers pointed out that absolute proof would be necessary.

It was the day on which Jackson came home from the hospital that Wentworth learned through a news flash that the Avenger had struck in Chicago; he wounded two men and left two others helpless prisoners beside the looted safe of a large jewelry concern. It was unfortunate, the Avenger 'phoned the newspapers, that he had been unable to save the loot.

Nita was with Wentworth a few hours later when the newspapers reported that the Avenger had struck again, that he had deposited near police headquarters the body of a gangster who, the Avenger said, had slain a witness to a killing. The gangster was one of the chief aids of the dead gang leader, O'Burke, a man who might logically have succeeded to his scepter. It was the Avenger's first kill and Wentworth smiled thinly over the entry and summoned Ram Singh and Jackson to him.

"I shall fly to Chicago tomorrow," he told his faithful servants, keen eyes studying both. "After these victories of the Avenger, I expect that the poisoners will be busy in Chicago tomorrow and I wish to be there to investigate. I leave to you the running down of such clues as we have here.

"Ram Singh, look over all of Mannley's associates.

There must have been a connection between him and the Avenger."

The Hindu bowed, sweeping his cupped hands to his turbanned forehead.

"*Han, sahib,*" his nasal voice was strong.

"I want you also to check up on three men: Commander Samuels; the croupier at Mannley's who is built like the Avenger and wears a green eye-shade; and Mr. Kirkpatrick's deputy, Marshant."

"*Han, sahib,*" Ram Singh repeated. He turned and strode from the room.

"Jackson," Wentworth said his eyes boring into the clear blue gaze of his ex-sergeant. "I want you to investigate Patsy Malone."

Jackson's expression did not change, his eyes did not waver, but Wentworth thought he detected a tensing of the prominent muscles along his wide jaws, a heritage from some Gascon forebear.

"I am not ready," Wentworth continued gravely, "to accuse her of deliberately assisting a plot against me. Her behavior at the time I invaded her apartment might well have been gratitude for the Avenger returning that forged check to her brother. But I do believe that the Avenger used her and her brother to set a trap for me."

"If the major pleases," Jackson interrupted, his voice wooden, "might it not have been possible for this crook, Mannley, to trap Shane, then have a man of his get nasty to Pat—to Miss Malone—in the restaurant where they knew I ate?"

Wentworth nodded slowly, his eyes serious as he studied Jackson's loyal face.

"Yes, that would have been easily possible," he agreed. "I want you to discover that man's identity and learn whatever else is possible about the connection between Patsy Malone and the Avenger.

"I have prepared to disappear from sight and completely wipe out my identity as Wentworth if the Avenger acts against me," he added slowly. "But it is a step for dire emergency only. It would hamper me

228

terrifically in my work. I want to locate the man and clip his claws first. I know I am asking a great deal of you, Jackson, to ask that you investigate a girl in whom you evidently are deeply interested, but it is for that very reason that I assign you to the task."

Jackson's brows tightened down over his eyes. "The major asks nothing. If I hadn't horned in and got myself shot . . ."

"We won't mention that angle of it, Jackson," Wentworth said kindly. "Just push on with the investigation and learn what you can. Also, I will arrange a *Spider* disguise for you. I want you to show yourself in it once or twice while I am in Chicago to mislead police and the Avenger and so to give me a possible alibi."

Jackson saluted, about-faced and stalked from the room with his shoulders set stiffly. His wound had begun to heal and would not hinder him in his work, provided he did not tangle in a rough-and-ready fight with the criminals. When Jackson had gone, Wentworth turned to Nita and found a faint smile upon her lips.

"Jackson loves that girl," she said softly.

Wentworth nodded agreement. "But he is loyal to me," he pointed out, "and because the girl must know his affections are involved, I think she will be truthful with him."

Nita obviously was not thinking of Jackson and the girl. Her eyes were intent under lowered lids. Her head was thrown back against the wine-red of the velvet-covered davenport and a shaded lamp made bronze lights among her curls.

"Is what you told Jackson true, Dick," she asked gently. "Are you prepared to disappear entirely?"

"Yes," Wentworth told her. "You are thinking that it was perhaps unwise to tell a man of divided loyalties my plans?"

"That, yes," Nita agreed, "and also—" she hesitated, lifting her head and looking down at a cigarette she tapped absently against a case, "and also you hadn't told me your plans."

Wentworth did not smile as he stepped swiftly forward and snapped flame to Nita's cigarette. "I'm not going to tell you, sweetheart, either," he said quietly. "If I disappear, it will be because Kirkpatrick has in his hands evidence that will convict me of being the *Spider*. You wouldn't expect me to involve you in any such mess as that would you?"

Nita rose slowly to her feet, tossing the cigarette into a tray. "But if I insist on being involved?" Her red lips were curved invitingly, but her eyes were deadly serious.

Wentworth caught her close in his arms. His mouth shut grimly. Nita leaned backward in his arms, hands upon his shoulders, eyes gazing steadily into his. Wentworth's stiff lips twisted into the mockery of a smile. "I cannot, dear," he told her. "I refuse to involve you."

And though Nita first coaxed, then grew angry, he would not reveal his plans. She smiled wanly as she prepared to leave, then suddenly flung herself into his arms.

"Oh, Dick," she gasped. "For both our sakes, be careful!"

His answer was a kiss and Nita left pushing her way disdainfully through a group of questioning newspapermen who waited always outside his door.

Wentworth prepared swiftly to leave the city. He packed no clothing, carried no luggage, He merely picked up a cane, shrugged into his dark overcoat and stalked out of his apartment a few minutes behind Nita.

The reporter, Eddie Blanton, was immediately at his side, a grin on his horsey face. "Going out to make a kill, *Spider?*" he jibed.

Wentworth nodded gravely. "Yes, I've decided your city editor must answer for his sins. He abuses his men."

Blanton swept a bow so low that he threatened to

230

pitch forward on his face. "I shall be your eternal debtor," he swore.

The other newspapermen watched narrowly, piled into the elevator behind Wentworth. He stalked through the lobby with the entire straggling crowd on his heels. Outside the door of his building, a group of people stood. Bedraggled boys, dirty faced and scantily clothed, pointing their fingers.

"There goes the *Spider!*" one yelled shrilly.

Men stared at him with speculative eyes from behind the line police had set up, for Wentworth had been compelled to ask Kirkpatrick for a guard against the mobs that newspaper publicity had set upon his heels.

Among the watching crowd were women also. They seemed strangely pale and for a moment that fact puzzled Wentworth. He stared again and found that fear made their countenances haggard, but more than that, not one of them used cosmetics. Powder and rouge and lipstick had been abandoned since acid burns had forced hundreds of women to go through life with faces scarred and welted and disfigured.

The discovery struck Wentworth with the sharp pain of a knife wound. His lips tightened. Something must be done at once to relieve the terror of these people. But how could he act, hampered as he was? Everywhere he went the newspapermen followed. His picture had been smeared over the pages of every newspaper in the city and on the streets, crowds turned to stare at him and urchins pointed grimy fingers. Worse than that, there were dozens of amateur detectives always upon his trail, seeking a share in that sixty-thousand reward.

At the curb, Wentworth signaled a taxi and cursed as he saw recognition even in the driver's eyes. Damn it, he must elude this constant surveillance! The cab buzzed swiftly up Fifth Avenue. Wentworth could find only one cab that seemed to be following and that dropped off before he had covered five blocks. Wentworth frowned heavily. It was probable that Blanton

231

had signaled some other newspaperman, one Wentworth did not know by sight, to take up the trail.

He sent his taxi on a zigzag course until he spotted the cab that trailed him, then he alighted and walked directly toward the machine, climbed in while the passenger looked at him with frightened eyes.

"As long as we're going the same way," Wentworth said, "I may as well save you taxi fare."

The man forced a smile to his lips. "You understand how it is, Mr. Wentworth," he said. "I've got a job to do. . . ."

Wentworth said, "Sure, you have a job to do."

The cab driver was staring back at them, a frown of painful thought wrinkling his face like a monkey's. "Newark airport," Wentworth commanded.

At the airport, three quarters of an hour later, Wentworth, politely but firmly refusing to permit the newspaperman to 'phone his office, bought two tickets for Washington and ushered his prisoner onto the plane. When the co-pilot swung aboard with his passenger list fluttering on a clip board, Wentworth walked excitedly to the door.

"This isn't the plane for Pittsburgh," he said violently. "Let me off of here!"

He thrust the astonished co-pilot aside, climbed to the ground. "I should think you'd keep intelligent attendants around here," he continued angrily. "Telling me this was the Pittsburgh plane!"

The co-pilot apologized and shut the door. The plane took off with the newspaperman aboard, gently sleeping. In about an hour he would recover from the narcotic Wentworth had needled into his veins. By that time the plane would be past Philadelphia and sweeping on toward Baltimore . . . and Wentworth would be well on his way to Chicago.

Dawn was gray in the east and the yellow sprinkling of lights that dusted over Chicago proper was dwindling when Wentworth's plane set down on the field there. He went directly to a hotel and once in his room, flung himself down to sleep. At noon he arose, had lunch and made some purchases. The afternoon papers made no mention of the poisonings he expected, but he was still sure they impended.

In his room, he took his stand before a mirror and went to work on his disguise. He affixed to his upper lip a mustache that followed the line of his mouth and extended below its corners, giving his whole face a slightly discouraged droop. He made his cheeks puffed and ruddy, then oiled his hair and brushed it straight back from his forehead. He grayed the temples and finally donned thick-lensed glasses. He put on a suit of Scotch tweeds, topcoat and a crushed slouch hat, then swaggered out of the hotel with pigskin gloves and a cane in his fist. He walked with a quick, choppy step, tapping the cane briskly, beaming from behind his thick glasses, a smile upon his lips that were thick and much too red. But the smile was forced. Here, too, the women had pale, haunted faces, bare of cosmetics. It seemed to him the men, too, moved with a furtive, frightened air.

Wentworth turned back to his swift, choppy pacing, and a block further on, entered police headquarters. They accepted him and his forged police-card at face value. Carl Southers, it said, of the New York Press had arrived to do a story on the Avenger in Chicago. He was in the station press-room, making himself pleasant to the half-envious, half-sneering newspapermen of Chicago, when the reports of fresh poisonings began to tap into headquarters with the regularity of drum-beats.

A family of five had been stricken in South Chicago. These were Negroes and three had died before they reached the hospital, the other two soon afterward. A relay from nearby Cicero reported two men and a woman had collapsed in a restaurant. In each case, the victims had dined on canned salmon. Wentworth watched these reports with mounting rage. They confirmed his theories about the Avenger, but it was horrible to sit helplessly while human beings died.

Wentworth took a taxi directly to the restaurant

where the last attack had been reported and found that police had closed the place. The cop at the door fended Wentworth off, only grunting at his presscard, and Wentworth paced briskly away with his assumed choppy stride, tapping his cane. He circled the block, entered the alley back of the restaurant. He fished a salmon tin from the restaurant's garbage can. He made a note of the brand and the manufacturer, then paced away again.

When he got back to headquarters there had been fifty-seven more deaths from poison and in each case the victims had eaten salmon.

The deaths were mounting and still the reason for the attack was not apparent. His guess that an outbreak was due in Chicago, based on the fact that the Avenger had shifted his operations to the city, had been confirmed. But he was still as far as ever from discovering motive and methods. And meantime, the slaughter went on.

At the hotel, he went directly to his room—he had retained the key—and found a man leaning against the door with an expression of weary patience on his face. As Wentworth came into sight, the man swayed his weight away from the wall and blinked at him with shrewd, amused eyes.

It was Eddie Blanton. "Howdy, Mr. Wentworth!" he said, grinning.

CHAPTER NINE

A Clue—and Death!

Blanton broke off with a low curse of amazement as Wentworth, opening the door, allowed the light from his room to stream over him.

"That's a damned clever get-up," the reporter said. "You're a dead ringer for one of the boys on the paper. In fact, if I hadn't taken a tip from you and used disguise, come all the way here with you in the same plane, I'd think I'd made a mistake."

Wentworth felt a sinking sensation within him. He had thought himself safe from surveillance for a while. It had been a relief to walk the streets without seeing startled, half-frightened recognition on the faces he passed. Now Blanton had arisen to harass and hamper him. But Wentworth's face showed only annoyance.

"You must excuse me," he said with stiff boorishness, "if I seem inhospitable, but despite your familiar manners, I have no idea what you are talking about."

He entered the room and shut the door, hearing Blanton curse through the panels, and stood staring blankly across the room, hat and coat still on, cane gripped in his hand. He did not for a moment think that his attitude had fooled Blanton. But the fact that the reporter had followed him was a severe handicap. Apparently the newspaperman was keeping a detailed check of his movements and the fact that Wentworth and the *Spider* made a simultaneous appearance in a city would make a nice story for the Press.

Furthermore, the Avenger held evidence that would convict him. Indeed, he might already have turned it over to the police in New York. A feeling of panic, new to his years of battling against unbelievable odds, rippled over Wentworth. He found his muscles tense, found himself listening acutely for the approach of the law's myrmidons. The only sound was Blanton's weary knocking at the door.

Wentworth evaded Blanton by summoning a hotel porter to his room to remove a trunk, bribing the man and walking out in his clothing, face disguised. Blanton trotted after him but Wentworth grinned and would not talk and Blanton went back to the hotel room door to watch.

Wentworth spent the night and all the next day making a list of the firms competing with the handlers of Gold Moon salmon and with the companies which were being driven into bankruptcy by the poison in canned corn beef and the acid in cosmetics.

On the third day after his arrival in Chicago, as he prepared to begin the final phase of his work there, a 'phone call from Nita brought him disquieting news.

"Jackson was almost arrested last night, dear," she reported in a voice she tried vainly to keep unfrightened and calm. "He was out in that *Spider* disguise, wearing the steel mask you prepared for him, and some one saw him and called police. He was surrounded and, in escaping, his mask was torn off. They recognized him as your chauffeur. The newspapers are going crazy with it."

Wentworth went slowly back to work on the disguise, still frowning. His jaw was set grimly as he finished making up his face and left his rooms to begin a rounds of the companies.

Then Wentworth put the matter out of his head for the time being while he followed down the details of his new theory of the poisoning. In each office of companies that distributed canned salmon, he forced his way into the presence of the firm's active head and asked questions.

Had anyone attempted to obtain money from them under threats?

Had anyone offered them an inspection service as a guarantee against poisonings?

Had they been offered insurance against poisonings?

Had they ever had any dealings with racketeers?

In every case, Wentworth met only denials, but in fully half the places he visited, he read fear and evasion in the faces of the officials. The pale, unrouged cheeks of office girls goaded him on. Finally, entering the offices of the Silver Sea salmon company, he saw that he had been preceded by a lean six-footer who rolled his shoulders in a brown camel's-hair coat. The man had a lowering, dark face beneath the turned-down brim of a brown felt and he scowled with feeling when he saw Wentworth.

For Wentworth's disguise screamed that he was policeman, from his broad-toed shoes to his brown derby, from his swagger manner of unaccustomed authority to the piercing suspicious gaze of his eyes. And Wentworth recognized the man, a private detective named Nettleton whom he had once employed. He felt his heart leap with hope. If the company was calling in a private detective, it more than half-confirmed his theories. A firm might fear to inform the police, yet use private agencies.

When the man in the camel's-hair coat scowled at him and jerked his broad shoulders angrily in passing, Wentworth turned and walked out behind him.

"Just a minute," he growled.

The man in the long coat spun about and came at him on pounding feet, jabbing a rigid forefinger against his breastbone.

"Listen, dick," he said sharply. "I've got enough

237

of being ridden by headquarters, see. Just lay off." He spun on his heel.

"I said wait a minute!" Wentworth snapped. He went, heavily heeled, down the hall behind Nettleton.

The detective swung about and his neck was red and swelling with anger.

"I told you I had enough of it," he said in a slow, thick voice. "First off, you frame my partner for blackmail, then you frisk my office, and now you start shadowing me. I'm sick of it, and. . . ."

Wentworth listened to the tirade with his brows knitted, his eyes peering up sharply from under bushy eyebrows. It was apparent the cops had been riding this fellow and he probably had it coming to him. He was hard-boiled and not overscrupulous. But that wasn't going to help Wentworth any in getting information. It was probable that Nettleton had been called in by this firm partly because of his known hostility toward police. He crowded up close to Nettleton and jabbed the muzzle of his automatic against the hard muscle plates of his belly.

"You're coming with me," he said shortly. Nettleton quit talking in the middle of a word and his mouth stayed open. Wentworth whirled him with a punch at his shoulder, slapped over his pockets and took out two guns. Then he herded Nettleton ahead of him out of the building.

"What the hell is this?" the detective demanded furiously.

"It isn't a pinch," Wentworth told him and volunteered nothing else.

He jabbed the man into a coupé he had rented, handcuffed him to the steering post before he, too, climbed in. Nettleton's eyes were small black beads that glittered through lid-crowded slits. Wentworth shoved the car downwind between high factory walls and ignored his prisoner. Gradually Nettleton's anger gave way to a half-fearful bewilderment.

He cursed explosively. "You're no dick!"

Wentworth admitted that without hesitance. "I just

238

wanted to talk to you," he explained, "and I wanted you to be in a reasonable frame of mind. I'm willing to pay for information."

Nettleton's eyes were still narrow, but the gleam in them now had to do with cupidity. "What do you want to know?" he growled. "You sure got your nerve with you, strong-arming me this way."

"What did the Silver Sea people want?" Wentworth asked. "I'm willing to pay five thousand for an answer I can believe."

"Go to hell," Nettleton said savagely.

Wentworth smiled quietly. He knew his man and he knew the meaning of that gleam in Nettleton's eye. In the end he got his information—at a price. The firm had called Nettleton because it feared to go to police. The afternoon before a mild-mannered old professor calling himself Gottstalk had offered an inspection-service as a safeguard against poison getting into their canned goods. He had demanded a hundred thousand a year for the service.

CHAPTER TEN

The Gentle Professor

The president of the company, naturally, had turned him down flat and the man had arisen with a vague smile and said he hoped nothing would happen to poison consumers of Silver Sea salmon. He mentioned that the Golden Moon people had turned down his help.

Nettleton snorted. "It's the old racket in a new dress," he declared. "The old protection racket. In the old days, a man paid or his shop was wrecked. Now they gotta pay or they get wiped out by damage suits and criminal prosecution. Silver Sea wants me to put guards on their plant to keep out poison."

Wentworth heard the story without outward excitement, but inwardly he was burning with his discovery. This was a final confirmation of all that he had speculated. His theory of the explanations behind the poisonings and the use of acids had been purely guesswork, but Nettleton's story confirmed it down to the last detail. Now he was on fire to be rid of the detective and tackle the men behind these murders.

There was a cold certainty within him that he would strike without mercy. Men who could so heartlessly wipe out thousands and mutilate hundreds of women simply to line their pockets deserved not even the break of having a gun in their own hands. They should be shot on sight like the mad dogs that they were. But first he must be rid of Nettleton.

Wentworth pulled the coupé to a halt where a street car line meandered between brick walls, unlocked Nettleton and gave him his guns, empty, plus seven thousand dollars in cash.

Wentworth got rid of his broad-toed shoes, and the rest of the disguise, purchased new materials and had dinner before he drove a newly rented car toward the residence of Professor Gottstalk, which he had previously scouted.

The car seemed almost to sidle up Michigan Boulevard as it fought the howling wind, then turned and scampered down wind on a side street. He drew to a halt in the shadows a half-block away, then walked swiftly up the dark street. Houses sat well back, their glowing orange through the shrubbery. Trees rattled bare boughs overhead. As he pushed along into the wind, windows began to go dark about him.

He had purposely dallied over his supper, taken time to assemble the articles for disguise and now, halting in the dark shadow of a hedge, he swiftly affixed a mustache he had prepared, twisted his mouth with a false scar and used acid to pucker one eye into a squint. Blond wig and brows completed the swift transformation. Then he hurried on. It was nearing midnight and he wanted to enter by the door of the house, rather than risk an invasion by window. He suspected the racketeers would have thrown many guards about the professor and would be painfully alert on the night after he had made his contacts with the potential victims. It would be much more difficult to enter this isolated house than to force his way into apartment quarters in the city.

Minutes later, he swung from the street up the sidewalk to a large house that sat even farther back from the roadway than most of the mansions along Hamilton Avenue. His footsteps rang sharply. His hands in his overcoat pockets, grasped tear-gas bombs. Under his arms nestled two automatics; a blackjack dangled from each wrist, concealed up his sleeves. What he proposed to do was enter the house openly, overpower any guards that showed themselves and take the professor a prisoner.

Wentworth's lips twitched in a small smile and the scar he had executed upon his cheek twisted it into an evil grimace. An open frontal attack would be the last thing these criminals expected—especially from the *Spider*.

The lights blazed out on the porch as he mounted wooden steps. Wentworth took his hands out of his pockets and walked directly to the door, rang the bell. It raised a dim, echoing clangor within and for moments afterward there was silence. Then the door swung inward on comparative darkness. The lights from the porch shone on the bright canary of a girl's dress; it glinted on her hair. Wentworth raised his blond brows and let the scar distort his smile of greeting. The girl was Patsy Malone!

Wentworth could scarcely suppress the mocking laughter that rose to his lips. Here was a sharp and instant confirmation of all suspicions of the Avenger. The girl's connection with the Hooded One was well established in his own mind and now he found her in the home of the collection man of the racketeers! Another fact sent angry blood pumping through his veins. Patsy used cosmetics. *She* had nothing to fear.

Her opening of the door upset his plans. He had planned to knock out the guard at the door, follow that up with a swift and ruthless sweep through the house until he could seize and carry off the professor. But he could not bowl over this girl.

"What do you want?" she asked sharply.

Her small, shapely body was tense with alarm, and there was an artificiality about her voice, a strained, unnatural quality that told Wentworth more plainly than any words that she was not alone. Somewhere in the dim reaches of that hall, Wentworth knew there were

242

guns centering upon him. But there was no change in his manner.

"Howdy, Patsy," he said and stepped forward.

The girl shrank back, and Wentworth was upon her in a bound, left arm sweeping her from her feet and against his breast. His foot kicked back and slammed the door and instantly his hand flicked a gas bomb from his pocket and tossed it back into the hall's shadows. The girl's cry of fright and surprise blended with the muffled blast of the bomb. Wentworth saw its gray vapors rise ghost-like in the half-light, saw two men reeling. They coughed and wheezed frantically, fled into the deeper darkness behind them.

One man came toward him, bounding with long-legged leaps, gun glinting in his hand. Wentworth saw that it was Patsy's brother, Shane. He went toward him with the struggling girl still locked against his breast. One of the blackjacks swung into play and Shane went down and out.

Patsy had knocked off Wentworth's hat and fixed both hands in the hair of the wig. She tugged at this now and it came free in her hands. She gasped and Wentworth set her down, whirled her about so that her arms were behind her and locked them there with the grip of his left hand.

"Take me to the professor, Patsy," he ordered softly. "Little girls ought not to mix in gangster affairs."

The girl was sobbing, striking out with her high heels. "You killed Shane," she gasped. "You . . . you . . . !"

Wentworth skilfully dodged her kicks and shoved her toward broad stairs that led upward.

"His skull's too thick to kill that easily," he grunted. "But I'm not sure yours is. Take me to the professor."

Feet were pounding along the hall upstairs. Wentworth had heard the two men he had gassed flee out of the back door, but now that door slammed again and more men came in.

243

"Let me go! Let me go to Shane!" Patsy pleaded. She was writhing, sobbing and fighting and it taxed Wentworth's strength to pinion her with his one hand while he held his automatic ready for the impending attack.

"Tell me where the professor is," Wentworth insisted, "and you can go." He dragged Patsy to the right, to a doorway where the two of them were half-protected by the walls.

"He's upstairs," Patsy panted, "in his laboratory. Now, let me . . . !"

Wentworth released her and she plunged across the hallway and dropped on her knees beside her brother. Wentworth's scar-twisted mouth was grim, but there was a pleased light in his eyes. After all these days of wasted effort, he was at last tangling with the killers. The odds were great, but the *Spider* was used to facing impossible situations—and winning. He crouched in the hallway and the attacking footsteps above and in the back hall ceased.

The men on the floor with him beat a hurried retreat, coughing and sneezing from the remnants of the gas. Wentworth blinked. The tear fumes were beginning to reach out toward him. He would have to climb those stairs, or . . .

Behind him, in the darkened room, a man stumbled.

Wentworth flung a second gas bomb violently at the spot and slid out into the hall. At the head of the steps, a gun glinted and the *Spider's* automatic crashed. The gangster gun bounced against the railing, fell to the steps and from the overhead darkness, a man cursed raggedly. Wentworth flung two more shots at the voice and sprang for the stairs.

In the darkness, the white ghost of a face rose behind the bannister and Wentworth flung a fourth shot at it, saw the glimmer of it go backward and heard a body thud to the floor. He whirled at the head of the stairs and a heavy gun boomed below. Lead crunched into the bannister by his hand. Wentworth could not wait to answer that. In moments, that gunman would be blinded by tear gas anyway.

244

He began a hurried canvass of the second floor rooms, yanking their doors open and spraying the diffused beam of a pencil flashlight over them. Four were empty. A gun blasted from the fifth and Wentworth's answering lead wrung a dying scream from the gunman. The *Spider* flipped his nearly empty gun to his left hand, caught a fully loaded one from his holster with his right and streaked toward the third and top floor.

Directly ahead of him was a wide open door that was blindingly bright. White light blazed from it and through the dazzle, Wentworth could make out the cold glisten of glass tubes in racks, of shelves of bottles: the laboratory! He took the final stairs in a single leap, and went in behind his gun. The figure of a gray man, warped by age, half-straightened from where a retort bubbled on the bench. The man continued to stir a brilliant, blue liquid with a glass rod, but he twisted a scrawny neck about so that his beady eyes, shadowed by thick white brows, peered directly at Wentworth.

"What do you want?" he demanded in a rasping voice.

"You!" Wentworth said softly. "Come on! Get your coat. You're going with me!"

The professor blinked as his gaze dropped to the automatics in Wentworth's hands. It lifted again to his face.

"Who are you?" he demanded. "And why should I go with you?"

Wentworth's acutely atuned ears heard heavy feet pounding the stairs, knew that the gangsters were rushing upward to prevent him from escaping with the professor. He did not answer the old man, but strode to where a long gray cape hung from a peg beneath a black hat. He returned to the professor with the garments.

"I haven't time to argue," he snapped, "but unless you come at once, I'll have to knock you out and carry you."

The professor stood still stirring the retort, his beady

eyes glittering. "Just let me finish this experiment," he pleaded and reached for the shelf before him.

His hand grasped a bottle, then moved with incredible speed. It snapped the glass cover free and a globe of white liquid flew from the receptacle directly at Wentworth's face.

He flung up his arm on guard and the liquid splashed upon it. Flying cold fragments struck his face and an overpowering, sweet scent cloyed his nostrils. Wentworth stopped his breath in the middle of an inhalation, wheeled toward the door. He took two staggering steps and pitched forward on his face, unconscious.

Professor Gottstalk chuckled gustily deep in his throat. "Come and get him, boys," he called. "He can't hurt you now." He chuckled again and kept on stirring the blue liquid with a glass rod.

CHAPTER ELEVEN

The Avenger's Mercy

Wentworth came loggily to his senses. He felt that he was riding in a smoothly moving automobile, riding over city streets, but he did not open his eyes.

A harsh voice at his right side growled: "Ain't this punk ever gonna come out of it?"

A voice from the front of the car—Wentworth judged it was the driver—snarled back: "Slap him some more! Go on! Slap him 'til he comes out of it, like the boss said."

Wentworth felt the man beside him grip his shoulder roughly, felt the fellow's calloused hand slap his face ringingly twice—three times. For a moment he took it, let the other go on striking him. Then he made his eyes flutter open, gagged: "Hey! What the hell?" in a falsely weak voice.

He looked into a square, hard face, looked at a typical gangster type. "O.K.!" the burly man growled. "So you've come around, eh?"

Wentworth choked again, nodded with simulated feebleness. "Yes. What are you going to do with me?"

"Stop the bus, Jake," the gangster called to the man in the front seat. "He's O.K. now." Turning back to Wentworth, the hood pulled out a letter, shoved it into the *Spider's* hands. "There! The Avenger said to give you this." He opened the door beside him when the car had drawn to a halt. "Now scram, buddy. Get out. On your way."

Wentworth waited no second invitation. He gripped the letter in one hand, scrambled out the open door. The driver made the gears grind, and the auto careened away. Wentworth was standing on the curb in a residential section of the city. He tore open the letter, read the words inside:

WENTWORTH—THE SPIDER:

Next time I won't save you when your foolhardiness gets you into a tight place. But I had to keep Martin from disposing of you, because I'm saving you for later on. Right now I haven't time to see that you're convicted. I have to stop Martin. He plans to poison thousands in the East as a build-up for organizing the patent medicine industries. He plans to poison the cold cures in New York. However, if you'll be kind enough to mention the time and place, after we're both back in New York, I'll meet you on even terms. And when that happens, I'll see that you, Richard Wentworth, are proven conclusively to be the *Spider*. And so until we meet, dear enemy. . . .

THE AVENGER.

Wentworth was astounded by the calm effrontery of the man. He read the note again; realized how cleverly the Avenger had foiled him. He whistled at a cruising taxi, piled in, shouting: "The airport!" And as he settled back in the imitation leather upholstery, he muttered grimly to himself: "And I'm still not sure that Martin and the Avenger aren't the same person!"

At the airport, hangar doors were tight shut against gusty gray skies, and except for a few mechanics and necessary port officials, there was no one about. All mail and transport planes had been grounded. No word had come from the East for hours. Only crashing static sounded on the wireless when Wentworth tried to establish contact. He finally succeeded in buying a plane. Wentworth smiled thinly at officials, ignored their dire warnings and took off in the face of a gusty wind that spat snow. He whirled, took the wind on his tail, and fled eastward before it.

Snow that had been feathery when he took off turned to bullets in the lash of the wind. The ceiling was right down on the earth and within moments he was ripping through an impenetrable screen of clouds. It was incredibly cold. Mist began to freeze on Wentworth's goggles. He threw a narrow-eyed glance at his wings. Ice was there, too, forming on the leading edge.

Slowly the ice piled up and the plane became loggy and lifted sullenly to the gusts. Finally Wentworth was forced to the realization that he had only a few minutes of flying time left. The earth was covered thickly with snow. An attempt to put the ship down in that would mean a certain crackup when the soft drifts clutched at his landing gear. Wentworth felt despair welling up in him, but he fought it down, raging silently. Damn Kirkpatrick and his premonitions of disaster! He *would* get through!

Peering down through the night that had dropped upon the earth while he fought the skies, Wentworth caught an occasional gleam of yellow light from scattered houses, but they were far apart. Then, stabbing across the white plains, he caught the long blue-white ray of a train's headlight. It was only a glimpse, then a curtain of whipping snow dropped over his plane. But Wentworth yelled aloud in sudden triumph.

He fished his automatic from under his tunic, pumped lead into the plane's gasoline tank until it caught fire, then hurled himself out into space. He snatched out the rip-ring of his parachute, felt the great bell snap his body like a whip. Down he shot, peering through the welter of white. Finally, he spotted the glow of the train's headlight, the plume of sparks that thundered from its stack.

Staring toward it, Wentworth was scarcely aware of the ground, deep in snow, flashing upward. He smacked into a drift that swallowed him completely. He fought furiously out of the parachute and struggled through the soft, enveloping frigidity of the snow that was almost to his armpits. The plane plunged into the snow, but burning gasoline continued to smear crimson across the sky. The train streaked on.

Wentworth shouted despairingly. Like an echo, the train's whistle keened across the white flats. Sparks showered from its drivers as the brakes were thrown on. A gasp of thankfulness rose in Wentworth's throat. He ploughed toward the stopping train.

An hour later, the train crawled into Cleveland. There, Wentworth finally got a coded message in wireless through to New York. He could only hope that Kirkpatrick would realize the fierce need for action and get after the poisoners. He hoped so, but there was only one way to make sure—dash on to New York himself.

Planes were coated with ice, even as they stood on the ground here in Cleveland. Officials would not hear of starting a special train eastward. They had no telegraph.

But Wentworth, by kidnapping a locomotive, engineer, and fireman at pistol point and offering them a ten-thousand-dollar bonus, managed to leave Cleveland.

The train went through almost to Buffalo before it stalled in a snowbank and Wentworth foot-slogged on until he found a jumping taxi that took him to an airport. He bought a seaplane and used its boat bottom to wallow a take-off track through the snow.

It was four hours and fifty-two minutes later that Wentworth sloshed the seaplane into the drifting pack ice of the Hudson and whirled into the protection of an unoccupied pier. He leaped stiffly ashore and moored the craft. He gazed toward the glimmering beacons of New York's high towers, cold against the night sky, and he sucked in a deep breath.

"Now," the *Spider* muttered, "the battle begins!"

CHAPTER TWELVE

The Spider Is Doomed

Wentworth strode swiftly along the pier's snow-blanketed planks toward the shore. West Street, along the waterfront, was a wide white desert without a track. He floundered across it to where a greasy-fronted diner showed a yellow glow.

Wentworth ordered coffee, then spotted a pay telephone in a booth at the rear. He scuffed through the sawdust on the floor and called police headquarters. Kirkpatrick's answer was sharp, but there was a weary drag in his voice.

"This is Dick, Kirk," Wentworth said rapidly. "I've been trying to reach you for twenty hours. Did you get my warning from Cleveland? The poison gang is going to switch to patent medicines now. Cold cures first. I can't see any way to stop it except to slap an embargo on all patent medicines."

The cold silence at the other end of the wire stopped Wentworth then. He held the receiver to his ear and slowly a frown gathered a vertical pucker between his eyes. It hurt his cold-flayed face. His cheeks were burning and stiff after the cold.

"What's the matter, Kirk?" he demanded roughly.

"I warned you, Dick," Kirkpatrick's voice was more tired than before. "You've been indicted for Mannley's murder—as the *Spider*. The best thing to do would be to surrender to me here at once.''

"I'll talk with you about that in a minute," Wentworth said in a voice that was husky despite his effort at calmness. "Here's what's in the wind—and here's the motive behind the poisonings." Wentworth swiftly told him of his discoveries in Chicago, interrupted by Kirkpatrick's sharp monosyllables. New York police had never heard of the gang leader, Martin, any more than Wentworth had.

"I'm pretty sure that it's O'Burke's gang under new leadership that's handling the thing," Wentworth continued, "but this man, Martin, is the brain of the outfit and I have no idea who he is."

"O'Burke's tie-up in New York is with the McMurty outfit," Kirkpatrick asserted. There was new life in his tones. "We'll watch them, but if it's racketeering, it's a foregone conclusion that we won't be able to get any convictions unless we can catch some men in the act of spreading the poison. And those will not include the leader. We'll never get him."

"And that means the racket will never stop, eh, Kirk?" Wentworth asked. His voice was soft, but there was a hard, wild light in his eyes. "Do you still advise me to surrender, Kirk?" He slammed the receiver and burst out of the booth. His face was without expression as he sat down to eat, then he caught a gleam in the eyes of the pasty-faced counterman and knew suddenly that he had been recognized—recognized as Richard Wentworth, the *Spider*. Damn this newspaper publicity! The man was sidling toward the telephone even now to call police and seek his share in that sixty-thousand reward.

Wentworth bolted from the diner and shoved out into the fierce bite of the wind, turned the corner and ran. Police would come fast in answer to the counterman's call. Good Lord! Had it come to this, that Wentworth was to be hounded wherever he went? That he dared not appear without disguise? He realized with a start that it was for such situations as this that he had made his preparations for disappearance.

He had a passport in another identity. He had money banked abroad which that identity could claim. But Wentworth knew, even as the thought flashed across his brain, that he had no intention of vanishing. Not while so grave a danger menaced the people of his country.

His breath was pumping noisily. The cold was a sharp pain in his cheeks and in his panting lungs. His feet skidded and slipped in the snow. A Ford roadster, whirling dark around a corner ahead, skated into a snow drift, rocked and darted toward him. Wentworth flung flat down in the snow. It had not been cleared here, and well over two feet deep, it covered him entirely. He had no doubt as to the identity of that roadster. It was a police radio patrol car, running dark and silently to seize the *Spider*.

He heard the muffled roar of its engine as it wallowed through the snow. Had he been spotted before he flung himself flat? Would the policemen spot the abrupt termination of the broad track he had made through the snow? His mouth was bitter and harsh. Snow might cover him, but it would be no protection against bullets. If they halted and opened fire. . . .

The Ford droned rapidly nearer, its chained tires whining on the slippery snow. He heard the motor falter and instinctively, he snatched for his automatic, lips skinning back from his teeth. But, damn it, he couldn't use his gun on police. He lay rigid, waiting. The motor picked up again, the Ford hammered on. Wentworth crawled to the wall of the warehouse beside him, got to his feet in its shadow and ran on. The Ford was a dark blur receding down the street.

Two blocks further on, he found a taxi and flung into it. The driver turned with his hand on the meter flag, then his mouth sagged open. He, too, had recognized the *Spider!*

His hand snapped from the flag, darting toward his coat pocket. Wentworth reached over and slapped him across the forehead with his gun. His face was like frozen steel, his eyes burning. He yanked the driver into the rear of the cab and rapidly bound and gagged him. Then he took the man's cap and operator's button and got behind the wheel.

It was clear that he could do nothing until he had got hold of a disguise, and he was without the means of creating one. There was no doubt that Nita's apartment would be watched, his also. Though he might manage to steal into the secret dressing room he had built into his penthouse, he could not risk that now. There was not time. Already the minions of Martin might be distributing the poison.

He jammed on the gas so suddenly the taxi's tires skidded instead of taking hold. He cursed, tried again and got under way. Snow creaked beneath the rubber. A link of a chain was broken and made a regular, tinny slapping on a fender. As he pushed on uptown, with his unconscious passenger behind him, he began to run into groups of street cleaners. Thousands of unemployed had been drafted for the work. They had fires boiling up out of high cans and, clad in ragged overcoats, with their ears bound up, they leaned on snow shovels that they pushed with puffing clouds of breath. They moved slowly. Every man of them was conscious that when the snow was gone, the work and the pay ceased. They would make the snow last as long as possible.

Wentworth singled out one apart from the rest and slewed the taxi to a halt beside him.

"Want ten dollars, buddy?"

The man stopped pushing his shovel, and stared at him.

"You wouldn't kid me, mister?"

"Hop up here," Wentworth ordered and held out a bill. The man climbed in after it, standing up in the seatless space beside the driver's seat and Wentworth let him have it. The man watched him covertly, ignored the shout that came from behind.

A half-dozen blocks away, Wentworth halted the

cab. "I want your clothes," Wentworth told the street cleaner. "I'll give you mine and another ten dollars to boot. Okay?"

"Lord lumme, yes!" the man gasped.

They made the exchange and the bum donned a fur-lined flying suit while Wentworth tugged into a worn-out overcoat and a ear-flap cap and wrapped a burlap sack about his throat as a muffler. It hid half his face, too.

Wentworth slopped off down the street, head down into the brash cold, until he found a subway entrance. His shoulders were slumped and his feet scuffled. Now and again he sniveled and dragged a ragged sleeve across his nose. His face was unchanged, but he doubted that police or other reward-hunters would look for him in this garb.

In the subway station, he entered a telephone booth and called Nita.

"Don't come here, Dick," she said rapidly before she even greeted him. "I'm watched. You've been indicted for Mannley's murder."

Wentworth laughed softly. "Thanks, my beautiful," he said. "I talked to Kirkpatrick. I just wanted to warn you not to take any cold medicine. It's going to be poisoned. Will you call the newspapers and tell them that? Also expose the whole thing as a racket."

He told her swiftly what had happened in Chicago.

"I don't have to call the newspapers," Nita said, acid in her voice. "I just open the door and the newspapermen fall in. But, listen, Dick dear, I think you'd better ring off now. I don't know that police aren't tapped in on my wires and they might arrest you.

"Here's some information: Your newspaper clippings show that before each poisoning outbreak, there has been a series of robberies of groceries or cosmetic shops. There haven't been any reports of drug store robberies yet."

Wentworth cried, "Good work, Nita! That's what

255

had been worrying me. The method of distribution. Sweetheart, will you go to my apartment at once?''

Nita abruptly clicked off the telephone and Wentworth smiled wryly. That meant she had detected a listening tap and feared he might be traced. Well, he had been talking more than long enough to be traced. He glanced toward the change booth, along the empty platform. The station agent was not looking toward him. He took a single stride and leaped to the tracks, three feet below. Crouching, he ran swiftly into the darkness.

The tracks were lighted at long intervals by dim electrics. Red lights showed emergency exits and blue bulbs revealed telephones. Steel uprights marched off into the dark distances between the double line of tracks. On each side of them was the deadly third rail, carrying hundreds of volts of electricity. Distantly, he heard the humming of the rails that heralded a train. It was impossible to tell yet on which track it was.

His feet made thumping noises that echoed dimly. Abruptly, he heard voices clatter out behind him and he ducked to the right hand wall and ran on, up on his toes now for quietness. The police had done quick work in tracing that call. If the snow had not slowed their dash, he undoubtedly would have been captured already, he realized.

Peering back over his shoulder, he saw a policeman lean out with a flashlight in his hand. Wentworth flung flat down against the wall, motionless. The beam of the torch did not penetrate the darkness where he lay, but he saw the officer spring to the tracks and come toward him at a swift run. He darted a glance ahead. Another policeman coming that way. The roar of the train was heavier and he could determine that it was on the other track. He was surrounded.

Wentworth felt his heart tightening within him. He was trapped by men against whom he could not fight, just when he had learned at long last how he might battle with the slaughterers.

Slowly, his face twisted in self-mockery, Wentworth drew his automatic. The police were very close now. The passage of that train howling down the tunnel would throw light upon his hiding place. For the sake of thousands of lives, the *Spider* was being forced to do what he had sworn he never would: Shoot down police!

He raised the pistol and his hand rubbed against cold metal that was not the track. The police had halted and were calling back and forth to each other.

Wentworth laid the automatic down and feverishly felt the metal. It was a bar three feet long, hanging on hooks against the wall. He knew what it was, a heavy, soft, iron bar with eyes in each end, which was used to hoist cars back onto the tracks when they jumped. They were placed at intervals throughout the tunnels. A germ of an idea flashed into his brain. There still was a way to escape . . . if it was not too late.

Quickly, Wentworth thrust the pistol back into its holster. He eased to his knees and heaved one of the bars off its hooks. His teeth clenched, his neck corded with the effort to move the heavy ingot without sound. Its weight was over a hundred pounds. He got the bar clear and lifted it vertically so that it stood upon its end before him. Then he hoisted it slowly straight upward. It was ticklish work. He dared not sway far out from the wall, lest his shadow become visible against the dim lights. The clank of the bar would betray him. Yet he must work swiftly, against the onward rush of the train.

But the need for quiet was rapidly passing. The tunnel filled slowly with the hollow roar of the speeding wheels. Wentworth got the bar high enough to get his palm under it and, balancing it on one hand, steadying it with the other, he muscled the weight upward until its lower end was shoulder high, his arm braced as for a shot-put. He staggered to his feet, let the bar begin to plunge earthward. Then, with a strong thrust of his arm, his weight behind it, he sent the bar like a javelin across the tracks toward those twin third rails. Instantly, he hurled himself flat again, panting heavily.

Wentworth literally held his breath, then there was a blinding blue-white flash of light. Electric flame leaped up in a fan from the iron bar that had flopped across the two third rails, short-circuiting a combined power of over a thousand volts. There was a hissing blast, then the bar bounded clear and darkness shut down on the tunnel. Every light save the dim blues that marked the telephones and the reds that marked the exits, widely spaced and insignificant in that Stygian gloom, blinked out. The train's brakes squealed in an emergency stop.

In the sudden silence that followed, the police shouted in frightened voices to each other. But Wentworth, alone of all those in the tunnel expecting that blinding flash, was on his feet the moment darkness shut down. In two long leaps, he sprang between the steel pillars to the opposite track and raced toward the train.

That would be the one place police would not expect him to run, toward the train whose few scattered emergency lights, battery operated, made a faint yellow spot in the darkness. He ran without sound, on his toes. The stabbing beams of the police hand-torches were scouring the spot where he had been. Within seconds, Wentworth reached the train. Crouching low, he darted past the cars to the back, there he swung up and opened the one unlocked door of the train, the one at the rear. No one noticed him. The few passengers on the train had all crowded forward to stare out into the darkness, seeking the cause of the stop. Wentworth slipped in among them.

Five minutes later, the motorman had removed the bar from between the tracks, had 'phoned to have the current turned on again and the train clattered away. In a corner, a bum with a burlap bag for a muffler swayed and snatched a nap, his face relaxed beneath its dirt.

But behind that grimy mask, Wentworth's mind was racing on to the next step in his warfare.

It still lacked two hours of dawn, the time of night when the gangsters undoubtedly would do most of their work of distributing the poison. The clippings had given him the clue. They broke into stores as burglars and took whatever of value they could find, but they did more than that. Behind them, they left the poisoned goods, whether it was canned food, acid-tainted cosmetics, or cold medicine that would stretch its users in writhing death upon the floor. If only, now, he could work with police, the gangsters might be wiped out in no time.

Somewhere in the city, during these burglaries, one criminal was sure to be spotted. If police headquarters kept on its toes and shot radio cars to the drug store where the burglary was spotted with its siren silent and orders to trail, instead of arrest the robbers . . . Wentworth shut his mouth grimly. Kirkpatrick would have to listen to him, that was all. He, himself, might not be able to participate, but at least he could direct the battle. As a safety precaution, Kirkpatrick could close every drug store that was burglarized pending an examination of its stock.

Leaving the train, Wentworth made a series of 'phone calls from widely separated 'phone booths before he got the entire information in Kirkpatrick's hands.

He was reasonably sure that Kirkpatrick would follow out his suggestion, but he knew that Kirkpatrick would have to depend on the men in the radio cars to trail criminals. And that would not be easy. The prowl cars were conspicuous and there might be no opportunity for the officers to commandeer a car to do their trailing. But it was a vital work. It had to be done, if Martin's gang were to be eliminated. In Wentworth's mind, his whole plan of battle fell into neat array. The first task was to stop the medical supplies from being broadcast over the city. Police could take care of that, now that the means of distribution was apparent. The next was to locate and wipe out the men who were dealing out the poison. Police might be able to do that, but Wentworth intended to make sure by taking the field also.

He had no hope that Martin would be captured. Undoubtedly the man was still in Chicago, for there was no great need for him to rush eastward as Wentworth had. His plans were all set, his men had their orders and he could come latter to reap the profits of his diabolical plot. But wiping out the gang would accomplish one thing. It would destroy Martin's one ready weapon. He would have no trouble in gathering more men to work for him, but for a while he would be forced to halt his wholesale slaughter. And before he got organized again, Wentworth thought the *Spider* might be able to force a settlement, if—his eyes grew hard and bleak—if police and the populace he fought to save did not before that time destroy their benefactor!

Taxis nearly all carry radios now. Some few passengers turn them on, but chiefly they while away the waits between fares while the drivers park beside a fire hydrant with the engine running for some small warmth against the winter night's cold. Wentworth, foot-slogging through the snow, shoulders bowed, head pulled down into the muffling folds of the burlap bag, hunched up to such a cab. The driver jerked up his head from a tabloid paper and threw his arm in an angry gesture.

Wentworth opened the door and presented his automatic, muzzle first. The radio made low music at his elbow.

"Get out," Wentworth said. His voice was rough and the driver spun out like a snipe dodging a bullet. Wentworth watched him around a corner with the gun still in his hand, then got in and drove away. The cab would be reported stolen within minutes, but it was Wentworth's guess that the radio patrol cars would have something else to do this night than watch for stolen cabs. Besides, Wentworth did not expect to cover much territory. He drove a dozen blocks away and parked beside a fire hydrant, turned the radio to the wave-band of police calls. The first one that came over was a description of the taxi and himself.

"Be careful of this man," the announcer's rasping voice intoned. "He is dangerous and carries a thirty-eight caliber automatic pistol. He is believed to be Richard Wentworth, alias the *Spider*."

The short laugh that barked from Wentworth's lips was harsh. He had not anticipated that swift deduction. Well, Kirkpatrick had said he would prosecute the search to the last iota of his strength and ability. Wentworth settled himself deeper into the taxi seat, waiting, listening. Finally the announcement came.

"Car one-five-two, car one-fifty-two. Signal thirty at drug store, corner of Second Avenue and Harper Street. Proceed silently and follow burglars. See order two-thousand seven forty-five."

Wentworth nodded as he sped along, headed for Second Avenue and Harper Street. The order referred to would have been Kirkpatrick's general order for action when burglaries of drug stores were reported. It would direct that they follow and attempt to locate the head-quarters of the poison gang. He jolted across the rutted tracks of Second Avenue and turned north. Two blocks behind him, he spotted a Ford roadster coming fast and without lights. He cursed softly to himself. If those police were on their toes, they would commandeer his cab as less conspicuous than their own car. They might identify the taxi, recall their report on "Richard Wentworth, alias the *Spider*."

He was still five blocks from Harper, but if the police had decided to commandeer the cab, turning into a side street would not help. The Ford came up fast, pulled alongside and a cop stuck out his head. "Pull over!" he snapped.

"Who, me?" Wentworth stammered. "What did I do?"

"You haven't done anything," said the cop. "I'm commandeering this cab."

Wentworth sighed wearily, "Okay! I hope it don't

get messed up none." That sigh expressed genuine relief. If there had been a fight, it would have scared off the burglars, destroyed all his careful plans.

"Get moving," the cop ordered, "and when you get to Harper Street, go one block beyond and find a parking place."

Wentworth glanced sideways at the policeman. He was young and Irish, a broad six feet with blue eyes glinting under blond brows. He was excited and the fresh color of his face was not all from the bite of the wind. Wentworth wondered what reward Kirkpatrick had promised in that special order of his. This youngster was all keyed up.

"Want I should get the police signals?" Wentworth asked and reached through into the back compartment to work the radio.

"Good idea," grunted the cop.

He was paying no attention to Wentworth, but was staring toward where Harper Street intersected Second Avenue. He had crouched low in the empty space to keep out of sight, his visored cap laid on the floor beside him so its shield would not catch a gleam of light. He was showing rare sense, Wentworth thought. The police Ford swerved off Second Avenue, still running dark, and wallowed on east toward the river. It would cover the other end of Harper Street.

CHAPTER THIRTEEN

Death for The Spider!

Wentworth knew that he was sitting on a keg of dynamite. His face was not disguised and his identity was so well known, thanks to the newspapers, that a counterman in a greasy diner and a taxi driver had recognized him easily. Furthermore, the license number of this cab had been broadcast as stolen, and he was "believed" to be the thief. It was not alone for himself that he feared, though capture would be disastrous. He thought he might be able to handle this bouncing young cop if it came to a showdown. But the chase might be endangered, and he must not miss the trail to Martin's headquarters.

If the cop identified him, he would abandon all thought of this other chase. To him, the capture of the *Spider* was much more important than merely trailing burglars, even if those men were tied up with a thousand murders.

So Wentworth snuggled his chin down into the protection of that scratchy muffler, watched the young policeman's bulldog profile and listened for radio reports. His cab muttered along under the elevated. He spotted a man's figure in the black shadows across from the drug store. The lookout of the burglars?

"Say, officer," he whined, "I don't know what

you're looking for at Harper Street, but there's a guy over on the left hand corner in the shadows."

"I see him," the cop said shortly. "Keep on past, turn the next corner and park."

"Car one-five-two. Car one-fifty-two. Call headquarters when you can. Call headquarters when you can. Do not interrupt last assignment."

The cop grunted, pulled down farther behind the steel cowling. Wentworth cranked down his window, stuck out his head and yelled, "Taxi, mister?" at the figure in the shadows.

The man did not move, but Wentworth heard the cop cursing under his breath, felt the grate of a revolver muzzle in his side. He cranked up his window and kept on, turned the next corner west.

"What's the big idea, mug?" the cop growled and his blue eyes were narrow and hard. "I believe you was tipping that guy off."

"Honest," Wentworth gulped. "Honest! If I'd sailed by without trying to get a customer, with my flag up like it is, he'd get suspicious. I was trying to help."

The cop kept the gun grinding against his side and his eyes stayed small and hard. "You're damned smart, ain't you, mug?" he asked softly.

Suddenly, he reached out and yanked the muffler from Wentworth's face. Wentworth didn't wait to see whether he'd be identified. His hand dropped on the policeman's revolver and wedged the chamber tight with hard-gripping fingers. If that chamber didn't revolve, the hammer couldn't go back, the gun couldn't be fired. He held the chamber and lashed out with his fist.

The cop was crouching on his thighs, and in his excitement, he tried to straighten up. He caught Wentworth's blow rising and his head slammed against the roof of the cab. It batted his head down again and Wentworth snatched for his automatic. The cop hit out with his fist. Wentworth took two hard knocks in the face before he could slap the man down with the flat of his automatic.

He scanned the street behind him and saw a sedan go past fast with five men in it. With a curse, Wentworth threw open the door and rolled the cop out, thoughtfully retaining his revolver. He jerked the cab into motion with skidding tires and took the next corner so fast his rear-end slammed into banked up snow.

Wentworth was still muttering oaths as he whirled off in pursuit of the sedan. He was only guessing, of course, that it was the gangster car, but he had had another purpose in yelling at that lookout in the shadows. He had wanted to start the quarry before the other policeman or the excitement at headquarters should bungle the game.

He leaned forward and switched off his lights, swung back to Second Avenue and spotted the tail light of the sedan flickering along four blocks ahead up the middle of the street. He got outside the elevated pillars so that the long line of thick steel columns formed a screen for him and pushed on. He would be able to spot the other car if it turned off, but it was unlikely that he himself would be seen.

There was no way of telling whether that young policeman had identified him or not, but at any rate he would have police on his trail within minutes. The cop would regain consciousness quickly in the cold snow. His companion probably had seen the burglars take to their heels and would be after them. A telephoned report would set the whole network of radio cars after them.

The car ahead swirled right and Wentworth braked and pivoted two blocks short of the other. When he reached the next street, he parked and waited. The sedan shot into sight and kept going east. A taxi turned south. Wentworth leaned back in his seat and pretended to be asleep. His cab was by a fire hydrant, but this was an unlikely spot for a cab stand. If his hunch was right, and the gangsters had switched to this cab . . . Wentworth's hands were locked upon the butts of his guns. He had the car in low gear, holding his foot on the clutch, his right on the accelerator pedal.

The taxi drifted down the street slowly, abruptly swerved out between the elevated pillars into the outer lane nearest Wentworth. He caught a glint of metal at the rear window. He had been spotted, then. He stamped the gas, yanked his foot off the clutch pedal and his cab shot forward, straight across the path of the other. Excited shots sputtered from the rear of the taxi Wentworth heard them smack into the metal of body, heard a window crash, then he was dead across their path. He threw up his own gun and blazed away.

He blasted out his window without bothering to lower it and his first shots smacked into the rear of the other cab. He saw the chauffeur yank up a gun just as the taxi crunched into his side and he put a bullet through the man's shoulder.

But he was firing carefully. The revolver in his right hand held only two more shots. His automatic was nearly empty and that prowling police car, if it had missed the trail, could not fail to hear these shots. The still, cold air would carry the sound a mile. Wentworth flung himself toward the far side of his cab and out into the snow, circled its rear cautiously. There had been no sound, no movement from the other cab for thirty seconds. He had fired enough shots to account for every man in it, but he was by no means sure that they weren't lying in wait for him now.

But he could not hesitate. He had deliberately refrained from killing the one man in the other car that he could see clearly, the chauffeur. The chase was spoiled now, but it might not be hard to make a wounded man talk. It better not be, Wentworth told himself grimly, for the man's sake.

He went toward the other cab in a swift rush, ducking to the protection of the taxi's own body, but no movement came from within. He yanked open the door. Still keeping under cover, he blasted one more shot into the interior and got no reply. Cautiously, he peered inside. The ceiling light had clicked on when he pulled open the door and it revealed three men in a contorted huddle on the floor and seat. Two were dead. The other had taken a bullet through his chest high up. Well, police would be here within minutes. They could take care of the wounded.

Without ceremony, Wentworth dumped the three out on the ground, shoved the semi-conscious chauffeur from his seat to the floor and yanked the cab backward. It had not been damaged by the collision, taking the entire force of the blow on the bumper. Wentworth dropped from the cab then for a space of moments and daubed upon the forehead of the two dead and the one wounded gangster the seal of the *Spider*. There was a reckless light in his eyes. Let the police and the under-world know that, for all the hue and cry on his trail, the *Spider* could still strike terribly! Let them know he still fought when any other man would have fled in terror!

He flung back into the cab and sent it roaring and skidding away. The man on the floor groaned weakly and Wentworth threw him a glance, snatched up a revolver from beside him. He whipped back to the west, past more stalling groups of snow workers, turned south on Seventh Avenue. After five blocks he cut west again and brought the cab to a halt beneath the Ninth Avenue elevated. He got out and threw a double handful of snow in the wounded man's face, rubbed it into his temples. The gangster stirred feebly, regained his senses cursing.

"Hurry up!" Wentworth said urgently. "That guy blasted the daylights out of us. Got everybody except me and you. Hurry up! Where was you going to take us?"

Wentworth was taking a chance, playing the fact that Martin had a Chicago gang. There was a chance only the chauffeur knew where to go. If it didn't work, he'd have to force the man to talk, but . . . He bent low over the wounded man, heard him mutter an address and grinned in triumph.

A radio in the taxi began to squawk. Wentworth straightened, listening.

"Calling all cars! Calling all cars! Richard Wentworth, alias the *Spider* just killed three men at the corner of First Avenue and Thirty-second Street. When last seen . . ." A description followed. "Bring him in, dead or alive," the order concluded.

Wentworth's short laugh was rasping in his throat. Killed three men, they said, and didn't explain that they were murdering gangsters who had just planted poison to kill thousands, didn't explain that the *Spider* had fired only in self defense, though the evidence of that must be plain upon the wrecked cab he had occupied. Well, it was not police business to justify the kills of the *Spider*.

Wentworth stared down at the wounded gangster on the floor of the cab. The man was conscious now, staring up wildeyed.

"Cheez!" the wounded man gasped. "Don't hoit me, *Spider*, I told you what you wanted to know."

"Yeah," said Wentworth. He hauled the man into the back of the cab and bound him tightly. Then he mounted the driver's seat and sent the taxi purring southward. The address the driver had given was on the lower east side, the headquarters of the Martin gang. At the thought his foot grew heavier on the accelerator and the cab's tires whistled and shuddered over the snow at his increased speed.

He forced himself to slow down. He could not afford to be even bawled out by a traffic policeman, not with the bullet-pocked taxi, with a wounded man in the tonneau. Wentworth realized abruptly that he was utterly worn out, recalled that he had not rested since the night before when he had slept under the professor's narcotic. He had not eaten since leaving Cleveland. The radio made a constant dinning in his ears now, orders flying thick and fast for the capture of the *Spider*.

Someone had spotted the fact that he had left the scene of the killing in a yellow taxi cab and radio patrolmen were ordered to halt every yellow cab and check the driver's identity. A slow anger was growing in Wentworth's heart. He was fighting for the lives of people who were trying their damnedest to kill him. He realized abruptly that he could not hope to carry his fight to a successful termination unless he ridded himself of his present garb. His ammunition, too, was nearly exhausted and there was no fresh supply in the taxi.

Slowly, unwillingly, Wentworth faced the realization that unless he wished to risk the escape of those gangsters with the consequent blow to his plans; unless he wanted to jeopardize ultimate success—which meant Martin's death—by his own capture, he must turn this phase of the battle over to police. It was madness anyway, such madness as only the *Spider* could carry to a victorious conclusion, for one man to invade a headquarters of gangsters as powerful as Martin's mob.

Wentworth swerved the yellow cab to the curb and walked hurriedly back the way he had driven, turned a corner and shambled toward a subway. His eyes quested alertly for police. A passing radio patrol car gave him an uneasy moment, but the men were occupied in stopping a yellow cab for questioning. Wentworth quickened his pace. Within minutes they would find the taxi he had abandoned and begin combing the side-streets for him. He ducked down a subway entrance and did not 'phone until he was well uptown.

When Kirkpatrick answered, the flat, mocking laughter of the *Spider* grated over the wire.

"Dick," Kirkpatrick's voice was hard, but there was a quiver in it. "Dick, for God's sake! Give yourself up, before you're killed. After that last kill of yours, after you knocked out that policeman I had to give a dead or alive order. Give yourself up, before. . . ."

"Save your words, Kirkpatrick," Wentworth spoke still in the artificially deep voice of the *Spider*. "I called to give you something that your bungling police almost kept me from getting, the address of the gang headquarters.''

Kirkpatrick broke off his pleas. His voice came coldly over the wire as he repeated the address Wentworth gave him.

"Hit them with everything you've got, Kirkpatrick," Wentworth said heavily. "I'll be seeing you."

He hung up, hurried from the booth to catch a subway train. The slump of his shoulders was not feigned now. He was tired—tired to the soul. He had struck a blow at the gangsters who had been murdering the thousands; he had opened the way for Kirkpatrick to wipe out the lesser members of the mob. The main fight was ahead, the elimination of the steel-helmeted chief. For so long as that man remained alive, the rackets would go on. Wentworth had a plan in mind for trapping Martin, too, but it was a task to which he drove himself grimly, as to a hated duty.

It was not that he had weakened for a moment in his service of humanity. He was still as earnest as on that first day when he had pledged his life to mankind's protection against the underworld. But he knew that the end was near, even as Kirkpatrick had said. With the evidence that the Avenger had piled up against him, there could be no hope this time for the *Spider*. He was doomed.

Slowly, his shoulders straightened. Doomed, yes, but he would make this, his last fight, the most glorious of his life. When he went, Martin and the Avenger would go with him. The world would ring for years with the thunderous echoes of the cataclysm that had destroyed the *Spider*. He laughed sharply, and a pale-faced woman, lips and cheeks carrying a pallor that was not all lack of cosmetics, stared at him curiously. Wentworth arose and left the train.

Once more he shuffled through the snow, but this time he was nearing the apartment building in which he lived. There was a lightness in his feet, a rising hope in his breast, engendered by his determination that the end should find him fighting gloriously. In that se-

270

cret room, he would find a haven for a few hours, until he could set the stage for the *Spider's* end.

Wentworth made the service entrance of the apartment building apparently without being seen. He started up service stairs and heard a man shout, heard heavy feet beat after him. He swung inside the panel of his secret room just in time and stood with his shoulders against the wall, panting heavily. His eyes were wide open, but he could see nothing in the dark.

He didn't need to see the man who had pursued to know that he was a police guard. He didn't have to be told that the guards had seen him and deliberately allowed him to enter the building to make his capture certain. Well, they would have a hard time finding this spot. Heavily, he pushed himself away from the wall and groped for a light switch, clicked it on. He crossed the room to where a black, cloth hood was attached to the wall. He put that over his head and looked through peepholes into his music room. No one was in there.

He went back into the secret room. From a small refrigerator set into a wall, he took out emergency rations and ate. He stripped off his clothing then and, setting an alarm clock to ring in four hours—at noon— he flung himself down upon a bed to rest. He had done all that could be done for the present.

When he awoke, the dullness was gone from his eyes. There was a new springiness to his stride as he walked quickly about, clothing himself. When he was dressed, he dropped down before a mirror framed in a neon-light tube and went swiftly to work on his face with make-up equipment. There was once more a mocking twist to his lips. The whole city was hunting the *Spider*, wasn't it? Well, it would be the *Spider* who walked abroad this day!

Wentworth's hands moved deftly, sallowing the wind-burnt skin, building the beaked, hawk nose and painting out lips. There was a reckless light in his eyes. They glittered with inner fires. When his disguise was complete, even to the black hat that sat low upon lank hair, the long black cape that emphasized the grotesque hunch of his shoulders, he crossed to the far wall where the cloth hood showed and put his eyes to the peepholes again.

He looked into his music room, austere, high-ceil-inged, its walls great gothic arches atop cathedral columns. Before a concert grand, Nita sat upon a bench. But she was not playing. Her back was to the keyboard and her smooth elbows were upon it. Her head was flung back so that the ringlets of her hair swept smoothly from her brow and she was smiling in mockery up into the face of Stanley Kirkpatrick.

There was a high lamp just behind her and it showed her face brightly even while her body was in shadow. Wentworth picked up an ear-'phone connected with a microphone near the piano, and Nita's voice came to him clearly.

"I am glad to hear Dick is back in the city," she said. "Now the number of murders may decrease."

Kirkpatrick stood very erectly above her. He wore a belted overcoat and his derby and his stick were in his hand. There was a stiffness in his poise that told how weary he was.

"If Dick is in the city," he said quietly, "one sort of murder will increase: Kills by the *Spider!*"

Wentworth moved his head to the left and swept a glance over the rest of the room. Just inside the main doorway stood Kirkpatrick's deputy, Marshant. His head seemed squeezed down between the breadth of shoulders that diminished his height. If this man were the Avenger, he had made a quick trip back from Chicago. . . .

Kirkpatrick's voice came to Wentworth again. "I warned Dick that this time was the end," he said harshly, "that he would slip and be caught. And I warned him, too, that I would prosecute to the full extent of my power. I'm repeating that now to you. The evidence is air-tight. The pictures show that the man who killed Mannley wore Dick's signet on his left hand. There can be no question of a conviction."

Nita rose from her seat upon the bench. Her lounge pajamas were wine red and they emphasized her tall grace.

"What you say is ridiculous," she said swiftly. "If Dick were the *Spider,* he certainly would have more intelligence than to do such a thing."

Kirkpatrick looked at her without a sound. Marshant laughed harshly from his stand beside the doorway.

"He wasn't expecting the Avenger to take a picture of him," the deputy said. "And he intended to kill Mannley. It would have been quite safe."

Kirkpatrick braced his shoulders, bowed stiffly to Nita and left. Marshant lingered to laugh again, then he, too, left. Wentworth stood motionless behind the door and waited. His eyes were smiling, without mockery. Kirkpatrick had been positive that he was within hearing and he had spoken loudly so that Wentworth might hear and know the evidence that was against him. He wondered what had been the result of the attack on the gangsters. It was a difficult part that Kirkpatrick had to play, but Wentworth knew that he need expect no mercy if he fell into his friend's hands.

The smile faded and a frown took its place. The evidence was puzzling. Wentworth remembered distinctly removing the signet from his finger before he had entered Mannley's room, just as he had removed from his buttonhole the rosette of the *Légion.* Obviously, someone had done a clever piece of fake photography, but that made the evidence no less damning. The Avenger was reinforcing the evidence of the automatic.

Wentworth waited until Nita turned to the piano and began to play softly, her slender, white fingers rippling over the ivory of the keys. The silvery notes were blithe. Nita's voice came to him, a whisper into the hidden microphone near her.

"If you are there, Dick," she said, "be very careful. I am sure that the apartment is watched. There may be dictagraphs. . . ."

Nita's fingers trailed off the keys. She arose and

sauntered toward Wentworth's end of the room where an organ was installed. The door to the secret room Wentworth occupied was opened by patting the sound orifices of two treble tubes in a certain cadence but Nita made no move to do that. She passed close by the door, strolling.

"Thanks, my beautiful," Wentworth whispered.

He heard Nita's breath suck in sharply, but she continued strolling and passed out of sight. Wentworth pressed against the door, his arms spreading against the unfeeling wood. If only he could clasp Nita in his arms once more, then he would go willingly to this last battle, the battle that meant the end. . . . Marshant stepped into the open doorway.

Behind him were two men with axes. "We heard whispering in this room," he said harshly. "There is a secret panel here somewhere and we mean to find it." He waved his arm at the ax-men. "Smash in that wall!" he pointed toward where Wentworth and Nita stood on opposite sides of the panel.

Wentworth sprang back and crossed his secret room in long strides, reached the door that opened on the stairs. Cautiously, he opened a peephole and stared out. On the platform below crouched two policemen with revolvers in their hands.

"You have no right to do this," Nita cried indignantly, and Wentworth heard her voice dimly through the panels. He ran back to peer again into his music room.

He was trapped beyond any doubt. By a strange misfortune, one of those slips that had dogged every step of his battle against Martin and the Avenger, Marshant had spotted the very panel which opened as a door. Nita's standing before it had been a clue, but it was damned clever work. He flinched back from the panel as an axe thudded dully against the other side. A muffled cry of anger rose to his lips.

Nita was still protesting, but he knew that was vain. Marshant would not be taking such drastic action unless he had a warrant. Was this then the end? Wentworth cursed himself savagely. Kirkpatrick's premonitions had gotten under his skin. Each time he got in a tight spot, he was prepared to advance to surrender. But his anger accomplished nothing. Facts stared him in the face. The only two exits to the secret room were blocked by police with drawn revolvers, men against whom he could not fight. Yet he must escape them.

He peered once more into the music room. "This time, we've got the *Spider*," Marshant gloated. "The entire building is filled with my men." He drew two heavy revolvers and stood with them half-leveled at the door. The axe thudded again into the wood.

CHAPTER FOURTEEN

The Spider's Oath

Nita heard the axes ring on steel, heard the triumphant shouts of the axe men and their redoubled blows. The burly Marshant was barking short laughter from deep in his throat. He had a revolver in each hand and he stood well back from the spot where his men hacked, stood on the balls of his feet with a readiness that Nita recognized. When that door went down, Marshant planned to go in shooting. The *Spider* was not going to be captured alive!

Her heart's pounding suffocated Nita. She knew that even to save his life, Wentworth would not shoot at police. He might slug or fire over their heads, but his swift deadly bullets were not for the defenders of the law. What could she do? Was she to stand here helplessly while Dick was murdered? For murder it would be as surely as if he did not have a weapon in his secret room.

Nita smiled and stood away from the wall against which she had been leaning, strolled across the room as casually as the *Spider* could have managed.

"I suppose you're prepared to pay damages on all this, Mr. Marshant," she said, taking a cigarette from a case on the piano, lighting it.

Marshant barked his sharp laughter. "I'll pay it out of the reward money," he snorted.

Nita's laughter tinkled. "That, I believe, is what is known as counting the hens a bit before the incubation." She strolled to a high arched stone fireplace and tapped ashes into the hearth, stood staring down at the unlighted logs. She dropped a hand carelessly beside her and it closed about the handle of a heavy poker. A glance from the corners of her eyes showed that a single leap would put her within striking distance of Marshant. Then she waited, watching the work of the axe men. They had stripped aside all the wood now and were prying tentatively at the edges of the steel door.

One of them gave a violent wrench and the steel plate snapped aside into the facing. A choked shout rasped in Marshant's throat and he lunged forward, guns swinging up. Nita made her leap, the poker sweeping in an arc. Then both man and woman checked in midspring and Nita screamed. She darted forward, but Marshant's hand closed on her shoulder, thrust her roughly aside.

"No, you don't," he said harshly. "None of your tricks."

Nita pitched to her hands and knees and stayed that way, her head wrenched up, her eyes staring. The two policemen shrank back from the opening into which light streamed from the music room. Something dark and horrible swung limply in the doorway, something that turned slowly to left and to right, but had no other movement.

"It's a dummy," Marshant swore.

"No, chief," gulped a policeman. "It's *him!* He's committed suicide!"

They went slowly toward the figure of the *Spider*, hanged by the neck in the doorway. A chair had been knocked over and lay beneath his feet. His eyes bulged and his face was purple with congested blood, tongue pinched between his teeth. Marshant cursed suddenly and leaped forward to fling his arms about the *Spider* and lift him down. If he were not yet dead, Marshant wanted the glory of capturing him alive. The policemen crowded in behind him.

Abruptly, movement convulsed the *Spider*. Both his feet lashed out and caught Marshant in the stomach. The burly deputy doubled forward and sat down heavily and Wentworth dropped lightly to his feet, a blade slashing above his head to cut the rope. The policemen cursed, surging backward and squeezing together in the open doorway. They sought frantically to flee from the dead man who attacked them, the dead man whose face was still purplish with strangulation, whose tongue still pinched out between his teeth. Wentworth's able fists took care of them both. He stepped back and thoughtfully slapped Marshant across the base of the skull with a blackjack, then he snatched off the fearful mask made from implements of disguise, that had covered his features.

Nita surged to her feet and plunged toward him, flung her arms about his neck. "Ah, Dick, Dick!" she sobbed. "That was cruel!"

An end of the rope still dangled from inside the collar of his cape. It was fastened beneath his arm pits. Wentworth laughed lightly.

"Cruel, but rather necessary," he told her, holding her tightly. "If it hadn't been for your scream, they might have shot first and investigated afterward. Now, I've got to go, darling."

"The building is full of police," Nita said rapidly. "Every exit and every floor is guarded. How can you go?"

Wentworth shrugged. "I've got to."

He ripped off his cape and hat, picked up an overcoat that one of the policemen had discarded to work, jerked on the uniform cap.

"Go into the secret room," he said, "and when policemen leave the stairs, open the door and step out."

"But you!"

"I'll join you there."

While Nita stepped over the prone bodies of the police, Wentworth ripped out the telephone to prevent an

278

alarm, then he raced to the outer door with pounding feet.

"Quick!" he yelled into the hall. "We got the *Spider,* but he's fighting!"

He left the door open and ducked into the cover of the portières. He shouted hoarsely, grunted as if he struggled. He heard cries in the hall and the rapid pound of feet. Police raced toward the arched door of the music room. Wentworth slipped out into the hall and shut the door, wedged it fast with a bit of rasp steel. Nita walked toward him rapidly along the hall, drawing a cloak about her shoulders.

"I jammed the secret door shut," she said.

Wentworth nodded and signaled his private elevator. It rose swiftly while police pounded on the door of his apartment. A cop was running the cage and he gawped at the muzzle of an automatic staring him in the eyes.

"Down," Wentworth ordered casually.

The cage descended and as it stopped at the bottom floor, Wentworth sapped the policeman operator and opened the door himself. Nita sauntered out first into a ring of four police. There were two more at the outer door, another pair at the foot of the steps. She looked at them disdainfully, jerked her arm away when Wentworth touched it.

The deception worked for two seconds, until Wentworth was within reach of the four police. Even as they gasped with realization of the trick, Wentworth was in motion. Blackjacks slipped from each sleeve into the palm of his hands and, both arms striking, he charged the four.

"Save me! Save me!" Nita cried. She ran toward the two stair guards with her arms stretched out beseechingly. They bounded to meet her and she gripped an arm of each desperately. Needled rings she had picked from Wentworth's supplies in the secret room did their work and the two men stood foggily, then reeled back against the wall, already somnolent with narcotics.

One cursed, "You dirty little tramp!" He tried to raise his gun and Nita took it from his fumbling fingers.

Three of the police Wentworth had attacked were down now, but the other two from the doorway were closing in warily. They carried guns in their hands, but they hesitated to use them. After all, this man in a police uniform had fired no shots.

Nita leveled her captured gun. "Hands up!" she ordered sharply.

The cops cursed, their heads jerking toward her. Wentworth heaved up and dived at their legs. One man came down with both of his knees in Wentworth's side. The other reached out and slapped with the muzzle of his gun. It dug into Wentworth's shoulder. He gasped with pain, wrenched and tumbled the two men together. Nita sprang in and struck with the reversed revolver and one cop collapsed.

Wentworth reeled to his knees, then to his feet, slugging powerfully. The other policeman went down. He was still in the air, falling, when a blinding flash of light filled the hallway.

For an instant, it froze Wentworth and Nita in rigid surprise; then he was plunging toward two men in civilian clothes who stood by the outer doors, a reporter he recognized and a newspaper photographer whose flashlight had startled them. The photographer was already in motion, fleeing with his camera. The reporter remained to fight, but went down at the first blow.

Nita at his heels, Wentworth plunged through the outer doors to the street and saw a taxi spurt from the curb, snow flying from its wheels. He spun, hunting another, and saw two more police pounding toward him from a parked radio roadster with guns glinting in their hands.

"The chief wants that guy!" Wentworth shouted, pointing after the fleeing taxi. "He snapped a picture, and. . . ."

The cops raced up to him, staring at the fugitive taxi and Wentworth's two blackjacks flicked out. He sprang over their falling bodies to the police roadster and sent it racing and skidding up the street. Nita huddled beside him, shoulders hunched from the biting cold. She crowded as close to Wentworth as his wild driving would permit. There was a small, happy smile on her lips.

"Now, Dick," she said. "You can't disappear without me. We're outlaws together."

Wentworth skated around a corner in a shower of snow, heard the rising wail of sirens behind. His face was set in a hard, grim mold. Unless he could recover that photograph, what Nita prophesied was absolute truth. She was bound in outlawry with him, assisting a murderer to escape police.

He spun another corner, speeding toward the offices of the *Globe*, for it had been a reporter of that newspaper who had helped the camera man to escape. Two things to do at once, escape the police and recover that photograph. He wove around two more corners and slammed on brakes. The Ford spun completely about, bumped a snow bank and halted. A taxi was stalled in the middle of the street. By the side of it, the camera man whom Wentworth pursued stood cursing and shaking his fist down the street.

Wentworth spilled from the police car with an automatic in his hand.

"Where's that photograph?" he demanded.

"The Avenger!" snarled the newspaperman. "The Avenger held me up and took it!"

Wentworth heard what the reporter said with a sense of disbelief. The Avenger? But he was in Chicago, or had been twenty-four hours ago, blocked off from the East by the break-down of all communications in the blizzard. But there was no time to speculate on that. Police were on his heels. He hurled back to his car and it leaped away with whining tires as he sprang to the running board. Nita had taken the wheel.

Wentworth hurled a swift question at her. "Three planes got through from the west," she told him, "and they're hoping to get trains through by night. The need for foodstuffs, you know. They performed miracles in clearing the way."

Then the Avenger might have come on any of those planes. He recalled abruptly that the weather had been clearing when he had left Buffalo. It had been only necessary to arrange for a take-off and a landing and the planes could come through. But his battle eastward had not been in vain. Because he had reached New York early, Kirkpatrick had been prepared to stop the sale of medicines and he himself had learned the location of the gang headquarters.

His mind flicked back to the photographer. Needless to speculate on the Avenger's purposes. He had simply added another item to his evidence against the *Spider*. And this time, he had involved Nita also. And the Avenger had known uncannily where to strike. He seemed almost to have arranged for the picture to be taken. . . . Wentworth recalled sharply that the taxi beside which the photographer had stood had had no driver. That was the explanation then. The Avenger had posed as a taxi driver.

"Find an alley, dear, and park," Wentworth said swiftly. "We've got to get rid of this car."

While the car twisted and skated on icy streets, Wentworth made slight changes in his face. It had been well enough to defy the city in the garb of the *Spider* alone, but with Nita beside him, the situation changed. He made himself as inconspicuous as possible. Nita found an alley and charged the police car over a two-foot barrier of snow before it stalled. Wentworth led her rapidly to a subway station and they sped northward.

He had not lied when he had stated that everything was prepared for his disappearance. He had an apartment in the west eighties rented under an assumed name and it was to this he took Nita. In the small, plainly furnished living room, he relieved her of the long coat that had concealed her lounging pajamas, then faced her, his lips gravely smiling. Nita faced him joyously. Her violet eyes were sparkling.

"Now, Dick," she said, "you will have to take me

with you when you disappear. You can't leave me behind to face the charges alone. If the Avenger has that
plate. . . .''

Her voice died as Wentworth continued to gaze down
at her with compassion in his eyes. He lifted a hand
and stroked the clustering chestnut curls, lifted her chin
and pressed a light kiss upon her lips.

"Dick, what is it?" Nita asked him swiftly. "You
have everything ready to disappear, haven't you? Nothing has happened to destroy your funds?"

Wentworth's mouth twisted. He opened his eyes and
blinked away the blur that was before them and turned
to face Nita again, cupping her dear face in his hands,
fighting down the pain that was like a twisted knife in
his heart.

"I hate to tell you, my darling," he said gently.
"But . . . it just can't be."

"Why?" she asked.

Wentworth took his hands away from her face and
whirled to pace up and down the room.

"The evidence against me is complete," he said.
"The Avenger has enough a dozen times over to send
me to the chair. Every man and woman I pass on the
street recognizes me and says, 'There goes the *Spider!*'
All Kirkpatrick's police are hunting me with orders to
bring me in 'dead or alive.' ''

"I know all that, Dick," Nita's voice was deadly
still, stripped of all emotion. "I know all that, but none
of it would keep you from disappearing. Your plans are
well laid."

"Do you suppose I haven't told myself that ten thousand times?" he asked sharply, his voice close to cracking. "But the leader of this damnable conspiracy is still
alive. And I don't know him. There is only one way
to find him out."

"Still alive!" It was a cry from Nita. "But the police
smashed them this morning. Kirkpatrick was fair about
it. He told the newspapers that you had given him the
address. They killed twelve men, captured five or six

more with packets of poisoned cold medicine on them.''

Wentworth nodded. It was good to hear, but it was not enough.

Martin, damn him, was still alive, and while he lived, there could be no safety for the nation's millions. He need only whisper his dread threats and industry would bow to him. And now and again, when his hold threatened to slip, he would kill another thousand persons, or destroy another thousand women's faces. Nita was walking toward him, her deep, tragic eyes gazing into his.

"What are you trying to tell me, dear?" she asked quietly.

Wentworth still stood rigidly, hands clenched. "Just this," he said between clenched teeth. "That while that fiend is alive, I cannot disappear. I cannot run to safety. And to capture him means . . . the end!"

"But why, dear, why?" Nita's calmness broke. She was clinging to him suddenly, imploring him with piteous eyes. "Happiness seems so near, sweetheart. We have always realized that some day, the chase would grow too hot, that you would have to go away. Sometimes, when I was weak and lonesome, I have prayed that the day might come. And now it has come.''

"And I cannot go!" Wentworth's voice was harsh. "Would you have the *Spider* turn his back on a living enemy?"

Nita took her hands from his coat. She looked down at them and twined her white slim fingers together. She drew a deep breath and it made a shuddering noise in her throat.

"Yes, Dick," she whispered. She looked up at him and now her fists were clenched at her sides, her chin was up. "Yes, Dick," she said clearly. "I would have you run away. You have done enough for humanity. You have risked your life and given of your strength and brain without stint for years. You have saved thousands of lives, millions. You have saved your country time and again. And how has humanity repaid you?''

There was bitterness and anger in Nita's bearing. "How has humanity repaid you?" she repeated, her voice was like a challenging trumpet. "I'll tell you how: By hounding you until you are in deadly peril even when you walk along the street; by forcing police to spend their time hunting for you with drawn guns, instead of running down criminals; by putting a sixty-thousand-dollar price on your head!"

Wentworth lifted a hand wearily. "Does that matter?" he asked gently. "I do not serve humanity for a reward. I serve that men may have happiness, that the vultures of crime may be purged from the earth. The service is reward in itself."

He shook his head as Nita would have gone on. "Darling," he said, "Martin must die before we can go. And the only way to trap him is to offer myself once more as bait, and to do it publicly. If I can do that and still escape, I shall do it . . . but I can see no hope at all."

The anger was gone from Nita now, but she still stood rigidly. Slow, big tears were sliding down her cheeks.

Hoarsely, Wentworth cried: "For God's sake, Nita, don't—" He stood on braced feet, hands clenched. "Don't!" he repeated tightly. "God, Nita, I'm human as well as you. Don't you suppose that sometimes this gets to be almost more than I can bear? Don't you know that sometimes the torture of the service I have sworn tears at my heart?"

"Your heart, yes," Nita said bitterly, "but never your mind. Oh, Dick, don't you see? It's the sheer ingratitude of it all. Humanity hating you. And you giving your life, and more than your life. Your heart rebels, yes, but always the mind—the mind of the *Spider*, Dick, not that of Richard Wentworth—will not yield."

Wentworth's shoulders sagged. He stared down at the floor, lifted a hand to his weary head, pressing, pressing against the ache there. No, he would never yield! His heart ached, too. Suddenly Nita was in his arms, her lips lifted for his kiss.

"Forgive me, Dick," she said quietly. "I won't do it again. It's just that sometimes. . . ."

Wentworth took her close to his heart, buried his face in her fragrant hair.

A thunderous crash, a smashing tinkle of broken glass jerked up his head, but he made no move to seize his weapons. It was useless. Two policemen with leveled guns crouched in the window they had broken. The door hung crazily by one hinge and in the opening stood Kirkpatrick. He strode into the room and from behind him darted Patsy Malone, her eyes glittering with hate.

"You are under arrest, Dick," Kirkpatrick's voice was utterly without expression, "for the murder of Mannley."

Patsy Malone flung back her head and laughed. The laughter changed into a sob.

"And may you burn in hell for ten thousand years!" she shrilled. "You killed my Shane!"

CHAPTER FIFTEEN

Jackson Interferes

Wentworth put Nita aside slowly, still staring at the mixture of grief and triumph on the Irish girl's face. His mind still besotted with his own struggle. He was exhausted emotionally. He could only think dully that the end had come sooner than he had thought. Now his plans for Martin could not be fulfilled, that man would continue to prey upon the people. He jerked his head angrily. This was nonsense. Had someone cast a spell over him that he conceded defeat so easily?

Granted that he was captured, that there was no way to escape, did that mean the end? He flung his mind at the problem.

"Oh, Kirk," Nita was saying. "Couldn't you have allowed us this one last little moment?"

Kirkpatrick was bowing gravely, with his perpetual studied grace. Courteous regret was on his face, and his eyes were haggard. "I am sorry, Nita," he said.

That was all. Wentworth knew that Kirkpatrick had done much for him in making the capture himself. If it had been any one else the capture would have been made in the smoke of blasting guns that would have torn the life out of his body. But he must think of other things than this.

Patsy Malone said that her brother was dead and she

blamed him for it. Well, he might not be dead. But that was unimportant. It was obvious that she had led police to this hideout. She could have got information as to his whereabouts only from Jackson. That was clear, too. He shook his head sadly. Jackson had failed him utterly. The man was either a traitor or a feeble dupe in this girl's hands.

He looked to Kirkpatrick and found the commissioner's eyes alertly upon him.

"Kirk," he said desperately, "I must talk with you in private. I give you my parole not to attempt to escape during that time."

Kirkpatrick looked at him with cold, dead eyes and shook his head. "You are a prisoner, Dick," he said flatly, "and you must take a prisoner's treatment."

"The commissioner would listen to important information from any prisoner," Wentworth argued anxiously. "As to my parole, you do not need to accept that. Police can keep guard just out of hearing."

Kirkpatrick hesitated, then shrugged agreement. "It will do no good, but you may talk."

He walked with Wentworth to a corner of the room. "Now what is it?"

Wentworth drew a deep breath, his eyes holding his friend's. "I have a plan to catch both the Avenger and Martin, the gangster behind these poisonings."

Kirkpatrick waited, saying nothing, his eyes fixed on Wentworth's face.

"My plan is this," Wentworth continued rapidly. "The Avenger has agreed to meet me at any time and place I name. I want to arrange that and let Martin know the plans. He is anxious to remove us both, and will, I am sure, come after us. The rest should be easy."

"You want me to release you for this—meeting?" Kirkpatrick's voice was heavy.

Wentworth shook his head, smiling wanly. "No, nothing as impossible as that, Kirk. I only ask that you make the arrangements as I wish, and that at the proper time you allow me to go to the spot under surveillance—under guard of any number of men you can hide. And that, once on the scene, you allow me a free hand. I promise you that when the affair is ended, I will surrender to you."

Kirkpatrick was silent for a long time. Wentworth pleaded with him, pointing out how Martin could reorganize, and the total lack of clues to his identity. Ultimately Kirkpatrick agreed. "I want your pledge not to attempt to escape, Dick," he replied.

"You have it," Wentworth said simply.

Kirkpatrick's eyes met his sternly. "I'm risking everything, Dick," he said slowly. "I could never justify this, even to myself if there were a slip-up."

A faint smile touched Wentworth's lips. His face was very pale. "You're not risking anything, Kirk," he said slowly. "If my plans fail, you'll still have a prisoner and your evidence."

Nita was giving a fine exhibition of mass disdain. Apparently she saw neither the policeman, nor the gloating Patsy Malone. Only when Wentworth walked toward her, she smiled.

"Tonight, dear," he said, "you will receive a message from me. Follow it implicitly."

Her eyes questioned but got no answer. She looked to Kirkpatrick. "You mean you aren't taking me along, too?" she asked.

"There are no charges against you, Nita," Kirkpatrick said kindly. Then they filed out, taking Wentworth with them. Nita watched them go and for long after they had left, her eyes remained fixed on the door that sagged from one twisted hinge. Finally, she gathered her courage and went home to her apartment on Riverside Drive. Men and women turned curiously as she alighted from the taxi and walked across the walk. Even for these days when women dared use no cosmetics, she was strangely pale. Even the reporters clustered about her door gave way without a question.

Ram Singh awaited her. He had discovered the police at his master's apartment and reported to her instead.

He had found that all the suspects Wentworth had named, save only one, had been in New York throughout the time the Avenger had been operating in Chicago. The exception was Commander Samuels. He had dropped from sight for days together.

Scarcely was the report finished when the telephone rang insistently. Jackson calling from Chicago. He had made the trip west to help Wentworth. Communications had just been restored.

"I sent this information to New York by Patsy Malone by plane last night," Jackson said. "Hers was the first plane to go through after the storm. I tangled with Martin's men and got wounded, but I learned they are planning to use the poison in candy bars next."

"Did you give Patsy Malone Mr. Wentworth's secret address?" Nita asked, surprised at her calmness of voice.

"I had to," Jackson said swiftly. "I was afraid she wouldn't find him at home."

"Patsy Malone took the police there," said Nita in clear syllables. "Mr. Wentworth is now under arrest, charged with murder."

The wire hummed silently between them after that. . . . The operator broke to find if they were through talking and Jackson said hurriedly. "No, no!" There was another pause.

"Patsy took the police there?" he asked heavily. "You are sure?"

"I was there when they arrived," Nita said.

Jackson's voice dropped a full tone. "Will you give the warning about candy to the police? I'm flying to New York. Good-bye."

Nita did not know how much later it was that Ram Singh brought her newspapers with great screaming headlines across the front page:

WENTWORTH ARRESTED AS *SPIDER!*

The story narrated that the Avenger had 'phoned the information but that Commissioner Kirkpatrick refused to comment on the report. The Avenger had also said that it had been he who had directed police to Wentworth's hiding place; that he had turned over to police irrefutable evidence. A knot like a fist caught in Nita's throat and her breath got past it with difficulty. Did that mean the automatic that had killed Mannley? She read on, but the paper gave no details.

This great spread of news had crowded into a single column a new outbreak of the poison deaths, this time traceable to cold medicine. Despite embargoes and newspaper warnings, the toll for New York City was over a thousand. She skimmed on through that story. Throughout the United States, these mysterious poisonings were spreading. Seven thousand had died this day. The causes were various: canned meats and fish; medicine; package food of all varieties.

Nita read these facts without emotion. She became conscious of the fact that Ram Singh stood unobtrusively against the wall with arms folded, his hawkish eyes impassive beneath his turban-wrapped brow. He, too, was waiting. Nita sprang to her feet and began to pace the floor.

When the 'phone bell pealed finally, Nita stood and stared at the instrument for moments before she picked it up. The smooth, hard rubber felt cool and she realized her hands were fevered.

"Dick, darling," she said.

"Don't sound so mournful, sweetheart," Wentworth's voice was hearty. "Here's what you must do. Insert an ad in the *Times* personals for the morning, addressed to Mannley. It should read this way: Tonight at midnight in the Waldorf-Astoria, Main ballroom, unless you are the coward your actions indicate. No signature. Got it?"

Nita repeated the message breathlessly. "What does it mean, Dick?"

Wentworth laughed sharply. "It's a challenge to the Avenger. Send Ram Singh to give the same word to Patsy Malone."

"But, Dick," Nita hesitated. "How will you be able to meet the Avenger? How did you get to a 'phone?"

"I'm in Kirk's office," Wentworth's voice went emotionless. "We have an agreement. I'll see you at the Waldorf. Don't forget to get word to Patsy Malone. Ram Singh can carry the message. 'Bye, darling."

Nita groped twice for the 'phone cradle before she found it. Her eyes refused to focus on the instrument. Her heart was beating strongly, like a noisy drum in her throat. Was it possible that even in the face of doom, her Dick had found a way? But she dared not let herself hope. The Avenger's evidence was too much. And Wentworth had given his parole not to escape. He would not break his word. No, there was no hope. But her heart continued to sing and Nita felt a strange jubilance as she set about doing the things that Wentworth had requested. She even managed to sleep. . . .

Soon after dawn, Jackson's ringing of the bell awoke her. She wrapped a long black robe about her and went into the living room to see him. She felt hatred of him tightening her heart. This was the man whose bungling had helped to doom her Dick.

Jackson's wide-jawed square face was pale, but he seemed solid on his feet, and his eyes were like live coals.

"Where is the major?" he asked. His voice was quiet enough but it sounded forced out of his throat.

"In jail," Nita told him shortly. "Tonight at midnight he duels the Avenger. He wants to make sure that Martin hears of that fact. He desired that Patsy Malone hear of it, too." She masked her hatred, but her bitterness crept out. "Do you think you could get word to her?" she asked almost sweetly.

Jackson made no reply to her last phrase. "How is he to get out of jail for the duel?"

Nita shook her head. "He has made some sort of deal with Kirkpatrick. There is no doubt that the duel means his death. You read the newspapers?"

Jackson nodded his head woodenly. His face continued impassive. "Thank you, Miss Nita," he said, about-faced and stalked for the door.

"What are you going to do, Jackson?" Nita asked sharply.

"I'm going to see the major," he told her from the door.

Wentworth was in conference with Kirkpatrick when Jackson was announced. Kirkpatrick nodded jerkily. "In a moment," he said. "Are all our plans complete now, Dick?"

Wentworth checked over a list before him. "Every one of the suspects has been notified to attend," he said slowly. "Patsy Malone will be there all right, hoping to see her brother avenged. I'm depending on Martin learning of this through her; or through the ad. There can't be much doubt that he is in town. Certainly the capture of his men will set him to organizing a fresh gang."

"It sounds as complete as possible, Dick," Kirkpatrick said gravely, "but I am very dubious of success." He pressed a button and a policeman thrust in a carrot-topped head. "Let Jackson come in!"

Kirkpatrick had aged years in recent days. The deep-cut lines about his mouth corners were chiseled permanently into his face. Even his mustaches, usually sharply pointed, seemed to droop with age. He looked up heavily, both hands flat on the desk, as Jackson came in. The door closed and Jackson leveled a heavy gun.

"Please do not move, Mr. Kirkpatrick, sir," he said. He was polite, but there was menace in his voice.

"Put that gun up, Jackson," Wentworth snapped.

"Sorry, Major," said Jackson, his face impassive. "You're getting out of here."

"Put that gun up," Wentworth repeated. "I've given my parole."

"I haven't," Jackson replied.

Wentworth sprang toward him, snatching for the gun and Jackson dodged and slapped and Wentworth collapsed unconscious. Kirkpatrick had started to his feet, his hand going to a gun in his drawer. Before he could level it, Jackson knocked him out, too. Jackson was breathing deeply through his nose. It made small hissing noises. He crossed to the door and listened there, then he shifted his gun to his left hand and got Wentworth up on his right shoulder and stalked out of the door.

The carrot-topped cop gasped and went down with a gun-welt across his forehead. Jackson descended to the basement in the elevator with his gun in the operator's side, slugged the man there and carried Wentworth out of the door where patrol wagons delivered their charges.

He went passed a room where men were vehemently intent over pinochle. They didn't look up, didn't heed the starting purr of an automobile motor. Kirkpatrick's 'phone call was minutes late.

Nursing his aching head in his hands, Kirkpatrick sat behind his desk and stared down at the blotter. He had had one flash of doubt concerning Wentworth, then that had died. If Dick had given his pledged word, then he had not connived this subterfuge to evade that pledge and he had attempted to seize Jackson. No, Jackson had acted on his own.

Abruptly, Kirkpatrick jerked up his head. Jackson was infatuated with Patsy Malone. It had been Jackson, indirectly, who had betrayed Wentworth's hiding place. Was it possible that in kidnaping his Master, he had been working for the Avenger?

A sharp fear stabbed through Kirkpatrick. He had fought to put Wentworth behind the bars, but through every minute of the fight he had hoped that his friend would in some way elude him. It had been with a sinking heart that he had accepted the surrender in that hideout Patsy Malone had revealed, and there had been hatred in his heart for the Irish girl.

He was conniving a violation of the law in permitting Dick to meet the Avenger tonight and he had done it

294

willingly. Not so much to trap Martin and the Avenger, but in the hope that Dick might find a clean death and not be forced to go through the humiliation of trial and prison and execution. If Wentworth could achieve that, Kirkpatrick felt that he would be willing to accept whatever punishment was meted out to him for his part in the affair.

Kirkpatrick flung himself from his desk and paced his office floor with long, angry strides. He hurled the full forces of the police force into a search for Wentworth. At eleven o'clock, one hour before the scheduled meeting, he had learned precisely nothing. He left his home with an aching heaviness in his breast to take Nita to the Waldorf-Astoria, to the scene of the duel Wentworth had planned and now, perhaps, might never fight. . . .

CHAPTER SIXTEEN

The Avenger's Trick

Throughout the long day, Nita had gone emptily about her apartment, doing unimportant things as if they were the most important things in the world. She had spent a half hour feeding Apollo who was more than capable of feeding himself. She ironed lace which her maid could have prepared more prettily. For an hour she sat before her easel trying to mix the exact shade of a sunset cloud. Ram Singh watched her from his motionless post against the wall, and his eyes were brooding.

Nita had dragged through days before this when Wentworth's life hung in the balance, but never before, even when her Dick had been reported dead, had she known such an utter sense of futility and despair. Dick himself had given up. He was carrying on the battle to its bitter end, but not with any hope of escaping from the doom that overshadowed him. He hoped merely to do humanity one last service before he died.

And now Jackson had interfered even with that plan, as he had bungled so many others. Nita turned her eyes toward the ice-spotted river, but she did not see it. There was a prayer in her heart, a prayer she had never thought it necessary to say before for the all-powerful *Spider: Dear God, help Dick!*

When Kirkpatrick came, she went with him woodenly, her head held high and pridefully. A newspaper-man whispered audibly to a companion.

"Marie Antoinette goes to her tumbril," he snickered.

The other newspaperman shoved him violently against the wall and went toward him with his fists clenched.

"Keep your mouth shut," he snarled.

Nita heard all that in a vague way, but she ignored them as Kirkpatrick did. Loud-mouthed wrangling rose behind them as the elevator descended.

"Do they know anything?" Nita asked.

Kirkpatrick shook his head. He was frowning at the closed door.

"No one knows anything," he said slowly. "I called a conference to discuss means of combatting the poison-ers and promised to present such witnesses as might prove useful. It's a committee of citizens who are de-manding action by the city, an end of the poison deaths. Dick decided to use them. In underworld circles, we had it whispered that both the *Spider* and the Avenger would be there. By that means, Dick hopes to lure this man, Martin, into a trap. He says that Martin is anxious to dispose of the Avenger."

They were in Kirkpatrick's car now, purring eastward between head-high banks of dirty snow. It was five minutes of twelve when they entered the Waldorf and took an elevator directly to the ball room. Nita paced through the familiar halls with a sense of utter unreality. It seemed a flimsy trap that her Dick had built and now he might not even be there to lend it the strength of his own keen mind.

She was abruptly sure that there was much more to the plan than Kirkpatrick had said, perhaps more than he knew. Wentworth did not usually confide his full plans to anyone. Strangely, that gave her hope. It gave her the courage to walk, quietly smiling, past a group of newspapermen near the ballroom door. She even in-clined her head to Eddie Blanton, puffing nervous bursts of smoke from his long cigarette holder. He seized the opportunity to stride forward.

"I say, Kirkpatrick," he said in a whisper. "What's going on here tonight? There's more afoot than just giving evidence to this bunch of mugs that call themselves the Committee of Public Safety. Anyway, you've been refusing to see any of them, and now, all at once, you promise to put all your cards on the table."

"A matter of public policy, or politics," Kirkpatrick told him with a slight smile.

"Will you bring Wentworth here tonight to testify?" Blanton asked. "The Avenger 'phoned us he would be here, but that he didn't want it published beforehand."

Nita studied the reporter's shrewd, horsey face, so incongruously set on heavy shoulders, and felt a sudden distaste for the man. It was not his cocky self-assurance. That was an air that went with his job, a necessary adjunct to crashing in where he wasn't wanted. It was his sly satisfaction when he mentioned Wentworth. She recalled that Dick had said Blanton had long suspected him.

Kirkpatrick jerked a hand impatiently. "Would you mind stepping aside, Blanton?" He gestured Nita toward the broad, double doors.

"We know you've got Wentworth a prisoner, Kirkpatrick," Blanton clung to the commissioner's elbow. "Why not admit it?"

Kirkpatrick lifted his chin in a gesture toward a quiet man in tuxedo who stood just inside the doors. The man strode alertly forward, and Blanton fell back with a laugh. Nita and Kirkpatrick went in and were immediately the center of attention. Heads turned on all sides and a boy in a light-blue uniform hurried forward, clicked his heels and reported that Commander Samuels wished to speak to him on the platform.

Nita's hand had been resting on Kirkpatrick's arm. Her fingers closed tightly upon it.

"But, Kirk," she was a little breathless. "Is he on

298

the committee?'' She knew Wentworth suspected Samuels of being the Avenger.

Kirkpatrick nodded, his eyes veiled as they met hers. "Commander Samuels was in naval intelligence," he told her without expression. "He has been called in as a consultant by the committee."

Nita felt once more a sense of great things that were impending—things that would be unexpected and terrible. Her breasts were stirring with sharply accented breathing and she looked about her, half tearfully, seeking the reason. Blanton had felt it, too. She found that once more she was gripping Kirkpatrick's arm painfully. Her fingers ached with the tension.

Kirkpatrick seated her and hurried off with a deliberate bow. His face was expressionless as he strode toward the platform. Nita followed him with her eyes, saw the men assembled there. Commander Samuels was rising, ruddy faced wreathed in smiles as usual, the blond hyphens of his eyebrows raised. Something was utterly incongruous about his formally clad figure, but for the moment Nita could not place it. She saw then that, after the manner of service men, he wore high shoes instead of the proper oxfords or pumps.

Deputy Commissioner Marshant stood upon the platform talking with Kirkpatrick and Commander Samuels. The broad bulk of the two would have dwarfed a less commanding man than Kirkpatrick, but there was an arrogance in his carriage that dominated despite his lesser stature. Nita's eyes left them and turned to the audience.

Patsy Malone was directly opposite her in another bank of seats. Although she had known the Irish girl would be here, she felt anger sending a flush up her cheeks. That was the woman who, through Jackson, had trapped Wentworth.

On Patsy's right sat a man who almost cringed in his seat. It was absurd, but he held a baby in his lap. Nita recalled Wentworth's story of his fight with the Avenger in Patsy's apartment. That man would be the neighbor, Coxwell. A few seats away was a man with a stony, pasty-white face. He seemed to see everything yet look at nothing. Nita placed him, too: the croupier, Larue, from Mannley's gambling halls.

At a long table to one side near the front, newspapermen lounged in their chairs and smoked. Eddie Blanton, with studied insolence, had hooked his heels over a corner of the table. He snapped them down when he caught her eyes and sauntered forward, his horsey face longer than usual, smoke streaming over his shoulder from his foot-long cigarette holder. Curiously, Nita noticed that he was knock-kneed.

Blanton leaned over her confidentially. "What's coming off here tonight?" he whispered. "Something big's in the wind. My nose for news tells me that."

Nita continued to smile. She crossed her knees and tapped a cigarette on the knee cap. "Have you a match, Mr. Blanton?"

Blanton lit her cigarette with an exaggerated bow and walked purposefully toward the platform. The newspaperman was restless as a hound before the hunt.

A woman screamed.

Nita jerked her head to the right, staring at a woman who had half-risen in her seat. She was pointing and she had clapped a hand to her mouth, partly smothering her cry. Men had started to their feet. Their heads jerked, too, to the spot where she pointed, the platform.

A quiver shook Nita as her eyes took in the scene. Against the proscenium arch at one side of the stage leaned a man with a sub-machine gun in his arms. He had a black mask over his eyes and the gun's muzzle moved slowly back and forth over the assemblage.

"Don't move," the man said clearly, "and you won't be hurt."

Nita's eyes flicked from him to the other men on the stage. In a confused group, they were being herded off the platform, down a short flight of stairs and out into the audience. Behind them were three more masked men and as the last of the group descended, she saw that they, too, carried machine guns. Kirkpatrick still

300

stood on the bottom step. "Don't attempt to shoot it out with them," he said in a quiet voice that carried to the far corners of the room. "Too many bystanders would be killed."

Nita looked around and saw that the policemen at the doors were relaxing from tense poises. Their faces showed relief over Kirkpatrick's order.

An absolute hush lay upon the audience. The newspapermen sat rigidly, gripping the table, staring into the muzzle of a machine gun devoted entirely to them. The gangster who held it dropped down on the top step of the short flight from the stage. "You boys better sit quiet," he advised.

Nita was not thinking. She did not know what she had expected, but this was not it. Kirkpatrick sat down beside her, stolidly pulling up each trouser leg in turn to protect the crease. He gravely offered her a cigarette.

"Is . . . is this . . ?" Nita began.

"No," said Kirkpatrick quietly, "this is not part of the plan. Something has gone wrong."

Something! Everything had gone wrong. Nita fought down a mad impulse to burst into laughter. The despair she had struggled against throughout the day pushed up into her throat and strangled her. She did not realize that there was a renewed murmur of whispers all about her until, suddenly, that stopped. It was not a dying whisper such as the theater knows. It was instantaneous, breaths caught in the middle of a word. Her eyes flew to the platform.

From an ante-room of the stage, a swaggering broadshouldered figure strode. He stalked to the front of the platform and stood in the center, looking out over the people. One of the machine gunners turned his head and looked at him, then faced front again. Three of the gangsters were seated, but their weapons were trained on the people before them. If one of them squeezed a trigger, a dozen persons would be blown into bloody death.

But all eyes were focused on the new arrival. He was not formally clad, but wore a black suit, shirt and tie. Over his face was a hood mask that was tucked neatly into a black collar. The face was formless beneath the hood. Eyes glittered from the slits.

The hush broke into a running murmur of sound: *"The Avenger!"*

A few men started to their feet, but subsided as the machine gunners tensed. A newspaperman tried to argue with the crook that held them prisoner and was almost slugged down with a blackjack. Nita saw all these things subconsciously. Her eyes were fixed on the hooded man. He bowed suavely to the audience, then retired against the wall at the rear of the stage and stood on braced feet. His shoulders did not touch. There was about him an air of wary readiness.

"Damned clever," Kirkpatrick whispered in her ear, "if he really has kidnaped Dick."

Once more Nita felt the strange urge to laughter. Kirkpatrick could think of things like that when Dick might be dead! She touched her dress bag upon her knees, feeling the weight of the small automatic she carried there. She could kill the Avenger easily. It seemed unimportant that after she did that, she and a half-hundred others would be mowed down by fanning bullets.

She was aware that Kirkpatrick was still offering a cigarette. He leaned toward her, his eyes cool.

"No, Nita," he said. "Give Dick a chance."

Give Dick a chance? Didn't the fool know that he had no chance? Even if he survived this ambuscade, the law would reach out a merciless hand. Nita felt her breath coming fast and sharply in her breast. Dick must come in his own identity, if at all, she realized sharply. Subconsciously, she had been looking for the bent and sinister figure in the cape, the *Spider*. But Dick could not come in that garb.

His mere appearance on the floor like that would be an instantaneous admission of all charges. Was Dick prepared to make even that sacrifice to rid the country of this menace which only the death of the leaders could wipe out? For the first time, she remembered Jackson's warning that the poison would next be distributed through candy bars. She turned and whispered that information to Kirkpatrick. He shook his head slightly.

"If Dick fails here tonight, we'll do our best to guard," he said, "but actually we are helpless. Our guard over medicine accomplished practically nothing. They must have another means of distribution. When I left headquarters, the reports were still coming in. Yesterday seven thousand died of poison over the country. Today, there were more than ten thousand more. Dick has taken the only way. God help him!"

Nita flung the cigarette to the floor. Her lower lip was caught in her teeth. Movement to her right jerked her head that way. Eddie Blanton was on his feet and sauntering toward the motionless Avenger. He ignored a machine gunner's angry order. Smoke streamed from his long cigarette holder. There was no tension in his movements, only languid disinterest. His shrewd long face looked sleepy.

The Avenger's head swung toward him and he gestured imperiously with his hand, ordering Blanton back. The newspaperman sauntered on and an automatic snapped into the hooded man's hand. Women gasped sharply, but Blanton kept on.

"It would be poor policy to shoot me here," he drawled, loudly enough for all to hear. "After all there are quite a number of rather reputable witnesses."

The Avenger appeared to hesitate, then shrugged and shoved the gun out of sight. Blanton stepped squarely in front of him, rested his elbows on the edge of the stage. The Avenger stepped forward and Blanton's voice dropped to inaudibles. The deep rumble of the Avenger's voice answered him, then Blanton swung about and strolled away.

"That isn't the Avenger," Nita said sharply to Kirkpatrick. "It is his helper, who goes in his clothing."

Kirkpatrick asked, "Why?"

"The Avenger would not have pulled a gun in the first place, any more than Dick would have," she said

303

swiftly. "He would have known that Blanton couldn't be bluffed. And he would have realized that he couldn't do anything but bluff."

"I think you're right," said Kirkpatrick softly. "But I think that Dick has taken that into consideration, along with everything else." He drew a deep breath. "If only Dick is alive."

Abruptly the door by which the Avenger had entered swung open and a man stepped through and closed it behind him, stood with his twisted shoulders against it. The Avenger swung around, hand half-going to his gun, then he paused. The man in the doorway carried no weapon except a curved cane, on which he leaned.

Slowly, he shuffled forward, a long cape swinging from a hunched back, lank hair brushing out beneath a broad-brimmed, black hat. A beaked face peered upward from under it.

"My God!" A man's voice cracked thinly. "It's the *Spider!*"

CHAPTER SEVENTEEN

The Spider Dies!

The silence that dropped over the room was a shudder. People did not fear the Avenger. He was their Robin Hood, despite those four machine gunners who swung indolent legs from the edge of the stage. Those men were tense now. Two of them twisted their heads about on their shoulders to stare at the warped figure in the cloak that shambled toward the middle of the stage.

"Watch crowd," the Avenger's deep voice ordered and they turned stiffly back.

Nita had bowed her face into her hands and her shoulders shook with silent sobs. Oh, thank God! Thank God! Dick was alive. Alive, but . . . She jerked up her head, white-faced, eyes wide. He was alive, but why, why had he done this thing? Why had he come here in this disguise? It doomed him beyond any recall. It was a confession of guilt. It . . . Suddenly Nita *knew*. Dick had come here to die. He had come to kill his enemy and be killed. She sucked in a hissing breath and with it her shoulders straightened slowly. Her hand strayed again to the pearl-sewn bag upon her knee. Her fingers gripped it hard. But not alone! Dick should not die alone!

The twisted figure shambled on deliberately toward the Avenger, who faced him in a slight, tense crouch.

The *Spider* made no gesture toward the audience. He seemed totally unaware of it—until Blanton got to his feet once more and sauntered forward.

The *Spider's* face swung toward him, expressionless, wooden. His voice reached everyone clearly, thickened by accent.

"Sit down, my child," he said calmly. "I feel that I am about to make a speech that will answer all your questions."

Nita caught a full view of his face for the first time and a small pucker tightened between her eyes. Then abruptly, she understood. Dick was wearing that steel mask he sometimes used when he had need to change identities quickly. That explained the immobility of his expression.

The *Spider* fluttered a hand indifferently in Blanton's direction and Blanton shrugged and with a smile he tried to make jeering, went back to his table. There was subdued laughter from the other newspapermen. It was all strangely out of place.

Nita's blood was thrumming through her ears. She could feel the slow, hard pumping of her heart. She was excited, but no longer frightened or worried. Dick was here now. That was all that mattered. He had come to die with his face to his enemies and she—she was ready, too. She held her breath as the *Spider* halted within ten feet of the Avenger and faced the audience.

"I must admit," he said in his thick, accented voice that was so different from his own clear tones, "to playing a trick upon my most efficient enemy, Commissioner Kirkpatrick. I promised him that if he would call this meeting tonight, I would appear and give my testimony. I intend to do that, but what I actually came for is to punish a treacherous fraud, the Avenger. When I have finished my little speech, I shall challenge the Avenger to duel. I do not think he will refuse."

He turned his head slowly toward the Avenger and the Hooded One was regarding him with a fixed, unswerving gaze.

"The Avenger has violated his agreement with me

slightly," he said, waving an indifferent hand at the four machine gunners. "We were to meet on equal terms. Perhaps, he felt that this was making the arrangements quite equal, five to one."

The *Spider* laughed softly, mocking flat laughter that reached the farthest corners of the room, that made men shiver and women huddle their shoulders. Nita was listening with strained attention, a curious light in her eyes. Kirkpatrick's breath was audible to her. A fierce joy was pounding through her veins.

The *Spider* was speaking again.

"I had suspected the Avenger of complicity in the poisonings that have killed some twenty-five thousand persons in the United States in the last ten days. Now I am sure. I need not go into my reasons, except to say that every move the Avenger has made has reinforced some detail of the poisoners' work.

"I tell you that this man, the Avenger, is guilty of twenty-five thousand murders and that he has pocketed millions as a result of those crimes!"

The *Spider* paused and there was not a sound in the audience. The machine gunners were hunched over their weapons. The Avenger moved a hand carelessly, as if he waved aside all these charges as so much air.

"This is ridiculous," he boomed. "People know how I serve them. Poisoner is man named Martin whom I soon turn over to police."

The *Spider* waited courteously until the other man had finished; then he spoke again, rapidly now, as if he were in a hurry to be done.

"This is not exactly the Avenger," the *Spider* asserted. "He is an underling called Ivan who sometimes performs work for the Avenger, and in that way establishes alibis. The real villain—" during a pause in which not a breath was heard, the *Spider's* eyes swept the audience. "The real villain is among you gentlemen out there." The sweep of his hand brought gasps of amazement, turned every man's suspicious eyes upon his neighbor.

307

"Presently," said the *Spider* harshly, "I shall name this villain for you. But first—" He whirled and wrenched at the cane. It became a glittering arc of steel, a saber. "First, I shall deal with the underling. *En garde,* Ivan! Draw your saber. You first; then your Master!"

A deep snarl came from the Hooded Man. From his trouser leg, he whisked out a blade and instantly they were upon each other, steel ringing and clanging. The *Spider* was crouched army style, clenched fist behind his back. The straight-up stance of the Avenger's man made him look ineffectual. Ivan was walking into the attack, his blade a whirling smother of metallic light. The saber was everywhere, smacking at the head and shoulders, cutting at legs. And before the attack, the *Spider* retreated.

Nita sat tensely, hand gripping the automatic, her eyes following the swift give and take of the duel. She knew swordplay as only the *Spider's* mate could, and this . . .

Ivan's blade slithered past the *Spider's* guard and Nita gasped as the broad-brimmed hat was slashed from his head. The *Spider* crouched and his point jabbed home against the larger man's breast. Ivan reeled back under that blow and a harsh cry ripped from the *Spider*.

"A steel vest!" he cried. The Avenger's man wore armor! Nita felt a cold anger grow within her. She opened her bag slowly, gripped the automatic.

The *Spider* began a slashing attack that made the Russian's offensive seem a weak and futile thing. His blade was everywhere. Ivan stood up to it, abandoning all pretense of defense except that he protected his arms and legs. The steel vest made him impregnable to the assault. The *Spider* broke through and slashed to the head, and steel rang on steel.

Once more the *Spider* thrust with savage violence. The curved blade slithered out past the Russian's guard and once more grated on steel. But this time, from behind Ivan's hood came a muffled, fearful scream.

The *Spider* straightened, dropping the tip of his

sword and Ivan staggered back. His arms flew high and his saber clattered to the floor. No more sound came from him; he smashed down on his back. Two of the machine gunners pivoted toward the two duelists.

The *Spider* ignored them. Red-tipped sword in hand, he sprang to the side of the fallen man, ripped off the hood. A steel casque like a ball covered the man's head. The *Spider* tugged that off also and showed the Russian's face, blood streaming from one eye. The *Spider's* point had gone through the eyeslit into his brain.

Nita felt exultation leap in her veins at the victory, but there was a fearful menace in those two machine guns. She eased over behind Kirkpatrick, her fingers groping in her bag again, closing fiercely about the butt of the automatic.

The *Spider* held the steel casque high in his left hand and strode to the edge of the stage, still ignoring the machine gunners who pivoted with him, those dread muzzles gaping.

"This steel helmet," said the *Spider,* "proves what I have charged, that the Avenger and Martin, the head of the poison gang, are one and the same man. Martin never appeared before his gangsters unless his head was encased in this helmet. But this Ivan is not the man. He is an underling. The Master—"

Suddenly the *Spider* staggered. The steel casque dropped from his hand and hit the floor with a dull clangor. He caught at his throat, reeling. There was no sound at all then, except a woman's scream. Laughter lit the face of the machine gunner leaning against the arch. He thrust his body free and fondled his weapon.

"And that's that," he said calmly. "Everybody stand still, or—"

Nita was on her feet, the automatic clenched in her hand. The *Spider* was going backward, heavy-footed, and there was blood on his throat.

Suddenly the machine gunner stepped forward. "Drop those guns," he barked: then: *"Let them have it!"*

Two swift heavy shots put an exclamation point on his sentence, and he rolled backward, dead on his feet. Nita jerked up her automatic and emptied it in a swift, light shatter of sound. She poured lead into the face of another of the machine gunners. The man reeled back a step, standing there dead; then blood began to seep from a half-dozen wounds in his face and forehead. He pitched forward across his weapon.

Nita looked down at the gun in her hand and shuddered, then glanced up with a feeling of unreality as a familiar voice cracked out, the voice of Richard Wentworth! She jerked her head about. The pale-faced croupier, Larue, was in the aisle with a heavy automatic in each fist, and the voice that came from his lips was the voice of Richard Wentworth!

"Get to Jackson, Kirk," Wentworth called sharply. "The man in the *Spider* outfit, Kirk. It's Jackson. I've got to get the Avenger!"

He plunged down the aisle, still gripping his guns, kicked aside a chair that skidded into his path. He hurled aside Commander Samuels who had scrambled out into the space before the stage. He did not halt until he reached the spot where the newspapermen crouched behind their table.

As he reached the table Blanton straightened from behind a chair, holding his long cigarette holder carelessly in his fingers. His long face was pale.

"Give your name to the press, me lad," he said jauntily. "We want to tell the pee-pul who saved the day for us all."

"Get your hands up, Blanton!" Wentworth snarled.

The reporter started, stared, and threw back his head and laughed. "Why, it's my old friend, Wentworth," he said. "I thought for sure you were up there on the stage." He lifted the cigarette holder toward his lips.

"Get your hands up, I said," Wentworth snarled, and his two automatics centered on Blanton's chest. "You are the Avenger, the real Avenger, and you are Martin, too. When you shot the man you thought was the *Spider,* I saw that the bullet must have been fired from this side of the room. I could tell by the way your victim swayed, by the position of the wound. And then I knew.

"Nobody but a newspaperman would have known how to hound an enemy through the news as the Avenger did the *Spider* to keep him out of the way, while he cashed in on the poison plot. Nobody but you, Blanton, would have been smart enough to build the whole crazy plan. You had O'Burke and his lieutenant killed so you could take over his mob, and worked through it.

"I can prove that every time Martin or the real Avenger has appeared, you've been on the scene. You were a friend of Mannley's and many other crooks and you knew how to handle them. But it was your job to know them, so you escaped suspicion."

Blanton was fumbling with the cigarette holder and the grin was still on his horsey face. "Scarcely legal evidence, my dear Wentworth," he sneered.

"Quite right, Blanton," he said, "and you had me fooled for a while. I couldn't understand that play of hostility between the Avenger and Martin, but I gather now that you wanted me to carry word of that fact to Kirkpatrick. You were so confident of killing me that you even had Patsy Malone 'phone Jackson to come and free me. The fact that four of your men were killed made no difference to you so long as you got word to authorities of hostility between Martin and the Avenger. After I was dead, that would totally confuse them and you would have no trouble in arranging your getaway.

"You intended at this show tonight for Ivan to be killed, then for your machine gunners to kill the *Spider*. When police killed your machine gunners, there would be no member of the gang left. Martin and the Avenger could both disappear and the crime would be unsolved, while you pocketed your millions."

Blanton's grin was mocking now. "Is this all the evidence against me?" he queried. "It sounds like balderdash to me."

Wentworth shook his head. "No, but there are two other little matters that will convict you. First of all, Martin had weak ankles. It was clear from the way he ran and the fact that he wore high boots. You wear high-topped shoes yourself and have weak ankles. You're knock-kneed as hell. And you still have on your person the gun with which you shot Jackson as he was about to denounce you, as you thought."

The newspapermen were straightening from their frightened positions, staring with amazed eyes from Blanton, who was their idol, to this pale-faced man whom Blanton addressed as Wentworth, but who looked nothing on earth like that man. Blanton turned to his friends with a shrug.

"Did any of you see or hear me shoot?" he asked with a quizzical smile.

"A silencer," Wentworth interrupted.

"A silencer?" Blanton jerked. "They won't work on either revolvers or automatics, and you know it. The gases are kicked back and blast out through the back of an automatic or cut the side of a revolver and make almost as much noise as if the silencer weren't on them. Only a few fool fiction writers think silencers will work on hand arms."

"Give me your cigarette holder!" Wentworth snapped.

He lunged toward Blanton, but he was too late. He felt a numbing shock in his side that made him sway and knew he'd been shot. He saw Blanton drop the cigarette holder and snatch an automatic from beneath his arm, then both Wentworth's guns spoke together.

"Good God, Wentworth, you've killed him!"

Lanky Gallahan was pillowing Blanton's head in his arms. "You're crazy, Wentworth, crazy!" he gabbled.

Blanton's head rolled, his eyes opened slowly. Miraculously, the man was still alive despite two big-caliber bullets through his vitals.

"Not crazy, Gallahan," Blanton mumbled. "Damn . . . smart!" He closed his eyes, his chest heaving spasmodically. "Gang way . . . palsy. I'll mess up . . . your . . . !"

He wrenched. A torrent of blood poured from his mouth. He shuddered and lay still. Wentworth stooped heavily, and picked up the cigarette holder. It was much thicker than the one Blanton ordinarily used and no tobacco smoke ever had dribbled through it. He wrenched it open and revealed a single-shot pistol arrangement with a silencer on its muzzle.

"An automatic or a revolver can't use a silencer," Wentworth said slowly, "but a single shot weapon has no opening for the noisy gases to pop out of. It makes no sound at all. That's how he shot Jackson— and me!"

Jackson! The word sounded an alarm in Wentworth's mind. Jackson was wounded, perhaps dying because he had fought for Wentworth, taken the *Spider's* place, taken the bullet intended for the *Spider*. Wentworth turned heavily toward the stairs and the stage where Jackson stood with his shoulders braced against the wall. He had a gun in his hand and he was holding off Nita and Kirkpatrick and a half-dozen other men.

". . . This is the truth," Jackson was saying clearly. "I used Wentworth's home as a base of operations. I used the cover of his name. That is why he has so often been blamed. But I, and I alone, am the *Spider!*"

A woman went past Wentworth, shouldered through the crowd. "He's lying," she snapped. "He's not . . ."

Wentworth saw that the woman was Patsy Malone, he saw Jackson's gun coming up and shouted a hoarse warning. The gun convulsed and barked from Jackson's hand. Patsy's voice rose in a piercing cry and her small body slammed back against a man behind her. Even as his arms flew out to catch her, she slumped to the floor. She was dead before she hit.

Wentworth saw a man whip out a revolver and level it at Jackson, but he reached the wrist in time and put all his weight on it.

"Don't," he said hoarsely. "Don't! She had it coming to her." He slumped down on his knees, facing Jackson.

"The dirty . . . little tramp," said Jackson. "She tricked me from the start . . . !"

Wentworth reached out his hand and pulled off the *Spider* mask. Jackson was grinning weakly.

"Howdy . . . Major," he gasped. "I guess it's . . . taps this time . . . all right."

Wentworth felt something hard as stone in his throat. He was pressing the palm of his left hand against the wound in his side, staying the hemorrhage.

"Jackson, you damned fool," he said slowly. "All those lies." He worked a little closer on his knees. "Come on, Jack, we got to get you to the hospital."

Jackson shook his head wearily. It rolled on the wall. "No go, Major. I got it," he gasped. "But, say, is . . . everything all right? I kind of messed . . . you up."

Through his own swelling pain, Wentworth felt a stinging in his eyes. He had been a fool ever to doubt Jackson, but the weight of the evidence had been so strongly against him. He seemed to have gone haywire over that girl. And Jackson had made amends.

"Everything's swell, Jack," he said. "But, damn your soul, why did you do it? You're a hell of a swell soldier and nothing could ever make it different. You're loyal, square. . . ."

"Save the bouquets, Major," Jackson's breath was coming in short gasps now. "I'll . . . need them later."

Wentworth heard a woman's sob and was aware that Nita was on her knees beside him.

"Good-bye, Miss." Jackson writhed. "Good . . . bye . . . Major."

The life went out of his body in a breath. Wentworth felt as if his own life was gone, too. He lifted his head slowly. "A good soldier," he said heavily, "but an awful liar. Everybody knows he wasn't the *Spider*. It's . . . silly . . ."

Wentworth did not see Kirkpatrick's hand grasping a

314

gun, did not see Kirkpatrick, stooping forward as if to help him, slap that gun heavily behind his ear. He felt a blaze of light. Then soft black darkness and dived into unconsciousness. Kirkpatrick straightened. "Get this man to a hospital, quickly," he snapped. "He's wounded!"

CHAPTER EIGHTEEN

Long Live The Spider!

When Wentworth regained consciousness, he was in the hospital with Kirkpatrick and Nita beside him. He found that his voice was weak and that intolerable pain throbbed through his side. He twisted toward Kirkpatrick.

"Kirk," he said weakly. "You didn't let Jackson take the rap like that, did you? The fool was lying, lying to make up to me for his blunders."

Kirkpatrick smiled thinly. "You've been pretty sick, Dick," he said. "You'll be glad to know we wiped out the last of the O'Burke-Martin gang. You killed the Avenger and Martin in one man. We found both disguises hidden among the toys of Blanton's kid."

Wentworth tossed his head fretfully. "Listen," he said, "you're stalling. I won't let Jackson be buried with a blot on his name. He never was against me. He just blundered in trusting that girl. When he kidnaped me from your office, I didn't know. He took me to a rooming house and tied me up tight. I told him that he was jeopardizing my entire plan, that he had made me break my word by kidnaping me. Being a prisoner forced me to tell my plans and Jackson said he'd take my place. He executed all my plans marvelously. He got that *Spider* kit somewhere, God only knows where, and used the saber as I had taught him to do."

Wentworth stopped, closed his eyes, fought them open again. "I finally got free of Jackson's ropes, disguised myself as the croupier, Larue, and made my way to the hall. It had been my intention to force the Avenger and Martin to kill me, thus convicting themselves. They would then have been executed and I would have escaped the humiliation and pain of the courts.

"When I found it was impossible to locate and stop Jackson, I decided to carry on with the same idea in a different way. I would sit on the sidelines and block any attempts to hurt Jackson. I watched the suspects, Commander Samuels and Marshant. I'll admit Blanton eluded my suspicions, until I saw that the shot that killed Jackson must have been fired from the news table. Then I knew."

Wentworth was very tired. "Listen, Kirk," he said. "I want Jackson cleared."

Kirkpatrick interrupted roughly. "Don't be a fool, Dick. Jackson is the most honored soldier who ever went to his grave. The entire city turned out for his funeral. Newspapers are singing paeans to his glory, recalling all the services the *Spider* rendered to mankind. Soldiers marched behind his coffin and the President himself ordered that he be buried in Arlington."

"That'll help a lot now that he's dead," Wentworth said bitterly.

Kirkpatrick leaned forward. "What I am pointing out to you," he said shortly, "is that there is no sense in your making a foolish sacrifice of yourself. Jackson took the blame and the glory with him.

"Incidentally, he made it impossible for you to be convicted. He explained every bit of evidence that we have against you. He stole the automatic that killed Mannley, wore your signet ring on his finger, so the motion picture the Avenger took is useless. Another motion picture that was taken out in Chicago showed Jackson fighting the Avenger, but the latter half of it was too dim to be properly developed. The Avenger said it showed you, but we couldn't find you. The

317

Avenger said he had another bit of evidence that went to smash, literally, a picture of you and Nita escaping police from your apartment, a thing for which Jackson takes blame. But that plate was broken when the Avenger took it from the newspaper photographer who snapped it.

"If you insist on making a confession, the courts will have to consider it, of course, but I doubt that you could convict yourself even if you tried after that grandstand finish in which Jackson killed the Avenger's man. Personally, I believe you're out of your head with fever." He smiled slightly, parting his mustache with thumb and forefinger.

"And by the way, don't feel too bad about Jackson and Patsy Malone. He didn't kill her exclusively because of her betrayals of you. She was the wife of that man, Coxwell, who brought their baby to the meeting. She fooled Jackson the whole time."

Wentworth's hand was upon Nita's now. There was a great pain within him at the loss of Jackson, but there was a great peace, too. Jackson had been loyal to his salt. He smiled wanly at Nita.

"It seems," he said slowly, "that the *Spider* is dead."

"Let him stay dead," Kirkpatrick urged.

Wentworth turned his face toward him. "I suspect that a *Spider* must always rise to help the people when they need a champion. As long as the nation is held in the thrall of criminal madmen, there must be a *Spider* to fight them. One *Spider* is dead. A more gallant man never lived."

"The *Spider* is dead!" Nita said, and there was a sob in her throat. It was both sorrow for Jackson and for the happiness she had dreamed of that now was fading. For Wentworth had been washed clean of crimes by Jackson's blood sacrifice. The book was wiped clean of charges against him. For the brief hours that had passed between Jackson's death and now, she had nourished a little, secret dream that she knew in her heart was false. She had known, actually, that

Wentworth would never cease his crusades of justice while life was in his body, but the dream that they might go away together had been so sweet. . . . Her hands tightened upon Wentworth's, and the sob welled up once more and died. She was proud of this warrior man of hers. She would not have him otherwise. Her head came up.

"The *Spider* is dead," she said, with a breathless little laugh. *"Long live the Spider!"*

FINE MYSTERY AND SUSPENSE
TITLES FROM CARROLL & GRAF

☐ Ambler, Eric/BACKGROUND TO DANGER	$3.95
☐ Ambler, Eric/A COFFIN FOR DIMITRIOS	$3.95
☐ Ambler, Eric/JOURNEY INTO FEAR	$3.95
☐ Brand, Christianna/TOUR DE FORCE	$3.95
☐ Brand, Christianna/DEATH IN HIGH HEELS	$3.95
☐ Brand, Christianna/GREEN FOR DANGER	$3.95
☐ Carr, John Dickson/THE DEMONIACS	$3.95
☐ Carr, John Dickson/THE GHOSTS' HIGH NOON	$3.95
☐ Carr, John Dickson/THE WITCH OF THE LOW TIDE	$3.95
☐ Collins, Michael/WALK A BLACK WIND	$3.95
☐ Fennelly, Tony/THE CLOSET HANGING	$3.50
☐ Gardner, Erle Stanley/DEAD MEN'S LETTERS	$4.50
☐ Gilbert, Michael/OVERDRIVE	$3.95
☐ Graham, Winston/MARNIE	$3.95
☐ Griffiths, John/THE GOOD SPY	$4.95
☐ Hughes, Dorothy B/RIDE THE PINK HORSE	$3.95
☐ Hughes, Dorothy B/THE FALLEN SPARROW	$3.50
☐ Kitchin, C.H.B./DEATH OF HIS UNCLE	$3.95
☐ Kitchin, C.H.B./DEATH OF MY AUNT	$3.50
☐ Pentecost, Hugh/THE CANNIBAL WHO OVERATE	$3.95
☐ Queen, Ellery/THE FINISHING STROKE	$3.95
☐ 'Sapper'/BULLDOG DRUMMOND	$3.50
☐ Stevens, Shane/BY REASON OF INSANITY	$5.95
☐ Symons, Julian/THE BROKEN PENNY	$3.95
☐ Symons, Julian/BOGUE'S FORTUNE	$3.95
☐ Westlake, Donald E./THE MERCENARIES	$3.95

Available from fine bookstores everywhere or use this coupon for ordering.

Carroll & Graf Publishers, Inc., 260 Fifth Avenue, N.Y., N.Y. 10001

Please send me the books I have checked above. I am enclosing $_____
(please add $1.25 per title to cover postage and handling.) Send check
or money order—no cash or C.O.D.'s please. N.Y. residents please add
8¼% sales tax.

Mr/Mrs/Ms _____

Address _____

City _____ State/Zip _____

Please allow four to six weeks for delivery.